THE RICH PART OF LIFE

THE RICH PART OF LIFE

JIM KOKORIS

ST. MARTIN'S PRESS

NEW YORK

ISBN 0-312-27479-3

To Johnny, Michael, and Andrew,
but most of all to Anne

ACKNOWLEDGMENTS

First novels owe a great debt, so special thanks are due the following people: Lynn Franklin, my agent, for her persistence, guidance, dedication, and willingness to take a chance; Joe Veltre and Alicia Brooks, my editors, for their insights and enthusiasm; Gordon Mennenga, my teacher, who helped show me the way; Bill Contardi, my film agent, for his influence and support; and my business partner, Jonni Hegenderfer, for her support as well.

PART ONE

CHAPTER ONE

THE DAY WE WON the lottery I was wearing wax lips that my father had bought for the Nose Picker and me at a truck stop. We were driving back from my great-aunt Bess's house in the old Buick and we stopped for gas at a place called Ammo's along the interstate, where my father bought the lottery ticket along with the bright red wax lips.

"It's been thirty years since I've seen wax lips," my father said in his tired way as he reached into his pocket for money. My mother had died in an accident one year earlier on the same interstate and ever since then my father had seemed defeated like one of his Confederate generals that he read so much about. When he walked, he pitched his shoulders forward and bowed his head in a sad, thoughtful way that reminded me of grieving nuns. Earlier that day, I had heard him tell my aunt that he hadn't been sleeping well.

"My God, you shouldn't be driving then," Aunt Bess had said. She had insisted on our staying overnight at her house in Milwaukee but my father had refused. Instead, he stopped for coffee at Ammo's, and for the second time in a year, our lives changed forever.

Ammo's was a dirty, loud place that stank of gasoline and oil. When the Nose Picker and I went to the bathroom, we breathed out of our mouths and didn't bother to wash our hands in the small, stained sink. Once we got back in the Buick, we rolled up the windows to shut out the screeching and whining of the large trucks and to escape the smell of the bathroom that we were sure was following us.

"Are your seat belts securely fastened?" my father said as he got into the car, balancing his coffee on the dashboard.

"Yes," I said, though mine was not buckled. I knew my father would not turn his head to check. He frequently had a stiff neck and kept head-turning to a minimum.

"Tommy's too?"

I looked over at the Nose Picker and then helped him fasten his belt. "Yes."

"All right then," he said as he turned the key. "We'll be home in an hour or so, I imagine."

IT WAS EARLY EVENING in August, the time of day when the fading light and growing darkness hang in balance. While we drove back to our home in Wilton, a suburb of Chicago, I drew pictures of the white clouds in the sky, large and soft. The clouds hung high and I imagined my mother living inside them, floating quietly and humming like she did when she used to draw with me. The Nose Picker hated it when I drew. He became restless and then angry. He chewed noisily on his wax lips.

"I want a crayon," the Nose Picker said. "I want to draw too." I handed him some paper and a green crayon whose tip was well rounded. I never gave my brother a crayon with a sharp tip for fear he would stick it up his nose.

"His interest in his nose isn't normal," Aunt Bess had told my father. "It must be some type of reaction to the death."

My father had not looked up from his latest Civil War book. "He picked his nose before the accident. He's only five years old. I'm confident that he'll grow out of it."

"Are they seeing a psychiatrist?" Aunt Bess had asked. My father hadn't responded, though. He just sat hunched over in a chair in Aunt Bess's living room, reading about the life of Joshua Lawrence Chamberlain, a Civil War general.

Later that night, when we returned home and were getting into bed, I asked him about the book even though I generally found his discussions about the Civil War dull and wanted instead to study the wax lips in more detail. The only thing my father showed any interest in, however, was the war and I wanted him to show interest tonight. He had been very quiet the past few days.

He seemed surprised by my question. "Well, it's about General Chamberlain," he said, clearing his throat. "He held the Union flank at Gettysburg." He was silent for a moment and I could tell that he was thinking. "It's probably best that I diagram his maneuver. It was really quite remarkable." He pulled up my desk chair and reached for the pencil and paper that were on my desk. "Chamberlain was supposed to hold the Union position at a place called Little Round Top at Gettysburg. Not only did he hold it, he performed one of the most extraordinary counterattacks in history. He split his men like this, like an L and swung half his regiment over like a door shutting. He routed the rebels."

At this point I realized that I had underestimated my father's interest in Joshua Lawrence Chamberlain and, as a result, feared a major discussion on the war was taking shape. I had expected and hoped for a brief lecture, just enough to revitalize him, but judging from the tone of his voice and comfortable way he was arranging himself in his chair, I knew a lengthy dissertation on maneuvers and strategy was looming.

My father's interest in the war had been the cause of many arguments between my mother and him. A few weeks before the accident, my father had begun planning a family vacation to Shilo National Park. He was explaining to me why the battle was important when my mother walked into his study, saw the maps and brochures spread out on his desk and erupted.

"Are you nuts? Why do I want to go there? There's cemeteries twenty minutes from here," she yelled. "It would be different if you had fought in the stupid war. Then maybe I could understand your obsession."

"No," my father quietly said, "I did not fight in the war. If I had fought in the war, I would be more than one hundred and fifty years old."

"You act one hundred and fifty years old," my mother said. She picked up a brochure and then slammed it down on his desk. "We should go some place fun like Las Vegas," she said. "It's very family friendly now."

My father looked hurt, his forehead pinched tight, his eyes faraway and resigned. It was a look that I would come to know well. "Family friendly," he repeated.

Sitting on my small desk chair now, his legs crossed at the ankles, his hands in his lap, my father prepared to launch into a new discussion that could last indefinitely. He was an average-sized man, sagging and soft in the middle, with thinning white hair that stood out in small tufts on the sides of his head like cotton candy. His small, narrow eyes were offset by a strong and hard chin that jutted out in a way that incorrectly suggested confidence and pride. Leaning forward in my desk chair, I saw his eyes take on a rare bright and eager look as he scanned distant horizons, probing the rebel lines, searching for a weakness, a direction to charge. Gettysburg, Antietam, Chancellorsville, Bull Run, Atlanta, Lookout Mountain, my father was a veteran of them all. He had ridden in the mud with Grant, stood his ground with Jackson, maneuvered brilliantly with Lee, burned cities with Sherman, and died many times with Lincoln.

"Daddy, my nose is bleeding," the Nose Picker said, walking into my room.

The blood was a startling bright red that dripped down Tommy's chin onto his yellow pajama top. Despite its redness, I wasn't concerned. Tommy had frequent nosebleeds, messy but harmless, and they required nothing more than a cold washcloth and a pat on the head to set things right.

My father, though, was concerned. "Dear God," he said. Jumping up, he grabbed Tommy and disappeared down the hallway. Ten minutes later, when he returned to my bedside, I pretended to be asleep in a manner that I had perfected: mouth open, head thrown back on the pillow. I heard my father sigh and felt him readjust my sheets. Then I heard him walk out. That's when I took the wax lips out from under my pillow and studied them.

They interested me, as most odd objects interest eleven-year-old boys. They were smooth and light and had a tiny ridge on the backside that slid between my teeth in a precise and perfect way. Putting them on, I imagined myself kissing Miss Grace, my soft and sweet teacher, full on the lips as we danced around her desk.

"Teddy," she would whisper, holding my face in her hands. "Teddy Pappas. Where did you get those lips?"

After my vision of Miss Grace faded, I quietly took the case off my pillow and wrapped it around my head like a turban, then grabbed a blanket and threw it over my shoulders and wore it like a cape. With my wax lips firmly in place in my mouth, I then crossed the hall and entered the Nose Picker's room, intending to wake and terrify him, something I occasionally did when the mood struck me. A few weeks earlier, I had hid under his bed and made vague growling noises until he screamed.

The Nose Picker's room was small and so cluttered with toys and clothes, that it took some time before I could safely navigate a path to his bed. Once there, I hovered close to his face to check his nose for blood, something I knew my father would forget to do. Finding it clean and dry, I began to lightly moan through the wax lips, hoping to wake him. I did this for awhile, waiting for him to stir. When he finally did roll over, however, I stopped moaning. In his hands I saw a blue and pink sweater. It had been my mother's.

I stood there and watched him hold the sweater. I hated and loved my brother in a way that only brothers can and worried about him and his strange behavior. I knew he missed my mother fiercely and had heard him crying many times in his sleep. Yet, this was the first time I had seen him holding her sweater.

I watched him for what seemed a long time. His thick black hair was pushed back off his forehead and his mouth was open. He looked small and still and young. Taking the wax lips out of my mouth, I bent down close to his ear and whispered the Hail Mary. My mother had always said this prayer with us at bedtime and my saying it then was as much for her sake as Tommy's. When I finished, I returned to my room, my cape, a blanket again, dragging behind me. I was tired.

A while later, after I had fallen asleep, I was awakened by the sounds of sobbing. At first, I thought it was the Nose Picker but then, as my head cleared of sleep, I recognized the crying to be my father's. This frightened me. I had only heard him cry once before and only briefly at my mother's funeral. Fearing that he was hurt or sick, I carefully made my way into his bedroom where I found him sitting on the edge of his bed holding the lottery ticket that he had bought at Ammo's. He didn't notice me at first, so I stood and watched him cry, his shoulders shaking, his eyes wet and red.

"Why are you crying?" I finally asked.

He looked up and quickly wiped away his tears, embarrassed. "The television, I just heard. I was watching the news on the television downstairs," he said. Then he looked down at the ticket, then back up at me. "I think we won quite a bit of money, Teddy," he said quietly. "Dear God, I think we won an awful lot of money."

CHAPTER TWO

W E WERE RICH in a way that I couldn't understand. My father didn't seem to understand it either for he went about his daily business of researching the Civil War with a heavier than usual grimness, a silence that deepened as time passed. Weeks went by and still he did not claim the ticket.

From time to time, news of the lottery would filter into our house, overheard bits and pieces from the television and radio discussing its size and speculating why the one winner who had purchased the ticket on the Illinois–Wisconsin border was not coming forward to claim the winnings. My father instructed me several times not to discuss the lottery with anyone and the unusually urgent and direct way he asked me ensured my silence and kept me from asking too many questions.

One night though I could not resist. "Are we going to get the money?" I asked as he passed my doorway on his way to his study.

"Yes," he said. Then he said, "I have to organize things first though. I have to take care of some things," and was gone.

As the days passed, I felt a growing excitement, a low heat simmering that warmed my skin, making it jump and tingle. The lottery and its mysterious winner were chief topics of conversation during those late summer days at my school, St. Pius, and my heart would leap forward whenever I heard it being discussed. Theories on why no one had claimed the ticket ran from the absurd (an alien had purchased the ticket) to the possible (the person had died immediately after learning he or she had won). My father, neither an alien nor completely dead, kept mum on the subject.

One day after school, I went up to my room and began making my List of Things, items I wanted our family to buy when my father finally did get around to claiming the ticket. While I was old enough to recognize that we already lived comfortably, my father was a professor at a major university and had written a very successful book on the Civil War, I wanted things that only the lottery could buy.

My list started slowly and predictably, with the usual computer games and art supplies such as paints, markers, colored pencils, easel topping it. The list developed a momentum of its own, however, as I progressed, expanding in different directions. Three new television sets were added since our old Zenith (bought, according to my father, when Richard Nixon was president) provided an unhealthy, greenish tint to every scene. I thought we could replace the Zenith in the family room with one of the new sets, then put another new television in my room and the third in my father's room. The Nose Picker would get the old Zenith since he was still too young to realize that people's faces weren't necessarily the color of peas. I also included a VCR since I was sure we were the last people in America that did not own one, a fact I kept hidden like a rash.

Three new bikes were then added, one for the Nose Picker and two mountain bikes for me. I reasoned I should have two bikes in the event one was lost, stolen, or forgotten in a place that was inconvenient for me to retrieve.

I then added a large farm in Wisconsin. When we visited Aunt Bess in Milwaukee, we would sometimes drive up to Green Lake, a resort town an hour northwest for lunch or dinner. It was during those drives that I would admire the numerous farms we passed, their bright red barns and gleaming white silos clear and clean against the pure blue Wisconsin sky. I was particularly impressed with the size of the farms, their wide rolling expanses wrapping around the earth, hugging its edges. I thought we could use such space. I imagined idling away long summer vacations riding horses and fishing in our own private lake surrounded by gentle black and white spotted cows and salty but kind hired hands.

I next addressed our car, the old Buick forged, I believed, by ancient Egyptian slaves during the completion of the pyramids. It was so old that even my father, a savant with dates and presidential administrations, was unclear on its birth, saying it fell somewhere between the Ford and Carter administrations. My list replaced it with one of those sleek and sporty red Jeeps that filled most driveways in our neighborhood and I imagined my father, the Nose Picker and me riding high up on its leather seats, darting through the streets of Wilton with a precision and authority that always seemed beyond us.

Finally, I added a new house. Our brick two-story colonial was in definite need of replacement. The upstairs shower leaked through the kitchen ceiling and during the spring, the basement flooded, forcing us to roll up the carpets and place important items on tables and couches away from the swamp. Our furniture had a respectable but faded look and smell about it that reminded me of the public library. The couch in the living room had two small puncture holes in it, the result of the Nose Picker sitting on it with a pencil in his pocket and our small, round kitchen table was unbalanced, tipping unevenly from one side to the other whenever we ate.

Nothing would be unbalanced in our new house. It would be sturdy and bright with large windows that would let the light in at all angles. My bedroom would be spacious and airy with a skylight that would allow me to feel the sun in the day and study the stars at night with the aid of a high powered telescope that would lower automatically with a quiet hum from a concealed compartment in the ceiling. My bed would be a water bed, I decided. Though I had never laid on one, or for that matter, even seen one, sleeping on water was an exotic notion that appealed to me. I also thought my room should have a small refrigerator, something in which to store my Cokes and 7-Ups, and a small robot to serve them to me while I gently rode the waves of my bed searching for undiscovered and unnamed galaxies.

I was sketching out additional details of the house when I heard footsteps approaching on the hallway stairs.

"Teddy?" It was my father, standing in my doorway, looking like a distant constellation. "Teddy, please get your brother. I was unable to find a sitter so

I'm going to have to take you with me downtown now. We have to do something," he said and then he was gone.

A FEW HOURS LATER at the press conference where we received the oversized check for a hundred-and-ninety-million dollars, a woman reporter asked my father if he was married. "Yes, I mean no," he said. "I mean, I was married, but my wife is not with us any longer. She's dead, actually." The reporters in the small, hot room in the hotel in downtown Chicago looked at each other and were confused. One man squinted his eyes and shook his head. Standing just behind my father on the small stage, I watched my father shift his feet.

"I selected, I played her numbers, you see," he continued. "Yes. I played her numbers, the numbers she always chose. They're my oldest son's birthday, actually. I guess that was a very lucky day for her, the day he was born." My father seemed to be saying this more to himself than to the reporters. "She picked the same numbers every week for nine years, and . . ." He stopped as if he just then realized that he was talking and cleared his throat again. No one said anything. Some reporters coughed but most wrote fast in their notepads. A TV camera light suddenly went on and I held on tight to Tommy's hand.

"When did your wife die?" a reporter asked.

"A year ago. A year ago today actually. Yes, today."

"She's up in heaven though," Tommy said. "She's up in heaven and we're going to pay some money to get her to come back."

There was a stunned silence, a moment when everyone stopped thinking and breathing. As we stood there, I felt a wave of pity wash over my family, our lives suddenly a spectacle, a sad parade.

My father was slow to react. He stood with his shoulders hunched at the podium forever, his face blank and open. Then he finally stepped back and took Tommy's other hand and mumbled something I couldn't hear. More camera lights went on. A woman holding a pad and pencil wiped her eyes with a tissue.

Finally a reporter asked how my mother died, but someone from the lottery office took the microphone and said something about respecting privacy and reminded everyone that children were present. Everyone looked at Tommy and me and then everyone was quiet for awhile.

"How does it feel to not have to work anymore?" someone finally asked.

My father, clearly shaken by Tommy's comment, was confused by the question and asked her to repeat it.

"Are you going to quit working?"

My father shook his head. "No. Well, I intend to continue working."

"You won a hundred-and-ninety-million dollars," someone from the crowd yelled. "Give the money back then." Everyone laughed.

"What do you do for a living?"

"Well, I am a teacher, a history professor."

"Why did it take you three weeks to claim the ticket?" another reporter asked. She was a short, squat woman with black hair that hung over her eyes. When she spoke, she pointed her finger at us as if she were angry.

"Well, I'm not sure," my father said.

"Three weeks is a long time not to claim a hundred-and-ninety million. What were you thinking? What were you doing?"

My father moved back up to the podium and gripped its edges hard to steady himself. It would be some time before I truly learned the answer to that question. "It was a bit much to comprehend," he said slowly. "I was very busy. Making adjustments."

"Three weeks though," the short reporter said again. She was about to ask another question when someone yelled, "I hope you were shopping," and everyone laughed.

"Yes," my father said. "I was very busy." And then we walked off the stage and began what I thought would be the rich part of our lives.

ON THE WAY HOME after the press conference, my father pulled over on the shoulder of the expressway and began breathing loudly and holding his chest. He had had a heart attack before I was born and took medication, "antiheart-attack pills" as my mother used to refer to them, for his condition. Due to the uncertain state of his health, I was convinced that Tommy and I daily walked the fine line that separates children from orphans. So real was this fear, that I had recently looked up orphanages in the local Yellow Pages to prepare for the inevitable and was both disappointed and relieved not to find any listed.

After a few deep breaths, my father started the car again and we drove in silence to the cemetery.

"I forgot the flowers," he said, as we pulled into the parking lot. "I left them in the kitchen."

It was a warm day in September, summer was fading and on the tips of trees the first shades of color were appearing. As we walked to where my mother was buried, I wished I had brought my sketch pad and colored pencils. I would only need two pencils though—orange and red.

When we got to the headstone, we stood. Surprisingly, we did not visit often as a family. I suspected my father thought it might be too hard for us. I knew he came alone many times though, disappearing for hours after dinner while Mrs. Rhodebush, our neighbor, watched us at home. The Nose Picker, finally tired of standing, lay on the ground, facing the sky, looking comfortable. I wanted to lay next to him and study the trees, but I didn't. Instead, I stood next to my father and stared at the memory of my mother.

"Your mother was born to be rich. That's what she used to tell me. 'I'm born to be rich.' Now . . ." my father wasn't able to finish. I thought he might cry but he didn't. He just sighed and bent down to pull a weed that was growing near the tombstone. He stayed in a crouch over the grave, smoothing over the dirt where the weed had been with his hand, patting it gently like it was my mother's hair.

"Your mother always bought lottery tickets," he said. "I never did. I'm fifty-five years old and my entire life, I never bought one. Your mother bought hundreds. We always fought about that. We disagreed about many things." Then he stood back up and said, "We should be going now."

When we got back to Wilton, Aunt Bess was waiting for us on the front porch. I liked my great aunt, though I suspected her presence annoyed my father. She was an outspoken woman given to wearing capes and owning cats. She had tall, black hair that rose upward at a crooked angle like the Tower of Pisa and large, equally dark eyes that could look at once both angry and soft. Despite being the age when most women shrink and shrivel, she remained very large and appeared to be expanding at a healthy pace. She spoke frequently in Greek even though she was born in Chicago and lived in Milwaukee where she used to own a bakery until it burned to the ground after an oven exploded. When I was younger, I used to think she was a witch. She believed in ESP and used to communicate with dead relatives and famous celebrities using tarot cards. Once she claimed to have spoken to President John F. Kennedy, though she never discussed what he told her. "It's very disturbing," she had said. "And I don't want to put you in danger."

Close to eighty now, she had lost a bit of her mystery, but none of her drama. When she saw us, she fell slowly to her knees on the porch and simultaneously started crying and speaking in Greek. When she was through, she looked up blearily at my father who cleared his throat and said, "So, I assume you've heard our news."

Without explanation, she moved in with us that day, taking over the Nose Picker's room. My father accepted this, as he did most things, without comment.

The next morning, was Saturday and Aunt Bess made bacon and eggs for breakfast, walking slowly and with great effort around our table as she poured juice and coffee and buttered and rebuttered toast. Off in the corner of the kitchen, eggs fried and bacon popped on the stove, sending a spiral of salty smoke up to our cracked ceiling.

I ate my fried eggs in silence, intimidated at this early hour by Aunt Bess's presence. Our kitchen, small and overflowing with the various baskets and vases my mother had collected, was overwhelmed by her large size and loud voice. Stavros, my aunt's oldest and favorite cat, lay motionless on the floor near the refrigerator. Even though Aunt Bess owned four cats, she brought only Stavros with her because he was partially blind and partially deaf and she wanted to be with him at the end, she said.

"You look terrible in this picture," Aunt Bess said to my father as she handed him the newspaper. My father was drinking coffee in his peculiar and delicate manner which used to infuriate my mother. Holding the cup with both hands, he closed his eyes and took two short sips before carefully returning the cup to the exact center of its saucer.

"I'm sorry?" my father said.

"This picture," Aunt Bess said pointing to the photo of him, the Nose Picker, and me standing with the oversized check at the Marriott Hotel.

"You look like Christ on the cross. You don't look like a man who just won a billion dollars."

"It wasn't quite that much, Aunt Bess," my father said, picking up the newspaper.

"You could have at least pretended to be happy."

"It was a poor photograph," my father said.

"And you looked miserable on TV. Miserable. You looked mad, angry. You know what they're saying about you on the radio this morning?"

My father remained silent.

"They're saying, what's the matter, is he angry he didn't win more? They're also saying you should buy a toupee. To tell you the truth, Theo, you looked very bald on TV. Well, not bald, but balding."

My father flipped slowly through the newspaper. "I don't think hair is on my list of, well, immediate needs," he said quietly.

"Well, what is then?"

My father just shook his head and said nothing. Since the press conference, he had said little, retreating into his remote space. He reminded me of a kite in the sky, flying higher and higher, getting smaller and smaller, with just a fragile string connecting him to the earth and to us.

"Your brother called last night," Aunt Bess said, walking over to the dishwasher holding greasy plates.

"Frank?" my father said, looking up from the paper. There was an unusual trace of annoyance in his voice.

"You have more than one brother?" my aunt asked.

"Why didn't you tell me this last night?"

"Well, so many people have already called this morning," she said. She loaded the plates into the dishwasher. "I can't keep track. It's craziness. People have been driving up and down the street all morning honking their horns and pointing at the house. I don't know how you slept so long. I can hardly think. I called the police and complained."

My father looked startled. "The police?"

"Yes. The police. They said they would keep an eye on our block. Personally, I'm glad Frank's coming. Maybe he can keep those cars away."

"Dear God. Frank is coming here? To this house?"

"He's flying in from Los Angeles."

I detected an almost silent sigh from my father as he went back to his paper.

"Frank can help you," Aunt Bess said. "He's an attorney. The phone hasn't stopped ringing. You'll need advice now. Besides, we have such a small family. All we have is Frank, really." Turning toward me she said, "Your father and his brother Frank were inseparable growing up. Inseparable. They were the two smartest boys in the neighborhood. The two. Everyone knew they would be rich and famous. And now . . ." she looked up toward heaven, closed her eyes and began mumbling in Greek.

My father looked at her and then nervously glanced over at me and said quietly, "You're going to frighten the boys."

"I'm just giving thanks for being blessed with two genius nephews. Oh, your parents would be so proud. Geniuses."

"Aunt Bess, please. I assure you, I am not a genius. I just happened to pick the right truck stop to buy coffee. And Frank, well . . ." here my father stopped and carefully sipped some coffee.

"His last movie didn't do too well," Aunt Bess said.

"I don't think any of them have ever done well," my father said. Then he quickly added, "At least according to Frank."

"It was about vampires," she said. "Vampire cheerleaders." She turned to look at me. "Isn't that amazing? Such creativity. Where does he get such ideas?"

I nodded and finished my eggs. "How come he just makes movies about vampires?" I asked.

Aunt Bess picked up my plate and walked over to the dishwasher, considering my question.

"Well, because they're interesting. They're interesting people," she said. "Vampires."

Aunt Bess started the dishwasher, turning the dials slowly. "Well, he's done a lot of other things too. He made that one movie about all those pretty maids being murdered. Oh, I almost forgot," she said, turning to face my father. "The man who owns the truck stop called too, a . . ." she put on her glasses that had been hanging around her neck and looked down at a long piece of paper on the counter where dozens of names and numbers were written. "A Tony Ammosti. He wanted to thank you since he gets a percent of the winnings. He couldn't make the press conference, he got the days mixed. He thought it was today, but he wished you a long, healthy life and said that you can stop by for coffee on the house anytime." She took off her glasses. "Well, that's very nice."

My father nodded silently as Aunt Bess put her glasses back on and glanced down at the paper again.

"Someone from *People* magazine called too," she said. "They want to do a story on you."

My father looked over at her. "What's *People* magazine?" he asked.

THE PHONE RANG early the next Monday morning. I got up and went down to the kitchen to answer it, something I had been instructed not to do by my father. He was in the process of having our number changed because people kept calling and asking for money.

"Who's this?" a loud voice shouted over the phone. There was music in the background.

"Who's this?" I asked back. Stavros, the cat, wandered gingerly into the kitchen and lay down under the table.

"The Kink Man," the voice said louder. "WROLL Radio. You're on the air. Now, who's this?"

"Teddy."

"Teddy. You must be one of the rich kids. Tell us, Teddy, how does it feel to win a hundred-and-ninety-million dollars?"

"Pretty good," I said, then hung up as soon as I saw my father make his way sleepily into the kitchen. He looked at me with small eyes and squinted. Then he cleared his throat and walked stiffly over to the counter to make coffee.

I stood next to him and quietly began making my cheese sandwiches for school, a responsibility I had undertaken since my mother's death and would soon relinquish to Aunt Bess. I also made a half a peanut butter and jelly sandwich for the Nose Picker's kindergarten snack and packed it away in his backpack. Out of the corner of my eye, I watched my father take his anti-heart-attack pills, listened to him cough, and assessed his chances of survival for that day.

"Well," he said, after clearing his throat. "I imagine you're going to school today."

I nodded my head and carefully wrapped the cheese sandwich in wax paper, folding over the ends of the paper in the manner my mother had used. Upstairs I heard Aunt Bess's heavy feet make their way to the bathroom.

"Well, please, Teddy, remember what we discussed. Please be discreet."

My father had briefly considered keeping us home from school for a few days, thinking our presence would be a distraction. After some discussion, he had changed his mind and decided to let us go, instructing us not to discuss the lottery with anyone.

"Don't discuss it," he said again now at the counter. "It's really no one's concern but ours."

"Okay," I said and went upstairs to get dressed for school.

As soon as I got to the St. Pius playground, Johnny Cezzaro ran over to me and began demanding ten thousand dollars in twenties and tens.

"Come on, Pappas, I know you got the money. It's just a lousy ten grand. That's nothing to you. Your old man wipes his ass with ten grand."

"No, he doesn't," I said. The image of my father wiping himself with ten thousand dollars raced through my mind only to be quickly replaced by the sweaty head of Johnny Cezzaro, a short, wide boy with greasy black hair who everyone disliked. Johnny was particularly despised by Mr. Sean Hill, the custodian who was almost a priest when he lived in Ireland. I had once heard Mr. Sean Hill tell Mrs. Plank, the principal, that "the good Lord should have just made another rat instead of Johnny Cezzaro. They don't live as long and you can hit them with a broom handle."

"Come on, Pappas, I'll sell you a Pay Day for ten grand. Just give me the money."

"I don't have any money," I said as I tried to walk past him to the lines that were forming in front of the door. I could see my best friend, Charlie Governs, walking ahead of me and I wanted to catch up with him and ask him if he could come over and paint with me after school.

Johnny Cezzaro ran in front of me and fell to his knees. When I tried to walk past him, he reached out and grabbed me by the legs.

"Johnny, quit it," I said. Other children in the playground were beginning to look our way.

"Okay, just fifty bucks," he said. "That's nothing. You won a billion dollars. If you don't do it, I'm gonna eat this gravel and choke to death. Look." Johnny grabbed some rocks off the playground and held them close to his mouth. He was known for threatening bodily harm and physical violence to himself rather than to others which was why he never was considered an effective bully.

"I swear I'll do it, Pappas. Look! Look! Just ten bucks. Look!"

I wrestled free of Johnny and ran near the head of the line and stood right behind Charlie Governs. Charlie was the second best artist in class and I enjoyed drawing and painting with him. He could draw people better than me, capturing expressions and character in a way that I couldn't and I respected this talent. Even though I won most of the school art contests, I knew he was good. Very few of the other children, especially the boys, cared about drawing. But Charlie and I did. I was the only person Charlie ever spoke to which consequently made me his only friend. But he never talked to me in school or at recess. Instead, he would pass me notes with cartoons or illustrations on them, inviting me to his house or asking if he could come over. The St. Pius teachers were forever trying to get him to speak in class but he refused, staring stoically past them at the blackboard. If he hadn't always received the highest scores in math and reading in the class and if his brother Joshua hadn't graduated college when he was eighteen and gotten a job at a computer company, people probably wouldn't have thought him smart.

Charlie slipped me a note when I approached him. I opened it and was treated to a very good likeness of the Monopoly chance card, "Bank Error," featuring the little old man winning money from the bank. I nodded and smiled. As a rule, I didn't speak to him in public much. I knew this made him uncomfortable.

"Do you want to come over today?" I whispered.

Charlie looked hard at the back of J. R. Lawler who was standing directly in front of us in line, then he shook his head very slowly and carefully.

"How about tomorrow?" I asked.

Charlie nodded this time.

When we got into class, Miss Grace smiled at me and said, "Well, there

20

he is! We've been seeing a lot of you in the news, Mister Teddy Pappas!" I looked at her and smiled, then looked down at the floor, my cheeks burning red. Earlier that morning while I was still in bed under my covers, I had wondered what her breasts would look like with tassels on them. Over the summer, Johnny Cezzaro had shown me a picture of a naked woman with tassels on her breasts. He had said that the woman used to be an exotic dancer but now worked as a receptionist at his uncle's auto dealership.

Before we started history, Miss Grace asked me to tell, "in my own words," what it was like to win the lottery. Her face was unusually flushed and looked like my mother's used to after she did her sit-ups or drank too much Jim Beam.

"My father told me not to talk about it," I said, standing next to my desk. Miss Grace made us stand when we spoke for vague reasons, distantly related to posture and diction.

She looked surprised, but said, "Of course, of course," and cleared her throat. "And we will respect his wishes for privacy." Sensing her and the class's disappointment however, I quickly said, "We're probably going to buy a farm. But we're not sure."

"Oh. I see," she said. Then she said, "My."

"A lousy farm?" Johnny Cezzaro whispered. But he whispered it too loudly and Miss Grace gave him a punishment penmanship assignment and then we began a discussion about the Fertile Crescent.

During Enrichment period, when I was writing my letter to Ergu, my Christian pen pal who lived in poverty in a mud house in a remote part of Africa I could never locate on the map, Miss Grace walked over to my desk and softly asked if my father was planning any major charitable contributions.

"I'm not sure," I said. Miss Grace was a small woman with soft brown hair and large green eyes that I frequently lost myself in. I enjoyed having her close so I could smell her scent that reminded me of fresh rain on flowers. Hoping to keep her near me another moment, I said, "I think we might give some money to Ergu and his family so he doesn't have to eat as many roots."

"That's very Christian," she said, her eyes watering. Miss Grace always seemed to be on the verge of tears for reasons we could only guess at. Her poems about barren trees, gray skies, and squirrels that had been run over by semitrucks, frequently appeared in the Wilton newspaper under a pen name, Sylvia Hill. Everyone knew they were her poems though. Even Mrs. Plank, the principal knew. She was always calling Miss Grace our "secret poet" in the hallways even though it was apparent that Miss Grace was embarrassed by this, her face growing stop-sign red.

"Is Ergu still poor?" I asked, looking up at her. When she smiled at me, I wondered whether breast tassels hurt to wear or were instead painless like wax lips.

"Yes," she said. "It's especially hard during the flood season."

I looked over her shoulder in what I hoped was the direction of Africa, then asked, "How long is the flood season?" I received virtually all of my information about Ergu from Miss Grace since Ergu had never actually sent me a letter even though I had been his Christian pen pal for almost two years.

"A long time," she said, patting me on my head and walking away. "A long time."

Since Miss Grace saw all of our letters before they were mailed to Africa, I wrote a longer letter than usual to Ergu telling him that we had won some money and that I was going to see if we could send him some. I also suggested that, with the money, he and his family might consider buying a raft to use during flood season and paddle to another, drier country that might have modestly priced restaurants. Then I asked what his school was like, reminded him that I was praying for his family and handed my letter in to Miss Grace. Later that afternoon, during Reflection period, which was when we were supposed to reflect about Jesus but usually just looked out the window and reflected on the St. Pius parking lot, I watched Miss Grace silently read our letters at her desk, her sweet face intense and focused. When she came to my letter, she looked up and smiled. A few moments later though, she called Johnny Cezzaro to her desk and slowly ripped up his letter in front of him and made him throw it away, piece by piece in the wastebasket by the side of her desk. Johnny was always asking his Christian pen pal for money and I concluded that he had done so again.

When school was over, Mrs. Plank, our aged principal and Miss Polk, the assistant principal (whom everyone said was a woman-loving lesbian, because she had short hair and used to be a disc jockey) pulled me out of line in the hall and started asking me questions.

"Were you excited when you won?" Miss Polk asked. She was chewing gum and cracking it in her mouth, lesbian-style.

"Tell your father that St. Pius needs a new furnace," Mrs. Plank said, laughing and rubbing my head with a very old hand.

I nodded and smiled. Mrs. Plank had never touched me before and I began to feel nervous that Miss Polk would soon feel the need to start touching me too.

"You're going to become very popular around here, Teddy. You and your brother," said Miss Polk. I smiled at her and noticed for the first time that she had facial hair. Thin, almost transparent whiskers lay calmly on her upper lip, unrepentant and growing.

"Your father's going to be pretty popular around Wilton too, I suppose," Mrs. Plank said.

Miss Polk said, "Oh, Mary, really, that's terrible," and then Miss Polk laughed through her soft mustache and they let me go.

Near the front door, Mr. Sean Hill stopped mopping the floor and smiled at me as I tried to pass. He had thick red hair, a thick red mustache, and a blotchy, dirty-white face that reminded me of snow in March. Whenever I was near him, I sensed a strange current of anger lurking just out of reach of his smiling face. Rumor had it that he had been a member of the Irish Republican Army before almost becoming a priest and then moving to America to become a janitor.

"Jesus Christ himself would trade places with you now, Teddy Pappas," he said in his Irish brogue that sounded like off-key music. "Jesus Christ his own fuckin' self." Then he smiled violently and slowly started moving his mop over the floor, wiping my invisible footprints clean.

On the way home, a group of older girls from sixth grade kept yelling "Moneybags" at me from across the street. Embarrassed and flattered, I swallowed hard and tried not to look over at them. I was at the age where girls were starting to matter, moving slowly but steadily up my list of priorities. Up until that point, I had occupied a very low rung on the social ladder at St. Pius, a step above Charlie but several miles below Benjamin Wilcott and other members of the school football team, an arrogant group of boys with sharp elbows and hard knees. Tall and thin with red hair and freckles, awkward at sports, and recently made motherless, I received occasional pity but little else in the way of attention from the plaid-skirted girls of St. Pius. When the girls yelled again, I ducked my head and walked faster.

When I got to our block, Mrs. Rhodebush, our next-door neighbor, was sitting out on her lawn, fanning herself with a large pink fan that Mr. Rhodebush had brought back from the Far East before he died of massive heart failure while cleaning his gutters. He had rolled off the roof and onto a large evergreen bush where Mrs. Rhodebush found him some time later, suspended in the bushes, and dead.

"So you're rich now," Mrs. Rhodebush said. I looked at my shoes. I had always found it difficult to talk to Mrs. Rhodebush. She was old and had clear, liquid eyes that slid quickly through her wrinkled face. She lived alone and spent most of the day observing and, I thought, judging my family. My father said her mood was due, in part, to a gum disease that made her legally disabled. She didn't have any permanent teeth, a condition she allegedly took advantage of by parking in handicapped spaces whenever she shopped at the mall.

"You should ask for a big allowance now," Mrs. Rhodebush said. When she smiled I noticed that she had once again lost her false teeth. She had lost them the week before and had called my father and asked him to send me over to help her find them. After I located them behind the television, she had given me a can of creamed corn as a reward. When I gave the can to my father he studied it for awhile, then put it quietly away into a cupboard, after saying, "Well."

"I never played the lottery," she said. "I'm surprised your father did. I never would have taken him for a gambler. I never gamble. Except for the stock market and then only dividend-paying utilities." Then she said, "It's a shame your mother isn't around to enjoy this. A shame."

"Yes," I said. I was surprised that Mrs. Rhodebush even mentioned my mother. They hadn't liked each other much and had fought frequently over the condition of our house, Tommy's behavior, and the bathing suit my mother would sometimes wear while cutting the grass in the summer.

"You have your mother's red hair," she said. "Your mother had pretty hair. She was an attractive lady. Everyone knew that. More and more, you look just like her."

"I know," I said. People were always commenting about how much I looked like my mother and how the Nose Picker, with his dark looks, looked like my father.

"You're very rich now, young man, very rich," Mrs. Rhodebush said. "I suppose you won't be wanting to help me find my teeth anymore. Rich people don't do many favors. They just take cruises on big ships and sit in large chairs and allow negroes to fan them."

Her description of our future was very different from anything I had ever pictured for my family and I tried hard for a moment to imagine it. Finally, when I realized that she was staring at me I said, "I can help you find your teeth anytime you want," though I had no intention of ever doing so again. I had found the experience (as well as her teeth, slimy and covered with rug fuzz) disgusting. I had already decided to send the Nose Picker over to help if and when she called again.

"You're a fine young tycoon," she said. She pulled me close to her. She smelled like old flowers. "Tell your father to be careful. There are snakes and weasels in the garden. Snakes and weasels."

"I will," I said. The old flower smell was overwhelmingly sweet and I began to take short breaths.

"Being rich isn't as easy as you think. I know. Mr. Rhodebush made a basketful of money. But with that money came responsibility and guilt," she said. "And guilt."

I nodded my head and wondered what act, event, or disturbance had to take place in order for Mrs. Rhodebush to stop talking so I could go into the house. She was being unusually nice to me though, a fact I attributed to the painkillers I knew she sometimes took for her disabled mouth.

"Wilton is full of people who have money. Look," she said, sweeping her hand around the neighborhood. Our block, like most blocks in Wilton, was very nice. Large, old homes framed by large, old trees dotted the wide streets. A magazine had recently listed it as one of Chicago's nicest suburbs. There had been three movies filmed in Wilton since I was born. My mother said they were all about rich families in big homes who had children who hated them. Our house was a bit small and run-down and was never in any of the movies.

"No one in Wilton has as much money as your father does now though," Mrs. Rhodebush said. She leaned back in her chair and nodded her head. "No one," she said.

One house over, Mr. Tuthill, whom everyone called the Yankee Codger because he once lived in Vermont, started his lawn mower. I watched him pull the cord once, then heard the engine slowly sputter and come to life.

"What are your father's plans for the money?" Mrs. Rhodebush asked. "Are you going to move?"

"I don't think so," I said. Then I said, "We might move to Paris."

"Paris?" she said. "My Lord, why?"

I shrugged and looked at the ground again. Even though I was scared of Mrs. Rhodebush, I sometimes felt the responsibility to confuse and shock her.

"Well, Paris would be a big change," she said.

"I know," I said. "It's in France."

"Before you go moving, you should do some work on your property. It's an embarrassment to the neighborhood. Your father should get some new landscaping, some new grass and shrubs. The Yankee is always complaining about your lawn and he's right. I shouldn't have to look at that jungle all day. And you should get a new roof, too, while you're at it. It's sagging. And a new car. That car your father drives around is older than me."

I looked up at our roof and noticed that it seemed to be bending a bit in the middle. Then I looked over at our wild lawn, tall grass and waving weeds. I didn't have to look over at the Buick in the driveway though; I was well aware of its prehistoric origins.

Mrs. Rhodebush kept fanning herself and looking at me. A bee hovered near her head but she didn't seem to notice or mind. Except for the hum of Mr. Tuthill's lawn mower, the block was perfectly still. I felt the afternoon sun on the back of my neck and moved over a few feet to stand in the partial shadow of a tree.

She sighed and looked over my shoulder into the street. "You're too young

26

to realize what's going to happen to you," she said quietly. She stopped fanning herself and waved her hand at me. "I can only imagine," she said.

I nodded my head and said, "Thank you." Then summoning up my courage, I said, "I have to do my homework," and walked away.

When I got inside the house, the phone was ringing. Thinking that my father was in his study, I answered it in the kitchen.

"Let me just first say that I wouldn't be doing this if I wasn't desperate," a man's voice said. He was talking very fast. "I wouldn't be calling you if I had not exhausted every other option. You are my last hope. If I do not have the transplant, my doctors are afraid I'll die. All I'm asking for is a second chance for life. I know you don't know me, I know that I am just a voice on the phone. But of all the things you could spend the money on, what could be more important, what, besides my new organs?"

"A new furnace for St. Pius," I said, then I hung up the phone and went over to the refrigerator to get a glass of milk. While drinking it, I thought about the lottery. Up until that point, I hadn't believed that it would have much impact on our lives. I assumed we would buy some things, but I wasn't prepared for the interest it was generating. People like Mrs. Rhodebush, Mrs. Plank and Miss Polk, the girls on the way home, even sweet Miss Grace, all seemed drawn to me, like to a light at night. Standing in front of the open refrigerator, feeling the dry, cold air against my face, I saw my father, my brother, and myself as very small people in a very large room. Then I thought of our large, peaceful farm in Wisconsin and my drink-serving robot and I immediately felt better.

"Please close the refrigerator door," my father said as he put his coffee cup carefully into the kitchen sink.

"Are we rich now?" I asked.

My father's eyes widened then narrowed. He coughed then said, "Yes, I suppose we are. By most people's standards."

"What are we going to do with the money we won?"

"I don't really know. I guess we'll just have it, in case we need it."

"When are we going to need it?" I usually didn't ask my father many direct questions since he was easily confused, but I wanted to talk about the lottery.

"Well, I'm not sure, to be honest," he said. "I don't know yet. I'm sure we'll need some of it and find, and find a use for the rest." Then he asked, "Are people talking about it, about the money?"

"Yes."

He rubbed his hand over his chin. "Well, that's to be expected, I suppose," he said. "The prospect of money excites people. It interests them. They speculate over what they would do if they had won. People dream of being rich."

"Did you dream of being rich?"

The question surprised him. His eyes narrowed further, compressing to slits and I could tell that he was thinking. My father was a man who measured conversation carefully, believing that all words had eventual consequences. "No, not really. No." Then he added, "I bought that ticket because I was thinking of your mother at that moment." He looked down at me, his eyes whole again and tried to smile, but he just looked awkward. "Anyway," he said, clearing his throat. "Everything will quiet down soon. You'll see."

"What happens if it doesn't?" I asked.

"I'm sorry? If it doesn't settle down? Well." He took a step back, almost stumbling when he did. I knew then that I had asked too many questions and that he was getting flustered. "Well," he said again. "It just will, Teddy. Things, well, things always quiet down. In time things take care of themselves."

I wanted to ask my father more questions, to talk to him and hug him like I used to hug my mother, but before I could say anything else, he had drifted away upstairs and I was alone.

CHAPTER THREE

THE NEXT DAY, Uncle Frank arrived. He entered our lives loudly, with a sneeze and a smile.

"Shit," he said, after he sneezed. He was standing in the front hallway holding a black briefcase. "Goddamn airplanes are like flying petri dishes. They should pass out surgical masks for chrissakes. Everyone breathing the same air. All the damn germs. Everything's airborne. You could almost see the microbes." He stopped when he saw me standing at the foot of the stairs. "Well," he said suddenly smiling. "There you are. You must be little Tommy," he said.

"Teddy," I said.

"Teddy," he said. He walked over and extended his hand. "Put 'er there, little millionaire. Little *multi*millionaire. I'm Uncle Frank." Then he said quickly and seriously, "Your father's brother. Your father's only brother." He took a step back and studied me, nodding his head. "Bet you didn't know you even had an uncle, did you?" he said smiling again. "But you do," he winked and pointed a finger at me. "You most certainly do."

Since it was late, I was not allowed to stay up and visit with him. So I slowly brushed my teeth and washed my face as Uncle Frank and my father had a late dinner downstairs. I then went and laid on my bed for close to an hour, waiting for Aunt Bess to make her way upstairs and into her room.

When she finally did, I ventured out into the hallway and sat down on the sixth step, a location that allowed me to observe without being noticed. Because of where I was sitting, shielded for the most part from the dining room by a wall, my father who was sitting on the other side of the table, could not see me. If he knew I was up at this late hour, he would not approve. Uncle Frank could easily see me however, if he turned his head, but he seemed oblivious to my presence.

"This gets me sick," Uncle Frank was saying. He was holding a copy of the newspaper that Aunt Bess had bought at the supermarket. It had a picture of the Nose Picker, my father, and me on the cover with the headline: DEAD WIFE SPEAKS BEYOND THE GRAVE—"PLAY MY LOTTERY NUMBERS!"

"They should have at least paid you for the photo."

My father said nothing. Uncle Frank put down the paper.

"This is the way it's going to be, Theo. Get used to it. Every asshole, every Joe Shmoe. Every Tom, Dick, and Mary is going to be coming after you. Leeches, leeches, Theo," Uncle Frank said.

I heard my father sigh then say, "My comments during the press conference were, well, I regret them. They've had . . . repercussions. Yes. It's been distressful."

"You have to be careful about who you tell your story to," Uncle Frank said.

"My story?" my father asked. "It's not much of a story really." Then I heard him clear his throat which was his way of not talking about something he didn't want to talk about. "So," he said. "How is the movie business, Frank?"

"Don't ask. My last film cost me. Cost me big. People don't respect the genre," he said. "There just aren't that many outdoor theaters anymore."

I found my uncle's sudden appearance in our lives extremely exciting. He was shorter and slightly younger than my father, with wavy, thick black hair, a sharp nose, and a large jaw that he thrust at the people he chose to talk to. It was his voice, though, that distinguished him. It was loud and deep and strong in an unfamiliar but reassuring way. I had heard little about his work in Hollywood, though he had once sent me a poster of a movie he produced, *Centerfold Shewolves*. My father was upset when he saw the poster and immediately made me take it down from my bedroom wall. He never mentioned Uncle Frank to me.

"What are you going to be doing with the money?" Uncle Frank asked.

"Truthfully, I don't know, yet," my father replied. "I haven't been able to focus properly. It all seems very, well, very removed from me still."

"Where is it now?"

"What?"

"Where is the money now?"

"Oh, it's in the bank. The Bank of Wilton. In our savings account."

Uncle Frank shook his head. "The Bank of Wilton? You mean it's just sitting there? Jesus, Theo. You have to be a little more sophisticated than that. You should have some of it in the market. Invest it."

"Invest it? Well, why?"

"For the future."

"I think we have more than enough for the future, Frank."

Uncle Frank shook his head again. "Well, we can talk about this later. But we should consider some specific options."

"Options?" my father asked. "May I ask, what kind of options?"

"I'm not really sure yet. Land probably. Commercial real estate. There are some other things we can go into later. I have some ideas I want to bounce off you. Cattle."

"I'm sorry, cattle?"

"Cows, bulls. A few herds."

Just then the phone rang. Even though my father had changed our number, it rang constantly, filling our answering machine with sad, desperate, and sometimes angry voices, all asking and wanting.

"Let me get this one," Uncle Frank said. He disappeared from view as he walked into the kitchen. Then I heard him say, "Yes it is. This is his butler."

"Frank, please be polite," my father whispered. "It might be a neighbor."

"Listen," my uncle said to the caller in his deep voice. "I don't care how many veterans went blind in Vietnam. I served two tours in 'Nam and I didn't go blind." Then he slammed down the phone.

"Frank!" my father said, appalled. "That was rude. And you weren't in Vietnam."

"And neither was that guy on the phone," Uncle Frank said, returning to his seat. "Remember, Theo, there's people out there whose full-time job just became trying to get your money. Con artists, thieves, crooks. Everyone who calls you from now on is going to be blind, deaf, dying, paralyzed, impotent." He stopped here. "You can't trust anyone anymore. No one."

"All I'm saying Frank is that I urge you to be polite," my father said.

Uncle Frank shook his head and laughed softly. "Theo, you're too rich to be polite."

"Frank," my father said. "I appreciate your coming all the way from Los Angeles to help me in my . . ." My father paused. "My hour of need. But I ask that you respect my wishes as long as you are in my house."

Uncle Frank crossed his legs and looked at his shoe for awhile. "Okay, okay," he said, "point well taken." He picked up his glass of wine and slowly began to swirl it. "So," he said. "When are you moving?"

"Moving?" my father sounded surprised. "We're not moving."

"You're not going to stay here are you? I mean in this house?"

"It's a perfectly fine house."

Uncle Frank waved his hand. "That's just the point. It's a perfectly fine house. You can afford a perfectly perfect house now. A huge house. A pool. Ten pools. A pool in every room. Anything you want. Jacuzzis, a steam room, extra toilets. This house only has three bedrooms. You don't even have a guest room."

"I don't anticipate having many guests," my father said.

"What do you call me?" Uncle Frank said. "Looks like I have to sleep in the basement."

My father didn't reply. I heard him get up and begin to clear the table of dessert dishes. My father didn't like to talk at length. Questions, in particular, made him uncomfortable, throwing off his equilibrium, which always seemed to be in a delicate state. When asked a direct question, his body would stagger a bit as if he was trying to regain his footing on a slippery surface. Uncle Frank didn't appear to know any of this, however. He just kept talking and my father kept slipping.

"The problem with you, Theo," he said, "the problem with you is that you're too nice. You're too nice to be this rich. If you're going to survive, you're going to have to develop a little edge. A little attitude. A little anger."

"I don't understand." My father was back in the dining room, clearing more dishes. "I don't have much reason to be angry. I won an enormous amount of money. With whom should I be angry exactly?"

"Angry at people. It's your turn to get even."

"Even with whom?"

"With everyone. Everything."

"I'm sorry, Frank, I don't understand."

Uncle Frank appeared upset. He quickly uncrossed his legs and pointed a finger in the direction of my father. "People used to laugh at us growing up. They looked down at us. I'll never forget that. Never."

My father's voice sounded confused. "People looked down at us? In what way? In what way do you mean, exactly?"

"The only way it mattered. Down their noses. You never noticed anything. You always were hiding behind some book. Have you forgotten the fact that we used to take in other people's laundry?"

My father paused before speaking, "We owned a chain of dry cleaners, if that's what you mean," he said.

"Well, I call that pretty humble. We started from nothing. All those goddamn kids' fathers were doctors and lawyers. Orthodontists. You never saw the hurt and the pain in Mom's eyes when she didn't get invited to all their parties. The closest she ever came was using Woolite on their goddamn clothes afterwards."

"I think you're dramatizing a bit," my father said.

"Am I?" Uncle Frank asked. Then he drained his glass of wine and said angrily, "We were like sharecroppers, for chrissakes. Greek sharecroppers. Do you remember Debbie Cabot Swanson? Do you remember her and her whole goddamn Pilgrim-ass Wasp family? Do you remember her sisters? They all looked like Julie Andrews?"

"No, well yes, yes I do. They lived down the block from us. They had that large house with, with the . . ."

"A gazebo. They had a goddamn Wasp gazebo. Their house was like a goddamn plantation. I'm surprised they didn't own slaves, for chrissakes. Do you remember how she used to treat you and me? Do you remember what that bitch said to you when you asked her to prom?"

There was a long silence coming from my father's end of the room. "No, no, I don't," he finally said. "That was quite a while ago. I don't recall anything about anything like that."

"Well, I do. She said, 'I don't go out with people like you.' Do you remember her saying that? People like you."

"I don't recall ever asking her on a date. I don't recall ever speaking to her. I think you're confused on this point, Frank. I believe it was you who asked her out, asked her on a date. Yes, I believe it was you."

"People. Like. You."

My father was quiet again. Then he said, "Frank, I'm afraid you've had too much wine."

"I haven't had enough," Uncle Frank said. He reached over for the bottle and poured more wine, filling his glass to the brim. "You know, big brother, we have a different perspective on life, different, well, different world views, so to speak. Remember, I didn't go to Harvard like you. I went to the school of hard knocks."

"Oh, Frank, please, not this again. You went to Stanford."

"It's not Harvard," Uncle Frank said quickly. "It doesn't get the same reaction at parties."

I heard my father walk back into the kitchen and then return again.

"Let's face it, big brother," Uncle Frank said. "We were the Joads. We were the goddamn grape-picking Joads. And now it's our turn for the gazebo, Theo. It's our turn."

"Yes, well. I think I'm going to bed," my father said as I ran back upstairs.

That night I tried to draw my father again. I had tried many times before, but I could never capture that faraway look, that distance that separated him from the rest of the world.

Before the accident, my father didn't have much to do with our lives. Though he was always polite, he seemed continually startled by our presence and awkward at family functions, of which there were few. He frequently ate dinner alone after we were in bed and could go days without saying much more than a few words when our paths did cross. He displayed little interest in our activities and even less affection toward us. This apparent indifference led me to a sad conclusion: he did not love us like my mother had.

On all levels, he was a mystery. He certainly was smart; he was regarded as one of the country's leading authorities on the Civil War and his book, *A*

Civil War Companion, never went out of print. But despite his intelligence, he lived in a fog, a slumber from which I wanted to wake him. I wanted him to be like the other parents of Wilton who seemed to be in a constant state of family frenzy, shuttling back and forth between soccer games and birthday parties, laughing and talking. Yet these simple things were beyond him. He was trapped, it seemed, in a remote place and accepted his fate with a hopeless inevitability that frustrated, worried, and sometimes angered me.

I could not count on him for much. He frequently got lost when he drove, misplaced his wallet and keys almost daily, and drifted off in the middle of most conversations. His wardrobe and total disregard for clothes bordered on the ridiculous. He seldom wore socks that matched and his ties and suits all had a tired, mothball look and smell about them that used to embarrass my mother who took pride in her appearance. Once in the third grade, he picked me up at school, a rare event, wearing a very short, tight fitting white jacket whose sleeves barely extended past his elbows. As I approached him on the playground, I realized to my horror (and the amusement of my classmates) that he was wearing my mother's coat. When I pointed this out to him, he was confused. "I must have taken it by mistake," he said, then quietly took the jacket off and draped it over his shoulders, making a bad situation much, much worse. "Well, it is chilly," he said in response to my pleading glares.

While he was hopelessly disorganized, he was also very rigid in his routines. He ate his meals, worked in his study, and read the *New York Times* at the exact same times everyday. He had no hobbies that I knew of, no close friends, demonstrated no great acts of charity nor had any real temper.

He did love my mother though, that much was clear. Many times I would see him staring at her while she was working in the yard or cleaning the kitchen. Once he shocked us all by presenting her with a dozen roses at dinner for no reason other than it had been a sunny day, he said. He had a soft look in his eye when he watched her, a look I came to recognize. Men always stared at my mother. She was quite beautiful.

After she died, my father stopped talking entirely, passing the days in silence in his study or his bedroom. He communicated through notes, ("Dear Ted, Is spaghetti and a salad all right for dinner?") which he left on the kitchen table. I never questioned his silence, I assumed it was in response to the accident and I believed that if I left him alone, he would eventually start talking again or at least begin leaving longer notes. It was during this silent time that he suffered a horrible spastic bowel attack ("Dear Ted, I have an intense pain in my backside.") brought on, according to the doctors, by depression and stress. When we visited him at the hospital, he finally spoke to me. "Don't worry, Teddy, I'm not going to die," he said. "And when I get home, things will improve." He was right. When he came home, he began talking more, inquiring about our homework and after-school activities, answering questions about the Civil War, and occasionally playing a board game with us, which was something the family therapist from the hospital encouraged him to do. Even though I could sense that he was uncomfortable with Tommy and me and that talking still required an effort on his part, things gradually seemed less sad around our house and we got by.

In bed now, I tried to draw that look of soft pain around his eyes, the pain that I knew he felt every day, but I couldn't. Giving up, I slid my sketch pad back under my bed and laid down. When I closed my eyes, I could see my father's face perfectly.

THE NEXT MORNING, Uncle Frank offered to take me and the Nose Picker to school. My father was hesitant.

"They usually walk," he said. Any type of change from our routine caused great confusion for him.

"I rented a Lexus for a couple of days," Uncle Frank said. "It's nice. Besides, I always go out for breakfast. Always. I can't eat breakfast at home. What would I eat?" My father reluctantly relented, only after he wrote detailed directions to St. Pius on a piece of paper which Uncle Frank stuffed casually in his pocket without so much as a glance.

Once in the shiny, black car, Uncle Frank looked at his watch.

"What time does school start?"

"Eight-thirty," I said. The leather seats of the car felt slick and cool on the backs of my arms. I made a mental note to replace our red Jeep with a Lexus on my List of Things.

"Eight-thirty or eight-thirty*ish*?" Uncle Frank asked. "Is there some leeway there? Some give and take? A little wiggle room?"

I wasn't sure what he meant so I said, "Eight-thirty in the morning."

He nodded. "Well," he said. "What would you say if your favorite uncle took you to breakfast?"

"Yeah," the Nose Picker said.

"But we'll be late," I said, even though I had no overwhelming desire to go to school.

"What's a few minutes? I'm always late. I like to make an entrance. In L.A. I'm always thirty minutes, an hour, late, whatever. I want people to be relieved and excited to see me. It's an art. The more important you are, the later you can be. You two guys should start practicing it. Everyone can start waiting for you now," he said as he pulled into the parking lot of Will's Pancake House. "Hell, I'll wait for you."

Once in the restaurant, Uncle Frank looked concerned. "No way they have cappuccino here, no way," he said gloomily as he looked around the tired and dark coffee shop. "They probably don't even have fresh squeezed orange juice here. Out in L.A., I always have fresh squeezed. Always. With pulp. I'm not afraid of pulp."

Uncle Frank fell quiet for a few moments and I suspected that he was thinking about all the fresh orange juice with pulp that was being consumed by other fearless people that very moment back in Los Angeles.

"Well, anyway, I'm sure they have good pancakes," he said, as we slid into the booth by the window. Outside, I could see traffic, moving slowly. Uncle Frank picked up his fork and knife and squinted at them, shaking his head. "Jesus Christ, these things are infected. They may as well give us dirty syringes to eat with." He started wiping them furiously with his napkin.

Will's was a forgotten place that smelled of coffee and burnt toast. It was frequented by senior citizens and foreign-looking limousine drivers who came to Wilton to take business executives to and from the airport. It never seemed to be more than a quarter full. My mother used to wonder how it managed to stay open in our neighborhood next to the high priced gourmet coffee and bagel shops that lined the three blocks that made up downtown Wilton. The booths had a permanent sheen made of some unknown but resilient substance and the formica tabletops were dull gray. The floor was alternately sticky and slippery and walking on it could be a noisy and sometimes dangerous affair.

"I remember this being a nicer place. Maybe we should get the hell out of here," Uncle Frank said looking around the restaurant. Before we could get up to leave, however, the waitress came over and asked if we would like coffee.

"What the hell, we'll stay," he said. "You don't have cappuccino do you?" When he asked this, the waitress looked frightened and took a step back, away from our booth.

"What?" she asked.

"Relax," he said. "Relax. Just coffee. Do you want coffee?" he asked me.

I had never been asked that question before. "Yes," I said.

The waitress looked suspiciously at me, but walked away. She returned a few seconds later with two cups. "How do you drink yours?" she asked, raising one eyebrow. She was old and had teeth like unshined pennies and I considered hating her.

"I want some too," the Nose Picker said.

"He doesn't drink coffee." Then, turning to the waitress I said, "I like it like this, thanks." I picked up the coffee and took a sip.

"Bring the little guy some Kool Aid or something," Uncle Frank said. He looked at me. "Kids still drink Kool Aid, right?"

Just then, Uncle Frank started ringing. He quickly retrieved a small phone from his pocket and began talking.

"Frank Pappas. Sylvanius? I can barely hear you. What? Yeah, I know. I just got here. What they say? That's bullshit. I hope they all have heart attacks. I'm going to pray that they have heart attacks. I'm going to get on my goddamn knees and pray."

I took another sip of black coffee. I liked my uncle. There was an excitement and confidence about him that I found both exotic and appealing. I instinctively wished my father was more like him. If I wanted to, I would have no trouble drawing Uncle Frank. He was distinct in every way, his edges sharp and clear.

"Joan Collins would never play a vampire," he said. "It's too close to home."

At school, Miss Grace was probably wondering where I was. Johnny Cezzaro was probably writing his Christian pen pal another letter asking for money, Charlie was probably looking for me without turning his head or his eyes. They all seemed very far away as I took another sip of coffee.

Since I was feeling happy, I started doing something I almost never did, I began talking to the Nose Picker in public.

"Tommy, what are you drinking?" His glass looked like it was full of Hawaiian Punch.

"I don't know," he said. "It's good."

"So is my coffee," I said even though I was pretty sure it tasted terrible.

When the waitress came to take our order, Uncle Frank covered the phone with his hand and said "Order whatever you usually get." Then, returning to the phone he said, "Have you seen her lately? She's huge. Vampires are supposed to be thin. They live off blood, not pie á la mode." He looked briefly over at me and the Nose Picker and then he said, "No. Not yet. This is going to take some time," and hung up.

"So," he said when the waitress brought us our food. "You guys usually get banana splits for breakfast?"

"Yes," I said. Tommy and I began spooning up the whipped cream of our banana splits.

"Well, I'm stuck with oatmeal. Cholesterol. It's hereditary you know. You guys better watch it." He turned to Tommy. "What's your cholesterol, Tommy?"

Tommy stopped eating, his spoon in midair. He glanced sideways at me, his eyebrows raised high, his mouth full of ice cream.

"He doesn't have any," I said.

I turned my full attention back to my banana split and ate it in large scoops that dripped and slid down my spoon. My hand was soon sticky, all the way up to my wrist.

"So, you like being rich?" Uncle Frank asked as he poured skim milk over his oatmeal.

"Yes," I said, "it's okay." The Nose Picker poured syrup on his finger and then stuck it up his nose.

"Tommy, don't," I said, pulling down his arm gently. "Don't."

Uncle Frank looked over at Tommy, then back at me. "So, have you asked your father to buy anything for you yet? Some new toys? A horse? Anything?"

"No," I said.

"Isn't there anything you really want? A new basketball? Some kind of bike?"

I thought about my List of Things and the farm. I also thought about Ergu and his raft, but didn't say anything.

Uncle Frank sipped his coffee. "Have a lot of people been asking you for things? For money?"

"Not too many," I said.

"Well from now on, they have to go through me. I'm going to head up the Pappas Charitable Foundation. I'm going to be around for a little while to help your dad out."

"How?"

"How what?"

"How are you going to help him?" I asked.

Uncle Frank swallowed some oatmeal. "Well, I'm a lawyer. I can help him with taxes and investments. I can help him save money."

"But you make movies," I said. I took another sip of coffee and held it in my mouth for a while before forcing a swallow.

"I'm a lawyer who makes movies." He shrugged. "It happens."

"I wish my father made movies."

"Hey, your father is a very smart guy, even though he doesn't say much. He's as smart as they come." Then he said, "In some areas."

I took another sip of coffee and considered what Uncle Frank said. "In some areas," pretty much meant the Civil War.

"Have you guys ever seen any of my films? My movies?"

"Our father won't let us. We started watching one on cable, the one with the vampire sharks, the ones that attack those people on the beach."

"Blood Ocean," Uncle Frank said quickly. "Those weren't sharks, those were dolphins. That was the twist. Evil dolphins. They were a pain in the ass to work with. They're not as smart as you think. They're not all Flipper."

"My father made us turn it off."

"You've never seen any of my movies, then. Not one? They're on cable all the time. How about *The French Maid Murders*? That wasn't too violent. A little sexy, maybe, but the violence was understated. What about *Microbes*? That actually got a few good reviews. That was my best one I think."

"Our father doesn't let us watch much TV," I said. "Except for PBS."

Uncle Frank's initial look of surprise immediately gave way to disbelief, then finally concern. He put his coffee cup noisily down on the table, spilling some. "What? No TV? No child should be deprived of television." He picked the cup back up again. "Not in America, at least." Then he asked, "What do you watch on PBS?"

"Nature shows," I said. "History shows. Last week we watched a show about the construction of the Mackinaw Bridge."

Uncle Frank absorbed my comment in silence. "The Mackinaw Bridge," he finally said. "They have shows like that. On TV?"

I nodded. "Yes."

"Well, I'm surprised they didn't save that for sweeps' month." He shook his head. "The Mackinaw Bridge."

"My father watches the news sometimes too," I said.

"I love vampires," Tommy suddenly said. His lips were red from the Kool Aid.

Uncle Frank was confused. "What? Oh. So do I, especially when they make me money. Which they haven't been doing lately." He drank more of his coffee. "You know, you're the first kids I think I've spoken to in about thirty years. I just realized that they don't have kids out in L.A. They probably eat their young."

"Did you know my mom?" the Nose Picker asked.

The question surprised Uncle Frank. When he answered, his voice sounded softer and moved slower.

"Of course I did. Your mom was a very beautiful lady. You know," he said looking back at me, "you look just like her. It was a sad day when she died, a sad day." He drank more coffee and wiped his mouth with a small paper napkin, while the Nose Picker finished his Kool Aid. Then Uncle Frank leaned across the table.

"Let me ask you something here," he said quietly. "Just between, you know, us Pappas guys. Your father, how's he doing?"

"Okay," I said.

Uncle Frank nodded his head and scratched his chin. "Okay is a very general term, Teddy," he said. "Do you mean, okay as in just okay, or okay as in great, ass-kicking fantastic? Could you narrow the range here and be a little more specific?"

I looked out the window and watched a large truck stop at the red light. Inside the cab, the driver yawned, then opened his window.

41

"Just okay," I said.

"That's what I was afraid of. Listen," Uncle Frank said, leaning farther forward, his head now inches from mine. "We guys have to do our best to, you know, make him feel better. Keep an eye on him. He's lonely, I can tell. And lonely people can do, well, strange things. I want you to let me know what he's up to, you know, what he's doing, who he's talking to. Your father is very trusting, especially around, well, especially around women, so we have to keep an eye on him. Both eyes. Can you do that for me, for him?"

Uncle Frank's large head was so close to my face that I could see two small hairs growing out of his nose. I looked away. "Okay," I said, because I knew that's what he wanted me to say.

He leaned back and sighed. "Atta boy," he said. "I knew I could count on you. We Pappas men have to stick together." He made a fist and punched the air. "Trust no one. Words to live by, boys, words to live by."

"No one!" Tommy said. He too punched the air with his fist.

Uncle Frank went back to his oatmeal while I scooped up the melted remains of my banana split. Despite the fact that I enjoyed being with Uncle Frank, I was beginning to feel the first pangs of remorse over missing class. Even though I generally found school uninteresting, I felt a responsibility to Miss Grace and didn't want to disappoint her in a way that might make her less likely to fall in love and marry me.

"So," Uncle Frank said. He finished his oatmeal with a flourish, grandly flipping his spoon into the empty bowl and pushing it to the center of the table. "One-hundred-and-ninety-million dollars. Jesus Christ. We have to do something with that money. Something. We can't just ignore the goddamn money. We have an obligation to do something with it. Don't you think?"

"Yeah," Tommy said. He punched the air with his fist again, then began stacking small packets of sugar on top of each other.

"Something, goddamnit." Uncle Frank held his hands out, palms up. "Something."

Since Uncle Frank seemed almost annoyed with the fact that we won the lottery, I decided to tell him about Ergu.

"We should give some money to Ergu," I said.

Uncle Frank, dropped his chin and looked at me suspiciously. "What the hell is an Ergu? Some type of group?"

"He's a boy. He lives in Africa in a mud hut. He's my Christian pen pal."

Uncle Frank kept looking at me.

"He eats roots," I said. "Sometimes bark."

Uncle Frank nodded his head. "What is he, half beaver?" he said. "Ah, this is some type of Catholic thing, isn't it? I see, they make you do this in school. Yeah, okay, well, we can send him some money. Twenty-five, maybe fifty bucks. That goes a long way down there."

He took another sip of his coffee and smiled. "You know," he said his voice low and thoughtful. "I was thinking we should do something else maybe with the money, you know, something worthwhile, something that might make a real difference. In people's lives, I mean."

"Like what?" I said.

"Produce a television show," Uncle Frank said. "A very thoughtful, very, what the hell word am I looking for here, a very *good* television show. A talk show with a game show twist. With me as the host. And you know what it would be called, don't you?" He leaned back in the booth and when he smiled again, I saw excitement and possibilities, our large farm, our new televisions, and our new house gleaming in his eyes. "Come on, guess, guess!"

"I don't know," I said.

"Come on, guess."

Uncle Frank's animated behavior was getting me nervous. He was jumping around in his seat, pointing his finger. "Come on, Teddy, guess. You too, Tommy!"

I looked down at the table. Tommy kept stacking sugar packets.

"*Frankly Speaking!*" Uncle Frank said. He clapped his hands when he said this then pointed one last finger at me. "The show will be called, *Frankly Speaking*. It will be just me at large, so to speak. Me and one, just one, celebrity guest. I'll interview the celebrity for awhile, say Paul Newman, I know someone who knows him, and then members of the audience will participate in a kind of trivia contest about Paul Newman's career. I'll ask questions, about *Cool Hand Luke* or *Hud* or Joanne Woodward and maybe three audience members try to answer them. And the winner, right then and there, gets to go out to dinner or lunch or whatever with Paul Newman. They leave right there from the show. Alone. Just the two of them. Except for me. I'll go along too. And the camera crew so we can film the thing."

Uncle Frank's face was red from talking and he leaned back in the booth. "So, what do you think? Be secretive about this, by the way, but what do you think?"

I looked back down at the table and was about to say, "I don't know," when the waitress walked up with a copy of *USA Today*.

"I didn't know I was serving famous people," she said as she unfolded the paper to reveal a picture of my father, the Nose Picker, and me. It was the photo of us at the big press conference, except this time it had a different headline: WHAT WOULD YOU DO WITH $190 MILLION?

"Give me that," Uncle Frank snapped.

"I know what I wouldn't do," the waitress said looking down at the headline before handing over the paper. "Eat here," she whispered.

The three limousine drivers in the restaurant were staring at us when we got up to leave. Gus the owner of Will's, came out from behind the counter and shook my hand. He knew my father. They would talk about Greece and local politics during our occasional visits. "Where's your father, he too rich for my restaurant now?" he asked.

"He's at home," I said.

"You know where Gus would like to go if he had money, where I would live?" he asked my uncle.

Uncle Frank stared at Gus. "Don't make me guess," he said.

"No guess. Key West? You hear of Key West?"

"Yes, I've heard of Key West," Uncle Frank said handing some money over the counter to the waitress. "I was born and raised on Earth."

"Key West is beautiful. The most beautiful place."

"Yep. Nice town," Uncle Frank said as he counted his change. "Nice town."

Gus looked down at me. He had a big nose and was bald. He looked like an old parrot. "Tell your father that I need a loan," he said. "Tell him he give me a loan, I give him free pancakes. Tell him, Gus of Will's, he got bills!" Gus smiled after he said this and looked proud.

"We'll be sure to make that a priority and pass that on immediately," Uncle Frank said, taking the Nose Picker and me by the hands. Before he walked out, he said, "Hey, just a word of advice. That silverware was god-damn filthy. If I get sick or get some type of sore, I'm reporting you to the goddamn Department of Health. You're playing with people's lives here, people's lives." Then we walked out.

Back in the Lexus Uncle Frank's phone rang again. While he talked, I read the newspaper article about us.

The One-Hundred-And-Ninety-Million Dollar Question:
"What Would You Do If You Won the Lottery?"

If you won $190 million, would you quit your job? If you say yes, then you're not alone. According to a *USA Today* poll, more than 80 percent of Americans would quit their jobs and pursue leisure activities. Among those activities:

- travel 34%
- ski 25%
- golf 19%
- gourmet cooking 14%
- sail around the world 5%
- learn another language 3%

How would you share the wealth? Fifty percent of respondents said they would share it with family members; 30% with friends; 20% would give to charitable causes.

Theo Pappas, of suburban Chicago, winner of one of the largest lotteries in U.S. history, said he wasn't sure what he was going to do with the money. Pappas, author of *A Civil War Companion,* plans to continue teaching at Northwestern University where he is a tenured professor. Widowed last year, with two young sons, he played the numbers his deceased wife had played every week for nine years. His wife died in a . . .

"TELL HIM THAT the whole point of the sequel is that it continues a story. Tell him slowly because he's stupid," Uncle Frank yelled into the phone. "He doesn't process information normally. He processes it like a dog. So you have to treat him like one. And tell him to lose that touchy-feeling scene at the end. This is 1994. That stuff went out with *The Waltons*. I want him burned alive as the sun is rising."

As we turned a corner, St. Pius came into view. It was an old building, with dark red bricks. Surrounded by a rusting fence, the school stood out in upscale Wilton, managing to look dreary even on the sunniest of days. My mother had insisted that we attend the school because she was Catholic. After a brief debate, my father, who never discussed or showed any interest in religion, agreed.

"Tell him if he doesn't follow the script, that he will be back directing porno movies in a week. Remember, a dog. He's a goddamn dog."

Uncle Frank flipped the phone shut as we pulled into St. Pius's parking lot. "This it? It looks like an orphanage, for chrissakes."

I looked over at Uncle Frank and swallowed hard at the mention of orphanage.

"Well," he said, spraying something into his mouth. "Let's go eat some shit."

MY FATHER WAS WAITING for me at the playground fence after school was over. He usually picked the Nose Picker up at lunchtime—Tommy only went for half days—but seldom picked me up. After my mother died, the university let him work at home, doing research and writing articles about the Civil War. He did most of his work in the afternoons, calling different libraries or other professors from around the country, hoping to confirm the correct temperature that fateful day at Appomattox, the size of Robert E. Lee's horse, or U.S. Grant's preferred whiskey. It seemed, over his lifetime, my father had exhausted the study of the War's major events and was now forced to hunt for the remaining bits and scraps. Earlier in the summer, I had overheard him debating William Tecumseh Sherman's exact hat size with another professor from Memphis. My father would devour this information, recording every morsel in a leather-bound notebook in his meticulous handwriting using a gold fountain pen the university had given him. Such attention to detail required time, so I was surprised to see him standing there on the edge of the playground. He looked upset as he took my hand and crossed the street.

"I received three phone calls today," he said quietly. "One from your teacher, one from Sister Foreman the school nurse, and one from Mrs. Plank, all asking where you and your brother were. You shouldn't have asked your uncle to take you to breakfast. You had a number of people quite worried." Then he said more to himself than to me, "I should have anticipated this."

As we were getting into the Buick, a young woman ran up to us. My father appeared frightened and said quickly, "Get into the car and lock the doors." The woman smiled at us. She had blond hair and was wearing tiny round sunglasses. I lowered the window.

"Mr. Pappas? I'm Leslie Baller from *People* magazine," she said. "I've been trying to reach you all week."

My father deflated at the mention of the magazine, his shoulders sagging and rounding into an apprehensive hunch. "I've been receiving so many calls lately," he said. "I haven't . . ."

"I understand," she said. Then she looked at me in the backseat. "And that must be your son, Teddy."

"Um, yes," my father looked back at me stiffly, straining his neck.

"I was wondering if I could ask you a few questions about winning the lottery. We'd like to do a story on you and your family. Our readers are very interested in you."

"Your readers?" my father said. "Well, I'm not sure this would be the appropriate time."

"That's why we've been calling you. We were hoping that we could set up an appropriate time. It will only take an hour or so."

My father cleared his throat and once again glanced over his shoulder at me. A car passed by on the street, then another. "Well, I'm not sure we have much to say on the subject that would be of interest to anyone."

"Oh, Mr. Pappas, you're living the fantasy of every American," she said. "We want to learn more about your family, your wife, how it feels to win all that money and why you took so long to claim the ticket. It would make a wonderful story."

"My mother used to read your magazine," I said suddenly.

The reporter looked at me and smiled. "She did, did she?"

"She always wanted to be in it," I said. My father looked at me with disbelief. "She always wanted to be famous."

The reporter took out a notepad and started quickly writing.

"Well," my father interrupted. "Why don't you follow us home where we can talk then, I guess that would work best, don't you think? Yes, yes, follow us home."

"Wonderful," the reporter said and began walking back to her car. My father quickly jumped into the Buick and drove off. "Make sure your seat belt is fastened," he said urgently. I had never seen my father do anything quickly in my life and this sudden outburst of energy and speed scared and excited me. I buckled my seat belt.

My father was silent as he drove. He clutched the wheel with both hands and pressed his face close to the windshield, squinting his eyes in a way that made me think they might burst. We were home in seconds.

"Please go inside and do your homework," he said. He was breathing fast, in spurts.

"I don't have any homework. And Charlie's coming over."

"Teddy, please. I'm sure Aunt Bess has a snack prepared for you. I have to move the car into the garage."

Just then the reporter's car came roaring up to the front of the house. "Let's run," my father said.

"Mr. Pappas, please wait!" the reporter yelled.

"Let me handle her," Uncle Frank said as soon as we entered the house. "I know how to deal with their kind. Goddamn parasite. I'm going to send her straight to hell."

I stood next to my father and peered out from behind the living room curtains at Uncle Frank as he waved his hands and pointed his chin at the reporter. Rather than leave as I had expected, the reporter appeared to be thoroughly enjoying being sent straight to hell. When she wasn't flipping her hair out of her eyes with her finger, she was smiling widely and writing in a notepad. For his part, Uncle Frank looked like he was enjoying himself too. Whenever the reporter laughed, he would point his finger at her and cock his head to one side like a robin. Once he went so far as to shuffle his feet a bit like he was dancing.

"What's a parasite?" I asked my father. I had obviously misinterpreted Uncle Frank's intentions. Judging from the looks on their faces, I thought the reporter and Uncle Frank might soon start kissing.

"It's a word," he said. "Something that lives off something . . ." his voice trailed off. He was breathing heavily and clutching the drapes.

After Uncle Frank flicked a leaf off the reporter's shoulder I asked, "Does Uncle Frank know that lady?"

"No," my father murmured. "At least I didn't think so."

When Charlie Governs's mother dropped him off in our driveway, the reporter tried to talk to Charlie. He stood rigid for a few moments then dropped his art supply bag and ran off down the block. After Charlie was gone, Uncle Frank waved his hand and I thought I heard him say, "What's he know anyway?"

"Dear God, I'm afraid he's encouraging her," my father whispered. Then he said softly, "He was waiting for her. Of course."

A few minutes later, the reporter went back to her car and returned with a camera and began taking photos of Uncle Frank and our house. Uncle Frank cocked his head again to one side, put his hands on his hips, and thrust his chin proudly in the air as he posed.

"Dear God," my father said. "The way he's posturing, he looks like Benito Mussolini."

After the reporter took a few more pictures, she put the camera away and she and Uncle Frank got in her car and drove off together.

THAT NIGHT AT DINNER, my father did not speak. Uncle Frank did most of the talking, touching on a wide variety of issues ranging from politics and history, to why a vampire dies when a stake is driven into his heart.

"When you think about it," he said, swirling his glass of wine thoughtfully and thrusting his chin out in the general direction of Aunt Bess, "they really shouldn't even have hearts. They're not human. It's obviously symbolic of the crucifixion. I always thought that was a flaw in the mythology. A major flaw."

"How interesting, the crucifixion," Aunt Bess said, looking at my father. She was nervously trying to engage him in the conversation. "Those vampires are really something, aren't they, Theo? I wouldn't want to run into any."

My father silently rearranged the food on his plate.

"Are there really such things as vampires?" the Nose Picker asked.

Uncle Frank took a long swallow of his wine and then slowly and delicately wiped the corners of his mouth with a napkin. "That's hard to say. If you believe in them, they exist," he said. His jaw seemed to extend as he spoke, expanding forward. "If people believe in God, they should believe in vampires. Because if people believe in God, they must believe in the devil. And if you believe in the devil, it's only natural to extend that belief to include his apostles, which could include vampires." Uncle Frank looked around the room at us as if he had just imparted some deep knowledge.

"That's interesting too," Aunt Bess said even though I knew she hadn't been listening because she had been picking up some lettuce from the floor that had dropped from the Nose Picker's plate. "Your uncle always had a wonderful imagination, even when he was young," she said sitting back up at the table. "We always knew he would grow up to be something special. He always directed the school plays. Do you remember that, Theo? The school plays, do you remember?"

My father pushed a small, orange tomato around his plate, his face a number of interesting shades of red.

"Theo was always too busy with the books to notice his little brother," Uncle Frank said. "Too busy writing and working hard. Now, of course, he doesn't have to work at all. Now, he's got it made. Mr. One-hundred-and-ninety Million."

I had only seen my father lose his temper once, when my mother accidentally threw out some of his Civil War books to make room for her Precious Moments collection of miniature figurines in the basement. The books had been signed by my father's idol, Civil War writer Bruce Catton. He ended up retrieving all but *Grant Moves South*, which for some reason he could never find. That night, he accused my mother of deliberately throwing them out, a charge my mother loudly denied. It had been the only time I could recall hearing my father raise his voice.

I feared I was about to hear it again. His cheeks were moving in and out, vibrating, as he continued to push the orange tomato around with his fork.

Uncle Frank was also observing my father. "Stop torturing that tomato and eat it already," he said casually, reaching for his wine.

With that, my father stood up and sharply threw his napkin on the table.

He looked at my uncle, then over at the Nose Picker and Aunt Bess, then finally at me.

"I'm leaving," he said evenly. "I'm going for . . . a walk."

As soon as my father left, Aunt Bess said something in Greek and began clearing the table. The Nose Picker slipped from his chair and began crawling on all fours and barking, something he had begun doing recently.

Uncle Frank looked at me and said, "What?" Then he too got up from the table, walking over to the dining room window, where he stood with his hands in his pockets. "Where the hell do you walk around here?" he said. "It's not like we're in Manhattan or anything."

That night I laid awake in bed and waited for my father to come upstairs. He passed by our room exactly at ten o'clock every night, on his way to his small study, to read the *New York Times*. When he finally walked past our doorway, I quietly called out to ask him who was a better general, Robert E. Lee or U.S. Grant. It was a question that I thought he would enjoy, considering his respect for both generals was high.

He hesitated before entering our room, then approached my bed slowly and carefully. "Well," he said, clearing his throat. In the next bed, the Nose Picker sighed deeply and rolled over, asleep. "Well," he said again, putting his hands in his pockets. His cotton-candy hair hung limply to the sides and he looked old and thin and in the fading light I thought I could see through him if I looked hard enough. "That's a question that has been debated for more than one hundred years. And I don't think we have time to discuss it tonight. It's late. We can talk about it tomorrow after school. There are some very good books I can give you."

"But what do you think?" I asked. As usual, I had no genuine interest in the answer, but I knew that my father needed some cheering and nothing cheered him up more than a good dose of the War.

"Well, Lee, of course was a proper man and a brilliant man, probably the finest general America has ever produced, the finest military mind. If he had accepted the command of the Army of the Potomac, the Union Army, as Lincoln had wanted, if he had, the Civil War would have lasted only four months. He would have attacked. I wrestle with the question of whether Lee was a completely moral man though. Despite his insistence that he was fighting for Virginia, and despite his being a proper man, he was fighting for slavery all the same, in defense of a horrible institution. Sometimes I think that if he was as great a man as we all claim, he would have chosen the greater cause—the freedom of men. Still he was a brilliant leader who had no equal. As for Grant . . ."

I tried to stifle a yawn, but failed. My father saw this and caught himself. "Let's talk about this some other time. Tomorrow," he said.

"You remind me of Abraham Lincoln," I said.

For the first time in a long time my father smiled what I thought was a real smile. "I am nothing like Abraham Lincoln," he said.

"Where did you go on your walk?" I asked.

He looked embarrassed and shifted uneasily on his feet. I had asked too direct a question and immediately regretted it. "Nowhere actually," he said. Then he cleared his throat. "I was afraid the neighbors would be confused if they saw me walking. I never walk. I thought it might invite suspicion or concern. Possibly alarm."

I looked at him.

"So," he continued. "Actually, I was in the garage. I stood there for a while. I needed some air."

The image of my father standing alone in our cluttered, dark garage saddened me. I wanted to ask him why he had gotten angry and why he didn't want to talk to the reporter from the magazine but instead I simply asked, "Do you feel better now?"

He squinted his eyes. "Better? Yes," he said, thinking. "Yes, I do. I felt things were closing in on me you see, tightening around me. So much has been happening that it seems difficult to grasp things. People don't understand the responsibility. They simply see everything on the surface. The things we can buy. They want to live their lives through us and they don't want to be disappointed. I feel that something is expected of me, something I cannot possibly deliver. And of course, they don't understand the consequences, in our case, consequences they can't imagine." He stopped talking and glanced down at the floor.

I looked at him. His rush of words and the intensity in which he had spoken them, surprised and embarrassed me. I felt I had been caught looking at something illicit and rare, something I had not been intended to see.

He stood in the middle of the room and predictably cleared his throat. Then he said softly, "I feel better now, though. Thank you," and quickly left. Across the room, I heard Tommy ask "Daddy?" but I told him to go back to sleep.

CHAPTER FOUR

Mrs. Wilcott stood on our front porch looking divorced. She might as well just wear a sign that says, "He left me," my mother used to say about her. I remembered Dr. Wilcott, her ex-husband, as a tall dark man with golf clubs and very white teeth. There were three children in the Wilcott family, two older girls in college and Benjamin, who was a year ahead of me in school and made it a point to ignore me at every opportunity.

My mother didn't like Mrs. Wilcott much. "She thinks she's Jane Pauley or something," she once said as she watched Mrs. Wilcott jogging past our house in her blue and pink running suit. Mrs. Wilcott had her own television show, *Access Wilton*, on Channel 87 where she baked cakes and bread and pies with holiday themes. Sometimes, though, she had guests on to discuss local issues. My father reluctantly made a brief appearance on it once to help raise money for Civil War Month that was being celebrated at the Wilton Public Library. Even though my father was a guest, my mother changed the channel after just a few minutes. "I've had enough of Mrs. Middle-Aged Miniskirt," she said.

"Hello, sweetheart, is your father at home?" Mrs. Wilcott now asked as I opened the door.

"He's at work in his study."

"Could you tell him that Gloria is here? Oh, hello, Theo!"

My father had emerged from the bathroom, the only room in the house with a lock, where he had been reading. He had begun this practice ever since Uncle Frank's arrival. He would disappear for hours, causing Aunt Bess great concern over the prospect of another bout of spastic bowel, an attack she believed to be imminent.

"Oh," my father said. Then he said, "Hello, Mrs. Wilcott."

"Gloria," Mrs. Wilcott said and smiled.

"What?" my father said. "Oh. Yes."

"I was wondering if you had a chance to consider our invitation to appear on *Access Wilton*. We'd love it if you could."

My father was confused and for some reason, looked at his watch. "Is it Civil War Month already?"

"No." She laughed a little. "We'd just like to interview you about your big news." Mrs. Wilcott's eyebrows went up after she said this and I thought she looked pretty. She was close to middle age but still wore bows in her hair and still bounced when she walked, her arms swinging like twirling batons. She had very clear blue eyes and a moon-shaped face that had a delicate but definite shine about it. Her blond hair hung over her forehead in bangs and was tied in the back today with a red bow that reminded me of an unexpected Christmas present.

"We'd like for you to come on our show," Mrs. Wilcott said again.

"Oh," my father said. Then he looked at me and I noticed that the zipper of his pants was down. "Oh, I see. Well, I am very busy right now on several projects."

"We would love to hear about them," Mrs. Wilcott said. "We want to know what you do all day now."

"What I do all day," my father repeated. "Now. Yes. Hmmm. Teddy, why don't you go find out what Tommy is up to?"

"He's trying to crap like a dog on his bed," I said truthfully.

My father looked down at me with his mouth open then back up at Mrs. Wilcott who was still smiling. "I really don't . . . could you call me and we can discuss this? Tonight, call me tonight. Thank you so much Mrs. Wilcott. Gloria."

As my father began to shut the door, Mrs. Wilcott stepped forward. "Oh, Theo, I almost forgot, I would like to invite you and your boys over for dinner."

My father was extremely confused now.

"What? Dinner? Now?"

"No, of course not. I was thinking Friday."

At the exact moment Mrs. Wilcott said the word "Friday," my father realized his zipper was down. "Good God!" he said. He began to fumble with it. Then he said quickly, "Yes, of course. Fridays are always good days. For dinner. Thank you." He shut the door and walked quickly up to our bedroom to find Tommy the Dog.

LATER THAT NIGHT when I walked past my father's study, he motioned me inside with a cautious wave of his hand. He was sitting behind his desk, typing on his old blue Royal typewriter. His study was a very small room that I realized years later was actually a very large, walk-in closet. It was decorated solely with Civil War souvenirs, mostly black-and-white pictures of generals, though a few faded maps depicting troop movements and battle sites hung on the walls. My father spent most of his time in this room after my mother died staring out the small rectangular window that overlooked our garage.

"Teddy, I have to ask you something," he said. I stood apprehensively in front of his desk. I seldom went into his study, it was his private and remote place and I respected it as much as I could. "Do you think your brother has been acting strange lately? I mean more so than usual, his preoccupation with his nose notwithstanding?"

"A little," I said.

My father looked worried. "Yes, yes. I think so too. This dog business, has it been going on long?"

Over my father's shoulder I could see the burning eyes of William Tecumseh Sherman, who, my father once told me, had been institutionalized for being thought insane. "Just a few days," I answered.

"He doesn't do it in school, does he?"

"Once I think." I decided not to tell him that the day before, I had seen him crawling on all fours on the playground, barking with his friend Steven Ryan.

"Well, we must keep an eye on him," my father said. "I'm sure he'll out-grow it. This desire to bark."

My father was about to go back to his typewriter when I asked him a question that I had been mulling over. "Do you think we can buy St. Pius a new furnace?"

He looked up at me slowly. "I'm sorry?"

I told him about Mrs. Plank's comment and also about the new fund-raising drive that had been announced, starting with a bake sale that was scheduled for an upcoming night.

"Your principal has specifically asked that I purchase a furnace for the school out of my own funds?"

"She only asked once."

"Is it cold in school now?"

"No, it's hot."

"It is? Oh, yes, of course, it's only September." My father looked back down at his desk. "Well," he said. "I see, a new furnace. Well, I'll have to think about it. I don't know anything about furnaces."

Just then Stavros wandered into the study, walking haltingly, his glassy eyes unblinking. When he reached the wall, he pressed his nose against it but remained standing.

My father was startled by his appearance. "Dear God," he said. "I didn't think he could climb stairs."

We both watched him stand for a few moments, his sides moving in and out unevenly. I began to breathe out of my mouth, knowing that his odd smell would soon fill the small room. He moved away from the wall and walked closer to my father's leg. When he reached my father's shoe, he looked up at him and then wandered slowly out of the room, his listless tail dragging behind him.

"Well," my father said. Then he said, "Yes."

"How old is Stavros?" I asked.

"Well, I'm not sure," my father said. He attempted to go back to work but I could tell that Stavros's presence had disturbed him. "He's quite old, but apparently he still has some life in him yet."

My father gave me a short tight smile and made a more serious effort to return to his typewriter. I knew I was asking too many questions, but having been invited into his special place, I wasn't quite ready to leave. And I had another question to ask.

"Can you come to Parents Night at St. Pius next week?" I looked at the floor when I asked this because I didn't want to see the fearful look that I was sure was in his eyes.

"I'm sorry?"

"Parents Night. Mom used to go with us," I said. "It's next week. You talk to teachers." Then I said, "They have cookies you can eat."

I kept my eyes on the floor while my father cleared his throat. I had debated whether to talk to him about Parents Night. I knew that he wouldn't want to go. He had never stepped foot inside St. Pius.

"Was there some type of notification about this? From the school?"

"Yes. I gave it to Aunt Bess."

"Oh, yes," he said. "I do remember her giving me something."

We were both quiet and I tried to hide my feelings on the subject. I didn't want him to know how badly I wanted him to come. I suspected that too direct of an appeal would frighten him. I knew it would be difficult for him to come and face questions about the lottery and my mother and everything in between, but still I wanted him to go. He was my father.

"Well, yes," he said.

My heart leapt.

"Yes. When is it exactly?"

"The Thursday night after next," I said. I looked up and watched my father check a small desk calendar.

"Oh, no, Teddy, I'm sorry. I can't attend," he said. "You see, I'm scheduled to be in Atlanta for a conference that week. I have to give one of my papers. I am sorry. I wasn't originally planning to go, but now that Aunt Bess and your uncle are here to watch you, I accepted."

We were quiet again. I tried not to show my disappointment. "That's okay," I said. I hadn't really expected him to come.

"Well, it might be possible that Aunt Bess could attend though."

"It's just for parents."

"Well, it might be possible that they could make an exception."

"I'll ask Mrs. Plank," I said, even though I knew I wouldn't. I didn't want

Aunt Bess to come. Her being there would just remind everyone that I no longer had a mother.

I looked up at my father. His face was tight and his forehead was beginning to perspire. He was clearing his throat so loudly that I decided to change the subject before he did serious injury to himself.

"What are you writing?" I asked.

"What? I'm sorry? Oh. Well, a paper or really a speech for the conference next week. I'm behind a bit, but I think I'll be all right."

"What's it about? Your speech?"

He cleared his throat. "Well, I was invited to talk about a specific issue, a specific supply issue of the War."

"What?"

He cleared his throat. "Footwear, actually. The shoes the soldiers wore."

My father waited for a reaction. I had none.

"It was one of those small but essential issues of the War that often gets overlooked."

"You're writing about the soldiers' shoes?" I asked.

"Yes, well, the types of boots and shoes the soldiers wore in battle and while marching is more interesting than people think. The fact that the South didn't have any regulation footwear played a subtle yet important role in the War." He leaned back in his chair and picked up his gold fountain pen. "The Union had a significant advantage with their footwear, an advantage they maximized. They were able to do, well, a lot more walking."

"Uncle Frank says you don't have to work anymore. Why are you still working?" I blurted this out and immediately regretted it.

But rather than clear his throat more, he merely gave me another tight smile and began typing. "Well, Teddy," he said without looking back up at me, "I suppose I don't know what else to do."

LATER THAT NIGHT I laid in bed and listened to Tommy the Dog whimper. He was having one of his nightmares again, kicking his legs and turning about. I walked over and nudged him awake, waiting for his eyes to open and register where he was. When his eyes finally did open, he looked at me vacantly then drifted back to sleep. Convinced he was fine, I got back into bed.

I decided to attempt to sketch my father again. I worked on the drawing for quite a while, focusing mostly on his eyes. I often struggled with them. I felt my father was forever peering out at life from behind something and I could never capture that sense of watchful, protected isolation that shielded his vision. I knew that to draw something, you had to understand it first and I didn't understand my father.

When my mother died I felt stranded, a terrible left-behind feeling that would overwhelm me at night in bed. It was during those first weeks that I waited for my father to comfort me but he was incapable of doing much. One night though, after I had been crying facedown in my pillow for some time, he came into my room, sat down on my bed, and hugged me. He hugged me a long time in the dark without saying anything. Then, after I stopped crying, he wordlessly left. It was the first time I remembered him hugging me. It was that father that I wanted to draw now, that father that I knew was there, waiting in the dark. So I stayed up late drawing. I drew until our house was quiet and my wrist was tired. I drew until I was sure that everyone else in the world had disappeared into sleep and then I drew some more.

WALKING HOME FROM SCHOOL a few days later, I noticed the red pickup truck for the first time. It was the first dreary day in September and the color of the truck stood out sharply against the gray skies I was sure were inspiring Miss Grace. She had spent most of the afternoon staring out the window in mournful repose. The week earlier, her first haiku, "Blind Butter-flies," had been published in the *Wilton Doings* and I was sure, with the weather turning gloomily haiku-like, others were in the works.

I didn't see the red truck right away because I was walking home with Johnny Cezzaro and Charlie Governs and Johnny and I were arguing over the ranch I had said we were going to buy. I had revisited my List of Things and decided to change our large farm in Wisconsin to an even larger ranch in Montana. The farm had begun to conjure up images of cow manure and square dances while the ranch offered open ranges, hunting, and cattle roundups, all in the shadow of majestic snow-capped mountains.

"You ain't gonna buy no ranch, Pappas. I don't think your dad even won the lottery," Johnny said loudly. His black hair was particularly greasy that day and I envisioned french fries cooking and sizzling in it. The first signs of pimples were forming on the side of his dark face as small red ridges. "You guys ain't bought nothin' yet. Your dad still drives that old car, you still live in the same lousy house, you don't have a butler or a butler lady, or a satellite dish. No swimming pool, nothing. My dad says the money's wasted on a nerd family like yours."

Johnny's accusations were hitting home. I had begun registering a subtle but growing disappointment from my other classmates on our lack of purchases and felt an explanation was in order. Yet, I had none to offer other than our winning a hundred-and-ninety million dollars seemed to have somehow slipped my father's mind.

"The ranch is in Montana," I said. Then remembering Johnny's grasp of geography I added, "That's a state. Out west."

"I know where it is," he said. Then he said, "Hey, do you know that guy?" He pointed to the red pickup truck that had emerged behind us, driving slowly. "He's following us."

When I looked over I realized I had seen that same truck the day before. I remembered noticing the Tennessee license plates and the dented front bumper. A man with long blond hair was driving the truck and when I stopped to get a closer look, he drove off, his engine sputtering, his tail pipe spitting smoke.

We started walking again. "Do you even get an allowance?" Johnny asked.

"No," I said quietly. Johnny's persistent questions about the lottery were beginning to annoy me.

"Man, you don't even get an allowance? My dad said that if he won the lottery, he'd give me a thousand bucks just for taking out the garbage."

"When I turn sixteen, I'm going to get ten million dollars," I said. I surprised myself by saying this, though having said it, it didn't seem at all unreasonable.

"Bullshit," Johnny said. Then he said, "Really?"

"Yeah," I said. "Tommy gets five million dollars."

News of my pending windfall silenced Johnny for awhile. I suspected he was trying to figure out how many years it would be until I turned sixteen.

"Hey, look at this," Johnny said when we got to a street corner. Traffic was unusually heavy for a school day and we had to wait before crossing. "I said look at this."

From a plain, brown envelope, Johnny pulled out a photo of an almost-naked woman. She was standing backward on a table, looking over her shoulder, holding what looked like a whip and smiling cruelly. Even though she had whiskers painted on her face, she was pretty in an unsettling, threatening way. "This is Carla the Cat Woman. My uncle just hired her as another receptionist."

I took the photo and studied it in detail. Carla had a small tattoo of a cat on her shoulder. A long, furry rope (that I quickly realized was a tail) protruded from her backside. Her shiny black high heels looked sharp and dangerous seams ran up the backs of her black stockings in perfect straight lines.

"What do your uncle's receptionists do?" I said.

Johnny shrugged. "They stand around and look hot so guys come there and buy cars. I'll sell you it for eight thousand dollars."

"What?"

"Eight grand. Cash. That's nothing to you, that's nothing."

I looked at the photo for a few minutes longer and felt my cheeks grow warm. I thought Carla, minus the whiskers and tail, bore a distant resemblance to Miss Grace—an evil, older sister perhaps. Over my shoulder, I felt Charlie's quick hot breath.

"I'll give you four dollars for it," I said. I had never owned a picture of an almost-naked woman before and thought Carla would be an impressive start to what I thought could eventually turn into a vast but tasteful collection.

"No way," Johnny said. He took back the photo. "Ten bucks. It's autographed."

"I don't have that much," I said.

"I'll give you the rest," Charlie said. Johnny and I looked over at Charlie, surprised.

"Done deal," Johnny said, handing me the photo.

After we paid Johnny, I went over to Charlie's house. Charlie's father was a surgeon and the McGoverns lived on the nicest block in the neighborhood, a wide street with a canopy of arching trees. His house was large, even by Wilton's standards and had tall white columns in the front and a sweeping lawn that somehow seemed green even in winter. The outside of Charlie's house had been in one of the movies filmed in Wilton and, according to my mother, the pond in the backyard had been the setting in a poignant scene involving a boy who tried to drown himself after he saw his father having sex with the family nanny.

When we got inside, we went straight upstairs to Charlie's bedroom and locked the door.

"If you hear my mom coming, let me know," he said.

For the next half hour or so, I watched Charlie scan the photo of Carla into his computer. Then he did something that truly amazed me.

"Watch this," he said. I looked on as he slowly and carefully cut out a photo of Mrs. Plank's head from the St. Pius *Meet Your Teacher* booklet the school sent home at the beginning of every school year and scanned it onto the body of Carla. He then printed it out and gave me a copy. I found it repulsive. Mrs. Plank was old and ugly and Charlie hadn't made her head nearly large enough. She looked like an ant.

"Can you do this with another picture?" I asked.

"Yes," Charlie said. He adjusted his glasses.

"Can you do that with Miss Grace's picture?" I asked casually.

Without a word Charlie went to work. Within minutes, Miss Grace's sweet, unsmiling face rested crookedly on Carla the Cat Woman's naked and tattooed body. My face felt warm again.

"Her head is on crooked," I said.

"No, it's not. She's turning her head in the picture," Charlie said. Then he said, "You love her."

"No, I don't," I said putting the picture carefully away in my backpack.

"Yes, you do." Charlie readjusted his glasses, pushing them back onto his head. He wore round wire spectacles that magnified his eyeballs, giving them an unfocused, fluid look. "She tried to kill herself once. When the man she was supposed to marry didn't show up at the church. They were supposed to be married at St. Pius but he never came. He wrote her a letter later saying that he discovered he was homo. My mom told me."

"Really? He was homo?" I thought about this for awhile, but instead of expressing concern over Miss Grace I asked, "How do you discover you're homo?" I thought there might be some type of process involved, a written test possibly.

Charlie shrugged and pushed back his glasses again, his eyeballs swimming. "I don't know." He shrugged. "You just do."

On the way home, I considered Miss Grace's suicide attempt and ran through a number of scenarios: Miss Grace tried to hang herself but the rope snapped just as her face was turning blue; Miss Grace tried to shoot herself but the gun misfired; Miss Grace jumped off a bridge into a river, but was pulled to safety by alert fishermen; Miss Grace tried to jump in front of a speeding train but mistimed her leap and rolled over the tracks, down a hill, into a camp of friendly and compassionate hobos. The images upset me and I felt immense guilt over the photo. Under no circumstances would Miss Grace allow herself to be photographed almost naked wearing a tail. I concluded that keeping the picture was wrong and vowed to look at it just one more time when I got home, before ripping it up.

I was deep in thought about Miss Grace when I saw the red truck again. This time it was heading my way from the opposite direction. As it approached, I saw the driver looking at me. He stopped the truck and lowered the window.

"Hey there, boy," he said. "I gotta talk to you." Then he smiled at me, a wide smile I can still see to this day. I looked away and started walking faster.

"Hey, I can give you a lift," he said, "Get in. Might rain."

"No thanks," I said.

"Your momma taught you not to talk to strangers, that's good. But I ain't no stranger."

"Who are you?"

"You don't recognize me? Come on," he said, leaning over to open the door. "Get in now."

"I have to go home," I said. And then I turned and walked away fast.

THE NEXT EVENING was dinner at the Wilcotts. My father wore a pained expression on his face as he attempted to flatten his fluffy cotton-candy hair in the hallway mirror with a comb I had won at the St. Pius Summer Festival by lowering a magnet into a fish bowl full of cheap prizes. Several times, he pushed the hair down on the sides of his head only to watch it slowly rise again like Jiffy Pop popcorn heating on the stove. I knew he didn't want to go to the Wilcotts and had overheard him discussing the possibility of canceling with Aunt Bess. Social activities frightened him. He

64

obviously was not comfortable with conversation and was known to disappear into bathrooms at parties, sometimes for hours. In the end however, he decided going would be easier than calling Mrs. Wilcott and canceling.

"I want you to keep a keen eye on your brother," he said as he once again tried to flatten his hair. "I think it might be best to keep all forks and knives out of his immediate reach."

"What about spoons?" I asked.

"Spoons are fine," he said, though he paused before answering.

Uncle Frank walked into the hall, holding a glass of wine. "What time is dinner?" When he saw my father, he took a step back and said, "Whoa. What the hell do you have on?"

My father stopped combing his hair and looked down at his clothes. He was wearing white pants, a white, short-sleeve shirt, and white socks. The entire ensemble was offset by the thick, black shoes he always wore and that reminded me of sturdy rubber life rafts.

"You look like a milk man, for chrissakes," Uncle Frank said. "Don't you have any other clothes? Something with some pigment?"

"Well," my father said, clearing his throat. "I was thinking of wearing a sports coat as well."

"What color?" Uncle Frank asked. Then he said, "Not white, I hope."

"Well, actually," my father said, his voice trailing off.

"Don't you have a blue one?"

"Yes," I said. "The one mom gave you last year. For the faculty dinner."

"Oh, yes," my father said. "That's right."

"Well, that'll help," Uncle Frank said.

While my father was upstairs, Uncle Frank took me by the arm and pulled me into the kitchen and whispered, "Let's keep an eye on this Wilcott woman tonight. Find out what her story is, what angle she's playing."

I nodded my head. I enjoyed being brought into Uncle Frank's confidence and despite the fact that I didn't really have any idea of what he was talking about, I was determined to help him in any way I could.

"We have to figure out what to do about her. We have to decide whether we let this thing play itself out or"—he paused here, his face grave—"or take matters into our own hands."

I nodded grimly. "Okay," I said.

When my father came back downstairs, Uncle Frank said, "That's better. A little. Anyway, are you bringing this woman anything. Some wine? A pie? A melon? Something?"

"I hadn't really thought of that," my father said. "That would be the proper thing to do, I suppose. Aunt Bess usually does the shopping. I wonder if she thought to pick up something appropriate."

"Well, you're a little late for that," Uncle Frank said. Aunt Bess had returned for a few days to her home in Milwaukee to pick up some more clothes and check on Baber, Aliki, and Asa, her three cats who were staying at a friend's.

"What the hell, I'll run to the store and pick up something," Uncle Frank said.

We were waiting for him on the front porch when he returned with three bottles of wine. Tommy the Dog was running in small circles on the lawn, chasing fireflies that no one else saw. My father, looking stiff in his blue jacket, was watching him intently, squinting his eyes in the fading light. When Uncle Frank arrived, my father took the bottles and thanked him.

"Let's go," Uncle Frank said.

My father looked surprised. "You're not coming, of course."

Uncle Frank looked equally surprised. "What do you mean? Of course, I'm coming."

"But you weren't invited."

"What do you mean I wasn't invited? I need an invitation to have dinner at someone's house?"

"Well," my father said, considering the question. "Yes."

"So she didn't invite me? She doesn't even know me. How could she not invite me?"

My father was confused and cleared his throat. Despite his social backwardness, he held manners and protocol in high regard, a fact I attributed to his admiration of certain Confederate generals like Robert E. Lee who, according to my father, was a very proper man when he wasn't defending slavery. "Mrs. Wilcott specifically said, 'I'd like to have you and your boys over for dinner.' She didn't say anything about me bringing, well, a grown man, my brother. It could prove very embarrassing, Frank."

Uncle Frank processed this information silently. Then he looked over at me so I looked down at my shoes. Aunt Bess had polished them before going to Milwaukee and despite the growing darkness, I could still see glints of the shine.

"I hope you understand, Frank."

Uncle Frank remained silent. He was wearing a black shirt, black coat, and black pants. He looked like night and against this darkness, his pale face stood out, deathlike. For a moment, I feared he was a vampire or at the very least, an apostle of the devil. His eyes narrowed as he aimed his chin directly at us.

"Well," he finally said. "Well, I see." Then he reached for one of the bottles of wine. "I'll just take one of these back then."

My father hesitated before turning to leave. He looked concerned. "What will you do for dinner?"

Uncle Frank shrugged. "I'm going to eat Stavros," he said. With that, he turned and walked slowly off.

"Well," my father said as Uncle Frank disappeared. "I suppose we should go, so we can . . . come back."

THE WILCOTTS HAD ONE of the largest houses on the block. It backed up to the Wilton Forest Preserve and the tall pine trees that ringed its sides gave it a majestic secluded look that reminded me of a castle. Up close though, the house lost its luster. Its white paint was peeling in small flakes and the red door that looked so impressive from the sidewalk had a large, crooked crack that ran jaggedly from the bottom all the way up to the door-knob. Leaves from the unraked lawn swirled and danced in the wind before settling in small piles.

Mrs. Wilcott was waiting for us in the doorway. "Hello, Theo. Hello, boys," she said in a high, cheerful voice that sounded like a friendly chipmunk.

She looked very different than I had ever seen her look before. She was wearing a very short dress that was cut low in front to reveal the tops of her breasts. My first thought was that we had come too early and she hadn't yet finished dressing. My second thought was that she might pitch forward because her breasts were so large. I stared helplessly at them. They were pressed tight together, almost angrily, and the crack that separated them wiggled when she opened the front door to let us in.

My father was startled by her appearance as well. He cleared his throat for such a long time that I feared he was choking. "Gloria," he finally said stiffly, holding out the bottles of wine. "We brought this for you. For your family, I should say. But not for the children, of course." He bowed his head deeply as he presented the bottles to her.

"Oh, Theo, you shouldn't have," Mrs. Wilcott said as she took the wine. Then she did something that astounded me: she leaned forward and lightly kissed my father on the cheek.

My father's reaction equally shocked me. He accepted her kiss as if it was an expected present, then he coughed into his hand and said, "Well, yes, anyway, I hope you enjoy it."

We followed Mrs. Wilcott through the spacious living room and into the dimly lit dining room, her high heels clicking loudly on the shiny wooden floors. Benjamin, her son, who played on the St. Pius football team and always had some form of dried blood on his arms or knees, was already sitting at the table, holding his head in his hands and staring at his plate. "Can we eat now?" he asked without turning to look at us.

"Benjamin, honey, why don't you take the boys up to your room and play for a while? Dinner will be ready in a few minutes."

"What am I going to do with them?" he said, looking at Tommy who was sucking his thumb. "Watch Barney?"

Mrs. Wilcott said nothing. She just looked at Benjamin and gave him a big chipmunk smile. Her breasts still looked angry though.

"Let's go," he finally said.

On the way upstairs, I noticed several framed pictures of Mrs. Wilcott on the wall. In one, she was standing on a stage, in a long dress, her hands over her mouth in apparent surprise as another woman placed a crown on top of her head. In another, she was playing a white piano in what I recognized as their living room.

"Hurry up," Benjamin said. He didn't stop or even slow down as we passed the pictures.

Benjamin's room reminded me of a gym. It was large with a high ceiling and a bare wooden floor that I imagined was cold in the winter. A small basketball net hung in the corner with several small balls on the floor underneath. Trophies and certificates lined the bookcase and walls.

Benjamin picked up one of the balls, yelled "Pop a shot," and threw the ball in the basket. Then he jumped on his bed and began reading *Sports Illustrated*. I watched him read. He was tall and wiry, his body abrupt angles and small muscles. "I want to go to Notre Dame," he said after a few minutes. "Where do you want to go to college?"

"Harvard," I said.

"Harvard? Why?"

"My father went to college there."

Benjamin snorted. "They don't have any good teams there. What's he doing?" Benjamin was looking over at Tommy who was laying down on the floor, still sucking his thumb.

"Resting," I said.

"How old's he?"

"Three," I said. Tommy was five.

Benjamin raised his eyebrows a little then went back to his magazine. I walked slowly around his room. I could quickly tell that Benjamin and I had nothing in common other than the street we lived on. The walls were covered with dozens of photos and posters of various Notre Dame athletes, most of whom looked like older versions of Benjamin. "My mother said she might let me go to a Notre Dame basketball camp if I didn't embarrass her at dinner," Benjamin said. "It costs about a thousand dollars. And we're not rich like you. We don't have a butler like you."

"We don't have a butler."

"Then who's that short guy always hanging around your house, driving you everywhere? I just saw him come back from the store with the wine. I can see everything from my window."

"Oh. Him. He's our uncle," I said. "He makes vampire movies. He made *Microbes: The Unseen Death*. That one wasn't about vampires though."

Benjamin was unimpressed with Uncle Frank's occupation. He continued to leaf through his magazine. "You should have a butler. And a maid. If I was as rich as you, I'd have a maid and I'd screw her every night. That would be part of her job."

I nodded my head. "Yeah, we were thinking about hiring a maid. But not to screw. Not right away, at least. We'd let her work for a while first."

Benjamin put down his magazine and looked over at me. "How old are you?"

"Eleven," I said.

He went back to his magazine. "How come you guys don't move? You can probably buy a mansion or something. What are you doing in Wilton? I mean, it's okay, but you're really rich. You could probably live anywhere."

I kept walking around the room, looking at the pictures of grimacing, smiling, and ultimately victorious athletes. "We're probably going to move next year," I said.

"Where?"

"We're going to buy a ranch in Montana and raise horses." I said this very nonchalantly.

"Horses?"

I nodded my head then put my hands in my back pants pockets like a cowboy. "Horses," I said.

"You ever ride a horse?" Benjamin asked.

I shrugged. I had once ridden a blind pony at the Wilton Carnival, but I suspected this would carry little weight with Benjamin.

"You don't seem much like a cowboy," Benjamin said.

WE ATE IN THE DINING ROOM, surrounded by flowers and flickering candles. The table looked like a page from one of my mother's old magazines about beautiful houses and diets. The gleaming dishes reflected the light from the crystal chandelier and the thin, tall glasses felt fragile and weightless in my hand. The silverware was much heavier than ours and the napkins were thick and embroidered, like the drapes in our living room. When I laid mine on my lap, I felt a serious responsibility not to drop any food on it.

I tried hard not to look at Mrs. Wilcott's breasts while we ate, but they had a strong gravitational pull, drawing my eyes in their direction every few seconds. Their immense size concerned me. They appeared caged-in by her dress and I feared they could break free from their restraints at any moment. Initially, my father seemed to be afraid of them as well. During the early stages of dinner, he kept his eyes steadfastly on his plate and when he passed things, he did not turn his head more than an inch to either side. He did have several glasses of wine, however, and as the evening progressed, I noticed that he seemed less fearful of Mrs. Wilcott's breasts and talked more, occasionally glancing at her breasts when he did. Midway through the meal, it was apparent that he had entirely overcome his fear of her breasts and was talking directly and solely to them in a very conversational manner, as if they were old friends.

"This is all quite delicious, Gloria," he said. "Quite delicious."

I looked over at Mrs. Wilcott's left breast to whom my father had directed the compliment, expecting it to answer. Instead Mrs. Wilcott's mouth did. "Why, thank you, Theo," she said.

While we ate the strange food Mrs. Wilcott had prepared, chicken with cooked peaches and walnuts, she mentioned that our neighbor, Mr. Tuthill, was selling his house.

"It's a beautiful house," she said. "It was in *Chicago* magazine."

"Ah," my father said. The wine seemed to have had an arousing effect on his hair which now stood out like small wings on the sides of his head.

"It has five bedrooms and a study with a fireplace."

"A fireplace," my father said.

"Oh, do you like fireplaces, Theo?"

"Yes," my father said, swallowing. "They are so, well, so warm."

"I enjoy a good fire on a winter night," Mrs. Wilcott said.

"Yes," my father said. "It would seem that that would be an appropriate time to have one. Winter is so, well, cold."

"We used to use ours quite often, but now that it's just me and Benjamin, we don't find as much occasion. We used to though, before everyone left, the girls left for school." Mrs. Wilcott stopped here and took a slight sip of her wine, then dabbed at her mouth, her lips pressed together. "Do you have a working fireplace, Theo?"

My father was confused by the question. "A working fireplace?" he repeated. "Yes, I think we do. I don't remember ever using it though."

"We used it once," I said.

My father looked at me, surprised.

"Mom did," I said, softly. "To smoke out that raccoon. The one that built that nest at the top."

"Oh, yes," my father said. He lowered his head over his plate and cut at a remaining peach. "That was quite an . . . event."

During dessert, while we ate a cranberry pie that made my lips pucker and sting, Mrs. Wilcott began asking my father questions about the Civil War which he answered at great length. When he finally finished talking, she leaned forward on the table, put her chin in her hands, and said, "It's all just so fascinating. And tragic too." Then she suddenly stood up and bounced into the kitchen. She was back within seconds, a copy of my father's book, *A Civil War Companion,* in her hands.

"Would you be so kind as to autograph this?" she asked. She handed him the book and a pen. "I just bought it."

My father accepted both the pen and the book with an uncommonly gracious nod of his head, then stared at her breasts for inspiration.

"Make it out to Benjamin," she said. "He's interested in history. Aren't you, Benji?"

Benjamin made a strange sound, half burp, half cough, then drank some milk.

The mention of Benjamin's name broke my father's breast trance and he began to write in the book, his pen moving with precision over the page, his brow furrowed. I imagined this to be how Abraham Lincoln looked when he signed the Emancipation Proclamation. "There," he said, handing the book back to Mrs. Wilcott, who read the inscription. My father watched her face as she read.

She smiled. "I think this book would make a wonderful movie, Theo," she said. "It's a fascinating subject we all need to know more about. There's just not that much information about that particular war available to the public."

To this, my father, who had once told me that tens of thousands of books had been written about the Civil War, simply said, "Yes."

"Tell us about your trip to Atlanta, Theo, your conference. What are you speaking on?"

My father swallowed some pie. "Boots," he said. "Soldiers' boots. Yes."

Mrs. Wilcott put her chin back in her hands and said, "Interesting." Then she said, "Do you mean, what they wore on their feet?"

My father nodded enthusiastically, obviously impressed with her immediate grasp of the issue. "Yes," he said. "Their feet."

Mrs. Wilcott paused for a moment, measuring my father's comment carefully. She finally chose to say, "That's just so interesting." Then she picked up her glass of wine. "I think it's wonderful that you have such a passion for your work. I used to have a passion for music."

She waited for my father to say something but he was dumbly silent, smiling vacantly in a way that was starting to annoy me.

"I used to sing," she continued. "I considered it as a possible career but," she stopped and smiled, "I chose another career instead."

"Ah," my father finally said. "And what was that?"

"Oh," Mrs. Wilcott smiled. "Parent, mother, wife." She began to finger a small gold necklace that hung delicately down her neck.

"Oh, yes, of course." My father quickly picked up his glass of wine and sipped at it.

I was wondering how much longer we were going to have to sit there when Mrs. Wilcott asked if we would like to hear her sing.

My father was confused by the request and leaned forward in his chair. He seemed to be considering the matter carefully, as if she had asked him a complicated three-part question concerning the Civil War or possibly physics. He put his hand up to his mouth and furrowed his brow once more.

"Well, I'm not sure, Gloria, I haven't sung in years," he finally said.

She laughed, a slight tinkling of ice against glass. "Oh, no, Theo, I said would you like to hear me sing?"

"Oh," my father said. Shaking his head. "Of course, of course, very much so. I thought you asked if I could sing, well, never mind."

"Let's go boys," Mrs. Wilcott said. She stood up. "Benjamin? Will you set up the piano?"

Benjamin threw his napkin on the table and groaned. Within minutes, he was lugging what looked to be a small, portable keyboard into the living room. As he adjusted its wobbly stand, I wondered what had happened to the white piano I had seen in the picture.

Mrs. Wilcott seemed to be reading my mind. "I'm afraid this electronic keyboard will have to do," she said as she pulled a chair up to it.

We all sat crammed on the couch in the living room as Mrs. Wilcott studied some sheet music, her lips pursed, her eyes small and intense. Then, she took a deep breath as if she were about to fling herself off a mountain top or jump head first into a freezing river and began to sing.

At first, I didn't understand the words. As the seconds passed, however, I realized that she was singing in a different language. Foreign words, rich and lyrical filled the room, smothering us. Her deep, resonant voice was also strange, mysteriously transforming from a friendly chipmunk's to that of a large man. I leaned back against the couch, trying hard not to make contact with Benjamin who was sitting next to me and closed my eyes, waiting for the moment to end. I could not bring myself to look at my father. I assumed he was mortified.

Mrs. Wilcott sang what I concluded were three separate songs, moving gracefully from one to the next with a slight smile and a quick glance back at us. As the minutes passed in slow agony, I became aware of my father's head hovering just inches off my shoulder. I glanced up, just as his mouth was opening, about to emit the first of what I knew could be a series of sharp snores. I nudged him gently awake. He snapped his head and readjusted his position on the couch, just as Mrs. Wilcott finished the last song.

"Wonderful, Gloria, wonderful," my father said. "*La Boheme.*" He made a brief attempt at clapping but quickly abandoned the effort when no one else joined in.

"This sucks," Benjamin said under his breath, but he said it too loudly and Mrs. Wilcott's head shook the moment after he said it. She immediately asked him to help her bring in some drinks from the kitchen.

"I'm afraid I had a bit too much wine," my father said after they left. He cleared his throat. "Wine always has a tiring effect on me."

"Can we go now?" I asked.

Tommy had started wandering toward the electronic keyboard. My father stood up and followed him. "In a few minutes. Why don't you see if you can be of some assistance in the kitchen?" he asked. "Help the boy Benjamin. I'll keep an eye on your brother."

I walked slowly through the living room and was pushing open the swinging door that led to the kitchen just as Mrs. Wilcott was slapping Benjamin hard across the face. She slapped him twice, her face red and her teeth bared. After the second slap, Benjamin smirked, then balled his hand up into a fist and took a swing at her, missing her face by inches. I let the door swing quietly shut and stood there, unsure of what to do. I was afraid that if I was detected, they might refocus their fury and take turns hitting me.

I was still standing there, when the door swung open again to reveal Mrs. Wilcott holding a tray filled with cups and glasses. Her face was still red but her teeth were back behind her lips. She took a few steps back into the kitchen when she saw me, startled.

"Oh, Teddy, I didn't see you there. Can I get you something?" She was smiling but her eyes were studying me. I looked down at the floor. When I looked back up, Benjamin was standing next to her, holding a coffee pot. Neither one of them seemed any worse for the wear.

"I'm okay," I said. I turned and headed to the living room.

"Benjamin? Why don't you and Teddy watch TV for a little while?" she said. "Up in your room."

Benjamin said, "Shit," as I followed him back up to his room, past the smiling pictures of Mrs. Wilcott.

"Your dad better not try to screw my mom," he said as he turned on a small color TV and laid down on his bed. "If he does, I'm gonna kick your ass."

"He won't," I said.

Benjamin got up off the bed and walked over to me. His face was still red from the slapping. He pressed a finger deep into my chest like a gun barrel.

"He better not."

"Okay," I said, "okay." Then I pretended to watch a football game that was on the TV until it was time to finally go home.

A WEEK LATER, my father appeared on *Access Wilton* with Mrs. Wilcott. I watched it with the Dog and Uncle Frank in the living room. Aunt Bess, who had returned from Milwaukee, watched it in the kitchen, on a tiny, black-and-white television with a crooked antenna she had brought back with her.

"He should have gone on *Oprah*," she yelled over the sound of running water and pots and pans banging. "Why did he go on this rinky-dink show? I never heard of it. My God, look how short that skirt is! She's making Theo nervous. His scalp is all red. He could have a heart attack or go spastic right on the show."

My father did appear particularly awkward, alternately bowing his head and clearing his throat before answering a question. Much to my disappointment, he did not discuss the lottery. Instead, he talked about footwear in the Civil War and held up an actual pair of Union boots that had been recently sent to him from a professor in North Carolina. When Mrs. Wilcott unexpectedly tried on one of the boots, the camera focused on her legs for a long time.

"For chrissakes," Uncle Frank said. "I'm sure she wishes there was a Civil War bra to try on."

Surprisingly, Uncle Frank watched most of the show, asking questions about how often and when it was on.

"You know," he said, his voice low, reflective. "You know, this might be a good place to try out *Frankly Speaking*. Test market it here. Did you ever mention that idea to your father? About buying airtime?"

"No." I had no idea what airtime was.

"Well, I might just bring it up. It can't be any worse than this." After a few more minutes of listening to my father talk about a hundred-and-forty-year-old insteps, Uncle Frank finally succumbed to the measured tedium of the show and fell asleep with his mouth open.

I feared that my classmates, to whom I had casually promoted the show, were having the same reaction. I had implied that my father was going to discuss our plans to build a new cafeteria and swimming pool for St. Pius, though they had seemed skeptical.

Rather than face their questions, I stayed home from school the next day, feigning a sore throat. Several times during the day, Aunt Bess checked in on me as I lay in bed, feeling my forehead in search of a fever. "Nothing," she would say. She was clearly disappointed. Over the years, it had become apparent that she thrived on illnesses and the rituals involved in tending the sick. She enjoyed applying cool cloths to foreheads, smearing Vicks VapoRub on chests and dissolving children's aspirin in spoons of water for Tommy and me to swallow. When she moved in with us, the first thing she unpacked was a plastic vaporizer which she diligently scrubbed with hot water and baking soda in preparation for use. Next, she unpacked a vast cough medicine collection that included an endless supply of old, sticky, half-empty bottles of cough medicine which she called suppressants.

After a lunch of chicken broth and plain toast, Aunt Bess took my temperature.

"Nothing. Normal," she said with disgust. "Does your throat still hurt?"

"Yes," I said. I coughed once to prove this.

"We need to suppress that," she said, walking off to the bathroom.

A few minutes later, as Aunt Bess was giving me cough medicine, a cherry-flavored Smith Brothers, my father walked in.

"And how are you feeling, Teddy?"

I was starving. Aunt Bess's meager meals just left me hungrier. "Okay," I coughed and laid back down on the bed, pulling my sheet up tight around my throat.

"Well, that's good." He turned to face Aunt Bess. "Aunt Bess, I won't be having dinner at home tonight. I've been invited to the opera by Gloria."

"Who?" Aunt Bess looked alarmed.

My father cleared his throat. "Gloria Wilcott. Mrs. Wilcott."

"Oh," she said. "That Gloria."

"You're going where?" Uncle Frank suddenly appeared in my room. He was wearing a black turtleneck and black pants and for some reason he was barefoot.

My father kept his hand on my head longer than I thought was necessary. "To the opera. It's a benefit. For the library."

"You're going with that neighbor? That woman?" Uncle Frank asked, suspiciously. "That woman with the big—"

"Frank please!" my father said. Then he said. "Yes. Gloria Wilcott."

"Tonight?"

My father looked down at the floor. "Yes."

They stood in silence around my bed, my father's hand still on my forehead. It was then that I detected a peculiar smell coming from his direction, a not altogether unpleasant musky aroma, that reminded me of tobacco and lilacs and black earth.

"What's that smell?" I asked. My father quickly took his hand away.

"What smell, what smell?" Uncle Frank asked. He started vigorously sniffing my father, his nose curling up into a ball.

"You're wearing cologne, Theo. You're wearing cologne. Since when do you start caring what you smell like? You don't even wear deodorant, for chrissakes."

My father cautiously sniffed the back of his hand. "It was just a splash," he said, though he looked concerned.

"The opera should be nice," Aunt Bess said. Then she said, "You're not planning on marrying this woman are you?"

My father ignored this comment and instead put his hand back on my forehead. "You feel quite cool, Teddy, quite cool," he said, smiling one of his short tight smiles. And then he quickly turned around and walked out with Uncle Frank and Aunt Bess close behind.

Later that night, after my father had left for the opera, I lay in bed and prayed that he wouldn't have sex with Mrs. Wilcott. Because of the delicate nature of the issue, I worded my prayer carefully, asking God that my father return "without having sinned." The fact that my father might actually perform a vigorous physical act was in itself worrisome; I wasn't sure his anti-heart-attack pills were up to the challenge of Mrs. Wilcott. And the fact that I might have my head banged on the sidewalk because of it heightened my sense of concern.

Downstairs, the muffled voices of my aunt and uncle mixed together, overlapping sounds of worry. I heard Uncle Frank say, "He's flattered. It's not like he's Robert Redford or anything. Let's face it, any time any woman has shown an interest in him, he falls."

"He's changing," Aunt Bess. "He's confused. The cologne. The hair combing." Then she started speaking lower and I could only make out a few words, like "tragic," and "sad," and "spastic bowel."

Laying in bed, it occurred to me that even if they had sex, Benjamin would have a hard time proving it. As much as Mrs. Wilcott seemed to like to talk, I didn't think she would discuss this at home, at least not with Benjamin. Regardless, I was concerned. Benjamin might draw his own conclusions.

As I waited for my father, I began to think of my mother. Since my father was possibly at that moment having sex with Mrs. Wilcott, I wondered what she would have thought. I couldn't decide whether she would be jealous, disgusted, or angry. I knew she hadn't liked Mrs. Wilcott, that much I was certain of.

Mrs. Wilcott and my mother didn't get along. It started with something Mrs. Wilcott wrote in the *Wilton Doings* while I was still in first grade. In her column, "Wilton Whispers," Mrs. Wilcott criticized the lifeguards at the Wilton Pool, claiming that "some were too old and not in the proper shape to perform the duties of their position." This upset my mother, who was a lifeguard at the time, having taken the unusual summer job out of boredom.

"I'm only thirty-two years old," I heard my mother yell into the phone when Mrs. Rhodebush brought the column to her attention. When my mother raised her voice, her Southern accent emerged, slicing through the air like a pocket knife. "It's not like I'm in a wheelchair, watching the kids swim."

After the column appeared, my mother began writing letters to the paper, defending her position as a lifeguard and attesting to her physical condition. "My body is firm and hard," she claimed in her letter that, once it was printed, was widely circulated around the neighborhood. Encouraged at seeing her opinion in print, she soon began writing other letters, all critical of the paper. She was particularly harsh on the columnists, taking issue on their—specifically Mrs. Wilcott's—views on the annual village Easter egg hunt (Mrs. Wilcott believed it should be restricted to St. Pius parishoners), to the opening of a shelter for stray cats (Mrs. Wilcott believed the cats should be shipped to another suburb). The letters, full of misspellings and grammatical errors, mortified my father who pleaded with her to stop.

"You must cease this crusade, or at the very least, begin using a dictionary," he said one day after a letter appeared that began with the sentence, "The primordial thing a newspaper should be is fair."

"What's wrong with that letter?" my mother yelled.

"The word you wanted to use was 'primary,' not primordial. Primary, for goodness sakes, primary."

After that, my mother began asking my father for help in writing the letters, but he always refused.

"I will not be drawn into this suburban Shilo," he quietly said one day at dinner.

Sometime during the letter-writing campaign, my mother smashed into Dr. Wilcott's car at DeVries, the local supermarket. "Shit!" she yelled, when our car hit Dr. Wilcott's in the rear. Then, when she realized whose car it was, she pounded on the steering wheel with both hands, and yelled, "Oh shit, it's Mr. Tanning Booth."

To my surprise, Dr. Wilcott was very nice about the accident and my mother and he spent quite a bit of time examining the damage, then talking about real estate prices in the neighborhood. My mother was thinking about becoming a real estate agent, something Dr. Wilcott said she would no doubt excel at.

"Well, he ain't so bad," she said when she got back in the car. Not long after that, one afternoon when I came home from school, I saw Dr. Wilcott trying to kiss my mother on the couch in our living room. I remembered peering through our swinging kitchen door as he leaned over and tried to pull her to him and saw my mother swing her fist at him, hitting him full in the face. A moment later, while I was at the refrigerator getting a drink, I heard the front door slam.

Thinking of my mother just made me miss her. She was pretty and she was funny in an easy and light way that drew people to her. I enjoyed simply being with her. She would tell me stories in bed at night about people she knew in Tennessee, stories that made me laugh so hard that my stomach would hurt and my mouth would feel stretched out and tired. "Everyone down there has at least three or four names," she said. "I was lucky I got out with only two."

My mother also liked to draw. "You get your talent from me," she used to say. She was an excellent artist. I would study her work long after she was finished and try to imitate her strong, flowing lines as best I could. She would tease me about how much time I spent drawing and how seriously I approached even the simplest illustrations. "It's supposed to be fun, babe, you don't have to work so hard at it," she used to say. "Just let it flow." But when I won first place and five hundred dollars in a Chicagoland art competition, she stopped teasing me. Instead, she started buying me markers and colored pencils.

Despite her generally easy manner, my mother didn't get along with my father. She grew quiet when he was around, her lips drawing tight and thin, curling around her teeth like a cornered alley cat. She would spend hours on the phone complaining about him to her friend Lillian from Memphis. She used to lean against the kitchen counter during these conversations, waving a Camel cigarette in the air and tell Lillian that my father was incapable of human emotions. Whenever she noticed that I was within earshot, she would shoo me away with her cigarette hand, the smoke chasing after me like a tracer bullet. Then she would go back to complaining about my father. "He got me out of Memphis, but that's about it," I once heard her say. Then she said, "I thought that would be enough but it ain't."

My mother was considerably younger than my father. At restaurants, waiters frequently mistook her for his daughter causing the top of my father's head to flash red. I wasn't sure how they met. I was vaguely aware that their marriage had some unspoken history surrounding it, but I knew no details. When I once asked my mother, she casually put me off, saying it was a long story. Laying on my pillow now, thinking about my mother and father, I wished that I had been more persistent with my questions. I was growing curious.

THE NEXT DAY was Saturday and I decided that I wasn't sick anymore. Since I hadn't eaten anything the day before, I got up early and ate the steady stream of pancakes that Aunt Bess made, pouring liberal amounts of syrup on each one until they were soggy and lush with sweetness.

"Your appetite seems to have returned," my father said. He looked at me from over the top of the newspaper. Outwardly, he did not appear to have recently had sex. I was hoping that Benjamin was drawing the same conclusion about his mother down the block.

I eyed him suspiciously. I had noticed that he had eaten a large number of pancakes himself and feared his appetite was somehow connected to physical exertion.

"Teddy, is there something wrong?" my father asked.

"What? No," I said. I went back to my pancakes. I had been staring at my father, trying to picture him having intercourse. I had trouble accepting the fact that this gray formless body sitting across the table from me was capable of performing such a complicated act.

"What's wrong?" Aunt Bess said. "Is something wrong with the pancakes?"

"No, everything's fine," my father said. "The pancakes were very good. Where's Tommy?"

"He's still sleeping." She poured a large cup of coffee. "He's like his uncle, they both sleep late. I have to go wake Frankie though. He said he had some important phone calls to make and I have to get him up." She added a drop of skim milk into the cup and stirred it with a spoon. "I think he's developing a sleeping disorder," she said. "He sleeps too much."

"Who?" My father curled back a page of his newspaper and looked over at Aunt Bess. "Tommy?"

"No, Frankie."

"Oh." My father went back to his paper. "I don't think that's a disorder," he said. "Sleeping too much."

"Well, something's wrong with him," she said. "Do you hear how he snores? My God, the house shakes." With that, she opened the basement door in the far corner of the kitchen and disappeared down into the black hole where Uncle Frank lived.

As I was finishing my breakfast, I soon became aware of my father's eyes peering at me from over the top of his newspaper. I cut into my last pancake, pressing down hard on my plate and causing the small table to tip in my direction. I felt a sudden rush of nervousness and apprehension; my father seldom looked at me for more than a few seconds.

"Sorry," I said, as I picked up my knife that had slipped to the floor.

My father continued to watch me. Then he cleared his throat. "Teddy," he said in a more formal voice than usual. "I have been meaning to have a talk with you. I wanted to ask you if you would like to play a sport of some kind. Soccer, for example. Gloria says it is very popular with boys your age. I thought maybe you, well, would enjoy it. She thought that possible."

"No, I don't think so," I said. I had no interest in or talent for soccer or any sports for that matter. I was always the last person picked on teams at recess and generally avoided all physical activities rather than risk the embarrassment my uncoordinated body consistently brought me.

"Well, you should consider it. Exercise is important for a growing boy."

"Did you play sports? When you were my age?"

My father's eyebrows arched in thought. "Not really. No, actually. Your uncle was more involved in athletics. I never participated in any extracurricular activities. Any sporting activities, that is. I was quite involved in the school newspaper. I was the editor. But I now wish I had been involved in athletics. I would have benefited, I think on many levels. It would have been healthy. Yes, I definitely think so."

I had a hard time swallowing my last bite of pancake.

"Gloria also thought you might enjoy spending time with her son Benjamin. He's only a year ahead of you in class. She thought that maybe you could do homework and play sports together. She thought the companionship might be good for you. You really should have more friends other than just, well, other than just Charlie. Though he is a nice boy."

"Benjamin Wilcott was suspended once from school," I said. I tried not to look at my father when I said this.

"Suspended? For what?"

"He beat up some boy from the public school."

I heard my father cough. "Was this recently?"

"Last year," I said. I looked up at him and thought I detected worry in his eyes. I was hoping he might somehow conclude that Benjamin had threatened me and for my safety alone he should stop having sex with Mrs. Wilcott.

"I'm sure there are two sides to the story," my father said.

"He's always beating people up. No one likes him," I said, even though Benjamin was actually one of the more popular boys in school.

"Well, he seemed well behaved at dinner the other night."

"That's because Mrs. Wilcott said she'd send him to a basketball camp if he was good. I have to go to the bathroom."

I went upstairs and stayed in the bathroom for a while, washing then rewashing my face and hands, scrubbing them clean with Uncle Frank's special antibacterial soap he had recently bought. I felt ashamed over what I said, but not very. I suddenly understood what Uncle Frank was talking about. In regards to Mrs. Wilcott, I had decided to take matters into my own hands.

SOON AFTER, I BEGAN a campaign to undermine Mrs. Wilcott's influence on my father. I felt justified, believing I was acting both out of concern for my father and self-preservation. If I answered the phone when she called, I would hang up or fail to relay her messages. Twice in one week, she stopped by unannounced, once with a plate of cookies and once with a basket of freshly baked apple turnovers that looked flaky and brown. I intercepted her both times, telling her my father was in his study and couldn't be disturbed. The second time, when she asked me to tell my father she was there, I went so far as to pretend that I had, then returned to the front door and told her that my father was on the phone with Mrs. Elkin, another divorcée who lived on nearby Chestnut Street. Mrs. Wilcott just smiled and handed over the turnovers, her breasts aimed at me like heatseeking missiles.

My aggressive actions were inspired by Benjamin's increasingly hostile attitude toward me. He had begun staring at me on the playground and giving me the finger at every opportunity, which was often. I knew that it was just a matter of time before my head was wedged in a crack on the sidewalk, so I made my campaign against Mrs. Wilcott a priority.

"Hey, how come Wilcott is always looking at you?" Johnny Cezzaro asked one day as we waited in line for the school doors to open. It was a cool damp day in early October and the thick clouds hung close and low.

"He's not looking at me," I said. I did not look in Benjamin's direction.

"Hey, he just gave you the finger!"

"No, he didn't," I said. "He gave you the finger."

Johnny was confused. "Did he?"

"Yes, he hates you," I said. "Everyone knows that. I would tell your brother." I didn't specify which brother. Johnny had six older vocational school-bound brothers, any one of whom could do serious harm to Benjamin.

"I'm gonna tell Big Tony," Johnny said.

"Yes, he's big. Tell Big Tony," I said. I was staring at the front doors. I thought that if I looked at them long and hard enough, they would miraculously open.

"Yeah, Big Tony will kick his ass."

"Yes," I said as the doors finally opened. "That would be good."

While I was at my locker, Mrs. Plank and Miss Polk walked over to me. Mrs. Plank patted me on the head. "So, are we going to see your father at Parents Night?" she asked.

I took off my jacket and hung it on the hook. "No, he has to travel. He has to go to Atlanta for the university," I said. I didn't want to talk about Parents Night.

"Well, that's a shame," she said. "We'll miss him."

"We wanted his autograph," Miss Polk said. Her long dangling earrings bounced and jiggled as she chewed her gum. I thought she was referring in some way to my father's dismal performance on *Access Wilton*, which was constantly being rerun on Channel 87, but instead, she showed me a copy of *People* magazine. Inside, there was a photograph of my father, Tommy, and me under the headline, MILLIONS CAN'T EASE HIS PAIN. In smaller letters I read, HE PLAYED HIS DEAD WIFE'S LOTTERY NUMBERS. There was also a small photo of my mother in her bathing suit at the Wilton Park Pool and another one of my Uncle Frank, smiling in front of our house, his jaw pointing downward.

"I didn't know your uncle was a big Hollywood producer," Miss Polk said.

I didn't say anything. I just looked at the photo of my mother in her bathing suit. She was smiling and standing by the water slide, the slide I was always too afraid to go down. The picture was taken just a few weeks before the accident.

"Well, the Pappas family certainly has its share of famous people," Mrs. Plank said, closing the magazine. Then she patted the top of my head again and they both walked away.

After school, I kept an eye out for Benjamin while walking home with Charlie and Johnny Cezzaro. As we walked, Johnny provided details on how we were going to kick Benjamin's ass. Somehow he had assumed that I was going to be part of this effort.

"We'll wait for him after football practice then we'll jump him. We'll wait until he's unlocking his bike at the bike rack. You'll grab him around his knees and I'll push him down, then we'll kick him in the balls. My father says that's the first place you gotta hit someone, in the balls. That wrecks their defense mechanism."

"I thought Big Tony was going to fight him," I said.

"We don't need Big Tony," Johnny said. "I can handle him alone, if you won't help."

Johnny was the runt of the Cezzaro litter and I had no confidence in his ability to fight. "I don't know," I said. "Big Tony is pretty big."

We stopped off at Uncle Pete's Place, a small store with a stale sweet odor and a checkered tile floor that could make you dizzy if you stared at it too long. I paid for the Twizzlers and Cokes for Johnny and me, something Johnny obviously expected me to do since he had told me before entering that he had no money. Charlie didn't want anything.

"Hey, there's the rich boy," the old lady behind the counter said. She bent down and picked up a copy of *People* magazine.

"Tell your father to cheer up," she said.

He seems pretty happy right now, I thought, thinking of Mrs. Wilcott. I didn't say anything though, I just nodded. When we got outside, I saw the red pickup truck parked across the street. I chewed my Twizzler and stared at the man with long hair. He waved at me, but I didn't wave back.

"Hey, there's that guy again," Johnny said, but I just started walking.

AFTER THE STORY appeared in the magazine, we started getting phone calls again, mostly from people asking for money. Some of them were already crying on the phone when I answered, their voices muffled and choked, their words wet. Others would speak softly and apologetically, saying they were too sick to talk any louder. One man said he had an advanced case of narcolepsy, the sleeping disease. While he was talking to me, he kept falling asleep and dropping the phone. Another man said that if my father could just give him seed money, he could begin his research proving that dogs were really aliens sent to observe us. "You don't have a dog, do you? No? Ah, smart boy, smart boy," he said.

The television stations and newspapers started calling again as well, overwhelming my father with demands for interviews. On a number of occasions, reporters would show up unannounced at our front door, their faces sheens of excitement, bright and alert. One television reporter, a pretty woman with short dark hair and big lips whose face I recognized from billboards along the expressway, came three times asking for an exclusive. My father politely refused all requests.

In addition to the reporters' calls, my father started getting photos and letters from women offering to marry him. I came to recognize the blue and pink envelopes with the sweet smell that lingered on the surface. I would retrieve them from the garbage after my father had thrown them out and read them. Most promised that they would be a good wife and mother. One included a picture of her and her three daughters who seemed about my mother's age. "Take your pick," the woman wrote. I saved that letter because the women in the photo were naked except for their tattoos.

As expected, my father was extremely upset by all the renewed attention. "I had hoped we had gotten past this point," I heard him tell Aunt Bess one day at breakfast after a phone call from a man requesting funding to support his proposed subway system that would circumvent the earth.

It was conference time though, so my father was too busy preparing his papers on footwear to focus on the situation. I would hear him working on his old Royal typewriter late at night or talking on the phone to other historians, confirming then reconfirming information. The tension showed on his face and body, which seemed to be caving in from the pressure.

"I don't understand why you're still working," Aunt Bess said at dinner one night. "You've won all this money and you're working harder than ever."

My father carefully put down his coffee cup, finding the exact center of his saucer. "The university has been very good to me, very loyal to me," he said softly. "I feel their loyalty should be honored. They don't ask me to do much, so I feel that I should do the best I can when I am called on to represent them."

"Can't you hire someone else to do your job?" Uncle Frank asked. "I know a lot of writers. You can pay them and when they're finished, you can slap your name on it. It's done all the time."

My father ignored Uncle Frank's comments and asked me to pass the salt. Over the past few days I had detected an unmistakable and unusual charge of anger coming from my father, an anger I sensed was directed at Uncle Frank. I suspected it had something to do with the *People* magazine story. When Aunt Bess showed the article to my father, he gasped and said, "He has no shame," and went to his study where he stayed late into the night.

Uncle Frank, for his part, seemed sorry about something. He spoke softer and began leaving the house early in the morning for meetings in downtown Chicago. Twice he flew back and forth to Los Angeles in the same day. Like my father, he also began to look tired and deep dark circles ringed his eyes, giving him a lost, hunted raccoon look.

"They're wrapping my film," Uncle Frank said, reaching for his glass of wine. "It's almost done."

"What's this one about, Frank?" Aunt Bess asked.

Uncle Frank seriously considered his glass of wine and then picked it up and swirled it delicately. "A good vampire," he said, still staring at the wine. "A vampire who doesn't really mean any harm. He can't help being a vampire though. He can't help the way he is. He didn't want to turn out the way he is, he just did. He does stupid things once in a while and he's sorry for them." He looked over at my father who looked away.

Later that evening, Mrs. Wilcott came over unannounced, holding a large pie in front of her like a shield. I had not expected her. She usually came before dinner, with hopes, I thought, of being invited to eat. I interpreted this late visit as a surprise attack, a violation of the rules and ignored her even after my father instructed me to say hello.

I found her sudden appearance that evening particularly annoying since we were preparing to play Stratego, a board game of military strategy. My father had surprised me by agreeing to play the game at dinner, despite his busy schedule. The object of the game was to capture your opponent's flag and I had devised a somewhat basic, but I thought effective, strategy of hiding my flag behind a number of bombs and sergeants to thwart my father and Tommy, who was assisting him. I had overheard the family counselor at the hospital recommend the game to my father while he was recuperating from his bowel problems, saying that it would encourage father-son interaction. We had only played once before, a dull and uninspiring affair during which my father had spent the majority of the time reading then rereading the instructions. I had hoped, with the rules now clear, the second game would prove more entertaining.

"I know you like apple-cinnamon," Mrs. Wilcott said, handing me the pie. Tommy ran upstairs. "I made this for you, Teddy, when we were taping this week's show." When she smiled it looked like she had saved two apples and put one in each of her cheeks.

My father looked at me expectantly, his eyebrows raised. I had a difficult time looking at him. I resented the bumbling, animated way he acted around Mrs. Wilcott.

"Thank you," I mumbled. I left the living room and brought the pie into the kitchen where Aunt Bess sat at the table with her chin in her hand, reading *Luxury Living!* a slick, thick magazine Uncle Frank had begun bringing home and, it seemed, memorizing. Stavros lay curled up at her feet silently emitting a variety of odors, all suggesting decomposition.

"Frank wants us to buy a heated toilet," she said, pointing to the magazine. "In the winter, the toilet seat gets warm. They cost two thousand dollars." Then she looked up at me and asked, "What are you doing with that pie?"

"Mrs. Wilcott gave it to me. To us."

Aunt Bess's eyes narrowed to a slit. "Did we get it in the mail?"

"No, she's here. In the living room."

"She's here? In the living room?" Aunt Bess looked at me with such alarm and suspicion that I was suddenly afraid of the pie.

"What kind is it?"

"She said it's apple-cinnamon."

She nodded her head gravely at this news. "Apple-cinnamon," she said. "What does she want us to do with it?"

"I don't know," I said. I wanted to put the pie down; I was tired of holding it.

"I don't want to eat that pie. Your uncle, does he know about this pie?"

"He went out."

"Where's your brother?"

"He went upstairs." Then I said, "He doesn't know about the pie either."

Aunt Bess looked hard at the pie again. I knew it was an insult to her. She prided herself on her baking and resented anyone else's efforts in this area, particularly Mrs. Wilcott's. She would shake her head and mumble in Greek whenever she watched *Access Wilton*, criticizing and correcting Mrs. Wilcott's every move behind the stove.

"Put it over there," Aunt Bess finally said, "on the counter." Then she slowly shook her head and went back to reading *Luxury Living!*

Since Mrs. Wilcott refused to leave, I went up to my bedroom. I wanted to be alone. I felt both jumpy and tired, and knew that drawing would make me feel better.

I stopped dead in my doorway though as I entered my room. There, standing by the window, was Tommy wearing a pair of my mother's old high heels. He also had breasts. Very large breasts.

"Tommy? What are you doing?"

"Nothing," he said. Then he thrust his chest out, fluttered his eyelids, and said in a falsetto voice, "I'm Mrs. Wilcott. I got big tits."

"Take those off," I said. I walked toward him and pulled up his shirt to reveal two rolls of toilet paper.

"Don't touch my tits!" he yelled and pulled his shirt back down.

I quickly shut the door. "Give me the toilet paper now," I said firmly.

"No way, Jose." He shook his body and closed his eyes. "I like my tits."

I sat on the floor and watched him parade back and forth in the high heels, his ankles twisting and turning with every step. The jumpy feeling had left me and all I felt now was tired, emptied out. I wanted to go to bed and drift and dream of our ranch in Montana, our shiny new Jeep and our personal French chef, a recent addition to my List of Things. Then I heard Mrs. Wilcott laugh—a loud, high giggle that felt like hot electricity. I sat there and listened to her, the woman who wanted to make me play sports, the woman who was probably having sex with my father, the woman my mother did not like. I opened my eyes and stood up.

"Tommy," I said. "Come here a second. Follow me."

WHEN I RETURNED to the living room a few minutes later, Mrs. Wilcott was sitting very close to my father, her spotless white running shoes touching his worn black wing tips. When I walked past them, my father inched away from her and cleared his throat.

I started putting away the Stratego game which was spread out on the low coffee table. I did this loudly to draw attention to the fact that the game was officially being abandoned. Neither my father nor Mrs. Wilcott seemed to notice my surrender, however. They continued to talk about a play Mrs. Wilcott had just seen.

"I cried, Theo, I cried," she said.

"My," my father said. "It sounds quite, well, sad."

"But it was beautiful too. The way they sang."

"Ah," my father said. "Yes."

"We will have to go then," Mrs. Wilcott said, briefly touching my father's knee. I looked up just in time to see his bald spot glow like Mars.

"Yes," he said. "That will have to be arranged. I think so." My father looked over at me and smiled.

"I'm thinking about playing the score at the country club Gala in November. I think it would be perfect during dinner. You'll have to come."

My father nodded his still glowing head.

Mrs. Wilcott sat up straight and smoothed the pant legs of her pink running suit. "I saw the article in that magazine," she said in a serious, hushed voice.

"Oh, that, yes." My father's face changed. He looked perturbed. "Yes.

That article was, um, intrusive. I don't know why our lives would be of interest to anyone," he said.

"It is a horrible magazine. I never read it. But since I am a working journalist, I feel I must at least browse it."

My father looked at Mrs. Wilcott, confused. "Journalist?"

"My column, Theo. 'Wilton Whispers.' "

"Yes! Of course," my father said quickly. He actually snapped his fingers. "I read it whenever I have the opportunity. It is always entertaining and informative." He said this loudly and urgently, as if he had just remembered something he was supposed to have memorized.

"I didn't know your brother and you are planning on going into television."

"We are?" my father asked. "The article said this? I never read it, never finished it, I mean."

"The article said you were going to produce a talk show. Your brother was going to be the host."

My father nodded his head and said nothing, though I noticed the muscles on his jaw grow tight.

A few moments later Mrs. Wilcott stood up to leave. "I have to pick Benjamin up from karate class," she said. "Teddy, I hear you might be playing soccer this fall."

I pretended I didn't hear her. I fiddled with a Stratego piece.

"Well, he's considering it," my father said, chuckling nervously. "Aren't you, Teddy?"

"What?" I asked, looking up.

Mrs. Wilcott smiled knowingly at my father and walked to the door. Just then Tommy walked into the room. He was wearing the high heels and the lipstick I had carefully applied to his mouth. He was also wearing one of Aunt Bess's bras on the outside of his sweatshirt which was stuffed with several pairs of my father's boxer shorts. "Hello, Theoooo," he said in his high voice. He shook his breasts a little and fluttered his eyelids. "Let's eat some pie! They make my tits grow bigger."

My father's reaction was initially delayed. At first, he just looked at Tommy with a smile on his face, the same smile he had when he was looking at Mrs. Wilcott. Then the smile vanished and he fell slightly backward against the wall, his face disbelieving. I thought he might slide down the wall to the floor when Mrs. Wilcott grabbed his arm and did something that, at that point in time, ranked as one of my life's biggest disappointments. She laughed.

"Oh, Theo," she said. "Stand up now. Stand up, that's it."

Tommy kicked off the high heels and ran upstairs.

"Are you all right?" Mrs. Wilcott asked my father. She had taken his hand and was holding it.

"Yes, of course, yes. That just startled me. I'm so sorry. That was rude of Tommy. Very, very rude. I apologize, I don't . . ."

Mrs. Wilcott stood close to my father and patted his hair down, pressing it softly against the sides of his head.

"Oh, Theo, really. I raised three children," she said. "I would expect that from a five-year-old." Then turning to face me she said. "Now I know Teddy wouldn't do something like that, not at your age, would you, sweetheart?" She smiled at me, but her smile looked different than it usually did. I felt my face flush.

"Well, anyway, I am sorry," my father said. "I'm going to make it a point to have a discussion with Tommy about this." He walked Mrs. Wilcott to the front hallway. When he opened the door, I heard a car engine start up and through the living room window, I saw the red pickup truck drive off.

"I wonder if Mrs. Rhodebush is having some work done in her garden," Mrs. Wilcott said as she and my father walked out onto the front porch. "That old truck has been parked in front of her house off and on, all week."

I walked out onto the porch where they were standing.

"I think she is," my father said absentmindedly. He was staring at Mrs. Wilcott, a trace of a smile on his face. I was furious. I couldn't understand how he could have recovered so quickly. Normally, such an experience would have thrown him into a throat-clearing fit that would have lasted for hours, if not days.

"No, she's not," I said, eager to break my father's trance. "That truck's been following me."

"What?" my father said.

"That truck has been following me home from school."

"What do you mean?" my father asked. "Following you?"

"I see it all the time." I enjoyed seeing the look of concern on his face.

"Are you sure?" Mrs. Wilcott asked.

"Yes. Charlie has seen it too. So has Johnny Cezzaro."

"How many times have you seen it?" my father asked.

"A few times. It has Tennessee license plates."

"Tennessee," my father said. His shoulders stiffened a bit when I told him this. "Do you know who it is? Is it someone's father or brother? Someone from school?"

"No."

"Oh, Theo, it's probably just another reporter," Mrs. Wilcott said.

"I thought it was but I don't think he is now. They don't drive trucks," I said. "He waved at me and tried to talk to me."

"Who did?" my father asked.

"The man driving the truck. He had long blond hair," I said.

My father repeated this then stared over my head into the street. He was very quiet. We all just stood there.

"Theo," Mrs. Wilcott said. "Is everything all right?"

My father continued to stare, his eyes looking at something that was approaching at a great distance, something that only he could see.

"Yes, yes, everything is fine," he said, his voice a whisper. "Good night now."

When we got back into the house, my father told me to go up to my room. Then I heard him lock the door.

CHAPTER FIVE

MAURICE JACKSON HAD seriously considered becoming a Muslim but had ultimately decided against it. I wasn't sure what that meant, but he told my father it took him years to realize that he wasn't devout or disciplined enough to follow such a demanding religion.

"I'm not strong enough to follow the faith," I heard him say. "I know my own limitations."

"Yes, well," my father said.

I was sitting on my perch on the hallway stairs listening to Maurice, my father, and Uncle Frank talk about Maurice coming to work for us. His job, according to Aunt Bess, was to keep Tommy and me from being kidnapped then buried alive in a pine box in a forest preserve while the ransom was being collected.

"It happens, honey," Aunt Bess whispered as she sat next to me on the stairs. "It happens."

Maurice was being hired partly because of the red truck and partly because of Edwina Hart, the orange-haired old lady who had handcuffed herself to our front door the day before, demanding that my father give all his money to keep the polar cap from melting any farther. She stayed on the front porch most of the morning, yelling "Save the cap!" As soon as Aunt Bess saw her, she called the police.

"Some nut is on our porch," she said when she called. I was surprised how calm Aunt Bess was about the whole affair considering that neither my father nor uncle were home to protect us and Edwina, with her shocking hair and gas mask, struck a very disturbing pose.

"Everyone's nuts," Aunt Bess said as she watched Edwina from the window. "Everyone's crazy."

The police had taken a long time in responding, so Aunt Bess finally offered Edwina some coffee which she gratefully accepted.

"The others were supposed to come, but I think they're lost," she said. She lightly blew on the surface of the coffee. "Great coffee. Decaf, dear?"

"That's all we drink," Aunt Bess said.

After a while Edwina stopped yelling "Save the cap," and instead sat on the front steps and waited for the police to come and cut off her handcuffs. She claimed to have swallowed her key.

"My God, I'm surprised you didn't choke," Aunt Bess said to her. "How big was it?"

"The key? Not very," Edwina said. "I've swallowed a lot bigger things. Here," she said. She dug into a brown duffel bag and pulled out a large "Save the Cap" T-shirt and handed it to Aunt Bess. Aunt Bess held it up against her chest. Under the words was a picture of what looked to be an ice cube melting.

"Do you have anything larger?" Aunt Bess asked.

When the police finally arrived, Edwina went willingly. She was disappointed that no television stations had shown up to cover her arrest and was eager to get back home and resume her crusade.

"This whole thing was poorly planned," she said to Aunt Bess as she was led away. "I think I gave the group the wrong address. They may come by later."

"I'll keep the coffee on," Aunt Bess said.

Upon learning about the incident, my father decided to hire Maurice.

"What happened with the protester, the woman yesterday, are you experienced in dealing with such situations?" my father now asked.

"Yes," Maurice said. "I've dealt with a lot of different situations. I can handle most anything."

Maurice was about ten years younger than my father and had played in the National Football League back when, according to Uncle Frank, it was a "sport, not a business." He played for the Chicago Bears. "I was an offensive lineman, that's why you probably never heard of me," he told my father. "I was much heavier back then." He had a low, quiet voice that seemed at first to hover close to the ground before lifting gently into the air. I liked the way it sounded and because of that, I thought I might like Maurice too.

After he left, Aunt Bess and I walked down into the dining room where my father sat at the table, quietly reading some papers Maurice had given him.

"He's good," Uncle Frank said eagerly. "He's got the right pedigree. He's worked for a lot of VIPs, a lot of celebs, when they come to Chicago."

My father continued to study the papers in silence. "I have some reservations," he said after some time.

"He's black," Aunt Bess said. "He'll scare the neighbors. Isn't there a white guard we can hire?"

Uncle Frank waved his hand and poured coffee into a cup. "I think that's one of the reasons we should hire him. It will send a message loud and clear to every creep out there. Some white guy isn't going to scare people away. Besides," he said, picking up his coffee, "the guy used to play for the Bears."

My father put the papers down and cleared his throat. "His discussion of religion. I thought that, well, I thought that a bit odd."

Uncle Frank shrugged. "He's a very serious guy. What's the word? Introspective."

"But he used to play football," my father said.

Uncle Frank quickly put down his cup. "Hey, now that's a stereotype," he said. "There's a lot of introspective athletes out there, Theo. Don't be so biased. Just because he didn't go to Harvard, doesn't mean he can't be introspective. I'm introspective. I'm introspective as hell. And I didn't go to god-damn Harvard."

My father sat back in his chair and took a deep breath. Then looking over at me he said, "Teddy, we are hiring this man to make sure that no one interferes with you and Tommy. We don't want anyone bothering you."

I immediately thought of Benjamin. Suddenly I liked the idea of Maurice immensely.

"Okay," I said.

"Well, we will try this for a month or so," my father said. "If the situation proves uncomfortable, I'll just rearrange my work schedule and take them back and forth to school myself."

"Theo, you're almost sixty years old and you have a bad heart," Uncle Frank said. "What are you going to do if something happens, someone tries something? What, go into cardiac arrest on top of him?"

"We shouldn't hire him," Aunt Bess said, picking up the coffee pot and walking back into the kitchen. "Emily Rhodebush and the Yankee aren't going to like having him around the neighborhood."

My father took another deep breath and looked out the window. "Well, it does seems a bit extreme to hire someone to stand guard over your children."

"Well, I think it's a good idea. A damn good idea," Uncle Frank said, but my father said nothing.

THE NEXT DAY Maurice walked us to school. "Walking is good exercise," he explained. "And it will give me the opportunity to get to know the neighborhood." As we walked, I surveyed Wilton with a new, critical eye. Familiar houses and streets were now suspect. I looked hard for lurking dangers, the red pickup truck or Edwina Hart, but didn't see a trace.

Maurice was tall and thin, with short cropped hair that was sprinkled with gray. He walked with an easy, smooth grace that I found hard to keep up with. Tommy walked a few feet in front of us, his eyes glued on the sidewalk. He was attempting to step on every crack he could because Jeremy Bodens said it would break Miss McHugh's, his kindergarten teacher's back.

"Am I going too fast for you?" Maurice asked.

"No. I'm okay."

"Well, you let me know now. I don't want to tire you out before you get to school."

A few blocks from St. Pius, a Wilton police car drove slowly by and stopped. The officer, a short fat man with pale skin and thick shoes, got out of the car and asked Maurice if he was our bodyguard.

"Yes," Maurice said as we kept walking. "I am."

"Just double-checking," the policeman said. "We were notified that you were starting today. We're there if you need us," he said. He got back into the car and drove off.

Maurice just nodded and took Tommy's hand as we crossed the street.

When we got to St. Pius, all the children on the playground stopped what they were doing for a moment and looked at us. Mostly, they looked at Maurice.

He didn't seem to mind or notice though. He walked slowly over to the fence, pulled out a large brown pipe from his coat pocket, and began inspecting it, rolling it around his large hands before carefully lighting it. Tommy ran off to the swings.

I just stood where Maurice left me. Since I had never been guarded before, I wasn't clear on exact procedures. I had a vague idea that I was in some type of protective radius and didn't want to anger Maurice by leaving it.

"Go on and play," he yelled and waved his hand. "Pretend I'm not here. You're okay."

"Can I go over there?" I asked, pointing toward the line of fifth graders forming near the door.

"Yes, that's fine."

I took my place behind Charlie who allowed himself one brief glance at Maurice before resuming his usual position of staring straight ahead at the front door.

As soon as we got into class, Mrs. Plank, the principal, came in our room, rapped her knuckles on Miss Grace's desk and said she had something to announce.

"For the next few weeks, Teddy and Tommy Pappas will be escorted to and from school by a private detective, so no one should be alarmed if they see Tommy and Teddy with a large black man."

Everyone in class already knew this, as did pretty much everyone in Wilton.

"Does anyone have any questions?"

"Will that man protect me if I get kidnapped?"

"No one wants to kidnap you, Johnny," Mrs. Plank said. Then I thought I heard her say, "Believe me," very softly, but I wasn't sure.

"Does he have a gun?" Johnny asked.

The question startled Mrs. Plank. "That's not important," she said, but I could tell that it suddenly was.

For my part, I enjoyed the attention that Maurice was generating on my behalf. I didn't believe I was in any danger and saw his presence more in terms of status than safety. Maurice was finally evidence that we had won the lottery and while he was no substitute for the new cafeteria or swimming pool I had promised my classmates, he was a start. The drink-serving robot no longer seemed so far off.

Near the end of the day, Miss Grace walked over to my desk, bent down, and whispered.

"You have a lot on your mind, don't you?"

At that exact moment, I had been reflecting about asking Charlie to make another picture of Miss Grace with a new photo I had found of her smiling.

"Yes," I said. "I do."

"Well, we won't let anything ever happen to you or your brother here at St. Pius," she said. "Ever."

I nodded. She smelled particularly fresh that day, like lemon and flowers and honey. I took a deep breath, and floated on her scent.

"That man your father hired sounds like a good idea." She stood up and nodded her head slowly, looking at me in an intense way that I had never seen before. I swallowed hard. For a moment, I thought she might try to kidnap me.

"You've been through so much," she finally said. Her eyes started to redden and in them I saw the first inklings of a sad haiku.

"But not as much as Ergu," I said.

She wiped the bottom of her eyes with a finger. "I have something for you. I know you've been waiting for this for a long time." She handed me an envelope with several foreign postmarks on it. I immediately knew it was from Ergu, my Christian pen pal.

"I thought I'd let you open it yourself," she said. Then she touched me on the back of the head and walked back to her desk.

I opened the letter and was surprised to see that it was typewritten. I had been led to believe that most things in Ergu's village were made of mud, twigs or stone. I read slowly.

Dear Mr. Tedde:

With happy heart We receive your letters and good news of your fortune. We are very poor here in Gabon. And do not eat much meat or milk. There is sickness as well. That is killing and hurting things greatly. It is sad.

We hope that You can please send money for medicine, food and tools for plowing. It is growing time now and we must plant.

I have nine brothers and six sisters. Our residence is small and has no television at all but two.

If you please, wire us some money, can it be $50,000? Send it to the number below, Switzerland. We will buy medicine and seeds and an ox.

I never been to USA but no it is a nice, strong Place where people are healthy and enjoy much success. I send you picture of my prideful family if you can send me money.

I love you. And God too.

E. Moosurlctd

Can it be more than $50,000? Please, thank you?

The letter confused me and ran somewhat contrary to my image of Ergu and his humble life. I thought it a bit forward to be asking for $50,000 which seemed like quite a bit of money. But before I could question Miss Grace, the bell rang so I folded it up and put it in my pocket.

ON THE WAY HOME from school, Maurice asked about my mother. "I understand that she died," he said.

"Yes," I said. "When I was ten."

We walked for a while in silence. An old yellow bus from the public school drove by creaking and groaning as it stopped at the corner then started up again. I put my hands in the pockets of my windbreaker. I really didn't want to talk about my mother at that moment. I wanted to think about the strange letter from Ergu. I knew something wasn't right and wanted to sort through things and come to some conclusions.

"My mother died last year too," Maurice said. "When I was forty-eight. It doesn't matter how old you are, you miss them all the same."

I didn't say anything as we crossed the street. The leaves on the trees were in full color now and soon would be falling in bunches. My mother used to rake the leaves and I wondered who would do it now.

"All this walking is going to keep me in good shape," Maurice said as we turned down our block. "This is my third trip back and forth. I picked your brother up at noon and walked him home."

"He only goes half days," I said.

"He's a funny little man. He makes me laugh."

"Tommy makes you laugh? What was he wearing?" My first thought was that Tommy had walked back and forth to school in high heels and Aunt Bess's bra.

"What's that now?"

"Nothing."

"He told me that he really misses his mother," Maurice said.

"Tommy told you?" I was surprised. I had more or less forgotten that Tommy could speak.

"He's a nice little boy," Maurice said as we made our way up our walk. "A very nice little boy."

My father was waiting for us on the front porch. Since it was a cool day, he was wearing his brown sweater with the pointed hood that made him look like an aging dwarf. It was an odd fitting sweater that had some connection to his college days at Harvard. My mother had tried to throw it out many times, but my father had always managed to rescue it from the garbage or the Goodwill.

"Well," he said, bowing his pointed head as we approached. "And how was everything today?"

"Fine, Mr. Pappas. A little cold though."

"Cold? Oh, yes. But other than that?"

"Fine," Maurice said. "Fine."

My father looked relieved then squinted his eyes as he scanned the street. "Nothing unusual?" he asked.

Maurice shook his head.

"Good then. Well." My father rubbed his hands together. "Aunt Bess, our aunt, has made an early dinner and we were hoping you could join us, Mr. Jackson." I was surprised by my father's invitation but Maurice merely said, "Why, thank you," and walked up the front steps.

While Maurice sat in the living room with my father, I went into the kitchen. Aunt Bess was quickly making her way around the cramped room, cutting vegetables and stirring steaming pots. The kitchen was hot and damp and smelled like thick soup.

"I don't have enough food," she whispered to Uncle Frank as he poured himself a glass of wine at the kitchen counter. "And I don't know what he likes."

"Well, don't insult him and try to make ribs or anything," Uncle Frank said.

"Ribs?" my aunt said, confused. "I'm making chicken. Is he expecting ribs?"

Dinner was an awkward affair. Maurice said very little and Uncle Frank, who usually did most of the talking when we ate, got a phone call and disappeared into my father's study, leaving us without his booming voice to fill the room. My father ate nervously, clearing his throat and cutting his chicken into small, then smaller, and finally tiny pieces that he had trouble picking up with his fork.

"Mr. Jackson," he said after some time. "I know you said that you were from Tennessee. Where in Tennessee, if you don't mind me asking?"

"Chattanooga," Maurice said.

"Ah, yes, Lookout Mountain," my father said.

Maurice looked up from his plate. "Excuse me?"

"Lookout Mountain. A great battle was fought there near Chattanooga. In the Civil War."

Maurice digested this information, as well as some baked potato. Finally he said, "I fought in the Vietnam War."

My father nodded his head. "Ah, yes, of course. A very interesting conflict."

"Conflict?" Maurice asked quietly.

"Yes. Technically, it wasn't a war. But—" my father stopped. Maurice was looking at him in a sad but stern way. "That's just technically, of course," my father continued. "I'm sure that it was very much a war to everyone who fought in it. Anyway, yes."

We fell back into an uncomfortable silence, the sound of our forks and spoons against our plates small and loud. Upstairs, we could hear Uncle Frank's muffled voice.

"So," my father said. "Mr. Jackson, do you have family in Chicago, may I ask, or are they still in Chattanooga?"

Maurice looked up again from his plate. "I have a sister in St. Louis. That's about all."

My father looked at me and Tommy. "No, children then?"

"No, I never married," Maurice said.

"Interesting," my father said.

Maurice swallowed. "Why is that interesting?" he asked.

My father, who was sipping his water, started coughing. He was embarrassed by the question. "Well, it's just . . ." He stopped there. "I don't know why I said interesting. Actually, it's really . . . not really interesting, it's just . . ." He paused again and took a deep breath. "It was a poor word choice," he finally said. "Yes."

We all watched my father drink his glass of water with his eyes closed.

"I'm on this voyage alone," Maurice said after some time.

"Excuse me, I'm sorry?" my father asked.

"I'm traveling through this life alone," Maurice said. "Some people are meant to be married and some people aren't. Some people are meant to be rich and some people poor. Some people happy, some sad. It's the balance of life."

I expected my father to start clearing his throat or drink more water in response to this strange comment, but instead he stopped cutting his chicken and looked over at Maurice. Then he nodded his head, once, as if he understood something I did not.

After Maurice left, Aunt Bess started speaking rapidly to my father in Greek so I couldn't understand.

"I don't understand you," my father finally said as he helped clear the table. "I don't know the language anymore. Please speak English."

"I don't think we need him here," she said. "I don't trust him. He might be a kidnapper himself."

"I assure you, he's not a kidnapper," he said, stacking some plates on top of each other.

Aunt Bess piled some silverware onto a serving platter. "He has an evil air about him." Then she turned and grabbed my father's arm and looked at him earnestly. "I had a dream last night," she said.

"A dream." My father repeated this slowly.

"Of dark clouds. They were moving fast. Toward us."

My father looked down at her hand as she clutched his arm. Then he looked over at me, embarrassed. "Well, they said it might rain tomorrow."

"That's not what the dream was about," she said.

"Well," my father said as he gently broke free of her grasp and picked up the plates. "I thought dinner went well enough."

"He's evil," Aunt Bess said again, walking back into the kitchen. "Nothing good will come of him being with us."

THAT NIGHT, I LAY in bed and revised my List of Things. I had studied a map earlier in the day at school and concluded Montana's distance from Wilton presented a logistical problem. My father was a terrible driver and I had little confidence in his ability to transport us safely to our ranch for summer vacations. The Dakotas seemed particularly ominous on the map and I imagined a number of catastrophes resulting from such a trip, all of them ending with my father, Tommy, and I wandering the Badlands, starving to death after our Ergu-ish attempts to locate edible roots failed.

A plane was then necessary. My father had a fear of flying and I believed a sturdy and reliable Cessna would help overcome this fear. I had recently seen a picture of just such a plane in the copy of *Luxury Living!* Uncle Frank had left on the scale in the bathroom. The plane would have leather seats, similar to Uncle Frank's rented Lexus, each with a television set, small drink dispenser, and computer terminal. Each seat would also vibrate, offering a relaxing but invigorating massage. According to *Luxury Living!* such seats were available for $3,600 each, plus installation.

I fell asleep with my list in my hand but woke a few hours later to the sound of Uncle Frank. His voice sounded so clear and near, that at first I thought he was in my room and when I sat up in bed I instinctively asked, "What?" After a few moments, however, I realized that he was downstairs in the living room talking to my father. Actually, he was shouting.

"Don't you think I know I'm a cliché?" he yelled. "Don't you think if you saw my life in a movie everyone would think my character was a stereotype? I've made fourteen movies in thirty years, and twelve of them had the word 'blood' in the title. I've had three wives. How do you think that makes me feel? I'm a cliché. I know this. But I'm also flesh and blood. Flesh and blood.

I make mistakes because I'm out there living a life, Theo, living a life. I didn't give up like you."

Though I could hear my father's voice, I couldn't make out the exact words. I crept out of bed and went halfway down the stairs.

"My God, Frank, exactly how much do you owe them?"

I couldn't hear what Uncle Frank said.

"And they've threatened you?" I heard my father ask.

"I needed the money. I owed everyone. Other people have borrowed from them. I didn't know they were so dangerous. I never would have done this if I did. I had to pay off so many people, I had no choice."

"Do you think they're following you? Or following the boys?"

"I don't know."

"This could explain things."

"That's why I'm telling you this now. I was going to pay them from what I made from this last movie, but distribution fell through. I've been on the phone all day."

There was a silence and then I thought I heard my father say, "Dear God, Frankie, dear God."

A FEW DAYS LATER, my father announced at breakfast that he had been asked by the St. Pius Mothers' Club to contribute to the new furnace fund.

"Apparently, the existing furnace is more than sixty years old," he said as he examined a piece of toast before taking a small bite.

"They asked you for the money?" Aunt Bess asked as she poured some orange juice into a pitcher. Aunt Bess never poured things directly out of bottles into glasses. Instead, she was forever pouring water, milk, and juice into other containers, then pouring them again into glasses, a habit that could turn a simple request for a drink into a very time-consuming affair. "That's some nerve. You're not going to buy them one, are you?"

"Well, I asked for more information," my father said, smiling tightly as he reached for his juice. "To be polite."

"Why don't you just give them ours and buy us a new one then?" Aunt Bess asked.

My father grimaced. "I don't think that would be appropriate."

"It seems like a crazy thing to buy," Aunt Bess said as she moved slowly over to the refrigerator. "Why don't you buy a new car, Theo?"

My father looked down at his glass.

"What about that old man's house?" Aunt Bess asked. "Are you going to buy that? It's the nicest one on the block and you need the space. He's been calling. He wants to talk to you about it."

"No," my father said. "I have no plans to purchase Mr. Tuthill's house."

"Are you ever going to buy anything?" Aunt Bess asked, her voice suddenly rising. "You won all that money. All that money. You have to do something with it. It's not right, Theo. It's not . . . *normal,*" she sighed. Then she said something in Greek and turned to face him. "Use the money, Theo. Maybe the money can make you happy. Maybe the money can help you find peace."

My father sat there, stunned, holding his small orange juice glass. I knew from the look on his face that he was disappearing and that the conversation between he and Aunt Bess was over. I put on my windbreaker and walked outside and waited on the front porch for Maurice.

As soon as I got to school, I was summoned to see Mrs. Plank. I had never been to her office before and naturally was apprehensive. I imagined it to be a large dark and dusty place with obsolete machines like a telegraph or a sun dial in the corners. I assumed it would smell like formaldehyde or stale bread.

When I got to her office, I found her sitting behind her desk, talking on the phone. She waved for me to sit down in an old wooden chair.

My picture of her office had been fairly accurate. It was larger than I thought though, almost the size of our classroom and had a low ceiling with an old fan that had just one blade. Against the wall, neatly arranged in a row, were several other wooden chairs. A brown couch sat in the corner next to a dusty bookcase that contained, I was sure, centuries-old books hand-copied by monks. It was the area behind her desk that drew and held my attention though, for hanging there was picture of Jesus Christ with very short hair.

I stared at the picture. It fascinated me in a morbid way. Jesus had a forgotten, lost, and searching expression on his face. His eyebrows rode up pensively on his forehead and his eyes were small, vacant Cheerios. If the words, "Jesus Christ, Our Lord," hadn't been inscribed on the bottom, I would have taken him for being anyone other than who he was.

"Pretty ugly, isn't it?" Mrs. Plank said in her matter-of-fact way when she hung up the phone. "A nun in Mexico, Sister Maria, painted it and sent it to me. I went to school with her." She turned and looked at the picture, shaking her head. "I had it at home for a while. I can't bring myself to throw it out. I'm going to have to do something with it though. It's upsetting people."

I continued to look at the picture. Mrs. Plank was right. There was something especially disturbing about it, something I couldn't immediately identify.

"He doesn't have any ears," Mrs. Plank said. "Maria is deaf. She was trying to make a statement. Anyway," she waved her hand, "I have to make one more call. Sit tight."

I sat back and looked out the window, away from the Earless Jesus, and saw Maurice sitting in his black car in the parking lot. I watched him lower the window and methodically light his pipe. Maurice always lit his pipe in the same manner and I enjoyed and respected his thoroughness. Turning the pipe upside down, he tapped it three times then sniffed it cautiously. Satisfied that it was empty, he next retrieved a small pouch of tobacco and took two pinches out, packing it gently but firmly into the brown wooden pipe that he then lit with a large silver lighter. His first few puffs on the pipe seemed to give him the most pleasure. His face, serious and considered during the lighting process, would noticeably expand and unfold before easing into a general expression of contentment. I was glad that Maurice smoked. No one was showing any signs of kidnapping Tommy or me and I was afraid that he might soon find his assignment uninteresting. Smoking a pipe at least occupied his time a bit.

"Teddy Pappas," Mrs. Plank said, hanging up the phone. She smiled at me but looked awkward. Mrs. Plank didn't have much practice at being cheerful and her small smile, in the close proximity of the Earless Jesus, unnerved me.

"Teddy Pappas," she said again. "As you know, there aren't many Catholics in Wilton. It's mostly a Protestant community. Not that there's anything wrong with that. But our numbers are small and the school is always looking for new sources of funding. The Archdiocese has been supporting this school for years. That's why we're thrilled that your father is considering our request for the furnace. Miss Polk is pulling together some of the specifics and will mail them off in the next day or so. In the meantime, if you could give him this personal note from me, I'd appreciate it." When she handed me a letter, I immediately thought of all the other letters my father received from women and instinctively shuddered. Mrs. Plank was beyond old.

"So," she said, after I put the envelope in my pocket. "How are you coping with your newfound wealth?"

"Okay," I said.

"Have there been a lot of changes?"

"No," I said. It was a truthful answer. From my perspective, winning the lottery had yet to have any real effect on our lives. The fact that Uncle Frank and Aunt Bess were now living with us, Mrs. Wilcott was having, or at least trying to have, sex with my father, and Maurice was now guarding us, did not represent significant enough change for me to comment upon. As Johnny Cezzaro constantly reminded me, we still hadn't bought anything.

"How do you feel about your bodyguard?" She looked briefly out the window at Maurice who was busily smoking.

"He likes to smoke his pipe," I said.

Mrs. Plank's mouth twitched to the side for a moment. "Well," she said. "That's good. We know it's been difficult for you and your family since your mother's accident. We're praying for you, of course. All of us. Oh," she said. "I understand you received a letter from your pen pal. And what did he have to say?"

I had forgotten about Ergu's letter. "He asked for some money," I said.

Mrs. Plank's face darkened. "He did what?"

"He asked me for some money."

Mrs. Plank's mouth stopped in mid-twitch. "And how much did he ask for, Teddy?"

"Five thousand, no, fifty thousand dollars," I said. I immediately regretted telling her this. I could clearly tell that she disapproved and feared that for some reason I might be held responsible for something, though I wasn't exactly sure what.

"Do you have it?" Mrs. Plank asked. Her voice was now low and controlled. "The letter, may I see the letter please?"

I dug around in my backpack and handed it to her. Though I had thought the letter was strange, I had yet to form a clear opinion about it and was curious what Mrs. Plank thought. She read the letter without any expression, then folded it back up and put it in a drawer. "I would like to hold onto this awhile," she said. "And, Teddy, if you have any more contact with this person, please let me know."

"Okay," I said.

THE NEXT MORNING, while I was still in bed, I thought I heard Stavros crying. It was very early and the sound pulled me from the bottom of sleep. At first I laid in bed, dazed, and listened to his whimpers. Stavros occasionally whined in the morning when Aunt Bess forgot to put food in his bowl the night before so I thought nothing of his complaints and tried to fall back to sleep. His whining intensified, however, and I soon recognized an unfamiliar depth and rhythm to it that concerned me. I thought he might be hurt.

I got out of bed and walked downstairs. Our house was silent and the cries cut sharply through the stillness like a telephone ring at midnight. I followed the sound into the living room, then back again to the front hallway where I stood and listened. The sound was coming from outside. Unlocking the front door, I opened it slowly, expecting to find Stavros curled up on the top step. Instead, I found a baby.

It was laying in a picnic basket, bound tight in layers of white blankets like a delicate miniature mummy. When I saw its tiny hand make its way free and poke out from underneath the mass, my breath left me in a rush. I had never seen a hand that small before and its size and exactness to detail amazed me.

Pinned to the basket handle was a note that simply said, "Baby Girl, four weeks old. Please love her."

I held the note in my hand and looked down at her. For a moment she stopped crying and looked at me with dark, urgent eyes. Then she squeezed them shut and started crying again, her face florid and angry, her cap of black hair, damp and wild. I looked around to see who had left her, but the street was empty.

I stood on our porch, uncertain what to do. I was sure that my first step would be the wrong one, so I watched Baby Girl's face tighten into a red fist. I was scared, convinced she was going to die.

I finally picked the basket up carefully by the handle and walked back into the house. Baby Girl kept crying. As I walked up the hallway stairs I began calling for Aunt Bess to come quick.

"What, what is it, are you sick?" Aunt Bess yelled from her bedroom. "What's wrong?"

"Come here. Please. Hurry, please."

"What's that noise?" she asked. I heard her get out of bed and saw her bedroom door open, saw her face explode.

"It's a baby," I said, holding the basket toward her like a gift. "It's a little girl."

WHEN MAURICE and the two policewomen came, Aunt Bess finally started crying. Sobs shook her body and the loose skin under her arms flapped as she waved her arms around like an angry windmill.

"That baby's been here for close to an hour. I had nothing to feed her, no formula, nothing," she said as tears rolled down her cheeks in thick streaks.

"We came here as fast as we could," one of the policewomen said. She was tall and thin and wore small glasses at the tip of her nose, like Charlie. Every time Aunt Bess said something, she would write it down in a small black notepad which she would flip shut then flip open again when Aunt Bess said something else. The other police officer, a small, gentle-faced woman, silently took the baby into the back of the police car that was parked in our driveway.

"Now where did you say you found the baby again?" the tall policewoman asked Aunt Bess.

"Right here, right where you're standing," she said, pointing to our front steps. "It was right there next to the door. How many times do I have to tell you?"

"Are you all right, Miss Pappas?" Maurice kept asking. He had come at his normal time to pick us up for school and was confused by what he had walked into.

"Yes, I'm fine."

"Is Mr. Pappas at home?" Maurice asked.

"No, I'm all alone. Theo left for Atlanta for his conference last night. I don't know where Frank is. He didn't come home last night."

"Is there anything I can do?" Maurice asked.

"You should have been here! You're supposed to be protecting us. Someone should have been here. I was all alone and someone left that baby on our porch. She could have died out here." Aunt Bess took a deep breath and wiped her eyes. "I'm fine now, though," she said quietly. "Take care of that baby, that's all I have to say." With that she went inside.

Maurice stayed on the porch with the policewoman but I went inside after Aunt Bess. I found her sitting at the kitchen table looking out the window over the sink, her face a mixture of sadness and relief, her tall hair leaning forlornly to one side.

I sat down next to her and listened to her breathe. Before the police arrived, she had been frantic, rocking the baby back and forth in her arms and talking loudly to herself in Greek. She made me call the police twice, panic rising in her voice.

"Are you okay?" I finally asked.

"Yes, honey, I'm fine now. The baby upset me. I was upset. I wasn't expecting it. I was afraid. I don't know too much about babies. I thought she was sick and would die in my arms, right in my arms."

"Why did someone leave her?" I asked.

Aunt Bess shook her head and waved her hand. "I made a coffee cake yesterday for breakfast and I think we should eat it," was all she said.

As she set out plates and forks and poured milk from her favorite glass pitcher, I continued to ask her questions. The whole incident had happened too fast and I felt cheated, like I had arrived at a party just as it was ending. Outside I could hear Maurice and the policewoman's low voices.

"Why did they want to give us the baby?" I asked again. The idea that someone had abandoned Baby Girl would not leave me.

"I don't know. People have pain, problems. Probably a young girl, no husband. Probably poor. People leave babies every day." She looked down at her plate and shook her head. "I can't eat this, what was I thinking?"

"Why did they leave it with us?"

"Because of the money, that's why. Because we won the money."

"What's going to happen to her?"

Aunt Bess shook her head again. "Someone will adopt her. She was a little doll, a perfect little doll. Someone will take care of her. There's people who do things like that. People who take responsibility. They're special people."

I nibbled on the coffee cake's sticky frosting and took a sip of milk. "Why didn't we keep the baby?" The idea of having a small baby around was suddenly appealing. I vaguely remembered liking Tommy as a baby.

"Who would take care of it? I'm almost eighty years old. And your father can't even take care of you." She put her thick arms on the table, causing it to tilt in her direction.

"This table is too small," she said. "The kitchen is too small. We have to get your father to spend some money around here. He hasn't spent any money and time is running out."

"Do you mean, if we don't spend the money, we have to give it back?" I was alarmed by this prospect though on a certain level, it made sense to me.

"No, it means I'm getting older that's all. So is your father. We should do something with that money, before something happens."

"What would happen?"

"I don't know, something," she said. "The money is forcing things upon us, forcing things out in the open."

We sat in silence, Aunt Bess's sadness and worry filling the kitchen.

"I don't think anyone will leave any more babies here," I said trying to make her feel better.

She sighed, her chest expanding to the size of a circus tent. "I don't know. Crazy things keep happening. Maybe your guard should stand at our door to keep people away."

"Maurice?"

"Yes. Do you think he'd be able to do that, if we ask him? I don't want this to happen again."

I imagined Maurice keeping a lonely vigil on our front steps, standing like a sentry all day and night, guarding against unseen and unwanted babies.

"I don't know," I said. Then I said, "I bet this won't happen again."

Aunt Bess waved her hand. "There's thousands of unwanted babies out there, thousands."

I pulled at a piece of the coffee cake and decided to change the subject.

"Is Uncle Frank in some type of trouble?" I asked. From the look on her face, I immediately realized that this subject was no better than the previous one.

"Who told you that?"

"I heard them talking."

She got up and walked over to the counter to get the pitcher of milk. "He needs a little money, that's all. A loan. That's all. He owes some people some money so he can finish his movie."

"Is my father going to give it to him?"

"I think so. I hope so. I don't know anymore, I just don't know," she said. "Do you want more cake?"

I glanced down at my plate which was still full. "No," I said.

"Frank, I worry about him too. He drinks too much. He doesn't seem happy."

She walked over to the counter and began wiping it with a dish rag, her arm moving in slow, sad circles. I thought she was going to say something else about Uncle Frank but instead she said, "I never had babies. I never had any babies and I've lived a whole life. I should have had children, a woman should have children." She put her hands up to her face and wiped away a small tear. "Oh, Teddy," she said. "Pray someone takes care of that baby. Pray that it's someone good like your father."

THE NEXT TWO DAYS were quiet around our house. My father was still in Atlanta discussing southern feet and Uncle Frank was a phantom, leaving early in the morning and arriving home late after we were in bed. Aunt Bess spent most of the time walking around in a hushed, thoughtful silence, a new copy of *Luxury Living!* unopened and unread. I knew she had been deeply upset by Baby Girl so I never discussed her, though the incident weighed on my mind too.

Near the end of the week, on the way to school, Maurice asked me how I was feeling.

"Okay," I said.

"Is your aunt still upset about that little baby?"

"I think a little."

"Well, that must have been hard on everyone."

It was a cool morning and the leaves on the ground were wet from frost. The sun was out though and I knew that by lunchtime it was going to be warm. Tommy walked a few feet ahead of us, dragging a stick on the sidewalk.

"What do you think will happen to her?"

"That little baby? I'm not sure. I'm sure she'll be fine. Someone will take care of her."

"Why do you think they left her?"

"I don't know for sure." Then Maurice said, "Maybe because they loved her."

"If they loved her, then why did they leave her?"

Maurice squinted his eyes, thinking. "They might have thought she'd have a better life with your family. My momma sent me to live with my aunt for awhile in St. Louis when times were tough, after she lost her job at the phone company. I was only eight and I missed her terrible. She did what she had to do though. She was looking out for my best interests. I know that now. You do what you have to do sometimes, you do what you have to do to get by."

Maurice lit his pipe, following the usual procedure. I regarded this now as a sacred ritual and was silent as he performed it.

"I talked to your father about what happened," he said after he took his first puff. "He wanted to come home, but I told him not to, told him everything was under control. He's been in contact with the police and they told him the baby was fine."

"When's he coming home?" I asked. Suddenly, I missed my father.

"Day after tomorrow. He said his conference was going well." Maurice took Tommy's hand as we crossed a street. When we got to the other side, he let go and Tommy ran up ahead again, still dragging his stick that was now bending in the middle.

"Your father seems to like his work," Maurice said.

"He likes the Civil War a lot."

"It's important that a person likes what he does. The money hasn't had much effect on him. It doesn't seem to be changing him."

"My father never changes," I said.

"How's that?"

"My father never changes," I said again, stating what I thought was the obvious. "He's always the same."

"I imagine being consistent is an important part of being a parent," Maurice said. "Maybe it's good then that he doesn't change."

"I wish he was a little different," I said.

Maurice puffed on his pipe. A thin trail of smoke lifted up into the air. "Now why do you wish he was different?"

"I just wish he was different that's all," I said.

We crossed another street. A police car drove slowly past and the policeman waved at Maurice, who waved back. The car drove away, leaving a small pile of leaves chasing it in its wake.

"Well, I'm sure he'll change a little," Maurice said. "All that money will probably bring some change I suppose."

"What would you do if you won the lottery?" I asked.

"What would I do if I had won," Maurice repeated my question. "I don't . . ." he stopped. "I don't think I'd wish that on myself." Then he said, "Your father, he's doing the right thing, I think."

This confused me. My father didn't seem to be doing much of anything. "What's he doing?" I asked.

"He's controlling the money," Maurice said. "Instead of having it control him." With that, Maurice puffed on his pipe a few more times and we walked the rest of the way without saying much else.

When I got to school, Benjamin Wilcott came up to me in the hall and pushed me against my locker. "Hey, asshole. Tell your dad to leave my mom alone."

"Okay," I said. Benjamin was pressing against me hard, his breath smelling of hot toothpaste.

"I don't give a shit how much money your old man has. He can't buy my mom. And your big guard can't help you in here." He gave me another short push and walked away.

During the first part of Reflection class, instead of praying silently for the cardinal who was sick again, I began praying for Mrs. Wilcott to relocate out-of-state. I decided that it would be best for my family, and me in particular, if they just moved away. Despite my best efforts, my prayer slowly dissolved into fantasies of vengence on Benjamin. Visions of me punching Benjamin in the face, pulling down Benjamin's pants on the playground, or insulting him in front of the St. Pius cheerleaders filled my mind.

My fantasies were interrupted when the fire alarm went off, a loud piercing sound that made me jump. Looking up from her papers, Miss Grace said, "This wasn't scheduled," then quickly led us outside in a single file. A few minutes later, two fire trucks pulled up in front of the school.

We waited outside for more than an hour and watched as firemen entered then left the school, moving at first in a quick and organized fashion, then noticeably slower. Miss Grace let us sit on the ground near the end of the playground and watch them. Johnny sat next to me and prayed out loud that the school would burn to the ground.

"Is there a saint of fire?" he asked. Then he said, "Hey, that's your brother."

I looked toward the school doorway just as Mrs. Plank, Aunt Bess, and Tommy were walking out. Within seconds Aunt Bess and Tommy disappeared into Maurice's car and drove off.

When we were let back into school, I was immediately summoned to Mrs. Plank's dark dusty office again. She was walking up and down in front of her desk, holding a pencil. I looked up briefly at the Earless Jesus, then stared at the floor. I concluded, from the way Mrs. Plank was acting, that Tommy had done something terrible.

"Teddy, your brother started a fire in the bathroom," she said as soon as I sat down.

She shook her head, twitched her mouth, then took off her glasses and rubbed her eyes. "This is very, very disturbing. It's a good thing Mr. Sean Hill decided to use the boys' lavatory, or else there could have been some real damage. He burned his hand though. Well, a finger."

"How did he start it?" I asked. I was amazed that Tommy could master something as intricate as matches.

"He dropped a lit matchbook into the wastebasket," she said.

"Oh." On second thought, I concluded that Tommy was probably capable of doing something basic like that.

Mrs. Plank looked at me so seriously that I decided to study my shoes awhile. "Teddy, we're very concerned about Tommy. Very concerned. Have you noticed any unusual behavior at home?"

I tried not to think of Tommy sticking crayons up his nose or barking like a dog. I was afraid that Mrs. Plank, through her centuries of living, had mastered the art of mind reading. "No," I said after some time.

Mrs. Plank frowned. "Well, we'll talk about this when your father returns from his trip. In the meantime, Tommy should stay at home. Your aunt knows this."

I nodded.

"Please keep an eye on him, Teddy. I know you've all been through so much. I heard about the baby. I can imagine how frightening that was."

I kept my eyes on the floor.

Mrs. Plank sighed. "Well, take care of Tommy."

"Okay," I said. "Okay."

After school, on the way home, Maurice didn't mention the fire or Tommy. Instead, he talked about the weather.

"Hot in the day, cool at night," he said. "Yes, sir, a real Indian summer. I'm going to miss the warm sunshine though. In a few weeks, it will be gone and we got a long wait til we feel it again."

We stopped at a corner and waited for the light to change. Maurice had a green baseball cap on his head that I had never seen him wear before.

"Why do you have that hat on?" I asked.

We crossed the street. "My lucky hat," he said. "I wear it once in a while."

"How come you don't always wear it?" I asked.

"Wouldn't be my lucky hat then. It would just be another hat."

"Why do you have it on today? You didn't have it on this morning."

Maurice squinted. "Oh, I like to wear it once in a while."

"Do good things happen to you when you wear it?"

Maurice shook his head, thinking. "No, not really. But nothing bad ever seems to happen. And, the way I see it, if nothing bad happens to you, well, you're pretty lucky. I was in Vietnam for nine months and the best thing that could ever happen to me over there was nothing. I got this hat over there, in Saigon, right before I got married."

This revelation startled me. "Married? You're married? You told my father . . ."

Maurice squinted his eyes again and looked straight ahead. "Well, almost got married."

117

"Why didn't you get married?"

He shook his head. "Well, she was Vietnamese and I was an eighteen-year-old boy from Chattanooga, Tennessee," he said. He looked down at me and smiled. "Anyway, that's a story for a longer walk than this."

We walked in silence the rest of the way home, the leaves crunching underneath our feet. When we turned into our driveway Maurice softly said, "Tommy is a lonely little boy. We have to keep an eye on him. We got to help him where we can now. He's too young to ask for that help. He's trapped inside himself. We have to help him get out."

I looked up at Maurice and saw an unfamiliar look of concern crease his face. Then he patted me on the head once, turned around and walked away.

When I got inside, I found Uncle Frank sitting on the leather couch in the living room with a glass of wine in his hand. I hadn't seen much of him the past few days and was shocked by his appearance. He looked run over, and at the end of things. He was wearing a tight-fitting gray suit and red tie, which was unusual for him. Up until this point, his wardrobe had consisted entirely of black shirts and black pants and this sudden change to clothes with color worried me.

"What the hell happened at school today?" he asked when I walked in. His voice sounded thick and wet, slippery like a just mopped floor.

"Tommy started a fire," I said. I looked around the room. "Where is he?"

"Your aunt wanted to take him to the doctor. She thought maybe he was sick." He took a long swallow of his wine. The large circles that had been forming under his eyes looked darker than ever. "She thinks he's a pyromaniac," he said.

"What's that?" I asked.

"Someone who sets fires all the time." He belched softly. "For the hell of it." He took another drink.

"Oh," I said.

Uncle Frank sunk lower into the couch and leaned his head back. He seemed to be studying the ceiling. "Teddy," he said. "I've come to the conclusion that I am a phony."

I didn't say anything. I didn't like the way his voice sounded.

"There's nothing real about me," he continued. "I have no center. No

118

foundation. I am a fake. A fake person. You have a fake uncle. Everything about me is false, made-up. Look." He reached up to his head and pulled off his black hair.

My jaw dropped. Uncle Frank was bald.

"Don't look so shocked. It's not like I pulled off my leg, for chrisssakes. It's a toupée. A wig. It happens," he said. "Cost me thirty-five-hundred dollars." He looked at the hair in his hands then tossed it onto the coffee table. "Thirty-five-hundred bucks for goddamn hair." He sighed. "You can't be bald in my business, though. I don't make the rules."

I stood in the living room, staring at what was once Uncle Frank. With his wrinkled forehead now pressing down on his eyes, he looked like a small, well-dressed ape.

"I just thought that you would like to know this," he said after some time. He sipped some more wine. "Let me ask you something here, Teddy, just a quick question, real quick. Do you believe in God?"

The question didn't surprise me. I thought that at that moment Uncle Frank was capable of doing and saying anything. "Yes," I said. I kept looking at his barren head and was reminded of a picture of a forest after a fire.

"You do. I find that interesting, very interesting. I really do. Me, I accept the randomness of life. I could have won the lottery, I could have been born taller, with hair, good hair, permanent hair. Your mother might have hit the brake instead of the accelerator." He stopped here and ran his hand over his face. "Hell, I shouldn't have brought that up. I'm a goddamn insensitive idiot." He closed his eyes. "I'm forty-nine years old and all I got to show for my life is a goddamn toupée."

I felt sorry for my uncle for reasons I didn't totally understand. Gone was his fierceness and energy and all that remained was a sadness I had never noticed before. For the first time, I saw my father in him.

"Can you tell Aunt Bess I'm in my room?" I finally said. I decided to leave before Uncle Frank pulled something else off his body.

I walked toward the hallway stairs. "Teddy," Uncle Frank said. "I shouldn't have brought up your mother. I'm sorry about that."

I turned back to face him. "That's okay."

"You're a good kid, you know that? A good kid. You've been graced.

You're overcoming everything. If I ever had the balls to have kids, the god-damn courage, I would have liked to have had one like you. Now I'm going to ask you a question, Teddy, and I want you to tell me the truth. Do you like me?"

"Yes."

"Ah, you probably say that to all your drunk uncles who wear rugs." He took another drink and finished his glass. "I remember the first time I saw you. I was back from L.A. You were about two years old when you moved in here. You looked scared. I remember telling your father not to do it, but he did it. You're too old, I said. She's too young. He did the right thing, though, because he got you and your brother out of the deal."

I nodded again and kept walking. I really didn't want to look at his head any more.

"Tommy, I mean, Teddy, one more thing. And it's important," he said. I stopped and turned again to face him. He was holding the toupée in his hands now, looking grave and lonely. With his eyes down and his chin trembling, I thought he might cry. "The toupée," he said. "It's, well, it's our little secret, okay?"

"Okay," I said and hurried up the stairs.

When Tommy came home from the doctor, Aunt Bess put him to bed, even though it was early. "Maybe he'll stay there until he's eighteen," I heard Uncle Frank say. I went downstairs to see if Aunt Bess would give me a piece of cake. When I walked into the kitchen though, I found Uncle Frank rummaging through the cabinet next to the sink, looking for more wine. I was relieved to see that his hair was back on, snug and secure, held in place by some unseen gravitational force that must govern all toupées.

"He has a fever," Aunt Bess said. "His forehead is hot."

"He probably burned himself," Uncle Frank slurred. "What happened to that bottle I bought last week? That merlot?"

"I threw it out," Aunt Bess said.

"You what?"

"I threw it out. It's in the garbage in the garage."

Uncle Frank stared at her. "That's what I thought you said." He teetered to one side. "I think I'm going to go lay down for a while," he said and went down the basement. Within seconds, I heard him snoring loud wet snarls.

Aunt Bess stood by the basement door and listened, her head cocked like a robin's. "He passed out," she said. She disappeared into the basement, returning a few moments later with a disgusted look on her face. "He's out like a light," she said, shutting the basement door.

"Is he okay?"

"He'll be all right." She began taking carrots and tomatoes and celery out of the refrigerator, sighing loudly every few seconds. "This house is becoming a crazy house," she said. "I wish your father would come back. I don't know why he still thinks he has to work. This is ridiculous. Everything," she said, "is ridiculous."

Dinner was a quiet affair. Since Tommy and Uncle Frank were presumably both unconscious, it was just my aunt and me, and Aunt Bess said little. When I tried to ask if she had had any more dreams recently, she said, "I dreamt I was on *The Price is Right* last night."

"What does that mean?"

She shrugged. "Nothing. I never liked that show." Then she went back to slurping her soup, an indulgence she allowed herself when my father wasn't around. He once quietly had told her that people, other than himself, might find slurping soup pedestrian.

"I don't know what to do," she said after an especially pedestrian slurp.

"About Uncle Frank?"

"No, your brother. He needs to see a psychiatrist. He has problems. We have to nip them in the bud or else he'll grow up deranged."

"What's deranged mean again?"

She began to explain but changed her mind, waving her hand at me. "It's not good," she said. "Just finish your soup."

After dinner, Mrs. Wilcott called. "I just heard the news about your brother," she said when I picked up the phone. "Is he all right?"

"He might be deranged," I said matter-of-factly. "And that's not good." Aunt Bess grabbed the phone from me. "Who is this? Oh, Gloria. He's fine. He's sick, but he'll be okay. He's fine." Then she said, "Oh my God. Why won't they leave us alone?" She quickly hung up and turned on the television where a newscaster was talking urgently about a school blaze. Suddenly, Mr. Sean Hill's wild-eyed face filled the screen with the word "hero" written below his smiling head.

"He's a crazy little character," Mr. Sean Hill said. "Crazy as they come."

The newscaster was interviewing a child psychologist from Wilton Memorial Hospital about "sudden wealth syndrome" and its effects on young children, when the phone rang again. This time it was Mrs. Rhodebush calling to see when Tommy was being sent to a prison for young nymphomaniacs.

"You mean pyromaniacs," Aunt Bess said. "And no he's not." She paused. "Yes, I know your house is made out of wood. Yes, I'm sure it's safe. No, no one has left any more babies today. Yes, I checked." She slammed the phone down and stomped around the kitchen like an old bull. I thought smoke might start coming out of her ears, she looked so angry.

"The nerve of some people! They think they can say anything! I wish Theo would move away from this neighborhood. It has a bad feel about it. The people here are rude!" She shook her head and let out an exasperated breath. "I'm going to go up and take a bath. Keep an eye on your brother. And your uncle. Call me if either one of them starts moving." Then she stormed off.

A few minutes later, while I was standing at the top of the basement stairs, listening to Uncle Frank's snores, deciding if it would be all right to use the computer that stood inches from the couch he had passed out on, the phone rang. I answered it in the front hallway. It was my father calling from Atlanta.

"Gloria just phoned me. Is your aunt there?" he asked. He was talking fast and breathing hard.

I could hear the bath water running upstairs. "She's in the bathroom."

"Teddy, exactly what happened with your brother?"

"He started a school blaze." I thought the word blaze might sound less alarming to my father than fire.

"Was anyone injured? Is he all right?"

"He's sleeping." Then, since I was concerned that my father had forgotten his antiheart-attack pills, I said, "It was just a small blaze. Mr. Sean Hill was burned a little, but no one was killed."

"Killed? Dear God, I hope not. Tell your aunt to call me at my hotel as soon as she is able."

"Okay," I said. I was about to hang up the phone when Aunt Bess screamed.

"Dear God, what was that?" my father yelled. Somehow, my father had been able to hear her.

I ran upstairs, two steps at a time, the cordless phone at my side. When I got inside the bathroom, I found Tommy standing by the sink, innocently drinking a glass of water. Aunt Bess was sitting in the half-full bathtub. She was trying to cover herself with her arms, but I could still see her big wrinkled breasts, sagging and hanging low like popped balloons. She kept screaming.

"Privacy, please! My God, I'm taking a bath!"

"What is going on there?" my father asked again, his voice tiny and loud.

"Aunt Bess is screaming because Tommy is drinking some water."

"Why is your aunt screaming then?"

"I'm naked!" Aunt Bess screamed. She struggled with one arm to pull the shower curtain. Tommy wandered out, his eyes half closed.

"Because she's naked." I had to yell this to be heard over Aunt Bess's screaming.

"Dear God, Teddy, you are being vague. Is your uncle at home?"

"He's in the basement. But he's passed out."

"What?"

"Out like a light," I shouted.

My father hung up and within seconds it seemed, Mrs. Wilcott and Benjamin were at our front door. Benjamin was holding a pie.

"Your father called me and asked that I come over to help settle things down," she said. She looked worried and expectant as she walked inside, stepping carefully as if a wrong move might trigger some type of explosion. "Everything seems to be quiet now," she said, though she still looked worried.

"Can I go then?" Benjamin asked.

"Why don't you stay and visit with the boys?" Mrs. Wilcott asked. She kept looking around the front hallway, waiting for Tommy, I was sure, to emerge from behind the drapes, holding a flamethrower.

A few moments later, Aunt Bess came downstairs, her hair wrapped in a towel and wearing an old white bathrobe. Underneath the robe I saw a "Save the Cap," T-shirt, extra large.

"Hello," she said, then she took a deep breath and looked at the pie which Mrs. Wilcott silently extended to her. Aunt Bess met Mrs. Wilcott's eyes, then looked down at the pie, then back up to Mrs. Wilcott. "Why not," she finally said, resigned. She accepted the pie and headed toward the kitchen. "Follow me," she said.

We sat in the kitchen and ate at the wobbly table, my stomach aching with every swallow. Sitting this close to Benjamin made me nervous and I avoided looking in his direction. Instead, I focused on Mrs. Wilcott's face. Even though I knew she was old, I grudgingly acknowledged her beauty; her blue eyes sparkled and her skin was smooth and tight and seemed to glow. There was a light about her and I thought it must be this light that attracted my father.

"I made this pie on my last show," Mrs. Wilcott said. She was chewing precisely, nibbling really more than eating. "I don't know if you watch my show."

"What show?" Aunt Bess asked, swallowing. "Oh, yes, that show that Theo was on. How much do you get paid to do that? Frankie wanted to know."

Mrs. Wilcott's eyebrows raised a little and she wiped the corner of her mouth with her napkin.

"Well, to be honest," she said. "I don't get paid anything. It's cable access."

Now it was Aunt Bess's eyebrows turn to rise. "Nothing?" she said. "Then why do you do it?"

"I view it as a community service," Mrs. Wilcott said.

"Community service?" Aunt Bess asked. "What, like picking up the garbage?"

Mrs. Wilcott looked over at me and smiled. "I think those are two very separate services," she said. "I'm hoping though that my show will be picked up by one of the local stations. I'm trying to make some connections downtown."

Aunt Bess didn't say anything and we ate in silence until Benjamin coughed and some pie shot out of his nose.

"Eat slowly, Benjamin," Mrs. Wilcott said. "I don't know how many times I've told you." She looked over at Aunt Bess. "As soon as Theo called, I came right over. I dropped everything."

"Everything but the pie," Aunt Bess said. "Things are fine now. The pie is good though. It's good pie. A little too sweet though. But it's good."

"Oh, well, thank you. Coming from you, that's quite a compliment. I know Benjamin likes apples. So does Teddy."

"I don't like apples." I blurted this out and Benjamin shot me a look. "But I like these apples though."

"How's Tommy?" Mrs. Wilcott asked.

"Who? Oh, he's fine. He's sick. A little." Aunt Bess said.

"He's sick? Just physically, you mean?"

"Yes. He has a fever. But he's fine. The doctor gave him something to put him to sleep. He's sleeping. He has problems."

"Well, I know a little bit about boys getting in trouble at school," Mrs. Wilcott said, looking at Benjamin who kept eating his pie.

"Is Theo's brother still around?"

"Yes. He's in the basement." Aunt Bess didn't say anything else and Mrs. Wilcott looked surprised.

"Oh. Would he like some pie then?"

"No," she said. Then she added, "He'd probably vomit it up."

"Oh." Mrs. Wilcott looked even more surprised. She went back to her pie, but didn't really eat any. She just rearranged portions of it on her plate, like pieces of a puzzle.

"I really shouldn't be eating so much," she said, smiling. "I didn't have time for my run this morning."

"Run?" Aunt Bess asked.

"Yes. I run one mile every day." She moved more pie around her plate, then sipped at her milk.

"Why do you run so much?"

"Well, I struggle with my weight."

Aunt Bess put an enormous piece of pie in her mouth and swallowed it in a way that reminded me of a PBS special we had once watched on pythons. "You?" she said. "Come on now, you're thin as a rail. I should be the one who's running, but I can hardly walk."

"I enjoy it," Mrs. Wilcott said. "But it's difficult to find the time. It's a commitment."

"How old are you? I say you're in your thirties, Frankie thinks you're closer to fifty."

Mrs. Wilcott's head jerked back a bit at this question and she looked over at me for a moment, a strained smile on her face. "Well, I'm somewhere in between."

Aunt Bess looked at Mrs. Wilcott hard for a second. "Theo is almost sixty."

"Is he?" Mrs. Wilcott readjusted herself in her chair, pulling it close to the table. "He looks younger. It most be all your wonderful cooking."

Aunt Bess said something under her breath in Greek and kept eating.

"It must be difficult being under such scrutiny," Mrs. Wilcott said after some time. "Everyone looking over your shoulder."

Aunt Bess was still quiet.

"Well, like it or not, you're all celebrities. *People* magazine. The newspapers. The TV. I know what it's like."

Aunt Bess stopped eating. "You do?"

"Yes. When I won the Miss Illinois contest a while back I was the center of attention. And the spotlight can be very bright—I know."

Aunt Bess leaned back in her chair. "You won Miss Illinois? For what?"

"Pardon me?"

"Oh, for beauty? Oh. A beauty pageant."

"Yes. It was a while ago. But I had my fifteen minutes of fame."

Aunt Bess looked confused. "Fifteen minutes? You were Miss Illinois for only fifteen minutes?"

Mrs. Wilcott looked confused. She spoke slowly. "No," she said. "That's just an expression."

"An expression," Aunt Bess repeated.

"Yes, an expression. More pie?" She cut Aunt Bess yet another piece then cut Benjamin one too, even though he hadn't asked for one. Out of the corner of my eye, I watched as he leaned forward on the table, holding his head in one hand and eating with the other. I thought that he might be trying to look at me, but I couldn't be sure.

"Benjamin, honey, sit up please." Benjamin didn't sit up. Mrs. Wilcott looked at him then turned toward me smiling. "It must be difficult for you too, Teddy. Being a little bit famous. Everyone watching you."

I didn't say anything.

"Oh, I'm sure you're under quite a bit of stress," she said. She patted me on the arm. "I want you to know that anytime you need someone to talk to, you can call me. Or Benjamin. I know he's been trying to keep an eye on you at school."

My throat shrunk, closing completely. I instinctively touched my unbroken nose.

"Has your father told you that he signed you up for soccer?" Mrs. Wilcott asked.

I stopped trying to eat at this news. "No."

"He did. He thinks it would be good for you. You'll be on Benjamin's team." When she smiled at me, she looked like Carla the Cat Woman.

I didn't say anything. At that moment, I never liked anyone less than Mrs. Wilcott, unless possibly my father.

I didn't even pretend to eat any more pie. I sat at the table, staring at my plate, as hopeless and alone as a single strand of hair at the top of Uncle Frank's head.

"Teddy, is something wrong?" Mrs. Wilcott asked.

"What? No," I said, picking up my fork.

"I can imagine, Bess, that money is a burden," Mrs. Wilcott said.

"Not around here it's not," Aunt Bess said between mouthfuls. "Theo won't spend a dime. You would have thought he lost a hundred-and-ninety million."

Mrs. Wilcott smiled. "Theo is a very intelligent man. I think he'll enjoy his newfound wealth when the time is right."

"Well, I hope that time is soon," Aunt Bess said. "Have you seen that old car he drives?"

Still smiling, Mrs. Wilcott rose from her chair and took her plate over to the sink. "I think Theo is just getting used to this new life. It will take time. It's an adjustment. Soon, he'll understand his new position, his new role in the community and society. So much has happened so fast for him."

"Let me tell you, everything happens fast for Theo," Aunt Bess said. "Grass growing."

"My advice to him has been to take his time," Mrs. Wilcott said.

Aunt Bess sat back in her chair again and nodded her head. "You've been offering him advice?"

"Well, I only offer it when he asks," Mrs. Wilcott said.

"Does he ask you a lot of questions? He doesn't say anything around here."

Mrs. Wilcott turned the faucet on and let the water run. Then she started rinsing her dish.

"He seeks my advice occasionally. I suggested that he consider buying Mr. Tuthill's house."

"He keeps calling," Aunt Bess said. "The Yankee."

"It is a beautiful house. Very large. Actually, I initially suggested that Mr. Tuthill approach Theo with the idea."

Aunt Bess folded her thick arms across her chest. I could see her working her tongue across her teeth on the inside of her mouth. She smacked her lips. "So you think we should buy that house?"

"Well, I think Theo should consider it. He could stay in Wilton, the boys could stay at St. Pius. It would be an easy transition."

"An easy transition," Aunt Bess said, nodding her head again. "For everyone."

Mrs. Wilcott turned the water off and dried her hands on a blue dish towel. Then she turned to face Aunt Bess. "Yes," she said, smiling like Mr. Sean Hill. "For everyone."

A few minutes later, Aunt Bess got up from the table to show Mrs. Wilcott and Benjamin out. From the heavy, stiff way she was walking, I could tell that she was tired and knew that an early bedtime was lurking. "Thank you for the dessert," she said to Mrs. Wilcott.

When she opened the door, I saw a thin old man with a cane standing on our front porch.

"Good evening," he said with a smile and a slight bow of his head. "I am Sylvanius."

That's when Aunt Bess screamed.

CHAPTER SIX

I APOLOGIZE ONCE AGAIN for startling you like that," Sylvanius said. He was sitting with his legs crossed on the couch in our living room, sipping a glass of red wine. "But your phone number is unlisted so I had no recourse but to arrive unannounced as it were." He drank some wine and smiled, his teeth white and sharp. "Despite my rudeness, you have been very gracious to accommodate me." Here, he bowed his head and raised his glass in the direction of my aunt. "And I thank you," he said softly, swallowing a belch.

Aunt Bess smiled. "Well, I was just so shocked. I was your biggest fan on *Dark Towers*. I recognized you right away."

"Ah," Sylvanius sighed. "My years in television. It was the support and, if I may be so bold, the love of affectionate viewers like you who sustained me during those hectic times."

"I thought you were dead," Aunt Bess said.

"Ah, the reports of my death are greatly exaggerated," he said. He winked at me. "Hemingway," he said. "Besides, everyone knows a vampire cannot die."

Sylvanius was the vampire who starred in most of Uncle Frank's movies. He needed to speak to Uncle Frank immediately, he said, to discuss "issues

129

of the utmost importance." When Aunt Bess told him he was under the weather, he smiled and said, "Ah, Frank has seen his share of weather."

MRS. WILCOTT AND Benjamin left soon after Sylvanius arrived. It was late and Benjamin had an early morning karate practice. It was apparent that Mrs. Wilcott wanted to stay, but Benjamin, through sighs and low moans, made it clear that he wanted to leave.

"I'll want to know all about his visit, Bess," Mrs. Wilcott said before leaving. Then turning to Sylvanius she said, "I am a newspaper columnist and my readers would love to know all about what brings you to Wilton." To this, Sylvanius merely smiled and bowed his head once again.

Sylvanius looked like a handsome serpent. He had a small head, with large lazy eyes that were both lifeless and wise. His slicked back hair was silver and his long, bony hands were sprinkled with brown spots. Though I had never seen or heard of him before, I was excited by his presence, as was Aunt Bess. She kept smiling at me with her eyebrows raised high as if in disbelief.

"More wine?" she asked.

"If it is not too inconvenient. May I ask what kind it is?"

"It's red. A merlot," she said. "I had thrown it out but found it in the garbage."

"Oh," Sylvanius said. "I see." He examined his glass, then sniffed the wine.

"Frank bought it," Aunt Bess said. "Let me get you some more."

"Thank you. The trip east was a dry one and I'm afraid I am a bit parched."

"What airline did you fly?" Aunt Bess asked, rising slowly from the couch.

"Airline? Oh, actually, I traveled over land." This confused Aunt Bess so Sylvanius added, "In a vehicle." Then finally after Aunt Bess looked even more confused, he said, "A bus. I took a bus."

"A bus? All the way from Los Angeles?"

"Yes. I thoroughly enjoy that mode of travel. It gives me a chance to see America the way the pioneers first saw it. Columbus, Washington, true adventurers." He smiled weakly and then Aunt Bess went out to the kitchen to get more wine, leaving me alone with the adventurer.

Sylvanius watched me. "Such a fine young man," he said. I said nothing. "Indeed, such a fine young man," he said again. I sat quietly, studying his face. I wanted to memorize his features, the thin nose, the sleepy eyes. I thought that I'd like to draw him.

"Your uncle," he said. "May I ask where he is resting?"

"In the basement," I said.

"Ah," Sylvanius said. "It must be very quiet down there."

"It is. Except when he snores."

"Ah, yes. That would probably disturb the peace."

"Are you in my uncle's new movie?"

"Yes."

"Do you play a vampire?"

"Yes. I am once again cast in the role of the great undead. But this time, I am a force of good." He picked up his wine glass, then noticing it was empty put it back down, and looked helplessly in the direction of the kitchen for Aunt Bess.

"Do you like being vampires in movies?"

Sylvanius brought his two index fingers up to his lips and nodded his head thoughtfully. "It is," he said after a few moments, "the role I was meant to play."

"Is Sylvanius your first or last name?" I asked.

"It is simply," he paused, "my name."

Aunt Bess emerged from the kitchen and poured him another glass of wine which he accepted with yet another tiny bow of his head. While I watched him drink it, I noticed that his shirt was missing a button in the middle.

Sylvanius crossed his legs again. It was then that I saw his shoes. They shocked me. They were large, black, awkward slabs with immense rubber soles. Rather than coming to a point in the front by the toes, they were cut at an odd angle, a sharp, harsh slant, that reminded me of the blade of a guillotine. They looked evil, something a monster might wear to crush babies, kick puppies. The shoes of a vampire.

"Where are you staying tonight?" Aunt Bess asked. She didn't seem to notice the shoes.

"Well, since I left somewhat in a rush, I didn't have time to make proper arrangements. I came straight from the station."

This surprised Aunt Bess. "Where are your bags then? Your suitcase?"

"My suitcase? Oh. Well, I travel very lightly. Just these heirlooms," he said, pointing to a large red handkerchief in his breast pocket and holding up his cane.

"How long are you staying here in Wilton?"

"Oh, that remains to be seen, I suppose." He drank some wine. "That remains to be seen."

Aunt Bess sipped at her own glass.

"You're not here to hurt Frankie, are you?" she suddenly asked.

This startled Sylvanius, his lazy eyes flickering to life. He uncrossed his legs and set his glass down on the coffee table. "My dear woman, whatever gave you that idea? Your nephew and I are friends and business partners. We co-produced the new film together. Or attempted to, I should say."

Aunt Bess was relieved. "Well, I'm sorry, but I had to ask. You know . . ." her voice trailed off and she quickly looked over at me. I knew what she was going to say next.

"Teddy, time for bed."

"It's only nine o'clock."

"You look exhausted and you've had a crazy day. We all did. Go on up. I'll check in on you in a little while. Go, now. Go."

I walked slowly upstairs and got ready for bed. The Fire Starter was still sleeping, buried under his blankets despite the warm night. After brushing my teeth, I laid down in bed for what I thought was a sufficient enough time, then crept over to the top of the stairs and sat down.

"I haven't been to the Midwest in years," I heard Sylvanius say. "I briefly played dinner theater in Biloxi when I was younger. But I suppose that's not really the Midwest. Technically."

"Biloxi? Where's that?"

"I'm not sure. I do remember something about a hurricane however."

"You must have led an exciting life," Aunt Bess said.

"I suppose, yes. Yes. Certain parts have been more exciting than others, especially the last few days, but on the whole it has been an adventure. I'm in the process of conceptualizing my memoirs."

"Tell me, have you ever met Elizabeth Taylor?"

"Who? Oh, no, no. Elizabeth and I have never had the opportunity to work together. Though it has long been a wish of mine, our schedules have never really allowed it. I, of course, do much darker films then she did, when she was working. I am classically trained. I don't believe Elizabeth is."

"You were once on *Gilligan's Island*, weren't you?" Aunt Bess asked. "I remember you played a vampire. You bit the Skipper."

There was a pause, then Sylvanius said slowly, "Yes, I suppose I was. My, you are a fan."

"It's on reruns all the time."

"It is, is it? Hmmm," Sylvanius said. There was a brief silence, then Sylvanius asked for more wine. "One more should do it," he said. "Then I am off, I suppose. I must call a cab."

"Where are you going to sleep?"

"I'm not sure yet. But I'm confident that there are suitable lodgings nearby. Maybe in the city. Simple accommodations, really. All I need is a small cot really, a bare mattress."

"The city? You don't want to go downtown now, at this time of night. Listen, why don't you stay here? Theo is out of town until tomorrow. You can use his room. He won't mind. He won't even know."

I didn't hear a response and I imagined that Sylvanius was bowing his head again. It seemed like something he would do after my aunt's offer.

"Under normal circumstances, I would never think of imposing," Sylvanius finally said. "But considering the lateness of the hour and my general unfamiliarity of this city, I can see no other option but to accept. So accept I shall."

"Good," Aunt Bess said. I heard her rising. "I'll go change the sheets. Theo is a heavy sweater."

"Ah," Sylvanius said as I scrambled back to my room.

THE NEXT MORNING at breakfast, Sylvanius walked into the kitchen wearing his red handkerchief around his neck and a white shirt of my father's. He attempted to pull out the chair for Aunt Bess when she sat down but this just seemed to confuse her.

"What's wrong?" she asked, alarmed. "Why are you taking my chair?"

As we ate, Sylvanius kept asking about Uncle Frank but Aunt Bess said simply, "He'll be up soon enough." Then she passed a platter full of bacon over to Sylvanius who bowed his head several times before taking five pieces. When Maurice came to the door, Sylvanius jumped to his feet.

"Good God," he said. "They've sent a black assassin."

"That's the boys' bodyguard," Aunt Bess said getting up to open the door. "He's on the payroll."

"Oh, I see," Sylvanius said. He stood up and introduced himself to Maurice with a deeper than usual bow. Maurice stared at him and nodded his head once. I put my jacket on.

"I'm sure the children are being well-protected," Sylvanius said. "I'm sure that they are quite safe. One cannot be too cautious nowadays."

"You don't have to tell me," Aunt Bess said as she poured orange juice into a glass pitcher. "There's crazy people everywhere. You don't know what we've been through."

"Oh, I can imagine," Sylvanius said, sitting back down at the table and picking up the last piece of bacon. "Sometimes I wonder where we are all headed."

When I got to school, Benjamin walked up to me on the playground and informed me that soccer practice was starting tomorrow afternoon. He stood very close to me when he said this, giving me a slight push when he finished. Over his shoulder, I saw Maurice walking on the far side of the playground, deeply engrossed in the study of his pipe. He seemed miles away.

"Are you going to be there?" Benjamin asked.

"I don't know," I said. I kept looking over his shoulder, hoping that Maurice would detect my situation, walk over, and punch Benjamin.

"You don't know what?" Benjamin said. He moved closer to me, his nose and mine almost touching. I saw small freckles on his cheek that I had never noticed before. "You don't know what?"

"Yes," I said. "I'm coming."

Benjamin nodded. A circle of boys, all St. Pius football players, formed a small knot around me.

"Okay, pussy. And just in case you forget, here's a little reminder," he said. He kneed me in the groin.

I fell on the ground, my stomach hot coals and fire. The pain was so intense I had trouble breathing. I squeezed my eyes tight and gasped for air.

"You're a pussy," I heard him say. "I can't wait to get you on the soccer field. And you better show up or I'll do a lot worse."

I opened my eyes just in time to see Big Tony Cezzaro, Johnny's older brother, whack Benjamin on the back of his head with a book. Benjamin fell forward, on top of me without making a sound.

The circle of boys parted and Johnny Cezzaro walked casually through the crowd, a toothpick in his mouth. "Thanks, Ton," he said, patting Big Tony on the back. Big Tony who never said much of anything, shrugged and walked away.

"You okay, Pappas?" he asked. Benjamin rolled over and lay next to me, rubbing his head, trying not to cry though his lips were trembling and his eyes closed. The other boys had widened the circle considerably and looked over at Benjamin from a safe distance, with open mouths and embarrassed expressions.

"I'm okay," I said standing up. "I'm okay."

Johnny helped me to my feet and dusted off my shoulder. Then he pressed his finger in my chest and said, "You owe fifteen thousand dollars for that. Half for me, half for Big Tony." He finished dusting off my shoulders and walked away.

I passed the rest of the day feeling sorry for myself. The incident with Benjamin was a harsh reminder of my standing at St. Pius. I was a coward, with few friends, little respect, and a bruised groin.

My brooding eventually led me to thoughts of my father. I was angry at him. On a number of levels he was to blame for my predicament. He was involved with Mrs. Wilcott, he was making me play soccer. And he was ignoring the fact that we had won the lottery, refusing to use the money to help us, to help me.

I couldn't understand his attitude toward the lottery. He wasn't acknowledging it, choosing instead to stand apart from it, something he had great practice in doing. Sitting there, I vowed to press the issue, vowed to discuss my List of Things with him and urge him to consider the ranch in Montana, as well as a new house in a different suburb, in a new school district where I could start my life over with new friends. The money, I concluded, could buy me this life.

When I got home from school, I found my father standing in the dining room, peering out through the window shades at Sylvanius who we had just passed sitting on Mrs. Rhodebush's porch, talking to her. Behind him, Aunt Bess set the table, placing forks and knives next to plates with deep, meaningful sighs.

"He's a talker," Aunt Bess said, polishing a knife on her apron.

"Yes," my father said. "I believe he is. Though he is polite. Why is he at Mrs. Rhodebush's?"

Aunt Bess looked annoyed. "I don't know, why are you asking me? He said he was going out for a walk. Next thing I know . . ." she shrugged and plopped the knife down hard on the table.

When my father turned around to face me, my anger left. He looked like old lettuce, wilted and soft. His eyes had a given up, heaviness to them and his puffy hair hung now in lifeless, confused strands.

"So, Teddy," he said. "How have you been bearing up?"

"Good," I said. He smiled, one of his short smiles that was gone before it was there.

"Good," he said. "And how was school?"

"Fine."

"Well," he said, "quite a bit of excitement the last few days."

"Yes."

"He's been a soldier through it all," Aunt Bess said. "A soldier."

"Yes, well, that's good," he said. "A soldier. That's good." Then, noticing that Aunt Bess was setting the table, he said, "Aunt Bess, don't set the table for Frank and his friend and me. I think we'll be going out for dinner. We have some things to discuss."

Aunt Bess was confused by the comment. She held a plate in one hand and a fork in the other. "What? You're not going to eat here? Why? Where are you going? I'm cooking. I'm setting the table now. Where are you going? I'm setting the table."

"We're going out for a quick bite so we can talk. We might go to Will's."

"What? Oh!" Aunt Bess said. "Oh," she said again. "Okay, all right, all right. You're going to talk. Okay." She quickly began to pick up silverware and plates. "I see," she said and walked back into the kitchen.

After she left, he glanced at me, then quickly at the floor. "Um, Teddy," he said, clearing his throat. "I've been meaning to tell you that I signed you up for soccer. I think it would be good for you to have some type of activity, other than your artwork. You need some exercise."

I was shocked that rather than talk about Baby Girl, Tommy, or even Sylvanius, he chose that moment to discuss soccer. The expression on his face kept me from saying anything though. The heaviness in his eyes had lifted and he looked expectant suddenly, hopeful for my agreement. I didn't want to disappoint him, at least not then. On some level, I understood that he wanted me to play soccer for my own good and I took some consolation in this.

I shrugged. "Okay," I said.

My father exhaled. "Good," he said. "Good. Well, then, I have some things I must take care of." Then he went outside to talk to Sylvanius.

During dinner, the Fire Starter asked where everybody was.

"Where's that monster?" he asked.

"He's with your father and your uncle. They're discussing business."

Tommy laughed. "Uncle Frank says he drinks blood in movies. He's probably drinking a glass of blood right now. I'd like to drink blood. I love blood. It tastes sweet."

Aunt Bess stopped chewing and stared at Tommy. She looked worried, even though I thought she would be relieved that Tommy was at least talking again. He hadn't really said anything since the fire.

"Sweet, sweet blood," Tommy said. "Sweet, delicious blood."

I glanced at Aunt Bess and saw that she was still frozen in midchew.

The phone rang, breaking her trance and she got up to answer it. We had changed our number again. After every change, the phone would fall silent for a few days, then the ringing would mysteriously resume, louder and more persistent than before, as if the callers had been angered by the disruption. Aunt Bess was the only one who ever answered it. She was always interested in whoever called, asking questions and listening intently to their stories, measuring their misery against the misery of previous callers.

"Hello?" she said. She listened for a while. "Oh my God, that sounds terrible. Well, I'll tell you something, honey, you got a better chance of winning the lottery yourself then getting a dime out of Theo Pappas. No, I'm his aunt and I still clip coupons. What? I can't hear you. That sounds terrible. Well, good luck, I hope you get your children out of Saudi Arabia. I'll pray for you. No, I'm sorry. I used to own a bakery in Milwaukee. The most I ever made was forty-two thousand a year. I have no money, but I will pray. I have to go now. I have another call." I watched as she removed the phone from her ear and squinted at the receiver. "Someone's beeping. How does this work? It's another call."

"Press the button that says phone," I said.

"What button?"

"The button on top."

She pressed the button and said, "Hello? What? I can't hear you? What? Who? What? No. Where? Gabon? Listen, I can't hear you. You'll have to call back." She hung up the phone and came back to the table, sitting down with a thud.

"Who was that?" I asked. I thought she had said Gabon which was where Ergu was from, but I wasn't sure.

She waved her hand. "Someone," she said. "People. Everyone's miserable. Everybody has pain." She looked over at Tommy and suddenly asked, "Why did you start that fire, Tommy Pappas? Are you trying to kill your only aunt?"

I was startled by her question. We had more or less gotten into the habit of not asking Tommy direct questions.

Tommy was sitting backward in his chair with his eyes closed. "Because the bathroom smelled. Like shit and farts."

Aunt Bess threw her napkin down on the table. "Go to your room, young man, and don't come out until I say so."

Tommy left the table and crawled up the stairs.

"Did you say Gabon?" I asked quietly after Tommy was gone. I could tell that she was in a foul mood and didn't want to provoke her. Still, I was curious.

"What?"

I picked casually at some broccoli with my fork. "On the phone, you said Gabon."

She waved her hand again and said, "I don't remember. Just eat." After a few minutes she said, "This is a crazy house," and got up and disappeared into the kitchen.

After dinner, while I was making my way to my room to do my homework, I stopped in the doorway of my father's study and peered in. I liked this room. It was small and orderly with cedar-paneled walls that filled the room with a fresh smell the rest of our house lacked. The sturdy brass desk lamp gave off a soft halo of light that sent shadows halfway up the wall. My father was always leaving the light on. I walked over to turn it off, but once inside I decided to look for letters from women who wanted to marry my father.

He had continued to get a steady stream of such letters and I had seen a number of the familiar pastel-colored envelopes on his desk that very morning. He usually let these letters collect unopened for awhile until he unceremoniously threw them out in a bundle. Rather than rummage through the garbage to retrieve them as I sometimes did, I decided to examine the letters in the quiet of his study with the hopes of finding photos of naked women, which some of the letters contained.

I quickly found three packets of letters in a drawer, each bound with a rubber band. On the top letter of one pile my father had written: "To consider." All of the envelopes in this pile had already been opened. I took a letter out and read it:

> Dear Mr. Pappas:
>   I work at the Chapter of Children with Communicative Disorders. I'm just an assistant therapist, but the work we do here for children who cannot for different reasons communicate in the normal way, is nothing short of a miracle.
>   We serve more than 500 children in the Danbury area and unfortunately are well behind in our taxes. We are a privately funded . . .

I stopped reading and put the letter back, concluding that there were no photos of naked women in this pile.

The second bundle of envelopes was marked, "Miscellaneous." They were all from banks and stockbrokers and I had no interest in them. The third pile of envelopes, the largest, was marked "Discard." This is what I was searching for.

I reviewed this pile carefully, looking for pictures. After slow examination, I selected an envelope postmarked Bettendorf, Iowa, turned it upside down, and shook it. Sure enough, two small snapshots fell into my lap. They were both of a small poodle, wearing a cowboy hat and a red-and-white checkered scarf around his neck. A brief note read, "We're lonely too! Call us, Laura and Brendan." Disappointed, I slipped the photos back into the envelope.

I quickly opened another letter and was just as quickly disappointed again. It was from "The Living History Society," a Civil War association I had heard my father mention from time to time. The letter read:

> Dear Mr. Pappas:
>
> Dr. Stephen Z. Larson of Dartmouth informed me of your good fortune. I was hoping that you will have the opportunity to review the enclosed literature on the Society and our most recent activities. As you will note, we are in dire need of support and would appreciate any effort you could make in this regard.
>
> Please forgive the formality of this letter, but I have been unable to reach you by phone.
>
> We hope you will consider us . . .

What I thought was a picture was actually a brochure, "Re-Live Manassas." Two Civil War soldiers were on the cover, superimposed over a silhouette of Abraham Lincoln's profile. Disappointed, I put the brochure down. Then frustrated by my poor luck, I impulsively picked up another envelope and checked its contents, even though it didn't feel like it contained any pictures.

> Theodore Pappas:
>
> You and me have to meet to discuss the situation. I don't want to be made out to be the bad guy here, but I know my rights. Maybe we can work something out and then we can all be happy. I'm coming to Chicago soon and then we can talk this out.
>
> Bobby Lee Anderson

I looked at the letter then folded it up and put it in my pocket. I heard my father's voice downstairs. He had returned earlier than I expected.

CHAPTER SEVEN

THE NEXT DAY, I went to soccer practice. All that day in school my stomach was in a terrible knot and I was unable to focus on Miss Grace who, with a powder-blue ribbon in her hair, looked particularly soft and sweet. Instead, I sorted through various scenarios involving Benjamin and me on the soccer field. Despite my efforts to hope for the best—Benjamin might be in a good mood, Benjamin might not have the opportunity to hit me, Benjamin might feel intimidated by Maurice, Benjamin might be struck by lightning—virtually all of the scenarios ended with Benjamin sitting on my chest, methodically breaking my nose.

The soccer league was run by the Wilton Park District. St. Pius didn't have a soccer team. They only had a football team. During most of the practice, I just stood on the sidelines with a few other boys, keeping my distance from Benjamin who seemed strangely uninterested in me and instead very focused on the drills. Our coach, Mr. Peterson, a short overweight man with a thick mustache that hung over his mouth like a curtain, was nice enough and didn't yell or scream, something I assumed all coaches had an obligation to do. Speaking in a very even, almost friendly voice, he tried to explain various plays to me, none of which I was able to grasp. Every few minutes, I checked my watch, waiting for practice to end so I could go home and play Mr. Verb, a new computer grammar game with Charlie Governs.

"Okay, Teddy Pappas, you play goalie," Mr. Peterson said, blowing his whistle.

I slowly made my way over to the net and crouched down in a position I had seen the other boys assume. Even though I had never been a goalie before, I tried to look nonchalant and experienced. I spat on the ground.

"Teddy, buddy," Mr. Peterson said, walking toward me, his silver whistle bouncing off his gray sweatshirt. The sun was setting and the field was slipping into shadows. Off in the darkness, my teammates lined up, a firing squad. "You don't stand inside the net, you stand in front of it."

I spat again and pretended not to hear the snickers from the other boys and nodded my head. Then I moved up a bit.

"Further," Mr. Peterson said. He was looking at me in an odd, sympathetic way that suddenly made me feel sorry for myself. I stopped spitting.

"Okay, everyone, one shot each," he said, dropping the ball on the ground.

For the next few minutes, everyone on our team scored a goal. Bob Poliski, who walked with a permanent limp, scored three times, pumping his fist hard in the air the last time to the cheers of the team. At first, Mr. Peterson was patient and tried to show me the proper way to play goalie.

"Try and get in front of the ball. Put your body in front of it," he said. He got down into a crouch near the ground and stretched his arms wide. "Didn't you ever play this in gym class?"

"No," I answered truthfully. Mr. Helpner, our gym teacher at St. Pius was seventy-two and concentrated most of his efforts in class to perfecting the jumping jack, an exercise with which he was obsessed. Usually during gym class, I just sat on the ground and watched Mr. Helpner clap his hands and say, "That's the way, kiddies, jumping jacks!" There was always talk of Mr. Helpner's retiring, but he never did. Every fall, he returned to St. Pius, eager and ready to do jumping jacks.

After Bob Poliski scored his last goal, Mr. Peterson abandoned any pretense of coaching me. Instead, he let everyone score goals at will, watching me in a detached, clinical manner that made me feel like a laboratory rat. After twenty minutes, he blew his whistle, ending practice. Walking off the field, I passed right by Benjamin who looked past me.

"Well, that was interesting," Maurice said as we walked home. It was getting dark and a trail of headlights passed us as we stood at a corner waiting to cross. Maurice held Tommy by the hand. Twice Tommy had tried to run onto the soccer field and join the practice and Maurice had had to hold him back. Tommy had asked to come along to practice, and my father, after quickly conferring with Maurice, had agreed.

"Did you enjoy it?" Maurice asked me, watching the moving headlights flow by. "Playing soccer?"

"No," I said, though I didn't feel as bad as I might have. Despite my humiliation, I had a general sense of relief that it was over and that Benjamin hadn't made an attempt on my nose.

"Well, maybe tomorrow, you, me, and Tommy can practice a little. I could use the exercise."

I didn't say anything. I was getting tired of everyone wanting me to play soccer.

"Yeah, let's play soccer," Tommy said and kicked his leg up in the air.

"Did you like practicing when you played football?" I asked Maurice. "For the Bears?"

"Did I enjoy practice?" Maurice repeated slowly. He was thinking. "To be truthful, no, I guess I didn't. I enjoyed the idea that I was improving, but I didn't actually enjoy practicing. It was the same thing all the time—I guess it was boring." Then he said. "But it had a purpose. An important purpose."

We crossed the street and walked a block without talking. My question seemed to bother Maurice.

"Practice made me a better player," he said. "I'm sure of that now. So it was necessary."

"Did you get nervous when you played football?"

"Only before and during every game. I still get nervous watching football. It's a violent game."

"Why did you play it then?" I asked.

"Because," he said, "I used to be a violent man."

When we turned down our block, we passed Sylvanius sitting on Mrs. Rhodebush's front porch again, drinking a glass of wine. He stood up and gave us a deeper bow than usual as we walked by and called out, "Hail the conquering heroes." When he tried to sit back down, he almost lost his balance and fell over. Mrs. Rhodebush wasn't looking at Sylvanius though. She just stared at Maurice through her sunglasses which she was wearing even though it was now almost completely dark.

When I got in the house, Aunt Bess told me that Charlie's mother had called and said that he couldn't come over to play Mr. Verb that day. He was being punished for something.

"What did he do wrong?" I asked.

"I didn't ask," Aunt Bess said. "Everyone has problems."

I went down to the basement to e-mail Charlie but was disappointed to find Uncle Frank sitting at the desk, working on the computer. I had never seen him on the computer before. When I tried to see what he was doing, he purposely blocked my view with his body.

"Sorry, Teddy, but I need to do some work for awhile," he said. "Why don't you go watch TV?"

"I can't," I said. My father never allowed Tommy or me to watch TV during the school week except on special occasions.

Uncle Frank stared at me and shook his head, concerned. "That's right," he said. "I forgot. That's unbelievable. Well," he said, "I'll be awhile."

"What are you working on?" I asked. Uncle Frank had a serious but satisfied look on his face and I could tell that he wanted me to ask him that question. "Are you working on your TV show?"

"Oh, no, no. This is something else," he said with a slight smile. "It's a novel."

"A book?"

He shrugged. "Novel, book. No biggie. Just a little something."

"Is it about a vampire?"

Uncle Frank laughed a little and thoughtfully arched one of his eyebrows. "No, no, no. Nothing like that." He pointed his chin at me and smiled. "Let's just say that it's a departure for F. Aris Pappas."

"Who?"

"Me," he said. "That's going to be my pen name. Aris is my middle name. I don't use it enough."

"Is it about microbes?" Uncle Frank was obsessed with germs, scrubbing his hands and face with special soap five or six times a day.

"No. It's something different," he said. "Something, well, something important. It's going to make people think."

"What are they going to think about?"

He nodded his head and looked deeply into my eyes. "About the human condition, Teddy," he said. "The goddamn human condition."

I nodded my head, disappointed. I was hoping for a book on vampires, apostles of the devil, or virulent strains of civilization-threatening disease. His book sounded as interesting as the Civil War.

"What's the human condition?" I asked. I didn't say goddamn.

Uncle Frank sighed, his knowledge a burden. "Well, how can I put this. It's, well, the things that make us human. Love, lust, hate, pain. Mostly though, it's about the things people want."

"What do people want?"

Uncle Frank considered my question, nodded his head. "Things. People want things. That's what makes them people. I'm going to tie the whole lottery into this." He shook his head. "Personally, I think it's dynamite stuff."

I looked at Uncle Frank for a moment. His description just furthered my disappointment. His book sounded dull.

"How much have you written?" I asked. Uncle Frank seemed unable to sit in one place very long without falling asleep with his mouth open and I wondered how far along in the process he was.

He gently waved a finger at me and my question. "Now, now, now. No more questions about the creative process. I have some real work to do here. *Real* work." With that, F. Aris Pappas took a deep breath and turned back to the computer.

Back upstairs, I found Aunt Bess in the kitchen cutting carrots at the counter, chopping hard with a large knife. After every two or three chops, she would bend down and peer through the crack in the drapes out the window at Mrs. Rhodebush's house and wistfully sigh. I poured myself a glass of milk, sat down at the kitchen table and began flipping through another magazine Uncle Frank had begun bringing home, *Eastern Estates*. I stopped at an article on home helicopter pads for the busy CEO.

Aunt Bess sighed again. "Cutting carrots at my age."

I didn't say anything. I kept reading the article and imagined myself, after a hard day at school, descending on our roof in a helicopter, onto our specially designed pad that guaranteed soft, skidless landings.

Aunt Bess sighed again. "I could cut off a finger."

I continued reading the article. The pad could be installed for less than $35,000 which seemed reasonable enough to me.

"A thumb."

I turned the page.

Aunt Bess suddenly stopped cutting and turned to face me. "Talk to your father," she said sharply.

I was sipping my milk when she said this and her abruptness caught me off guard. I coughed.

She took a step toward me, waving her knife. "Talk to him about spending a little money around here. I worked sixty-two years and I never made more than forty-two thousand a year. I'm not saying we have to go nuts, but a little comfort, a little convenience." She held her arms out wide like Mr. Peterson did on the soccer field. "Something."

"Okay," I said.

"The old man, the Yankee, keeps calling about his house. Tell your father to think about it. It's a beautiful house."

"The one Mrs. Wilcott likes?"

Aunt Bess's large body sagged when I said this. She slowly turned back to the kitchen counter and cut more carrots. Then she scrunched down and looked out the window again.

"What in God's name is going on over there?" She said. "He's been over there for hours. She's monopolizing him. The poor man needs his rest."

"Who?" I asked.

"Sylvanius. He's been over at Emily Rhodebush's all afternoon. I don't understand him at all. I'm half in the grave and she's older than me. I don't know why he spends so much time over there. She doesn't even know who he is. She never watched *Dark Towers*. I watched *Dark Towers* every day until he was killed off."

Sylvanius's death interested me. "How was he killed?"

Aunt Bess waved the knife. "I don't remember. However vampires die."

"Was it a stake through his heart? Or . . ." I paused here because I wanted Aunt Bess to seriously consider my question, "did sunlight destroy him?"

"What? I don't remember," she sighed. She cut up another carrot. "Sunlight. It was sunlight, I think," she said reluctantly. "He stayed out too late, or got up too early. I don't remember."

"Did he turn into ashes?"

"What?" Aunt Bess's knife came down sharply on the cutting board. "Yes, it was ashes," she said quietly. "But then he somehow came back to life again, for the reunion special. The ashes, something happened and they . . ." she stopped cutting and turned around to face me again. "What are we talking about this for? I don't want to talk about that silly show. I want to go home. I want to go back to Milwaukee. My cats need me. The family I left them with aren't taking care of them the right way. I need to go up there and be with them. At least they love me."

I was alarmed by Aunt Bess's outburst. I didn't want her to go back to Milwaukee. I had gotten used to having her with us and couldn't even remember how things were before she moved in.

"He likes going over there because he feels sorry for her," I said.

Aunt Bess stopped cutting, her knife suspended inches over an innocent carrot. "What?"

"Because she's so old. And has no teeth. Because of her gum disease. He thinks she's boring." Aunt Bess looked over at me. I glanced down at the magazine. "He told me that," I said.

She went back to her carrots. But I noticed that she wasn't chopping as hard anymore.

AT DINNER, Sylvanius made a toast. "To my host and hostess," he said standing unevenly. "For your graciousness. For your friendship. For your concern. For this wonderful, wonderful repast worthy of the finest chefs in Europe. And most of all, to you, Theo," he said, turning toward my father. "For everything." He bowed his head. Uncle Frank cleared his throat and said, "here, here," and raised his Diet Coke, which he was drinking instead of his usual glass of wine.

"Well, yes," my father said. He looked quickly around the table and began eating.

"I must warn you, Theo, that I am enjoying my sabbatical so much that I may be tempted to stay here forever and soak up the warmth and love of this unique and fortunate family. Imagine," he said, laughing, "a vampire in Wilton."

My father dropped a forkful of carrots onto his lap.

"Don't worry," Aunt Bess said, passing around the serving bowl of carrots. "I made too many of them."

After dinner, I worked on my List of Things in my room. I had decided that I would approach my father with the list within the next few days, possibly by the end of the week. I was preparing both a short and a long list, and would present one or the other, depending on my father's mood and interest at that particular moment.

On the other side of the room, Tommy looked out the window. He was wearing my now old wax lips.

He took the wax lips out of his mouth. "How long is that old vampire going to stay here?" he asked.

"Sylvanius? I don't know," I said. I decided to drop helicopter pad from my short list, concluding that while nice, it was not all that practical since we didn't yet own a helicopter.

Tommy kept looking out the window. He was clutching the wax lips with his hand and pressing his face against the screen. Outside, I could hear the steady rise and fall of crickets humming. Even though Miss Grace had said it was the first day of autumn, it was a warm night and I knew that I would be sleeping without my blankets again.

"Are more vampires coming to live here?" Tommy asked.

"No. I don't think so," I said. "Sylvanius is the only one and he's just an actor. He's not really a vampire."

"Is mom in heaven?" Tommy suddenly asked.

I looked over at Tommy. He was wearing gray Batman pajamas that were too tight for him. It was then that I noticed that he was also holding *When You Give a Mouse a Cookie*, a book my mother used to read to him.

"Yes," I said. I was as sure of this then as I am now.

"Is she an angel?"

"I don't know," I said. Tommy had his eyes closed and looked so small that for a moment, for the first time in my life, I thought I might want to hug him. "I think she is, Tommy," I said.

"Will she always take care of us, even when bad things and bad people are around?"

"Yes," I said. Then I said, "And I can take care of you too. Sometimes."

"You can't take care of me when he's around," Tommy said. He had his eyes opened now and was pointing his finger outside the window.

"Who?" I asked.

"Him." Tommy pointed again.

I got up and walked over to the window and looked out. There, across the street, under the street lamp, was the pickup truck. The man with long blond hair was leaning against it and looking up at us. He was smoking a cigarette and I could see its red tip glowing in the dark, burning bright like it was angry.

THE NEXT DAY in school, while I was sketching a laughing pumpkin during arts and crafts, Mrs. Plank walked into class, like an army general, her back unusually straight and rigid.

"Children," she said and clapped her hands. It was then that I noticed Maurice standing in the doorway with a policeman.

"Children," she said again. "I need your immediate attention. There has been a strange man loitering on the playground. He has long hair and drives a red truck of some sort. I want to remind everyone here that you are not to talk to strangers under any circumstances."

The room fell perfectly quiet. I felt a thousand eyeballs on me. I looked down at the beginnings of my laughing pumpkin and saw its eyes looking back up at me too, expectant and worried.

"Apparently, this is the second time he has been seen here this week," Mrs. Plank said. "We're trying to find out who he is. He may just be someone's relative or someone working in the neighborhood. We're trying to identify him, but in the meantime, you are not to speak to him."

"Does this man want to kidnap Teddy Pappas?" Johnny asked.

"No one's kidnapping anyone, Johnny," Mrs. Plank said. "We're not sure who he is or what he wants. Apparently he approached some children in another class during recess and spoke with them. I don't think we have to be overly alarmed but we just want to make sure." Then she said, "Teddy, can you come with me for a moment?"

I felt everyone's eyes follow me as I walked outside into the hall where Maurice and the police officer were waiting.

"Are you okay, Teddy?" Maurice asked.

I nodded.

"Did you see that man in the red truck today?" the policeman asked. He was shorter than Maurice and had a soft, white doughy face. Next to him, Maurice looked tight and lean. Even though the policeman had a gun holstered at his side, I didn't think I would feel as safe with him as I did with Maurice.

"No," I said.

"Well, he was there, Teddy," Maurice said. "Right outside."

"I didn't think it was necessary to alert the entire school of this situation," the policeman then said. "He's clearly interested in the Pappas boys."

"It's my responsibility to protect all of the children at St. Pius," Mrs. Plank said. "Heaven forbid something happened and we didn't warn them. We don't know what this man wants."

"Well, we'll post a squad out in front for the next couple of days," the policeman said. "I don't think there will be a problem. You going to be watching him right?" he asked Maurice.

"I'll be there," Maurice said. "I don't think there'll be any problem either. You go on back to your project now, Teddy, go back to your drawing. Everything's going to be all right."

During soccer practice after school, Maurice stood on the sidelines holding Tommy's hand. When he watched me on the playground during lunch or recess, he usually sat a distance away, under a tree or in his car, smoking his pipe, but this time he stood as close to me as possible, following me up and down the field on the sidelines, shadowing my every move. I could feel his eyes on me and sensed a tension coming from his direction, an alertness that put me on edge.

Near the end of practice, Mr. Peterson asked me to kick the ball. "I don't think I've seen you make contact yet," he said. I slowly lifted my leg and tried to kick it but when I did, my foot hit the very top of the ball and I fell on the ground. Laying on my back, I looked up at Mr. Peterson. I was hoping that he would somehow understand that I hated soccer and was only there because Mrs. Wilcott was having sex with my father. Mr. Peterson didn't seem to understand any of this though. He just said, "Try again. Use the side of your foot and kick it in the center."

I tried again. Even though I didn't fall, the ball only rolled a few inches before stopping in a patch of dry dirt. Mr. Peterson chewed on his curtain mustache for awhile. "You'll mostly play defense," he said.

Just then Tommy broke away from Maurice and ran toward us and kicked the ball right between Mr. Peterson's legs.

"Tommy!" I yelled. I feared he might attract the attention of Benjamin who had once again ignored me all practice.

"Hey," Mr. Peterson said, but he was smiling.

Tommy ran around the field, kicking the ball. The other boys stopped practicing and watched him. As I feared, Benjamin did notice and looked annoyed. He tried to stop Tommy and grab the ball but Tommy kicked it around and past him and the other boys. He kept running and kicking until the ball landed inside the goal, silently against the net.

"God, he's fast," Mr. Peterson said. "How old is he?"

I was about to say, "Five," but Maurice walked up behind me and put his arms on my shoulders and said, "He's six-and-a-half."

Mr. Peterson kept watching Tommy who was making his way around the field again, a small, streaking meteor. He kicked the ball into the goal three more times. Then Benjamin crouched down like a goalie and said, "Okay, try it now, little man," and Tommy kicked it past him twice. In between goals, he kept running and laughing. Finally, after another goal, he fell on the ground and looked up at the sky. I could see his chest moving up and down fast. He was breathing hard.

"That little guy's good," Mr. Peterson said. "Real fast. Real fast. How old did you say he was again?"

"Six-and-a-half," Maurice said.

"Well, he's old enough to play on our junior team then. It's really too late, but I can arrange it," he said. "Do you think he'd want to?"

"I know he'd want to," Maurice said. "He told me so."

"He did?" I asked.

"Yes," Maurice said. "He did."

ON THE WAY HOME, Maurice smoked his pipe. I sensed that some of his apprehension had left him and he walked loosely, with his usual easy stride. When we crossed the street, he hummed a little.

"Looks like you played yourself onto a soccer team, Tommy Pappas," he said when we reached the other side. "All that practicing you and I did paid off."

"You've been practicing with him?" I asked.

"Yes, sir. In the afternoons, while you're in school. Kept me busy. So he and I been kicking it around the playground a little. I could tell he was good. That's why I made him six-and-a-half years old. I hope you don't mind being an old man Tommy." Maurice laughed.

We didn't talk for awhile. The evening was warm and dry and still. Under our feet, leaves crunched quietly, like the parchment paper we used in arts and crafts class. The light was fading and as we walked, I heard crickets and felt the night reaching for us.

"Hey, you played pretty good yourself, Teddy," Maurice said, patting me on the back. "You're a player too." We turned down our block. "My rookie season with the Bears, I didn't play until the last game of the season. We played the Packers and . . ."

Maurice grabbed each of our hands and stopped talking. Up ahead, parked in our driveway, was the red pickup truck.

"Now what would that be doing there, do you suppose?" Maurice said. He held both of our hands with one of his and reached around and under his shirt for something with the other.

"A gun," Tommy yelled. I looked up at Maurice and gasped. He was holding a large black gun, its barrel sleek and terrifying.

"Come with me," Maurice said. We approached our house, slowly, Maurice's hand still tight on mine. When we saw my father standing on the porch, Maurice put the gun away but held onto our hands.

"Is everything all right, Mr. Pappas?" he asked.

"Yes, everything will be fine, Mr. Jackson," my father answered.

Maurice hesitated before letting go of our hands.

"Are you sure, Mr. Pappas?"

My father nodded. He was standing perfectly still, his face obscured by shadows. "Yes," he said quietly. "I'm sure."

Maurice finally let go of our hands and Tommy and I walked up the front porch steps.

"Tommy, why don't you run into the kitchen? Aunt Bess has a snack for you, I believe," he said. He turned and faced me, swallowing hard. "Teddy, I would like for you to meet someone."

Before we went inside, my father turned back to Maurice who was still standing in our driveway. "Thank you, Mr. Jackson," he said. "We will see you tomorrow." Maurice just stood there, looking like he didn't understand something.

"I'll be right outside, Mr. Pappas," I heard him say. "In case you need anything."

My father said nothing. He just closed the door.

Uncle Frank was sitting on the black couch in the living room next to the man with the blond hair. They both quickly stood up when I walked in and the man smiled at me, a long, slow grin that stretched tight across his thin face.

"Teddy," my father said. "Say hello to Mr. Anderson. Robert Lee Anderson."

"Bobby Lee," the man said. "Hey, son. What do you know?" He wiped the sides of his pants with his hands and smiled at me again.

I nodded hello. Uncle Frank coughed and I wondered where Sylvanius was.

"Mr. Anderson was a friend of your mother's," my father said.

"A good friend," Bobby Lee said.

"Apparently, he is going to be in the Chicago area, actually has been in the Chicago area for awhile, and has decided to pay us a visit."

"I heard a lot about you," Bobby Lee said. He examined me with a long steady look. "How old are you?" he asked.

"Eleven."

"Eleven years old. Hell. Eleven years old," he said. Then he said, "You look like Amy."

I didn't say anything. Amy was my mother's name and I wasn't sure I liked Bobby Lee saying it. I wasn't sure I liked Bobby Lee.

"Your mother and I grew up together," he said.

"In Memphis?" I asked.

"Yeah, in Memphis. Went to the same grade and high school. She was a lot smarter than me though. Always got good grades," he said with a short laugh. My father and Uncle Frank didn't smile.

Bobby Lee started walking around the living room, his hands jammed into the front pockets of his tight blue jeans. "Nice place you have here. Nice place. Hell of a lot nicer than where I'm staying."

"Where are you staying?" Uncle Frank asked.

"Here and there," he said. "I stayed at a hotel called the Mark Twain when I first moved to town. Ever hear of it? It's in the city. Near Rush Street where the action is. Cost me forty-three dollars a night though."

"Never heard of it," Uncle Frank said.

Bobby Lee kept walking around the living room, picking up pictures and books, pretending to look at them. He was thin and wiry and had a dusty, out-of-place look about him that made my stomach tight and my throat feel small again. His nose was hooked and his eyes dark bullets. He reminded me of a suspicious bird searching for something. "Chicago is a nice city. Lots of things to do, lots to see. Never been here before. Never been north of Louisville I guess." He looked over at me. "That's in Kentucky," he said. "I used to go there once in a while."

I stared at the floor and wondered how long I had to stay in the living room.

Bobby Lee kept walking. He stopped at the fireplace mantle and picked up a picture of my mother.

"She used to have longer hair," he said, putting the picture back. "Used to go all the way down to her shoulders."

My father and Uncle Frank were silent. Off in the kitchen, I could hear Aunt Bess's voice but couldn't understand what she was saying.

"Are you related to Robert E. Lee, the Civil War general?" I asked. I hoped that my father might start talking if the War was being discussed.

"Hell, I wish. Probably some money in that family somewhere. No, there ain't no relation that I know of. Hell, everyone's named Bobby Lee where I come from."

"Why have you been following me?" I asked.

"Following you!" Bobby Lee laughed. "Hell, I ain't been following no one. Just been driving around. I knew Amy lived here, so I thought I might check it out. A little too expensive for my wallet though. I didn't win no lottery." He laughed again, a short, high sound. My father looked back down at the floor.

Bobby Lee walked over to the front hallway and looked upstairs, then back at me. "So," he said, staring at my sneakers and shorts. "You play a lot of soccer?"

"No," I said simply.

"When I was eleven years old I fished a lot. You do any fishing?"

"No."

Bobby Lee stuffed his hands back inside his front pockets, and looked thoughtful. "Well, I guess there aren't that many places to go fish around here. I used to fish in a little creek near my house. Use to catch rock bass. They fried up all right. You ever fished?"

"No," I said again.

"Yeah, well, Amy never liked to fish either I guess. Girls don't on the whole, generally speaking." He nodded at me and smiled. Off in the corner of the room, I heard my father cough but my eyes were now fixed on Bobby Lee. I was trying to remember if my mother, in all of her stories about Tennessee, had ever mentioned him.

"Say," Bobby Lee said. "You got a little girlfriend or anything?"

"What? No," I felt my cheeks turn red. Bobby Lee's questions were beginning to embarrass me. I glanced over at my father for help, an explanation. But he was miles away, standing across the room, hugging his chest.

"Yeah, well, you're smart to steer clear of the girls. They're just trouble." Bobby Lee smiled again, then the room fell quiet.

"Teddy," Uncle Frank finally said. "I think we're about done here. Why don't you go up to your room and do your homework. We're done here, aren't we, Theo?"

My father mumbled something.

"Homework?" Bobby Lee said. "Boy just got home."

"Yes, he has homework to do now," my father said softly. "Teddy, why don't you go up to your room."

"Homework, huh?" Bobby Lee said. He seemed stuck on the word. "Homework. Well, I guess you got to do that." He let out a deep breath. "Well, I'll be seeing you there, buddy." He nodded and winked. "I'll be back soon."

LATER THAT EVENING, after Bobby Lee left, we had a quiet dinner, no one saying much, not even Uncle Frank. We all sat in a strange silence that reminded me of those first, terrible days after my mother died, a stunned, hopeless hush. I was confused by the silence, uncertain of its exact cause, though I was sure it had something to do with Bobby Lee's visit.

"Well," Sylvanius said, looking around the table and swallowing. "Everyone must be quite hungry." Uncle Frank gave him a look from across the table then reached slowly for his Diet Coke.

"Everything is quite delicious of course," Sylvanius said quickly. He lowered his head over his plate and cut up his pork chop. "Quite good."

I looked at my father for some type of clue or sign of what was or had just taken place. He was staring out the window, though, his food untouched. As expected, he was no help.

Sylvanius tried once again to start the conversation. "Emily Rhodebush and I have been discussing the need for professional theater here in Wilton," he said. He sipped his glass of wine, and peered out over the rim of the glass. "A suburb of this sophistication and resources should have an arts community that reflects its citizenry."

Aunt Bess covered her mouth with her napkin and started to cry.

"My God, Bess, is it something I said? In no way did I mean to upset you. If you feel so strongly against professional theater . . ."

Aunt Bess pushed her plate away and quickly left the table. My father surprised me by following her.

"Is something going on here that I am not aware of?" Sylvanius asked.

"Shut the hell up," Uncle Frank said. Then he too left the table and went down to the basement.

Sylvanius looked at Tommy and me with wide eyes. "My goodness," he said. "There must be something in the air."

"Yeah," Tommy said. "Vampires."

THAT NIGHT I lay in bed and waited for the discussion to start downstairs. I expected my father and Uncle Frank to talk about Bobby Lee but the conversation never began. Twice I went halfway down the stairs to listen, but heard nothing.

I eventually fell into a thin, half sleep, filled with familiar voices and feelings. I dreamt I was standing on our helicopter pad, looking up, waiting for something to land. Off in the distance, coming down from the sky like rain,

I heard my mother telling me about the colliding comets, a story she frequently told at bedtime. In her story, when the comets collided, they showered the earth with a magic that changed things; some things got better, some things got worse. Standing on the helicopter pad, my arms spread wide, my face turned up, I heard my mother's voice surrounding me, heard her whisper that the comets were flying.

I woke up some time later, my forehead damp with perspiration. It was another warm night and I lay on the top of my sheets listening to Tommy's deep breathing. Gradually, as the minutes passed, I detected a different sound, an isolated noise that I realized was my father typing. I got up and followed the sound. Suddenly, I needed to see him.

I found him in his study, typing, the index fingers of each hand poised over the keys. He was unraveling, like a ball of string. His puffy white hair stood up in sharp angles to the sides of his head and his shirt was rumpled and halfway unbuttoned. When he saw me, rather than seem surprised or concerned, he merely cleared his throat and motioned for me to sit down as if he was expecting me.

"Sit down, Teddy," he said. "Please sit down." I sat in the one chair in the room, up against the wall.

My father paused and I heard him take a deep breath.

"We should probably discuss this at another time, but my fear is that, well, my fear is that you will hear this from someone else and that would be unforgivable. There is never going to be an ideal time for this," he said. "We should have told you about this sooner, but your mother and I never agreed on when to do it exactly. She kept saying that she would tell you, but she never did."

I looked down at the floor and thought about the story about the comets. I knew that somewhere up in the sky, somewhere behind the planets, two comets were approaching each other, two comets were getting close.

"It's because of the money," my father said. "All of this. It has brought all of this upon us. I feared this from the start. The moment I won the lottery, this was my fear. That's why I almost didn't claim the ticket. You see, I made inquiries, I tried to locate him, but no one seemed to know where he was and in the end I thought, I decided that the money would provide for you and Tommy, you see. I was wrong, though. I made the wrong decision." He said all this in a great rush, and seemed exhausted for the effort.

I closed my eyes and heard my father clear his throat. When he started speaking again, his voice was soft and far away.

"My winning it, the accident, well, it was all uncommon. Yes. It seems like the past year has been full of uncommon occurrences. You know, Teddy, your mother and I, we, we . . ." He stopped here and I opened my eyes. He was staring at his hands. "We were different from each other. Very different. Of course, I suppose I'm not like many people. At least that's what your mother used to say." He smiled for a moment, and shook his head. Then he looked out the window into the dark, into the night, into a thousand miles away and eleven years ago and said, "That man, Bobby Lee, whom you met today, he was once involved with your mother. A long time ago." He looked back at me. I watched him open his hands wide then close them into two fists. "That man, Teddy," he said. "That man, well, he is, he is, your father."

PART TWO

PART TWO

CHAPTER EIGHT

THE NEXT MORNING, after my father told me everything, I lay in bed and remembered my birthday party when I turned ten. True to her spirited nature, my mother had decided to have a surprise party for me. I knew about her plans, because I had overheard her discussing them with my father one night while they were getting ready for bed and thought I was sleeping.

"I'm a bit hesitant about the surprise element, Amy," my father said. "I don't think it necessary. I believe he'll be quite happy with just the party. It might prove too much for him. He's only nine."

"What do you mean, too much?" my mother asked.

"The surprise element, it could prove disorienting. It could, well, shock him."

"What do you mean, shock him?"

"Scare him. Teddy doesn't seem like the type of person who would like surprises."

"*You* don't like surprises, you mean. He likes surprises fine. And he'll like this one. Just leave it to me."

For the next week or so, I walked around our house in a constant state of expectancy, thinking at any moment a party in my honor could and would erupt. I made every effort to look innocent, keeping my face as expressionless as possible whenever I entered a room or opened a door.

"What's that look on your face?" my mother asked as I entered our kitchen the morning of my birthday. "What's the big smile for?"

I touched my hands to my face, probing my mouth like it was a large scab. "I don't know," I said.

My mother went back to the magazine she was reading at the table. She was wearing a sleeveless white T-shirt, and her red hair was pulled back in a ponytail. "I thought we'd go somewhere for lunch," she said. "It's your birthday you know."

"It is?" I raised my eyebrows high when I said this and worked hard to keep the corners of my mouth in a straight line.

My mother stopped flipping the pages of her magazine and I thought I saw her bite down on her lip to keep from smiling.

"Why don't we go to Boogie Burger?" she finally said.

Boogie Burger was a restaurant where the waitresses and waiters dressed up as hamburgers and french fries and danced with hula hoops while they served you. I found the place loud and annoying—much more up Tommy's alley—and was disappointed in my mother's suggestion. I had hoped for bigger and better things than Boogie Burger for my first surprise party. In particular, I had my heart set on the Laser Zone, a place I had heard much about, but never been.

"Sure," I said. This time I didn't have to work at not smiling. The last time we had gone to Boogie Burger, a dancing cheeseburger had knocked over a real milkshake onto my father, who, caught completely off guard, reacted like it was hot lava and clutched his heart and yelled "Dear God," so loudly that the cheeseburger asked if they should call an ambulance.

"I asked Bobby and Michael to come too," my mother said. She had stopped flipping through her magazine and was now peering intently at a page. "They're going to meet us there."

"The Kopiks?" My heart sank. Bobby and Michael were twin brothers whose house backed up to ours. Their family was in the process of moving to New York City but unfortunately were still living in Wilton at the time of my birthday. They defined odd and spent much of their time discussing their braces and allergy medications when they weren't playing with their hand-puppet collection, speaking in a bizarre language they claimed to have invented. Despite being neighbors, I avoided them. They occupied a lower rung on the St. Pius social ladder than I did, a rung so low that it ceased to exist the day they finally relocated.

"What about Charlie? Can he come?" I asked.

My mother started flipping through the magazine again. "Who? Oh, I forgot to ask him," she said absentmindedly. "He's probably doing homework or something."

"It's summer vacation," I said, but my mother didn't seem to hear me. Then, without even looking at me, she told me to go upstairs and get dressed.

On the way to Boogie Burger, I asked where my father was.

"He's at the library," my mother said as she switched lanes. "But he did tell me to wish you a happy birthday. Actually, he asked me to sing it. You can help me, Tommy. Come on, honey!"

As we drove, my mother and Tommy, who was sitting next to me in the backseat, sang round after round of *Happy Birthday*, as I looked out the window, depressed, lonely, and more than a bit confused. I had imagined a number of scenarios for my birthday, none of which included my current reality.

"Oh, Teddy, honey. Do you mind if I just pop into Nancy's Fabric for awhile? I want to look at some new fabric. I want to make new curtains for your bedroom windows. It will only take about an hour."

"An hour?" I asked. My voice cracked a bit when I said this and I felt my face grow red.

"It's right there in the mall," she said as we pulled into the parking lot. "Come on in with me, honey, I want you to help me pick out some fabric."

"I don't want to go," I said. I slumped down in my seat.

My mother had already parked and was opening my door. "Come on birthday boy, it's right over there, right next to the Laser Zone. Tell you what, you can take Tommy in there while I go next door."

My mood immediately changed. "Oh, okay. Let's go, Tommy," I said, quickly taking his hand. "We only have an hour."

The first people I saw when we entered the Laser Zone were the Kopik brothers holding their puppets. They were standing right next to Charlie who was standing right next to Aunt Bess, who was standing right next to my father, who was standing right next to most of my fourth grade class, all of whom yelled surprise so loudly that I momentarily lost my breath.

I stood there in shock and then turned around to find my mother who was still standing in the door looking at me. Rather than leading the cheers and singing, she was simply smiling, looking at me in a way I had never seen before, as if she were studying and memorizing me. She held her hands in front of her in an unusually tentative manner, both nervous and hopeful. She clearly wanted me to be pleased. It was only when she stepped forward into the room, away from the bright daylight, that I saw her tears. It was the first and only time I ever saw my mother cry.

I couldn't hear her over all the noise and music, but through the commotion, I could still see her lips move. She was trying to tell me something, but I couldn't hear her. She repeated the effort, but I was swept away by the party. Her standing in the doorway, with her hair pulled back in a ponytail, wiping tears away with a finger, was the last real image I had of my mother. A few days later, she would get into her car, drive onto the interstate, and disappear from my life forever.

I was lying in bed, trying to recreate that party, trying to imagine what my mother was trying to tell me, wondering if it had any significance other than happy birthday, when I heard my bedroom door open. "Teddy," I heard Sylvanius's voice ask. "Are you still resting?"

I sat up in bed, the image of my mother fading. Sylvanius was standing in my doorway, a new, bright red scarf tied loosely around his neck.

He opened the door wide and bowed slightly. "Breakfast is served," he said.

WHEN I GOT DOWN to the kitchen, I saw that Sylvanius had set the table for one. It was late in the morning and Tommy and Maurice had already left for school. After our talk the night before, my father had said that I should stay home and rest the next day. "I imagine you have quite a bit on your mind," he said as he helped me back into bed. "Sleep as late as you wish." I tried to stay awake and sort things out, but I fell asleep while my father was still sitting on the edge of my bed.

"Your uncle and father had to go into the city," Sylvanius said. "And your aunt went to the market. So," he smiled, "it is just you and I. I had to convince your aunt that you would be fine, she didn't want to leave you." He paused and his lizard eyes dragged over me a moment, then he said, "Per her instructions, I have taken the liberty of pouring you a bowl of cereal with some fruit. Bananas freshly peeled. Now, exactly where did I put it?" He slowly rose and walked over to the kitchen counter. As I sat down, I instinctively glanced at his monster shoes out of the corner of my eye. They looked particularly immense that morning and I wondered if somehow they were expanding, feeding on some unknown food source.

Sylvanius found the bowl on top of the microwave. "Ah," he said. "And how did it get here?"

He returned to the table with the bowl and a pitcher of milk and sat down. "You were up late last night," he said.

I poured milk and started to eat my Cheerios, crunching them hard in a way that I hoped would discourage further discussion from Sylvanius. The bananas he had cut were brown and mushy looking so I pushed them to the side of the bowl and ate around them.

"I usually don't hear or see much from my lair in the basement," he said. "But unfortunately I heard all about this sad tale." He leaned across the table. "I can only imagine how you must feel. It must be very upsetting."

I shrugged and kept eating. I didn't want to talk about Bobby Lee. I didn't even want to think about him.

"Could I have some orange juice?"

"Ah, juice, of course." He sighed and stood up and walked over to the refrigerator. "Juice is important for children. It gives you vitality and, and"— he waved his hand—"other things."

He returned to the table and handed me a glass that he watched me drink. When I finished, he bowed his head and said, "Refreshing no doubt," and then sat down again.

I ate more cereal, now swallowing Cheerios whole, avoiding his eyes.

"I want you to know that everything will be fine," he said after some time. "Everything will be fine."

Stavros walked into the room, stopped and looked at Sylvanius, then glided by into the dining room and out of sight.

"Everything will turn out in your favor," Sylvanius said. "You'll see. That horrid man will never succeed with his plans. Never. Your father and uncle present a formidable team. He will never take you away from here."

I stopped eating and looked down at the Cheerios floating in my bowl. The thought of Bobby Lee taking me away from Wilton hadn't occurred to me.

"Where would he take me?" I asked.

"I'm not sure," Sylvanius said. "To the hills somewhere, I suppose. In the South. They have hills down there, I believe. But he won't get away with it. Your uncle assured me of this just last night. We were up quite late discussing the matter." He yawned and stretched his thin arms upward. "Yes, quite late, indeed. Planning your defense."

I tried eating again, but the Cheerios were fat and soggy, the milk warm. I could still feel Sylvanius's eyes on me and I knew he wanted to talk about Bobby Lee but I didn't. I was fairly positive I didn't want to discuss Bobby Lee ever again.

"Did you ever drink blood?" I asked. "In your movies?"

My question surprised him and he smiled when he answered. "No, no, no, of course not. I believe they used ketchup or some type of food dye."

"Were you ever anything besides a vampire in a movie?"

He eased back in his chair and folded his hands. "I occasionally played other roles, roles of a somewhat sinister vein. Once I played a professor or doctor of some sort. Dr. Gray Vatem. If my memory serves me, I was beheaded by an angry mob." He paused here, confused. "Or was I eaten by a large crab? Well, anyway, I came to some dastardly end that I no doubt deserved." He crossed his legs, his monster shoes now dangling close to my sneakers, dwarfing them. "I suppose I would have liked to have stretched myself a bit more. My last film, about the good vampire, the one that was never released, was different. It had some excellent writing in it. I had some very thoughtful lines. I gave this wonderful little speech at the end, wonderful, about love and people and family and growing. Frank, of course, didn't like the scene, he wanted me to be burned alive, but I actually cried when I first read it aloud, actually cried. It's a shame no one will ever see the film."

"Is it hard being an actor?"

Sylvanius closed his eyes and nodded, my question large and irresistible. "It is," he said, "the most challenging of professions."

"Is that what you always wanted to be?"

"Well, I thought briefly of becoming a surgeon, medicine has always fascinated me, but . . ." He took a deep breath and let the air out slowly, his chest falling. "I was born to be onstage. Everyone is born to do one thing well, I suppose." He was quiet again and looked over my shoulder, out the window. "Oh," he said. "I had such talent and dreams." He took another deep breath then stared silently out the window over the sink. I finished my Cheerios and looked up just in time to see him wipe a tear from his cheek.

"I am sorry," he said. He looked embarrassed and stood up. "My career is not without memories. Or regrets. I'm afraid I've grown quite reflective over the past few weeks. My recent ordeal, my escape if you will, has served to remind me of how far I have fallen, how far I have strayed from my dreams. And being here with you all, well, it reminds me of what I should have had in my life. A home. A family. A neighborhood to stroll. I should have had some sense of permanence at my age." He stopped here. "Especially at my age." Another tear slipped down his face and he didn't look much like a serpent anymore. He just looked thin and old.

"Well, if you will excuse me," he said. "I think I have to be alone." He made his way over to the basement, his monster shoes creaking and moaning like old ships. When he reached the door, he paused and looked back at me.

He started to say something, then stopped and merely waved his hand at me, a slow, sad wave. Then he vanished down the steps and into the darkness.

As soon as he left, I put my bowl away and went upstairs to my room. I had a sudden need to draw. Sitting at my desk, I sketched quickly, with no definite purpose or thought in mind as to what I was drawing. Many times when I drew, I would start with a vague emotion that would reveal itself and take shape as I worked. As I drew, my thoughts came into focus.

The night before, when my father told me about Bobby Lee, I didn't understand what he was saying at first.

"I thought you were my father," I said.

"I am. Of course I am. But I am your adopted father. He is your biological father." He cleared his throat. "Are you familiar with how that situation works? How that can be?"

"Yes."

"He and your mother conceived you. And then I met your mother and soon after she and you moved to Wilton. From Memphis."

"I don't remember moving here."

"Well, you wouldn't, of course. You were only two years old."

"Is Bobby Lee Tommy's father too?"

"No, he's not," my father said. "I am Tommy's father. Biological father." These words and the apologetic way he said them had given me a terrible, empty feeling.

"Tommy's still my brother though, isn't he?"

"Yes, yes, of course. Half-brother," my father said. "But he is definitely your brother. Yes, definitely," he added quickly.

I was thinking about that conversation and about Bobby Lee and my mother, when I heard my father's voice downstairs. Minutes later, he entered my room, walking directly over to my desk without stopping.

"Drawing again, Teddy?" he asked.

"Yes."

He peered over my shoulder at my picture.

"Very vibrant colors. What is it?"

I looked down at my paper. I wasn't sure what I was drawing, it was just a blur of colors and nothing yet had taken shape. "Different colors," I said.

"Ah," he said. I expected him to disappear into his study, but instead he sat down on the edge of my bed. "Teddy, do you have any more questions? About what we discussed last night?"

"About Bobby Lee being my father?"

He cleared his throat. "Biological father. Yes."

"No," I said.

He nodded his head. "Well . . ." He stopped and smiled briefly. "Well," he said again. Then he was quiet. Outside I could hear a car door slam. I looked over toward the window and saw the blue curtains blowing in the breeze, fluttering softly like someone had just breathed on them. I remembered my mother making those curtains on the dining room table late at night with a sewing machine she had borrowed from Aunt Bess.

"Teddy," my father said. "I was thinking that we should all take a family vacation."

I looked at him, speechless and confused.

He cleared his throat once more. "All of us. Together." I continued to look at him, not sure I heard him correctly. Other than our occasional trips to Wisconsin, we never took vacations. "A vacation? Where?" I asked.

He rubbed his hands on his knees and took a deep breath. "Well, where would you like to go?"

His question depressed me. I knew the reason behind it, knew it was because of Bobby Lee. Though I momentarily considered a ranch-scouting expedition to Montana I said, "I don't want to go anywhere."

"Well, how about Disney World?"

My heart fell. Marcia Broden from my first grade class had gone to Disney World after doctors diagnosed her rare bone disease. She died a year later.

"I don't want to go to Disney World," I said.

My father looked worried, his jaw moving in and out. The concept of planning a vacation was a daunting task and he was struggling to keep up the effort. "Well," he said, "we should all go somewhere."

"Will Aunt Bess come?"

"Yes, of course."

"Uncle Frank?"

He looked surprised. "Well, I hadn't really . . . I suppose if he would want to. Yes."

"And Maurice?"

My father's forehead tightened and his jaws tensed again. "I hadn't really thought of including Mr. Jackson, but I suppose that might be wise . . ."

"Where do you want to go?" I asked.

He seemed surprised again. "Well, I hadn't really planned on anything. I thought you and Tommy could pick out a place."

"Why don't we go to Manassas?" I asked. I remembered the brochure I had seen in his study, the one with the silhouette of Abraham Lincoln on the cover. I thought such a trip would please my father. Suddenly, going to Manassas made sense.

He was confused, his eyebrows coming together in a point. "What? I'm sorry? In Virginia?"

"We can see that Civil War battle. I saw that brochure. On your desk."

"Oh," he said, half turning toward the door and his study. "Oh, my desk. Hmmm, do you think you would enjoy that? Of course, it is near Washington, D.C., which would be educational. Yes. Well, I could make some inquiries. I believe that it, the reenactment, is coming up very soon. Immediately, actually. Do you think this is something you would like to do?"

"Can we fight in the battle?"

"What? Oh. Well, you are a bit young. Not many twelve-year-olds fought in the war, though there are records that show that a number of young boys served in the bugle corps. Well, I could call the Society. I really haven't had any contact with them in years. Are you sure you want to go there? Isn't there anywhere else? What about Epcot Center? Have you heard of it? It's very educational. I've been doing some research."

"Manassas," I said. "I want to go to Manassas."

My father uncharacteristically searched my face, then took a deep breath and stood up. "Well, I'll look into it right away." He was halfway to the door before he turned and said, "Oh, I almost forgot to tell you. For dinner, your aunt is preparing your favorite meal. Cheeseburgers."

My heart sank to unchartered depths, bouncing off the ocean floor. We never had cheeseburgers for dinner. I looked at my father, braced for news about my rare bone disease.

"Is Bobby Lee going to take me away and make me live with him?" I asked.

He shuddered and his head shook as if something small but solid had just struck and momentarily stunned him.

"No," he said, but suddenly I didn't believe him.

DURING DINNER, Tommy the Soccer Star, kept talking about the four goals he scored in practice. I knew that the mere fact that he was talking, that words were actually coming out of his mouth rather than high-pitched barks, pleased my father more than the goals. It was the most he had talked since the accident. My father kept nodding his head as words poured out of Tommy in breathless rushes.

"Mr. Peterson said that I was probably the best player on the team, even though I'm only six and a half years old," Tommy said.

My father took a bite of his cheeseburger. "You're only five, Tommy," he said.

"No, I'm not, I'm six-and-a-half now."

My father stopped eating. "No, I'm almost certain you're five. I mean, I am certain you're five. Quite certain."

"No, I'm not. Maurice made me six-and-a-half."

My father looked over at me for help but I just poured more ketchup on my plate for the french fries.

"Well," my father said. "Anyway," he smiled. "I'm glad you're enjoying the soccer experience, Tommy." He carefully took a sip of his coffee, placing it back down on the table with both hands. "As are you, Teddy, of course."

I didn't say anything.

"I'm sure you will score some points too. Once you play in an actual contest."

"You score goals in soccer, not points," Uncle Frank said. He had been mostly silent during dinner and wasn't eating much. Sylvanius had been in the basement since breakfast and I wondered if this was bothering my uncle in some way. Sylvanius's every action seemed to have an irritating effect on Uncle Frank.

"Well, I have some news," my father said, giving his throat a good double clearing. "We are all taking a vacation."

"What?" Uncle Frank said. "What do you mean vacation?"

"A trip, yes. Teddy has expressed a desire to witness the reenactment of the Battle of Bull Run. The first battle. There were two, of course."

Uncle Frank looked over at me and said, "You did?"

I nodded my head.

"We are?" Aunt Bess said.

My father picked up a french fry, then put it back on his plate. "Yes." He coughed. "Yes, indeed. This weekend."

Aunt Bess recoiled at this news, her eyes wide and frantic. "What do you mean this weekend? You mean, *this* weekend?"

"Yes. It's Columbus Day. The boys don't have school on Monday so there shouldn't be a problem."

"Where is this Bull's place?"

"It is in Virginia."

171

"Virginia," Aunt Bess said. She looked disappointed. "Virginia." She chewed on the word like a piece of gum. "Where is Virginia again? It's out east, but what's it near?"

"West Virginia," Uncle Frank said.

"I have made arrangements for all of us to fly to Washington on Saturday morning. We will fly together. We will stay in a very nice hotel and then go witness the Battle on Sunday." He looked up from his plate and for the first time in my life I thought he looked almost proud. "I made all of the arrangements, just this afternoon. It only took a few phone calls."

Uncle Frank picked up his glass of water. "Bull Run. I got to hand it to you, Theo. You know how to live."

My father ignored Uncle Frank, looking instead over at me. "It will be very educational," he said. "And it was Teddy's idea."

"Yes," I said. "It was."

That night, while I was doing my homework that Johnny Cezzaro had dropped off, my father returned to my room and once again sat down on the edge of my bed. His visits, once special occasions, now put me on guard. I knew they were related to Bobby Lee.

"And how are you this evening, Teddy?"

I didn't look at him. I was doing multiplication tables, something I didn't particularly enjoy doing even though I had been awarded the St. Pius Mathemagician trophy the year before because the contest had been held on the day Charlie Governs slipped on the ice and suffered a concussion. "I'm okay," I said.

He nodded his head. "Teddy, do you have any questions you would like to ask me?"

"What's twelve times fourteen?"

"What? Oh. Let's see. Let's see." He was quiet for a moment. "I think I might need a piece of paper and a pencil to . . ."

"It's a hundred and sixty-eight," I said. I wrote down the answer and waited for him to talk about Bobby Lee.

"Well, I suppose it is," he said, standing up. "Are you looking forward to our trip?"

"Are you done with your work?" I asked.

"Yes, yes, I'm done with the conferences. I have no pressing assignments at the moment."

I started on a new page of multiplication tables. On top of my workbook page, Johnny Cezzaro had written, "You owe me and Big Tony $15,000!" I made my way through one column of problems and tried to start on the next but felt my father's eyes on me. I put my pencil down.

"I think that Bull Run will be fun."

"Manassas? Yes. I think it will be educational. Though we could still go somewhere else if you would like."

"No, I want to go there." During dinner, I had thought my decision through again, and was convinced that it was the right one. Manassas would almost certainly make my father happy and less likely to send me off to live in the hills. I also had decided to learn as much as possible about the Civil War, thus making me indispensable in my father's eyes.

"How come it's called Bull Run and Manassas?" I asked.

He was relieved at my question, his face relaxing. "Manassas. Yes. In the Civil War, the same battle frequently had two names. The South would have a name for it, and the North would have a different name for it. The Union or the North called the battle the Battle of Bull Run after a nearby creek. The Confederates called it Manassas after a nearby railroad junction. I always thought that difference a microcosm of the war. The two regions couldn't even agree on how to name their battlefields." He let out a deep breath and looked pleased.

"Oh," I said. I sat back in my chair, my eyes, I hoped, bright and eager for the discussion on battlefield conditions and ammunition supplies to begin. Then I heard the doorbell ring and a few seconds later, Aunt Bess rushed in and whispered, "Theo!" She looked scared and that's when I knew Bobby Lee was back again.

"I THINK SHE WAS some type of dancer," Aunt Bess said.

She was sitting on my bed, trying to explain how my father and mother met, an event that seemed to be shrouded in some mystery. Across the room, I could see Tommy's leg sticking out from under his bed as he ate a piece of the German chocolate cake Aunt Bess had made for dessert. Downstairs, I was sure my father, Uncle Frank, and Bobby Lee were talking, but I couldn't hear a word. Aunt Bess had closed and locked our bedroom door when she came up.

"Where did she dance?" I asked.

"I'm not sure, honey. In Tennessee. Or wherever she was from again. I'm not sure, honey."

"Was my mother a ballerina?" I asked. I imagined my mother in pink tights, dancing and turning lightly onstage, her arms arched over her head, a holy and unapproachable look on her face.

"I don't think she was a ballerina, honey. I think she was a different type of dancer. You should ask your father. When you're older. When you're eighteen or twenty-one. He'll tell you then."

"Where were they when they met?" I sat at my desk and picked at a piece of chocolate cake with my fingers. Eating in our room was something Aunt Bess normally didn't allow. But I sensed that the rules were changing in our house, the old order vanishing, and I carefully licked a finger.

"I don't know, I'm not sure. He saw her dancing and they met. Your father was at a conference. That's how they met."

I looked at the chocolate cake again, turning the plate slowly around in circles on my desk. Bobby Lee's presence downstairs gave me a doctor's-waiting-room feeling, a heaviness that made my stomach clench. I stopped turning my plate and pushed it away.

I could tell that Aunt Bess was nervous too. She kept getting up off the bed and checking the lock on the door. Then she would walk over to the window and check to see if it was locked as well, in the event that Bobby Lee tried to scale the outside wall.

"I wish we had a phone in this room," she said. "I wish that black man, your guard, was around."

"Maurice!" Tommy yelled.

"Yes, him," she said.

"Why?" I asked.

"He's large. Eat your cake."

I pulled the plate back toward me, but made no effort to eat.

"Tommy, are you all right down there? Tommy?" She got down on her hands and knees, looked under the bed, then slowly stood up, shaking her head.

174

"Are you coming with us to Manassas?" I asked.

"Where? Oh, Virginia," she said. She walked back to my bed and sat down with a sigh. "Of course I'm coming. I hope the hotel is nice. And I hope we go to some nice restaurants. That's all I want. A nice restaurant. You know, we haven't gone out to eat once since we won the money? Not once." She shook her head. "Are you sure that's where you want to go?"

I nodded.

"You like the Civil War too. You're just like your father. Theo I mean. Not like your real father." She looked stricken after she said this and quickly stood up, her arms outstretched. "Oh, honey," she said. "This must be so confusing." When she kissed me on the top of my head, I smelled old soft pillows. "I don't know why they waited so long to tell you. They should have told you sooner."

I shrugged and looked down at my desk. I didn't really care when they had told me that Bobby Lee was my father. I couldn't really imagine there being a good time to learn this.

"Have you had any more dreams?" I asked. Aunt Bess sat back down, the bed sagging.

"Dreams? No," she said. "I don't have many dreams any more. I lost the gift. Every so often I get it back, but I lose it again. No one talks to me anymore, I don't see or feel things anymore. I'm over the hill."

"My mother told me you used to talk to dead people," I said.

"Oh, sure. I used to all the time," she said. She shrugged again, then waved her hand in a way that made me wonder if I was one of the few people who didn't talk to dead people.

"Do you think you could talk to my mother?" I asked.

"No, honey. I said I lost the feeling a few years back. It left me."

"Where did it go?" I asked.

"I don't know. Wherever it goes. It just went."

"How did you get it?"

"I was born with it. Some people are born with moles."

"Who did you used to talk to?" I asked.

"Everyone. Friends. Friends of friends. Relatives. Famous people sometimes. Near the end though all I could get was my mother. No matter who I tried to contact, I kept getting my mother. And I didn't want to talk to her when she was alive." Aunt Bess shook her head. "If I thought I could reach your mother, I would try, I would try. But I know I can't. Not anymore. I'm old. It's not my time anymore."

I turned my plate around again and looked out the window. It was dark and I could see the street lamp in front of the Yankee Codger's house burning bright, streaking the night with milky yellow light.

"Why is Bobby Lee here?" I asked.

"He just wants to visit. That's all. That's all he wants to do. He just wants to visit and see you."

"How come I'm not seeing him then?"

"Because he wants to talk to your father first. Do you want more cake?"

"No."

Tommy crawled out from under the bed and walked into the closet and shut the door. Aunt Bess looked at the closet for awhile, began to say, "Tommy," but changed her mind. Instead, she just shook her head.

"I don't know anymore," she said.

"Whatever happened to Baby Girl?" I asked. I knew this was a sensitive subject, one that could provoke tears from Aunt Bess, but I asked anyway. I was still very curious.

"She's in a foster home. Your father called and found out. A family in Chicago. A nice family. She's fine, honey, she's fine. I knew she would be."

Aunt Bess was about to say something else when a commotion broke out downstairs. I heard shouting, first Bobby Lee, then Uncle Frank. A moment later, I heard the front door slam. When I ran over to the window, I saw Bobby Lee get into his truck and drive off. Then Aunt Bess said something in Greek and made the sign of the cross.

CHAPTER NINE

MY HEART STARTED pumping like a Mr. Helpner jumping jack when they called our flight number. I had not slept much the night before in anticipation of our trip and even though I was tired, I was glowing, giving off heat as I stood up and held Aunt Bess's hand. The airport was bright and polished and the terminal hummed with a muffled current of noise and energy as people hurried past on their way to what I assumed were exciting journeys and exotic destinations. We were going to Washington, D.C., to fight in the great Battle of Bull Run, leaving Wilton and Bobby Lee far behind.

"I thought we were flying first class," Uncle Frank said as we got in line to board the plane. He was dressed in his usual black clothes and wearing immense dark sunglasses that wrapped around his large head, securing, I hoped, his hair. The night before I had briefly worried how air travel might effect his toupée.

"I only made accommodations for coach," my father said. He fumbled for our tickets in his front shirt pocket and squinted at them.

"I always fly first class," Uncle Frank said. "You can't sit back there. Those seats are for dwarves."

"Frank, you're not very tall," Aunt Bess said.

"I'm not a dwarf, for chrissakes," he said. "I'm five ten."

Aunt Bess and my father both looked at him.

"Five eight," Uncle Frank said. He grabbed his ticket from my father and walked away.

In line in front of us, a large overweight man in a bright orange sweatshirt and a baseball cap struggled with his luggage, finally dropping his bags and a book in a sloppy heap on the ground.

"Going to break my back," he said to my father who quickly looked back down at our tickets. The man bent over and picked his bags up again, kicking the book ahead of him as he walked. Behind us, a tall dignified man in a blue suit and red tie cradled a small phone against his neck while jotting casually into a thick book that was overflowing with notes and papers. He looked important, statesmanlike and I immediately assumed he was a U.S. senator. Aunt Bess had said we probably would run into a few politicians on the plane, considering our destination.

"I'll call you when I get on the plane," I heard the U.S. senator say. "I'm about to board. Tell him to fax everything to my hotel. The whole thing."

The flight attendant at the door smiled in a bored, mechanical way and looked past us as she tore our tickets in two. My father briefly studied the stubs she returned him before picking up his briefcase and entering the jetway.

I sat in the window seat, next to my father while Tommy and Aunt Bess sat in front of us. Uncle Frank and Maurice sat across the aisle, behind the U.S. senator. I was initially disappointed in the plane. I had imagined it to be more spacious and expected the flight attendants to be glamorous, if not movie stars. Instead, the inside was gray and narrow and the flight attendants old and washed-out looking. I liked the small tables that flipped down from the seat in front of me though. I opened and closed mine several times while my father struggled with our luggage in the overhead bin.

"I hope Sylvanius remembers to water the plants," Aunt Bess said, peering over the back of her seat at us with one dark eye. "And to feed Stavros."

"I'm sure he will," my father said, sitting down. His face was flushed from his efforts with our suitcases.

"Well, he's going to miss some wonderful meals at restaurants," she said.

"Who? Stavros?" Uncle Frank asked.

"No. Sylvanius," Aunt Bess said.

Aunt Bess had wanted Sylvanius to come with us, but Sylvanius had refused, saying he wanted to use the solitude to reflect. Uncle Frank said he wasn't intelligent enough to reflect on anything other than his next free meal and the real reason he didn't come was because he was scared of flying, something Sylvanius didn't deny.

"I don't know why you let him stay in the house," Uncle Frank said to my father from across the aisle.

"Well," my father said. "He asked me. And he really has no place else to go. Besides, he will keep an eye on things."

Uncle Frank shook his head as a man holding what looked to be a guitar case walked between them. Uncle Frank leaned forward and peered around the man. "I think you're pretty trusting, Theo. Pretty damn trusting," he said. "I would have chained him to a tree in the yard until we got back."

"I'm sure everything will be fine," my father said. Then he began to read the safety manual while a flight attendant with blond hair and bright red lipstick began talking about oxygen masks, emergency exits, and ocean landings.

When we took off, Tommy raised his arms up over his head as if he was riding a roller coaster. He also screamed. I gripped my seat handles tight and leaned forward, into the rush of noise and energy. As we climbed into the sky, I felt breathless for a moment, my stomach light and fluttering. The very notion that we were leaving the earth and entering the air thrilled me. I looked over at my father and was disappointed to see that he was calmly leafing through a magazine, our take-off just another opportunity for him to read.

After the plane leveled off, I looked out the window and watched the houses and cars shrink, then disappear altogether under sheets of clouds. I had the urge to draw, but my sketch pad was packed away, so all I could do was watch the clouds drift close and finally surround us.

"Well," my father said, putting the magazine back into the flap in the seat in front of him. "We seem to be safely off. A very smooth departure, don't you think, Teddy?"

"Yes," I said.

"Teddy, I thought you might like to read this, or at least browse through it," he said. He pulled out his briefcase and handed me a book, *Reflections on the Civil War*. "I hope it's not too advanced for you. I have others, but I don't have anything specific on Manassas unfortunately."

I opened the book with exaggerated gusto, turning the pages quickly. "This looks good," I said. "I'm going to read it all right now."

My father gave me a peculiar look then went back to his briefcase.

I tried reading the book for a while, but found my eyes glazing and the words blurring halfway through the first chapter, a tedious explanation of why the war was important. I was tired from a poor night's sleep and sensed a nap was dangerously close. Falling asleep while reading the first Civil War book my father had ever given me would do little to improve my standing with him though, so I closed the book thoughtfully and nodded my head.

"That's neat," I said.

"Excuse me?" my father said. "I'm sorry, you said something?"

"The Civil War, I think it's interesting," I said, sounding like Mrs. Wilcott.

"Well, I'm glad you find the book interesting," my father said. He gave me another odd look through his small, rectangular reading glasses. "The author, Bruce Catton, is quite good. I think he was the best at what he did. He brought the war to life in a way no other writer could. Though Shelby Foote is quite good too. I haven't heard from Shelby in years."

"Why do you like the Civil War so much?" I asked.

My father took off his glasses and rubbed his nose, then returned them to the perch on the tip of his nose. "Well, I suppose I just find it interesting. I find all history interesting. I am a history professor after all."

"But how come you don't like other wars?"

"Oh, well, the Civil War was unique, I suppose. It made this country what we are today. And it did away with a terrible thing."

"Slavery?" I asked.

"Yes," my father said. "I also think that, I think that the Civil War produced more heroes than any other war. Heroes on both sides really. Both sides truly believed in their causes. And the courage that this war required, the courage and faith it demanded were remarkable, just remarkable."

"Why was Bull Run so important?" I had decided that asking questions about the War would be much easier than reading the book.

"Well, as I mentioned, it was the first real battle of the Civil War. And its brutality and the fact that the South won, shocked the world. It made a hero out of Stonewall Jackson. Before that battle, he was just Thomas Jackson."

"How come they started calling him 'Stonewall'?"

My father cleared his throat, obviously warming to the subject. "Well, the Union side was initially winning the battle. For awhile, there were indications that the battle was turning into a route. Many rebel units were, in fact, retreating. Just as the battle seemed lost, a Confederate officer looked up and saw General Jackson's brigade holding its position against the Union onslaught and reportedly cried, 'There's Jackson, standing like a stone wall,' something to that effect. The other rebel units rallied behind Jackson and the tide of the battle was turned. It's really quite inspiring to the rebels," my father said, smiling. "Jackson refused to move. He made a stand. A remarkable stand."

"What was Stonewall Jackson like?" I asked.

"Well, he was a fascinating character really. I have some reading I can give you. He was a brave man, of course, a man of many contradictions. Despite his reputation as a ceaseless fighter, he was very religious and would pray before battle. His troops would see him sitting on his saddle, looking up to heaven, praying. He was killed in Chancellorsville, accidentally, by one of his own men."

"Was he a good fighter. In the War?"

"Yes, brilliant, though every so often he seemed to lose focus, show up late almost, to battle. Still, it was amazing what he did in the valley. He was very mobile and his mobility kept his opponents off guard."

My father was speaking in a fast and excited way, a tone I hadn't heard in awhile.

"What do you mean mobile?" I asked.

"Well, you see, one way to be successful in battle is to keep moving, keep your opponent guessing where your next charge will be. This is particularly effective when you're dealing with a dangerous foe. Simply put, Teddy, if you feel, well, if you feel you're the underdog, you don't want to attack head on. You want to flank them, if you can."

"Flank them?"

My father turned to face me, his eyes bright. "Yes, flank them. Basically, flanking involves movement. Coming at your enemy from an unseen direction. The key is to try and get *around* your enemy somehow, Teddy, and attack from the side or from behind. Draw and hold their attention in one direction and attack from another. Surprise and movement are often the keys to battle. Yes."

Satisfied, my father went back to his briefcase, sorting and rearranging papers and folders. I couldn't bring myself to read my book though. I was still afraid I would fall asleep.

"Did you bring your book?" I asked. "The one you wrote?"

"Oh. Yes, of course. I have it somewhere. Oh, here it is," he said as he handed me *A Civil War Companion*, by Theodore N. Pappas. He returned to his briefcase.

I studied the book. I had never really looked at it before. It was fairly large and on the cover there was a map of part of the United States colored blue and gray.

"It's probably too technical for most people, closer to a textbook really," my father said. He had stopped sorting through his briefcase and was looking warily at me over the tops of his small rectangles.

I opened the book with enthusiasm. On one of the inside pages were the words, "To my parents and to my brother Frank. Thank you for your patience."

"Do you mean Uncle Frank?" I asked, pointing to the page.

"Oh," he said. "I had forgotten about that. It was a long time ago. I wrote that some twenty-five years ago."

A young woman holding a baby walked passed us unsteadily in the aisle. The baby was crying loudly and other passengers turned to look at them. Across the aisle, Uncle Frank looked up, said "Jesus Christ," then went back to his newspaper.

"How come you didn't write any more books?" I asked.

My father looked surprised. "Well, this one book more or less covered everything I had ever wanted to write about. Besides," he said, picking up another book from his briefcase, "it took six years to write and I had to make a living. Writing books about history unfortunately doesn't pay as many bills as I would have liked. And I didn't have a grant. So I guess it was also a function of time and money. Ultimately, I went into teaching and research. I write quite a few articles and papers now, but I don't have time to tackle another book. I barely have time to do my research."

"You can write now," I said. "You don't have to work and do so much research now." Then I said, "We're pretty rich."

My father looked down at me and nodded his head. "Well, I imagine you're right, Teddy. I'll have to remember that. Yes, I'll have to remember that. Maybe I will write another book."

"Why do you like history so much?" I asked. I sensed my father had wandered past the safety of his tower and I wanted to lure him out farther and see him in the light of day.

"Well," he said. "I like to study things. I like to measure things and put them, well, put them in context." He was looking straight ahead, at the back of Aunt Bess's seat, as if he was reading. Then he turned and briefly smiled. "The study of the past fits me, I suppose. I'm comfortable with studying things from an objective view point, from a certain distance." He cleared his throat and returned to his briefcase, sorting through some more papers.

I was quiet for a few moments. "I think you'd be a good writer," I finally said.

He looked back up, surprised. "Well, thank you for your confidence, Teddy," he said. "Thank you." He smiled again, but this time in a different way, in a way that didn't totally disappear.

THE HOTEL WAS much larger than I had imagined, its size and elegance surpassing all my expectations. Walking through the spacious lobby, with its marble tables, thick burgundy rugs, and eager uniformed bellmen, I thought I had walked straight onto the pages of *Luxury Living!* or *Eastern Estates*. I was sure, high atop the hotel, a helicopter pad was silently waiting to receive busy CEOs.

"This is all quite nice," my father said as we made our way to the registration desk, gliding over a sleek polished floor that seemed made of ice.

A tall, thin man with a trimmed white beard was waiting for us by the desk.

"Theodore Pappas. Professor Pappas, is that you?" he asked.

"Yes, I'm Theodore Pappas."

"August Field," the man said as he shook my father's hand. "Dr. August Field. From the Society."

"Oh, yes. We spoke. On the phone," my father said.

"I just want to say that the Society cannot thank you enough for your very generous contribution."

"Contribution?" Uncle Frank said as he walked up behind us, carrying suitcases. "Contribution?"

"Yes," my father said quickly. "Well, it is a worthy cause. And thank you for accommodating us on such short notice."

"Accommodate you, dear sir!" Dr. Field laughed. "You have resurrected the battle, not to mention the Society. We considered renaming the battle Pappas Run." He laughed again.

Uncle Frank looked at my father who cleared his throat and said, "I hardly think that would be necessary. Or appropriate."

"We will be sending a car around to pick up you and your family tomorrow morning for the Battle," Dr. Field said. "We would once again like to extend an invitation to speak at tonight's dinner. You said you would consider it."

My father grimaced and shuffled his feet. "Yes, well, I don't think we will be able to attend. We'll just see you on the grounds tomorrow."

"Well, then," Dr. Field said. He bent down and picked up a long narrow, box that had been laying on the ground. "We were hoping to present this to you tonight, but since that's not possible." He handed the box to my father.

"What's this?" my father asked. He took a few small steps back, away from the box.

Dr. Field smiled. "An exact replica of Stonewall Jackson's sword. We would be honored if you wore it in battle tomorrow."

My father looked confused. "I wasn't planning on participating in the battle. We had just wanted to observe it," my father said.

Dr. Field raised his hand. "Mr. Pappas, please. We would like you to assume the role of Colonel Stonewall Jackson tomorrow and lead his Virginians in their defense against the Army of the Potomac."

The look of fear on my father's face quickly spread to panic. "Oh," he said. Then he said, "Oh my, no. No, no, no. I couldn't possibly. You want me to be Stonewall Jackson? Oh, no."

"If you would like to be someone of a higher rank, we could easily arrange for you to play the role of General Johnston or Beauregard. We have a uniform waiting for you in your room."

"A uniform?" My father was silent for a moment. "Ah, that's why you asked me how tall I was when we spoke on the phone. I thought that odd."

Dr. Field smiled and nodded his head. "Yes!" he said loudly.

"And how much I weighed."

Dr. Field clapped his hands and said, "Yes!" again, even louder.

Just then, Maurice and Aunt Bess walked up with more suitcases.

"Who's he?" Aunt Bess asked. "Is he the bellman?"

"Um, this is Dr. Field."

"August," Dr. Field said as he shook Maurice's hand. "August Field."

"August?" Aunt Bess said.

"He's with the Civil War Group, The Living Dead Society," my father said.

"The Living History Society," Dr. Field said.

"Yes, of course," my father said quickly.

Dr. Field looked down at me and Tommy. "We have two small uniforms for each of you. I understand from your father that you wanted to participate in the battle. You will be part of your father's staff."

"Thank you," I said. The prospect of wearing a uniform excited me terrifically.

"What battle? They aren't going to be in any battle," Aunt Bess said. "They're boys, young boys! Who are they fighting?"

"It's not really a battle, Aunt Bess," my father said.

"What is it then?"

"Well," my father said.

"It's a reenactment," Dr. Field said, cutting my father short. "An authentic reenactment."

Aunt Bess slowly nodded her head like she understood but I could tell that she didn't. Her eyes narrowed and began to suspiciously shift back and forth between my father and Dr. Field.

"So, it's like a play," she said. "You're playacting then and you want the boys to play with you."

"Well," Dr. Field said. "Not exactly."

"Frank," my father interrupted. "Why don't you check us in? I would like to speak with Dr. Field for a moment."

Uncle Frank shook his head and picked up the suitcases. "Let's go everyone."

WE HAD THREE ROOMS on the fourth floor. Maurice, Aunt Bess, and Tommy took the first elevator and my father, Uncle Frank, and I followed in the next. On the ride up, my father informed Uncle Frank that he would be sharing a room with Maurice, a fact Uncle Frank wasn't pleased about.

"What, you got me sleeping with a stranger? You put me with some guy I barely know. We're sharing a bathroom, for chrissakes. A shower. Towels, maybe soap."

"Well, it's just for two nights," my father said.

"He may be one of those guys who walks around naked all the time," Uncle Frank said. He looked down at me. "Some men are like that, you know. They just walk around naked like it's nothing. Especially jocks. They're used to locker rooms. That's all they know."

"Well," my father said. "The rooms here are quite expensive. I just thought we could economize a bit."

"Economize, Jesus Christ, Theo. You got a hundred-and-ninety million in the bank. What are you afraid of, inflation?" He was about to say more but the elevator doors opened, revealing Maurice in the hallway, still fully clothed.

"Jesus Christ," Uncle Frank said, picking up his bag.

Our room was large and airy with a high ceiling and dark blue curtains that were tied back in an elegant way that reminded me we were rich. The carpet was an endless, wall-to-wall lawn of colors, deep green and red. The beds were imposing with four column posts and swooping, white canopies; they looked like two ships docked in a harbor. There was a phone in the bathroom and a small refrigerator in the corner filled with an exotic selection of drinks: papaya juice, soda pop, tonic water, seltzer, lime juice, and cranberry cocktail drink. My father allowed Tommy and I each to choose one. After careful consideration, I decided on the cranberry cocktail drink, thinking it the most refined.

While we were unpacking, we found my father's uniform hanging in the closet. It was as gray as a storm cloud, with bright gold buttons and a black belt that glistened. When my father saw it, he softly said, "Dear God."

"Wow," Tommy said.

"Well," my father said. "I wasn't expecting this." He squinted, thinking. "I imagine your uniforms are here somewhere too." We searched both closets and dressers, but couldn't find them.

A moment later, Uncle Frank knocked on our door. He was holding two small, gray uniforms, miniature versions of my father's. "These were in my room. Or should I say our room. They were on Maurice's side of the room."

"Does Maurice have his clothes on?" I asked.

"So far." Uncle Frank shrugged. "But it's early." Then he left.

"Well," my father said as he hung up our uniforms. "Do you still want to participate in the reenactment? Is this something you would like to do?"

"Yes," I said. I knew he didn't want to, but the idea of wearing a uniform, of marching into battle next to my father, was proving irresistible. "Yes," I said again.

Tommy yelled, "Yeah. I want to shoot people."

My father shook his head. "I don't think there'll be any shooting, Tommy."

IT RAINED ALL DAY, so rather than go visit monuments, my father allowed Tommy and I to play video games in our room, further proof that things in our family were changing. My father held a dim view of video games, actually held a dim view of electricity, yet he allowed us to play for hours while he sat rigidly in a desk chair with a high back, and cleared his throat.

"Well," he said after we had successfully destroyed the last of the attacking Xenoites from the remote planet Xenon. "I think it's time for dinner, don't you think? Your aunt has picked out a special place so I think we should get dressed."

"Are we going to wear our uniforms?" Tommy asked.

My father looked warily over toward the closet. "No. We'll dress like . . . civilians tonight," he said.

We ran into Dr. August Field again in the hotel lobby while we were waiting for the others to join us. He was wearing a blue blazer and a sharp red scarf around his neck that reminded me of Sylvanius. I sensed my father's body stiffen when he approached us.

"Dr. Field," my father said.

"Dr. Pappas. I was wondering if I could have a word with you. I have some maps spread out," he gestured at a table off in the corner. "I would like to show you your position tomorrow. I thought it important that we review your tactics."

"My tactics." My father looked at me for a moment and sighed. "I'll be right over there, Teddy. Please keep an eye on Tommy. We'll leave as soon as the others arrive."

I sat down on an overstuffed couch, while Tommy circled a large fountain in the center of the room. I watched as trickles of water slipped up and over the top of the fountain, sliding down a column and falling into the small pool at the base. Next to the fountain, a sleek black piano played music by itself, a soft melody. Content, I sat back and let the couch swallow me, my only regret being that Johnny Cezzaro was not somehow outside the hotel, standing in the rain, watching me.

"Tommy, don't touch it," I said as Tommy approached the piano. He stared at it, transfixed, as the keys moved.

"There you are," a man's voice said.

I started and sat forward on the couch. A man had suddenly appeared in front of me holding a camera.

"Give us a smile there, buddy," the man said.

I stared at the man as he took my picture, his camera clicking. He had a long, white mustache and as he circled me, the two other cameras that were dangling from his neck swayed back and forth. He took several pictures, his camera whirring and clicking.

"You know, I've been chasing you around all day," he said. "Ever since I heard the news." He was talking fast and breathing heavy. "Okay, one more, and I'm gone," he said. His camera clicked a final time, then he turned and quickly walked away, across the lobby and out into the rain.

"Teddy, who was that?" my father said. He had appeared at my side.

"I don't know," I said.

. . .

WE WENT TO the Statesman, a restaurant Aunt Bess picked out of a magazine in her room because the ad promised elegant dining in a setting where history comes alive. When we got out of the taxicab, we were all disappointed to find a small, somewhat run-down building on a crowded street next to a computer repair store. Once inside, we were equally disappointed and confused to see a small plaque on the wall by the coat check that read, NEPTUNE'S BASKET. ESTABLISHED CIRCA 1973.

"Excuse me?" my father asked. A short man in a rumpled tuxedo who was standing behind what looked to be a podium, briefly looked up. "I think we're possibly in the wrong place."

The man looked over my father's shoulder, out toward the door. "You're in the right place."

"No, we were looking for the Statesman, I believe."

"This is the Statesman," the man said, picking up some menus. "Same restaurant, different name. Follow me, please."

We followed him through the crowded, hot restaurant, weaving between tables, booths, and weary looking waiters with wrinkled faces.

"Nineteen-seventy-three," Aunt Bess said as we were being seated. "What's so historic about nineteen-seventy-three?"

"Watergate," the man said. "Nixon ordered out here once." Then he handed us our menus and left.

When our waiter came to take our drink orders, I was surprised to see my father study the wine list and even more surprised to see him order a glass.

"May I?" Uncle Frank asked my father when the waiter returned with the bottle. My father gave him a disapproving look and Uncle Frank slowly sat back in his chair. "Make that a Diet Coke," he finally told the waiter. "Your finest year though."

The restaurant was long and narrow and reminded me of a PBS show I had once watched about Nazi U-boats in World War II. Our table was directly in the middle of the submarine, where the periscope would be, and had two small candles that threw tiny dancing shadows across the white tablecloth. All around us, older faded couples ate quietly over soft music and whispering waiters.

"This place reminds me of that pancake place," Uncle Frank said. "Back home."

"Oh. Will's," my father said, scanning the restaurant. I watched as his eyes stopped on a large blue swordfish that was mounted on the wall in the corner. "I think this place has a bit more character."

"Let's hope that's all it has," Uncle Frank said. He was holding his fork up to the dim light and studying it. "I haven't had a tetanus shot recently."

Everyone but Tommy ordered crab legs, which were the specialty of the house. When they arrived, a tangled mass of orange and white appendages, I was shocked by all that was involved in eating them.

"What's this for?" I asked, holding up what looked to be a pair of pliers.

"They're for cracking open your crab legs," my father said. He demonstrated with his own pair.

"Let me try," Tommy said, grabbing the pliers out of my hands.

"They don't work on cheeseburgers," Maurice said as he quietly took the pliers away from Tommy.

Throughout dinner, Aunt Bess kept talking about monuments and statues. She had read a tourist magazine in her hotel room and was eager to tour the city.

"I don't understand why there isn't a statue of Washington somewhere," she said. "There's just that monument."

"What's the difference?" Uncle Frank said. He was struggling with a particularly thick crab leg that looked to be still alive.

"What's that pointed thing have to do with him? Lincoln has a nice statue."

"Well," my father said. He wiped his mouth with his napkin and reached for his glass of wine, still chewing some crab. He seemed at ease in this dark restaurant and his face, usually a pinched frown, looked strangely relaxed. "Both Lincoln and Washington deserve memorializing. I think they are the two Americans who upon close study measure up to their, well, deification, if you will. In fact, the more you learn and study them, the more you realize how remarkable they really were. Other great Americans such as Jefferson, or even Roosevelt, don't hold up as well under close scrutiny. But Lincoln and Washington do. In fact, they should each have a dozen statues or monuments built in their honor." My father smiled after this last statement. Realizing that this was his attempt at humor, I smiled back.

He was about to say something else when a dark older woman wearing a brown uniform that stretched tightly over her body, appeared and tapped him on the shoulder. I had noticed the woman clearing off a nearby table while we were being seated, loading dirty dishes and silverware onto a tray. "Excuse me, I'm so sorry to interrupt, but are you the person who won the lottery?" she asked. "I seen the magazine."

My father jumped in his seat. "Yes, yes, I am," he said. "We are."

The woman wrung her hands together nervously. "I'm sorry to interrupt but my grandson, he's sick. He needs a machine to help him eat the food now. The machine, it cost eight thousand dollars. I don't have the money. He needs the money."

Out of nowhere the man in the tuxedo appeared at her side and took her elbow. "Let's go, Rosilita. Let's go now." He looked at my father. "I'm sorry about this. She's a little emotional."

As the man led her away, the woman started crying. "Please! I will pay you back all the money. The insurance, it won't pay for the machine. The doctors say he might die. Please, you must help him. God gave you that money to help people. Please. Help my child."

A confused silence filled the restaurant as people turned and craned their necks our way, their forks and knives frozen in midair. Several of the waiters stopped serving and looked over at us. My father kept his eyes trained on the table while Uncle Frank glared around the room.

"Well," my father said after a few minutes. He picked up his water glass then quickly put it down, spilling some. He cleared his throat.

"Why don't you give the lady some of the money?" It was Tommy.

My father's face reddened and he started to cough. "Well, Tommy," he said. Then he took a deep breath. "You see, it's not quite that simple . . ."

"We can't, Tommy. We can't help everyone," Uncle Frank said. I looked up at him, surprised at the gentle and slow tone of his voice.

"Who are we helping then?" Tommy said. He picked up a french fry and licked some ketchup off its tip. "We should give her some of our money. She was crying."

"Maybe we will, honey," Aunt Bess said. "Maybe we will."

We all started eating again. Out of the corner of my eye, I watched my father continue to stare at the table. His face was blotched alarmingly red, and his chin hung low.

"Well," he said, picking up his fork.

We pretty much cracked our crabs in silence after that and didn't order dessert.

WHEN WE GOT back to the hotel, Dr. August Field and another tall man with a beard whom he introduced as Dr. Henry Hunter, were waiting for us in the lobby. My father seemed to be expecting them.

"And how was dinner, Professor?" Dr. Field asked smiling.

"It was fine, it was fine," my father said. It was the first he had spoken since the incident in the restaurant and I could tell from his tone of voice that he was tired and wanted to be left alone.

"Well, we'd like to complete our earlier review of tactics." He made a fist and punched the air with it. "We have a battle to fight tomorrow, after all."

My father sighed. "Yes," he said. "I suppose we do. Teddy, why don't you stay with me for awhile? You might find it educational. Frank, Mr. Jackson, Aunt Bess, we'll see you all back at the rooms."

After everyone else left, Dr. Field and Dr. Henry spread out some maps on a low table in the middle of the lobby. Two men who were smoking cigars on a nearby couch looked over at us and eyed the maps. I sat down next to my father and watched Dr. Henry Hunter light his pipe.

"I'd like to start with a brief review of tomorrow's menu," Dr. Field said.

"Menu?" my father asked.

"Yes, we have secured three different caterers. Southern cuisine will be emphasized, particularly at the banquet. But we will have heavy appetizers throughout the battle, as well as a selection of wines."

Dr. Hunter drew on his pipe and nodded in agreement. "French wines," he said.

"We're eating? And drinking? During the battle?" my father asked.

"We are expecting more than three thousand people tomorrow," Dr. Field said. "Spectators as well as participants. We felt we had to offer them something throughout the day. We want to make this entertaining, as well as educational. We're competing with a number of other groups for members you know." He unfolded a piece of paper and tried to present it to my father. "Would you like to see the menu, approve it? The wine list is attached."

My father looked at the paper as if it were radioactive, then shook his head.

"We've also secured the very best Abraham Lincoln in the country, thanks to your funding," Dr. Hunter said.

My father, who had been sinking hopelessly back into the overstuffed couch, struggled forward. "Pardon me?" he asked. "I'm sorry?"

"A professional Abraham Lincoln impersonator, I should say," Dr. Hunter said with a laugh. "I saw him last year myself at the Cold Harbor event. Very inspiring."

"A professional," my father said. "I didn't know there were people who impersonated Lincoln. People who did things like that, for a living."

"Oh, yes, he's quite busy. He was scheduled to do something with the Fredericksburg group, but we snapped him up at the very last minute. Stole him away, actually. We simply outbid them."

My father was silent as the two doctors began pointing to the map.

"Lincoln, of course, was nowhere near the Battle of Bull Run," my father said after a few moments.

Dr. Field smiled and nodded his head while Dr. Hunter relit his pipe.

"Of course we know this, Professor," Dr. Field said slowly.

"Do you think it right then that he be there, tomorrow? For accuracy's sake?"

Dr. Field cleared his throat. "We, of course, debated this. But he is such a good Lincoln, such a wonderful Lincoln, that we simply could not resist. We've tried to get him before but have always lacked the funding. Now though . . ." Dr. Field didn't finish. Instead, he simply laughed.

"Well, what role will he have?" my father asked. "This Lincoln. What will he do exactly? Surely he won't fight in the battle. He's the president. Was the president."

"No, of course not. We think he's going to give a brief speech before hand, welcoming everyone. Then he'll work the audience, as they say." Dr. Field had a proud look on his face and nodded his head.

"Excuse me?" my father said.

193

"Meet some of the spectators," Dr. Hunter said. "Many of them are members of the Society. Others are considering membership and we need their support. We need to grow."

"Oh, I see," my father said. "So it's more of an ambassador's role."

"Yes, yes, yes," Dr. Field said. "That's an accurate description. And he has a beautiful voice. When he sings 'Dixie,' you'll be hard pressed not to stomp your feet and join right in."

My father was startled at this statement. "Excuse me? Did you say sings 'Dixie'? This Abraham Lincoln sings?"

"Yes," Dr. Hunter said. "He'll do a few period pieces. He and Mary. Mary Lincoln."

"Mary Todd Lincoln is singing also?" my father asked. He looked frightened.

"Yes, yes. They sing a duet," Dr. Hunter said. "Wonderful voices."

"Yes, wonderful," Dr. Field agreed. "You'll be very impressed. The songs themselves have historical value, in addition to being entertaining. Music had a definite role in the war, as you know."

"Yes, I know," my father said softly. "But I don't believe there is any record of Lincoln himself singing. Especially before a battle."

Dr. Hunter and Dr. Field were quiet for a moment. I could smell Dr. Hunter's pipe burning and watched a thin line of smoke rise from its center. It smelled sweeter than Maurice's pipe.

"Well, we can always reconsider his performance," Dr. Field said after awhile. "If you're opposed to it."

"No, no, please, don't make any changes on my behalf. I was just taken by surprise," my father said as he put on his glasses and began studying the map.

Afterward, on the elevator ride back up to our rooms, my father seemed worried. It was apparent that he had not liked the way the meeting had gone. Throughout the discussion, he had kept clearing his throat and mumbling about "inconsistencies," though when Dr. Field and Dr. Hunter pressed him, he merely shook his head. As the meeting was ending, he had once again tried to refuse the role of Stonewall Jackson, but the doctors were insistent.

"I worry that tomorrow's battle may not be quite as educational as I would have hoped for you, Teddy," he said as the elevator doors opened.

"There seems to be more of a theatrical element involved that I didn't anticipate."

"Do you want to be Stonewall Jackson?" I asked. I had a hard time imagining my father leading men in battle.

"Well, to be truthful, I have reservations," he said as we walked down the wide hallway to our room. "I don't feel comfortable. Fortunately, not much is required of me. Apparently, I'll just stand and wave my sword."

"Are you going to kill anyone with your sword?"

"No, no, no. I don't plan on, well, killing anyone." He sighed. "And neither will you, of course. You and Tommy won't actually participate in the battle. You'll be off to the side somewhat."

"I know," I said. Dr. Field had discussed this with my father and agreed that Tommy and I could wear the uniforms and possibly hold a Confederate flag up until the start of the battle. Then a slave would escort us off to watch the event from a golf cart, where we would have a cold pasta and salmon salad for lunch.

"Do you think Maurice minds?" I asked.

"What?" my father asked as he fumbled in his pocket for the key to our room.

"Do you think Maurice minds us fighting for the Confederate side? They liked slavery, didn't they? They had slaves."

My father stopped looking for his key. He was surprised by my question.

"Well, I never really had thought about that. That's very . . . perceptive of you, Teddy. The thought hadn't even occurred to me. I certainly wouldn't want to offend Mr. Jackson." He stood still and stared at the floor, thinking. Then he took a deep breath and began fumbling for the key again. "Well, I'll ask him about this tomorrow. Hopefully, he'll understand that we are merely recognizing history, not glorifying a cause. Well, then," he said as he opened the door.

THE NEXT MORNING while my father was clearing his throat in the bathroom, Abraham Lincoln called.

"Is Professor Pappas available?"

"No, he's in the bathroom," I said.

"Well, if you could please give him a message, Abraham Lincoln would be mighty obliged. Tell him that the entire Society would once again like to thank him for his generosity and for making this battle happen." I thought I heard Dr. Field or Dr. Hunter's voice in the background, then Abraham Lincoln said, "The president thanks and commends him for his duty to his country."

"Okay," I said. I was watching Tommy try to put his uniform pants on. He had worn both his little gray cap and jacket to bed and both were now wrinkled. I already had my uniform on and liked everything about it, right down to the black stripe that ran sharply down the side of my pant legs like a dark thunderbolt. I had already spent a good part of the morning admiring myself in the mirror.

"Can I ask you a question?" Abraham Lincoln asked.

"Okay," I said.

"Is there a particular song your father likes? Does he have a special song? I'd like to surprise him. It really doesn't have to be related to the war."

I tried to think of a song that Abraham Lincoln could sing to my father but couldn't.

"Maybe a show tune?" Abraham Lincoln asked.

I wasn't sure what a show tune was. "No. I don't think he likes show tunes," I said.

"Well, if something comes to mind, pull me aside at the battle and let me know. We want this to be a special day for your daddy. He's the man and we aim to please," Abraham Lincoln said, chuckling.

"Okay," I said.

As soon as I hung up, the phone rang again. This time it was Mrs. Wilcott. Her chipmunk voice sounded higher and more animated than usual, scraping my ears.

"Teddy, is your father there? I must speak to him. Right away, sweetheart. Please."

"He's in the bathroom," I said. Tommy was sitting on the floor still wrestling with his pants.

"Has anyone else talked to him yet?" she asked. "Has anyone else called?"

"No." I decided not to tell her about Abraham Lincoln. I wanted to get off the phone and look at myself in the mirror some more.

"Teddy, please this is important. Can you get your father?"

I heard the shower running from inside the bathroom and knew that in a few moments my father would begin turning into Stonewall Jackson.

"He's in the bathroom," I said.

"Well, please have him call me as soon as he can."

"Okay," I said, though I had no intention of relaying her message.

A few minutes later, my father emerged from the bathroom, a wall of steam rising behind him. I watched as he took the uniform from the closet and carefully laid it on the bed. Then he began to put it on.

He took a long time getting dressed. Moving between the bedroom and the bathroom, he struggled, first with the pants which were too tight, then with the shiny black belt. Finally, he decided against wearing the belt. "I doubt General Jackson wore one," he said. "I don't believe there's any record of it."

Once dressed, he stood in front of the mirror and stared at himself. Then he turned and faced us. I was amazed. My father had disappeared. His round shoulders had broadened and his soft face now had a lean alive look that I found thrilling. When he put his large gray hat on, his transformation was complete. He looked brave and stout, clearly in focus, and I suddenly wished my mother could see him.

"Well," he said.

Tommy looked up from the floor, his leg still tangled in his pants. "Wow," he said.

A SMALL REGIMENT of Virginia infantry greeted us in the hotel lobby, ten men wearing Confederate uniforms of varying shades of gray. A few of them held what looked to be old-fashioned rifles, their barrels shaped like snouts.

One of the soldiers, a large older man about my father's age with a drooping gray mustache stepped forward and saluted us as we approached.

"Atten-hut!" he yelled.

My father stopped dead in his tracks and instinctively grabbed my and Tommy's hands.

"Dear God," he said softly.

The group of soldiers stood ramrod straight, looking off in the distance, over our shoulders. A Japanese couple who had been drinking coffee in one of the overstuffed couches, quickly walked over and began taking our pictures, nodding and smiling furiously.

"Colonel Jackson," the soldier with the mustache barked. "Your limousine is waiting."

WE SAT IN THE BACK of the white stretch limousine and waited for Aunt Bess, Uncle Frank, and Maurice for awhile. The soldier with the drooping mustache, Sergeant Hardy, sat facing us, his back to the driver's. Rather than revel in the luxury of the limousine, I kept my eyes on Sergeant Hardy. He had a wild, Mr.-Sean-Hill look and feel about him that made me nervous.

"Nice car," he said.

"Yes, it is," my father said. He still held onto our hands.

"Big," Sergeant Hardy said.

My father agreed. "Yes, it is." Then he cleared his throat. "And where are you from?"

Sergeant Hardy drew a deep breath, looked out the window, his eyes a squint.

"Cold Harbor, Chancellorsville, and . . ." he looked back at us, his eyes full of meaning and suffering. "Gettysburg."

"Well," my father said. "You've been . . . busy."

"Made Pickett's Charge." He held up three fingers. "Three times."

"Ah." My father nodded. "That must have been tiring. That was . . . quite a charge."

"Keeps me in shape." As Sergeant Hardy talked, I began to notice that he was developing an accent, drawing his words out in a strange way like he was dragging them over a hot sidewalk. He sounded like Bobby Lee.

We were quiet for awhile. I kept looking out the window for everyone else. Despite its spaciousness, the limousine was beginning to feel cramped and hot. On the other side of my father, Tommy squirmed.

"Where are you from, geographically?" my father asked. "Where is your home. In, well, real life?" I was surprised that he was trying to make conversation. This usually wasn't his way, particularly with strangers.

"Pittsburgh," Sergeant Hardy says. "Born and raised. That's where my practice is." He stopped, then said, "Gynecology."

"Ah," my father said.

When Aunt Bess and Uncle Frank got in the car, I had to move over and sit next to Sergeant Hardy. He smelled dank and musty, like I imagined war smelled.

Aunt Bess seemed impressed with the limousine. Her eyebrows arched excitedly over the rims of her large, round sunglasses. Uncle Frank though, seemed uninterested and merely looked out the window.

"Where's Maurice?" I asked as the driver started the car.

My father cleared his throat. "Well, he said he had some friends here in Washington, so I encouraged him to go visit them. I think we'll be fine."

I was disappointed that Maurice wasn't coming and feared my comment about slavery the night before had something to do with his absence. I didn't say anything to my father though. I just looked out the window, away from Sergeant Hardy.

As we drove, first through the crowded streets of Washington, then through quiet country highways, Uncle Frank kept asking Sergeant Hardy questions about the battle.

"Who wins this thing again?" he asked. "Bull Run? Who won it?"

Sergeant Hardy smiled. "We did, the South! And it's all because of that man over there," he said, pointing to my father, who at that exact moment was seriously examining a small thread on the sleeve of his uniform, pulling it with his fingers.

"Is this thing orchestrated? Choreographed or anything? How does everyone know where to go?" Uncle Frank asked.

"That's all worked out," Sergeant Hardy said. "We pretty much line up on one side and the Yankees line up on the other and we start shooting. It all comes together pretty good. Everyone in this group is a veteran. They know what to do."

"They don't use real bullets, do they?" Aunt Bess asked.

"Naw, 'course not." Sergeant Hardy from Pittsburgh was dragging his words again. "We use black powder, makes a good noise. If someone points a gun at you and shoots, you drop."

Uncle Frank looked at Sergeant Hardy and my father, examining their uniforms. "I have to admit it, you guys look good, like the real deal," he said. "The real deal." Then he looked out the window.

When we got to the parking lot of the battle, Sergeant Hardy left without so much as a salute. Within seconds, Dr. Field found us. He was dressed resplendently in a blue uniform with a gold braid that hung down low from his jacket lapel, and a stiff, sharp blue cowboy hat that had two tiny swords crossing in the front. He was also wearing a monocle in his eye. Standing next to him was a fat woman wearing a long, hooped skirt and a bonnet on her head. She was holding an umbrella and when she smiled, she looked like a very pretty pig.

"General Jackson!" Dr. Field said to my father. "I'm so glad your uniform fits! We were so worried."

"Yes," my father said. He was looking around the parking lot at the countless campers and minivans that were dislodging fresh troops. Everywhere I looked, I saw men in blue and gray uniforms, polishing their weapons and boots and urgently grilling hot dogs and hamburgers on small, smoking barbecues.

"You look very, well, authentic, yourself," my father said, looking at Dr. Field. "Who are you supposed to be reenacting again?"

"McDowell," he said.

"I didn't know he had a vision problem," my father said, gesturing toward Dr. Field's monocle.

"It's my interpretation," Dr. Field said. Then, turning to the fat woman he said, "May I introduce Miss Anna Bell Smith?"

The fat woman curtsied and smiled.

"She'll be Mrs. Pappas's hostess this afternoon."

"Miss Pappas," Aunt Bess said. She looked suspiciously at Anna Bell Smith. "I don't need a hostess."

"You don't want to spend all day out in the hot sun," Miss Anna Bell Smith said. She had an accent and sounded like Sergeant Hardy wanted to sound. "That's no place for a lady of your breeding."

"My breeding?"

"Come on now," Anna Bell Smith said, hooking her arm into Aunt Bess's. "We'll stroll over to the pavilion and have some refreshments, then go watch the men fight."

As she was being led away, Aunt Bess looked over her shoulder at my father for help, but he merely waved his hand. "I think that might be the best

200

place for you, Aunt Bess," he called out after her. I tried to follow where Aunt Bess was going but soon lost her in the bright sun.

"Frank," my father asked. "Would you like to join her?"

"No," Uncle Frank said. "I'm going to stay here, with you."

Just then, a small, thin black man approached us. He was dressed in torn rags and walked with the aid of a crutch.

"Oh," Dr. Field said. "You found us. Wonderful. Dr. Pappas, this is Taupe. Taupe Bogi. He'll be your personal slave, Midas Johnson."

Midas Johnson smiled brightly, his teeth an amazing flash of white. "Massa," he said.

My father staggered backward a few feet and I was afraid he might fall. I tried to remember if he had taken his antiheart-attack pills that morning in the hotel.

"Taupe," Dr. Field said quickly. He looked worried. "Mr. Bogi, why don't you meet us at the battlefield. We'll be there shortly."

Midas Johnson smiled again. "Ah's goin' to da war, Mr. General. Ah's goin' to fight da damn Yankee. We goin' to whoop him, we's gonna give him such a beatin'." Then he laughed and put his crutch over his shoulder and sauntered off.

My father was speechless.

"He's an actor," Dr. Field said. "We don't have any African-Americans in the Society, so we hired him for his role. He's really quite accomplished. He's been in *Cats*."

"*Cats*," Uncle Frank said, impressed.

"The traveling troupe," Dr. Field whispered.

"I want to fight," Uncle Frank said suddenly. "What the hell, I want in on this too. I'm here, for chrissakes." He turned to Dr. Field. "Give me a uniform, what the hell. I want something comfortable. Pleats maybe."

A look of concern emerged over Dr. Field's face, spreading like a shadow. He took his monocle out of his eyes and rubbed his chin. "Unfortunately, Mr. Pappas, unfortunately, it's not that simple. You see, we have no extra uniforms."

"What?" Uncle Frank angrily took off his black wraparound sunglasses and pointed his chin at Dr. Field.

"Everyone brings their own uniforms," Dr. Field said. "The Society doesn't actually own any uniforms. The Society doesn't actually own anything, other than letterhead."

"What the hell kind of deal is this?" Uncle Frank said. "We're producing this goddamn show."

Dr. Field looked at my father who was still recovering from the shock of being told that he had a personal slave. Next to us, two more Yankee soldiers got out of a shiny black minivan and, with military precision, began to assemble a large barbecue grill.

"Well, to be honest, I don't know how we can accommodate . . ." Dr. Field said.

Uncle Frank cut him off. "I want to be one of those guys, you know," he said, snapping his fingers, "Grant or Lee."

"Frank," my father said calmly. "Grant was not here, at this battle."

"Where the hell was he?"

My father sighed. "He was out west."

"Where was Lee?"

My father cleared his throat. "Lee, well, was . . ." his voice trailed off. "Lee was somewhere else."

Uncle Frank's chest swelled and his chin looked like it was about to explode.

"Professor Pappas, may I have a word with you?" Dr. Field asked.

While my father and Dr. Field walked a short distance away to discuss the situation, Uncle Frank put his black sunglasses on again and folded his arms across his chest.

"*You* got a uniform," he said.

"Mr. Pappas," Dr. Field said, smiling as he returned. "We think we have a solution. You will work in the Union commissary."

Uncle Frank first absorbed this without reaction, then scowled. "Commissary! I'm going to be a cook! A goddamn cook!"

"Head cook," my father said quickly.

Uncle Frank looked back and forth between my father and Dr. Field then let out a deep breath. "Lee or Grant, one of those guys should have been here," he said. He stormed off, into the ocean of sunlight, soldiers, and Weber grills.

"Well," Dr. Field said. "If you'll please follow me, Dr. Pappas."

He lead us out of the parking lot and up a small wooded hill. Walking on the small path covered with soft brown pine needles, my heart began to race. Up ahead I could hear the low thunder of drums beating, of men moving. We emerged from the woods, back out into the full sunlight. My father took Tommy and me by the hand.

Below us, in a wide, grassy field were hundreds of soldiers, marching. They moved in small groups, synchronized blocks of blue and gray, their boots hitting the ground and kicking up dust with surprising precision. Cannons mounted on crazily large-wheeled carriages rolled by, pulled by sleek black horses with mean hooded eyes. Off to the sides, dozens of gray and green tents shimmered in the sun. When the marching band that was in the middle of the field, struck up the song "Dixie," I felt a lump in my throat.

Dr. Field faced us and smiled. "Welcome to Bull Run, Dr. Pappas," he said.

My father was dumbstruck, his mouth helplessly open. "Manassas," he whispered, "Manassas."

"THIS PASTA SALAD is heavenly," Midas Johnson said. "To die for."

Tommy and I were sitting in a golf cart by the woods finishing our lunch and listening to Abraham Lincoln sing the final verse of "Old Man River."

"If that old coot sings one more song," Midas said.

Despite its promise, the afternoon had proceeded slowly. There were a number of drilling competitions with the soldiers marching up and down the field while Dr. Field and Dr. Hunter and some other men judged them. Then there was a painfully dull uniform inspection that dragged on, followed by a brief rifle, shooting contest which my father made us stand too far away from for us to really see what was happening. Finally, there had been a number of speeches, lectures really, on the battle and why it was important. Throughout all these activities, no one had said a word about Tommy and my roles as flag carriers. I was beginning to feel left out.

"I want to go home," Tommy said.

"You and me both," Midas Johnson said, sipping some bottle water.

"Boys!" I turned and saw my father walking toward us, followed by Sergeant Hardy who was carrying a small cellular phone and a glass of wine.

At first I didn't recognize my father. He was walking at an unusually brisk pace, his arms swinging by his sides.

"Is everything all right?" he said. He was sweating heavily, large, dark circles spreading under the arms of his uniform. But he was smiling.

"Yes!"

"Daddy, I want to fight," Tommy said.

"Yes, that will be starting momentarily, yes. Since I don't know where your uncle is, would you like to go sit with your aunt, up there?" He pointed toward some bleachers full of people, across the field. Up at the very top, I thought I could see Aunt Bess.

"No, this is good. Can't we get closer though?" We were entirely too far away from the battlefield.

"It might be dangerous out there," my father said. "I think this is a safe distance."

"They'll be fine, Stonewall," Midas said. "Really."

My father looked briefly at Midas. His first official act as Stonewall Jackson had been to liberate him, freeing him to watch the drills and eat lunch with us.

Just then, a small man on a motorized wheelchair approached us, bouncing hard over the ground. A red pennant that was attached to the back of the chair hung limply in the heavy air.

"Dear God," my father said. "It's Otto. I thought he was dead. I recall sending his wife a condolence card."

"We received your card with great amusement, Professor Pappas," Otto said as his wheelchair came to a halt, inches from where we were standing. He was wearing a sharply starched Confederate uniform that had a number of red and blue medals pinned up and around the lapel. Despite the wheelchair, he looked vigorous and healthy and I wondered if the wheelchair was part of the reenactment, if he had been somehow already wounded.

"Dr. Hillcrest," my father said. "I don't know, well, what to say. I heard from the faculty . . ."

Otto raised his hand, motioning my father to stop. "Yours wasn't the only card I received, though it was the last." His eyes were keen and clear and when he talked his small gray goatee bounced along with his words, like a moving target. He looked briefly at me, but registered no reaction. Then he turned back to my father. "I'm here to say that I resent you. I was slated to play the role of Stonewall Jackson but apparently your newfound wealth has won you some important friends in the Society. Congratulations. I'm sure you'll perform admirably, considering you've had two or three days to prepare for the role I researched for twenty-eight years."

My father cleared his throat and looked at the ground. "To be honest, Doctor, I had no desire to usurp your command."

Otto once again raised his hand. "Please. I know I can't compete with what you bring to this event. Salmon, wine, singing Abraham Lincolns. I'm just a simple professor from tiny Coe College. I'm not here to debate that issue with you. Rather, I want to officially register a protest against your upcoming paper comparing Rommel to Robert E. Lee. I think it is an odious comparison."

My father looked up, startled. "How did you hear about that? I haven't even completed it."

Otto smiled. "I may not have your vast wealth, Professor, but I have friends. I know all about it. And I think it's reprehensible. Comparing the two."

"Well," my father cleared his throat. "Well, the similarities abound really," he said. "Both were superb military leaders, fighting for corrupt causes."

"According to my source, you imply that Rommel, a vital cog in the Nazi war machine, was morally superior to Lee."

My father stared at Otto.

"I demand an explanation," Otto said.

"Colonel Jackson!" Sergeant Hardy interrupted. He had been pressing the cell phone close to his ear. "We must report to our battle positions."

Otto leaned forward in his wheelchair, his face set and determined.

"Well," my father said. "I simply stated that Rommel participated in the plot to kill Hitler, in effect, attempted to end the war, while Lee continued to fight in what was obviously a lost cause. He had the power to end the war months before he finally did. I didn't make any moral judgments, none intentionally."

"I think it nothing but another contemptible attempt at grandstanding on your part. And I have officially resigned my post on General Johnston's staff today in protest! I wish you well in your battle now. I know you spent enough on it. What's next, Theo? Are you going to buy the Lincoln Memorial, drag it home with you? It might make a wonderful lawn ornament." With that, Otto whirled the wheelchair around and rode off, bouncing into the overwhelming bright sunlight, the little red pennant, a black and disappearing dot.

"Well," my father said. He looked at me, embarrassed, his uniform soaking wet.

"My, my," Midas said.

"Colonel Jackson!" Sergeant Hardy yelled.

My father cleared his throat. "Dr. Hillcrest and I have quite a history," he started.

"Colonel! The battle is beginning!"

My father was hesitant to leave. He sighed. "Well, Teddy, I originally came over to tell you that this is not how the battle really took place. They've taken a number of liberties, a number of them. We're not on the original grounds for example, and there's no creek, no Bull Run. Actually, other than the uniforms, nothing about this battle resembles the original, as far as I can tell."

"Are you going to flank anyone?" I asked. "Surprise and movement?"

My father looked confused. "I'm sorry? Oh, flanking. No, I, we . . ."

"Colonel Jackson!"

"Well," my father said.

Then a cannon fired and my father marched off to war.

THE BATTLE STARTED slowly, in a confused, halting way. The blue-coated Union troops advanced and then retreated several times, making their way back and forth across the field. Every so often a cannon would roar and some men would fall to the ground, flatten down to the earth, then rise up again. From where we were sitting, I couldn't see my father. Midas told me that he was positioned on a small ridge behind the other side of the field near the bleachers where Aunt Bess was sitting.

"We can't see anything here. Let's get some better seats," Midas said as he started the golf cart.

We drove around the perimeter of battle, near a number of small but brightly decorated food and refreshment stands that I noticed for the first time.

"Sushi," Midas said as we drove past. "Yum."

We were deep into the Union lines, weaving between the tents, when we came upon Uncle Frank standing by a huge smoking grill. He was holding a large fork in his hand, passing out food to a growing line of Union soldiers.

"This is your third filet, for chrissakes," he was saying to a fat Union soldier when we drove up. "This is a battle, not a buffet! Why don't you go try to kill someone?"

"Uncle Frank!" Tommy yelled.

Uncle Frank turned to look at us. "What the hell?" Nearby a cannon roared. Then he looked at Midas Johnson and took off his white apron and threw it on the ground. "Get out of that goddamn golf cart."

THE UNION WAS clearly winning. The gray line of soldiers was disappearing back into the woods that lined the rectangular field. Watching the battle reminded me of the board game Stratego, with one color overpowering the other. I still hadn't seen my father.

The fighting was intensifying though, so I didn't mind. The ground shook with cannon explosions and the air was thick with smoke. We were much closer to the fighting now and I could see the grim look of the soldiers' faces, hear their grunts and screams, the rattle of their guns and swords, as they charged and swarmed each other, throwing their bodies wildly about. Few, if any, were drinking wine.

Uncle Frank drove the golf cart right into the heart of the Union headquarters camp where we found Dr. Field peering intently at a map, holding his monocle with one hand and a chocolate-covered strawberry with the other. He was standing in front of a large, green tent that had an American flag hanging crookedly over its entrance. Nearby, three wounded men lay on the ground, holding their stomachs in bloodless agony, moaning for water. One was trying very hard, it seemed, to cry.

Dr. Henry Hunter rode up on a fat, white horse with bloodshot eyes and a dirty brown mane. He dismounted slowly, his foot catching for a moment in the stirrup. When the horse took a few steps, he had to hop along with it until he was able to free himself. He was dressed similarly to Dr. Field except he was wearing snow-white gloves that matched his spotless white hat in which a red feather was stuck, growing it seemed.

He approached Dr. Field, readjusted his feather, and saluted.

"General McDowell," he yelled. Nearby, a bugle sounded, piercing the air. Tommy covered his ears.

"General McDowell," Dr. Hunter yelled again, saluting once more.

Dr. Field put the strawberry in his mouth and smartly returned the salute.

"Mr. Custer," he said, swallowing. "How goes the good fight?"

"We've flanked them, sir, now we must finish them."

Dr. Field shook his historic head. At this news, other soldiers quickly emerged from the nearby Starbucks tent and gathered around him. They stood in silence around the map, waiting, blowing on hot cups of coffee and cappuccino. Dr. Field surveyed the group and filled his chest with air.

"Is Colonel Jackson in place?" he asked.

"Yes, I believe he is."

Dr. Field returned to the map, tracing some unseen line with his finger. The other generals drew tight, heads drawn to the map.

"Hell," Uncle Frank said under his breath. "I didn't know they had a Starbucks here."

Dr. Field, with great practice and deliberation took off his stiff hat and placed it over his heart. "May God have mercy on us all," he said. Then he placed the hat back firmly onto his head and raised his fist in the air. "Commence the attack!" he yelled.

"Oh, this must be the final scene," Uncle Frank said, backing up the golf cart. "This could be good."

We drove around and past some more tents and onto the edge of the battlefield where a large number of Union soldiers were massing, standing side by side, checking their guns. A man on a horse was in front of them, waving a sword, his face, fiercely red, his voice hard and bloody. Behind him, on the field, I saw another cannon roar and a group of Confederate soldiers who had been trying to advance, disperse, falling to the ground. The man's horse kicked up in the air at the sound of the explosion.

"Men, the rebels are beaten!" The man on the horse yelled. "That secess scum got itself an ass-whooping courtesy of the U.S. Army of the Potomac."

The group of soldiers, which was getting larger, cheered and hollered. One threw his hat in the air.

"Let's run those rebs back to their mammies," the man on the horse yelled. The men cheered again.

"There's one more brigade, holding out, back by that ridge that needs to be reminded who they're fighting against. Let's teach those boys a lesson."

"Stonewall Jackson," a soldier yelled.

The men cheered again.

"Yes. Mr. Jackson must be dealt with," the man on the horse yelled.

Uncle Frank started up the golf cart. "Let's go tip Theo off," he whispered.

"Hey, where are you going with that golf cart?" the man on the horse yelled as we drove onto the battlefield. His eyes were on fire, his face a beet. "You can't take that on the field."

Uncle Frank violently turned the steering wheel and stepped on the gas pedal. "Go to hell," he yelled.

WE DROVE AS FAST as the golf cart could go, me, Tommy, and Uncle Frank in the front seat. All around us on the battlefield, men were shooting, screaming, and dying. The air smelled like pepper and dirt and I felt an electric current humming through me as Uncle Frank maneuvered around dead soldiers.

I cupped my hand to Tommy's ear. "This is all make-believe," I shouted over the din, as much to calm myself as well as him. Tommy just clapped his hands and started screaming.

When I looked over my shoulder, I saw the man on the horse riding toward us, followed by a long, blue line of running Yankees.

I closed my eyes and held onto Tommy. "Uncle Frank," I yelled over the roar. "Hurry up! They're coming."

Up ahead I could see a hill, a small rise on the flat field. The golf cart was bouncing now, jerking violently from side to side, and I found myself fighting to keep from falling out. Several Union soldiers yelled at us as we passed, some even pounding on the cart.

When another cannon roared and a small group of rebels fell in front of us, Uncle Frank swerved sharply and the golf cart tipped over.

Tommy and I were thrown free of the cart, falling nearby on the hard ground. When I looked up, I saw that the Yankees were upon us, then passing us, advancing toward the hill.

"Are you all right?" Uncle Frank yelled.

"I'm okay," I said. I sat up and searched for my hat. Tommy stood up and pointed toward the hill.

"Daddy!" he yelled and started running.

"Tommy, don't!" I got up and ran after him, surrounded by grunting and screaming men. Up ahead, Tommy ran laughing.

As we approached the ridge, there was a terrible scream from behind it, the full-throated yell of rebel men. Then there was a dense blast of noise and smoke, followed by a repeated banging and thumping. The ground shook again, and everywhere Union troops fell in apparent agony. The man on the horse died gloriously, waving his sword over his head before slumping in his saddle.

I stopped running and stood there, swirling, caught in the moment. Then I started yelling too, raising my fist in the air, jumping up and down like a rebel.

Nearby, a soldier who had been shot, stood up, clutching his invisible wound in his chest, invisible blood leaking through his fingers. "Over there," he yelled, pointing his sword. "There's Jackson, standing like a stone wall!" I looked toward the small ridge and that's when I finally saw my father. He was slipping down the hill, crawling really, on his hands and knees, struggling to gain balance. For a moment, he disappeared entirely, stumbling backward and out of sight. Then there was another blast and I fell on the ground and covered my face. All around me, I felt soldiers rushing past and heard more rebel yells and Yankee cries. When I opened my eyes, I saw my father standing solidly in the midst of all the smoke and noise, standing in the midst of everything. He was waving his sword, dying and fighting men at his feet, a defiant look in his eye. Standing impossibly tall, like Stonewall Jackson.

CHAPTER TEN

IN THE LIMOUSINE, on the way back to the hotel, my father wouldn't stop talking.

"As you know, Teddy, that was not an authentic reenactment of Manassas. That was really more of a, well, representative interpretation of a Civil War battle. If anything, it resembled Pickett's Charge at Gettysburg with, of course, the Union and rebel roles being reversed. Still though, I found it interesting. Yes. The uniforms and weapons were remarkable and the quality of some of the drilling exercises, particularly the marching was excellent. And did you see the southern footwear? It was very realistic. The old boots and shoes. Did you notice how many of them fought barefoot?"

"We must have missed that, Theo," Uncle Frank said.

We had been among the very last people to leave the Blue and Gray Banquet that followed the battle. We stayed late into the night, my father reluctant to go back to the hotel. Throughout the evening, he had walked proudly around from table to table, almost strutting, his uniform splattered with mud, his sword sheathed at his side. Wherever he went, Union and Confederate officers congratulated him on his heroic stand, a job well done.

"The food was very good," Aunt Bess said. She looked exhausted and was leaning her head against the window. In her lap, Tommy slept deeply. "They had sushi. I never had that before. A little salty, but it was good."

"I hope you found it interesting as well, Teddy."

"I liked it. I liked it a lot," I said. I had enjoyed the battle and was happy that my father was happy. My plan of coming to Manassas, and of impressing my father with my devotion to the Civil War, had worked to perfection. I was extremely pleased, as well as tired.

When we arrived back at the hotel, Maurice was waiting outside by the front door. As soon as we got out of the car, I could tell that something was wrong by the look on his face. He quickly took my father by the arm and pulled him aside.

"Mr. Pappas, I think we have a problem," he said. But before he could say much else, a television camera appeared by our side. Soon there were four or five people surrounding us. I immediately recognized one of them as the photographer in the lobby. When my father turned to face him, his camera started whirring and flashing again, as did others.

"Mr. Pappas, is it true that you illegally adopted your son? That he's not even your son?" One of the photographers yelled.

We stood frozen as the cameras pressed upon us, a circle of flashing white and blinking red lights. I closed my eyes and saw spots and yellow circles, spinning and exploding. Then I heard Uncle Frank's voice.

"Get the hell out of here," he yelled. When I opened my eyes, Maurice was trying to part the crowd with his long arms. "You all stand back now," he said. "Just move back."

We made our way slowly through the lobby, the crowd following us close. All the way, with every step we took, people kept shouting questions. Once inside the elevator, my father slumped against the wall and held his chest. Uncle Frank kept pressing our floor's button hard.

"Damnit," he said. "What the hell was that all about?"

When we got back to our room, the phone was ringing. It was Mrs. Wilcott again, telling us that Bobby Lee had been on TV accusing my father of being a kidnapper.

AUNT BESS lay perfectly still on her bed in the hotel room, her hands folded on her stomach, her eyes staring at the ceiling, unblinking. I stood over her silently, then poked her arm gently with my finger.

"Don't worry, honey," she said. "I'm not dead."

After Mrs. Wilcott called and told us what Bobby Lee was saying, the phone started ringing in all of our rooms. Some of the calls were from my father's lawyer, Quinn, but most were from television stations back in Chicago asking my father for a statement. "I'll give them a goddamn statement," Uncle Frank said, but my father refused to comment.

"How do they know where we are?" Uncle Frank yelled. My father remained silent throughout the confusion, however, shrinking into his now baggy and shapeless uniform, a melting Stonewall Jackson.

Before my father made me go into Aunt Bess's room, Uncle Frank asked him about my adoption.

"This was done by the books, right? You got papers, right? The right procedures were followed, right?"

"Yes, of course," my father said. "I believe so."

"You believe so?" Uncle Frank said. That's when they made me go into Aunt Bess's room.

"Oh, honey, I wish I knew who to pray to," she said.

I sat down on her bed, watched her watch the ceiling.

"Do you say your prayers, honey? Every night?" she asked.

"Yes."

"That's good. I used to do that too, but I don't now. God doesn't listen to old people. He figures if we made it this far, we're on our own. I don't pray."

"I don't always either," I admitted.

She sighed. "I should have gotten married."

"Who would you marry?" I asked. The idea of Aunt Bess being married intrigued me.

"I don't know. Someone. Anyone. Spiro the Chicken Man."

"Who?"

"Spiro the Chicken Man. He had a meat store across the street from the bakery on the west side. He sold meat and used to give us chicken necks for soup. Before I moved to Milwaukee and got fat."

"You're not fat," I lied.

"I'm enormous, honey. But Spiro liked me enough. If I had married him, I would have had my own children. My own grandchildren. But I didn't like Spiro. I could tell his soul was not right. And he always smelled so odd," she said. "Chicken blood."

"Did you know Bobby Lee was my father?" I asked.

"Yes, of course I did. You were two years old when you came to live with your father. With Theo."

"Did you know Bobby Lee?"

"No. I had heard about him though. But I didn't know him. No. I knew he lived in the South. That's all I knew about him."

"Why is he saying that I was kidnapped?"

"I don't know. It's a misunderstanding. Everything will be all right though, you'll see."

"Do you think I'll have to go live with him?"

"No, of course not. He just wants some of your father's money."

"Is he going to give it to him?"

"I don't know, honey. I don't know."

I sat there and watched Aunt Bess breathe, her large chest swelling and filling itself before easing gently downward. From the other room I could hear Uncle Frank and my father talking. I was hoping they were deciding to give Bobby Lee as much money as he wanted so I could stay in Wilton.

"Money complicates things," Aunt Bess said. "It should make things easier, but it doesn't. It's like a weight that you have to keep pulling around with you. Poor Theo. He's not too good with weight."

I looked out the window and felt an emptiness I had not felt since the day my mother died, a terrible hollow feeling, a realization of being alone. I knew that if Aunt Bess wasn't there watching me, the emptiness might overwhelm me and blow me to bits.

"Don't cry, honey," she said.

"I'm not." I quickly wiped my face.

"It's okay if you do, though. Crying is good sometimes. It lets things out."

"I don't want to. I'm not." As we sat there, I thought about things, about Bobby Lee, my mother, my father, about who I was and who I might have to be. I held onto the edge of the bed as all these thoughts ran through me. Mostly though, I thought about my father not being my father.

I sniffed and wiped my nose with the back of my uniform sleeve. "Have you had any more dreams?" I asked.

"What? Oh, dreams. I've had a few."

"What were they about?"

"Trees blowing in the wind. I think that means that things are changing. Wind always brings changes. I think that's what it means." Then she slowly sat up and looked at me. "But I think the changes will be good. I think things will change and everything will be all right. You'll see," she said, reaching for me. "You'll see."

THE NEXT MORNING, when we got back to the airport in Chicago we saw a picture of my father on the front page of the newspaper, standing in front of the hotel in his Stonewall Jackson uniform. He looked hopelessly confused, his mouth open, his eyebrows halfway up his forehead. Directly underneath the picture, there was a story with the headline, LOTTERY WINNER ACCUSED OF CHILD ABDUCTION.

"Jesus Christ," Uncle Frank said.

Aunt Bess bought the paper from the newsstand and studied it. "Oh my God, Theo," she said. "Your zipper is down."

While we were waiting for our luggage at the baggage claim area, a tall man approached us and smiled. "Professor Pappas? My name is Keith Frandsen. May I ask you a few questions?"

"Get the hell out of here you son-of-a-bitch. Leave us alone. You people are vultures," Uncle Frank said. "You goddamn reporters are vultures."

Keith Frandsen looked down at my uncle and smiled briefly. He was very tall and had sharp blue eyes that I was sure had the power to burn holes through things.

"I'm sorry for this inconvenience, sir, but I'm just doing my job."

"Just doing your job," Uncle Frank sputtered. "You people are heartless vampires."

"He's a vampire!" Tommy yelled.

"Be still now," Maurice said taking Tommy's hand. He was looking at Keith Frandsen very seriously.

"I'm not a vampire, little buddy," the man said, smiling down at Tommy. "And I'm not a reporter either." He then took out a little black wallet and flipped it open to reveal a photo of himself and a badge.

"I'm with the Federal Bureau of Investigation, Mr. Pappas. And I need to ask you a few questions. If you could just step this way we can make this brief."

My father just stared at the FBI man, motionless and disbelieving. He looked stricken.

Uncle Frank took my father gently by the elbow. "We're coming," he told Keith Frandsen. "We're coming."

MY FATHER WAS standing in the middle of my bedroom looking like he was about to break into a thousand pieces. Outside, I could hear Tommy laughing and yelling as he played soccer with Maurice on the front lawn, his voice a foreign sound, high and happy, without weight.

"I met your mother while I was attending a conference in Memphis," my father said, clearing his throat. "I was giving a paper on Bedford Forrest. He was a Confederate calvaryman and he was from Memphis. But that's not important," he said quickly. He put his hands behind his back and began pacing.

"After one of the sessions, we all went out for a drink. Some of the other professors and I, we went out which is something I never did, or do. But it was my birthday, you see, and, well, they insisted, especially some of the younger professors, and we ended up at a nightclub where I met your mother. The others made her dance for me. I should say that your mother and I met and danced together."

Sitting up in my bed, I stared at my father. I couldn't imagine him dancing, even on his birthday.

"Well, you see, one thing led to another and we struck up a conversation and consequently I went back there every night I was in Memphis—I was there for a week—and I talked to your mother and we became friends. I was flattered that someone as attractive and young as your mother would have any interest in someone like, well, me, you see."

He kept walking around the room, opening and closing his hands, like he did that night when he first told me about Bobby Lee.

"Your mother told me about herself. She told me that she had a small child, that was you of course, Teddy, yes. And she told me that she had been, or was, in a bad relationship with a man. An abusive relationship. That person was Bobby Lee, you see. Well, to make a long story short, actually, it's not that long of a story really, when I went back to Chicago, to Wilton, she and you came with me. Shortly after, we were married."

"Then why does Bobby Lee say you kidnapped me?"

He paused and looked at the floor. It was late afternoon and the fall sunlight was filling my room at low angles. I watched my father's shadow move against the wall as he started walking again.

"Well, you see," he said. "You see, your mother failed to tell me that she was married to Bobby Lee, Mr. Anderson, at the time. And that they were living together, as husband and wife. Apparently, according to him at least, he came home one day and she and you were gone and according to him, once again, he never knew what happened to you. Until now. And now he says he wants you back. He's also claiming that your mother and he never were actually divorced. Legally divorced. You see, it's all complicated. Though I'm sure he's wrong on that last point."

"Does he want some of our money?"

My father stopped walking and turned to face me. "Yes. Yes, he does. He did, I should say."

"Why don't you just give it to him?"

"Well, I initially intended to. That was my inclination. If we thought he would go away forever, we would have agreed to that. But the lawyers believe that he would never really leave us alone until we resolved the matter, legally. We also thought that somehow it might someday be construed as an admission of some wrongdoing on our part. The lawyers think that it would look like we were well, buying you, Teddy. We have a very good case. We have very good lawyers. So we decided to settle this once and for all."

Outside I could hear Tommy yelling, "Kick it here, Moe Man, kick it here, dude man," and laughing again.

"Teddy, I have something else I have to tell you now too. This may come out in the papers, in the course of things, so I must tell you now." He cleared his throat and I hung on to the side of my bed, bracing for yet another storm.

"When your mother died, she was in the process of seeking a divorce from me. We had had problems, you see, difficulties, and she was . . ." He stopped here and shook his head as if trying to rid himself of something.

"She hadn't gotten very far, the process wasn't very far along I should say." He straightened up a bit. "This could complicate things further." He let out a deep breath. "So," he said.

"Why did she want to get a divorce?" I asked. My father's announcement hadn't surprised me. In some unspoken way, I knew my mother hadn't loved my father.

"There was the age difference, of course," he said. "I think we entered into the marriage for different reasons. Your mother was escaping an old life and I, well, I . . ." he stopped and shook his head again. "I guess we weren't very compatible. I guess I'm not a very compatible person." His smile looked like pain.

My head began to hurt, so I laid down on the bed and looked across the room at my father. The sunlight was almost gone now and he seemed to be vanishing. I watched him pace the room, walking in and out of shadows, then watched as he walked over to my bed and stopped. For a moment, I thought he tried to reach out for me, his hands slow and uncertain, but I wasn't sure because the sun was gone and the room was without light and my eyes were half-closed.

"Teddy?" he asked. "Teddy, do you want to stay here with me, with us?"

I sat back up. I couldn't believe he had asked me that question.

"Yes," I said. "Yes."

He straightened up again, his chin lifting. "Good," he actually said, as if he had been uncertain of the answer. "Good." Then he cleared his throat. "I have some things to do then," he said. "Things to do."

I DIDN'T GO to school the next day. At breakfast, I made the mistake of mentioning my headache so Aunt Bess insisted I stay home and rest while she furiously worked on a variety of cures, ranging from chicken broth to blueberry pie.

I didn't eat anything though. I just lay in bed and drew, aimless, incomplete pictures of clouds and planets. Most of the time I thought about Bobby Lee and considered what it would be like to live with him in Memphis, Tennessee, and be a banjo-playing hillbilly. On numerous occasions, I had overheard Uncle Frank describe my possible life using this term and the convincing, matter-of-fact way he referred to banjo-playing made me wonder if someone would actually take the time to teach me the instrument or if the skill would inherently come to me once I moved to Tennessee.

When Aunt Bess came in my room around lunchtime, I pretended I was asleep.

"Are you asleep?" she whispered. After she felt my forehead, I peered out from under my eyelids and watched her put a sandwich and a piece of pie down on the desk and leave. Then I really did fall asleep. When I woke up, Sylvanius was sitting at my desk alternately eating the sandwich and pie.

"Oh, I am sorry," he said. "I presumed you weren't interested in this food. So I took the liberty."

"That's okay," I said, sitting up. I was happy to see Sylvanius. Despite a vague fear of him and his shoes, I found him interesting.

"Your aunt asked that I look in on you," he said. He pretended to look worried. "How are you feeling?"

"Okay," I said. I was still tired. My nap had not refreshed me and my head felt soggy and full of sand.

He looked at me and swallowed a burp.

"Well," he said, wiping his mouth with the napkin, "is there anything I can get for you? Anything you need? Some type of medication? Your aunt has quite a selection."

"No."

"Well, I want to say that I feel for what you are going through. I truly do." He tried to keep from burping again, but couldn't. "I too had a traumatic childhood. A difficult childhood."

"What happened?"

He waved his hand and then continued to eat the pie. "Dear God, I don't know where to start. My parents were very insensitive distant people and my sister was also very remote, almost a stepsister really. It was unsettling to say the least. I left home as soon as I could. I fled."

"How old were you?"

"Twenty-seven. I went to New York and got a job in a hotel as a bellboy. Bellman, I should say. Still it sustained me and helped shape me. Until the theater rescued me."

"Have you ever been to Tennessee?" I asked.

"Tennessee. Tennessee," he repeated, his mouth full of pie. "The state? Yes, I think I have. I've been most places."

"What's it like?"

"What? Oh. I don't recall much. I remember that it had hills, or mountains in parts of it. And a river." He stopped eating and put his fork down, his eyes suddenly somewhere else. "Yes, yes, I remember a river outside my hotel room, or near my hotel. It must have been the . . ."

"The Mississippi River," I said.

He looked at me and nodded his head. "Yes, of course, that river. It was brown, I remember. Very dirty looking. The whole town was dirty. Memphis, I was in Memphis for a production. That's right."

Pleased with his ability to recall Memphis, he sighed and ate more pie. Some crumbs fell on the floor, but he didn't seem to notice or care.

"What were the people like there?" I asked.

"The people? Oh, people are people. One thing, I've learned is that everyone is more or less the same regardless of your location."

"Did you see a lot of hillbillies down there?"

"Hillbillies? Yes, some. From a distance, I believe I made out a few lurking by the river and alleys. Most of my knowledge is from two *Huckleberry Finn* traveling tours I did, however."

"What are hillbillies like?"

"What are hillbillies like?" Sylvanius repeated while he finished chewing. "Well, they hunt quite frequently, it seems. And they have quite a desire for catfish, but I may be getting that from your uncle. Well, anyway, they smoke little corncob pipes and what teeth they have are in very poor condition, if they have any at all. According to the adaptation of the play I was in, teeth seem to be in very short supply, a commodity." He took a sip from my glass of 7-Up. "They are not particularly ambitious people, I suppose."

"Why are they called hillbillies?"

Sylvanius crossed his legs, his monster shoes on full display. "What? Oh. Well, I suppose because they live in the hills."

"Why are they called billies then?"

Sylvanius chewed thoughtfully for a moment. "I'm not really sure," he said. "That's an interesting question. I understand the hill part, but I can only imagine how they came up with billy. It might possibly be something biblical, some reference to Satan perhaps. I haven't read the Bible in years."

I was about to ask another question about Tennessee and hillbillies when Sylvanius's lizard eyes blazed as if just realizing something. "Come now, I know why you are asking about hill people, young man. We'll have none of that. Your father and his legal team are quite brilliant, to say nothing of the depth of your father's resources. I assure you that this whole situation will soon vanish like a bad dream and that you will once again return to your idyllic and rich young life." Sylvanius pointed a long, bony finger at me. "I will not be party to any more questions on that topic. Your uncle has reprimanded me enough about saying and doing the wrong thing lately."

I watched him eat the rest of my sandwich, then carefully dab at the small corners of his mouth with a napkin. I wanted to ask him about his shoes, I was sure there was some history attached to them, but hesitated, unsure if it was too personal of a question. Instead I changed the subject to a more acceptable topic. "Were some men trying to kill you and my uncle?"

He stopped dabbing at his mouth.

"My," he said. "You do know things." He picked up a remaining piece of crust, and chewed on it. "No. I don't think they were going to actually do away with us. I don't doubt that they would have done some sort of bodily harm to us though, possibly more so to your uncle, who seemed to have quite an irritating effect on them. More than once they mentioned something about damaging our knees and legs. As for killing us, I don't think so. But then again," he sighed, "I have a tendency to look for the good in people. Well," he said standing up slowly. "I will take leave of you. Emily is expecting me next door for tea. Why don't you try to get some more rest? Sleep is the boon we all crave. And when you do come down, please make sure to bring the plate and glass down with you to the kitchen. Your aunt is very particular about certain things."

After Sylvanius left, I lay back on my bed and resumed contemplating life as a hillbilly. Images of hunting and fishing in my bare feet, of smoking a corncob pipe, and sharing a decrepit toothbrush with Bobby Lee raced through my mind. I envisioned my goodbyes to Charlie and my classmates to be full of tears, promises to write and in the case of Miss Grace, passionate kisses. I could not begin to envision my goodbyes to my family.

Laying in bed, I tried to remember my mother's stories about Tennessee. I remembered what she said about everyone having three names and I wondered what extra name Bobby Lee would give me: Teddy Lee Pappas. Teddy Boy Pappas. Teddy Lee Boy Pappas, Jr. Then I realized that my last name might not even be Pappas anymore. That's when my stomach started to hurt again, so I closed my eyes and eventually fell back to sleep.

WHEN I WOKE UP it was dark outside and Uncle Frank was sitting where Sylvanius had been. He was drinking the last of my 7-Up and reading a newspaper.

"Oh, you're up," he said. "Are you okay? Your father and aunt are worried about you. You've been sleeping a lot, I mean."

I nodded my head and sat up in bed.

He folded the newspaper and put it on my desk. "Your aunt has some food downstairs. For you to eat. She wants you to eat the food."

"I'm not hungry."

"Well, you have to eat something. Your aunt is going to call an ambulance if you don't eat something. She'll try to feed you one of her pies intravenously."

I didn't say anything. I just looked at him. My head still hurt.

"Hell, I'm not hungry either," he said after some time.

"Where's my father?" I asked.

"He's meeting with some of his lawyers downstairs. He sent me up to check on you. Do you want anything? Some 7-Up?" He looked over at the empty glass. "I drank yours. It was just sitting here. That was rude of me. I shouldn't have drank your 7-Up. It was warm too."

"Is Bobby Lee downstairs too?"

"What? No. He's nowhere near here."

"Am I going to have to go live with him?"

"No. Absolutely not. I'll go live with him before that happens."

"You will?"

Uncle Frank smiled. "I would do it if it meant that guy would leave us all alone. Son of a bitch didn't remember he had a son for nine years. Then all of a sudden he wants to be goddamn dad of the year. Piece of shit." Then he said, "Don't tell your father I talk like this around you. He's got enough god-damn problems."

"What did that FBI man want? Was he going to arrest my father?"

Uncle Frank crossed his legs. The dim light from the desk lamp threw a shadow that covered half his face and made him look mysterious, and other-worldly. "No one's going to arrest your dad," he said. "The FBI agent just had to tell us a few things. Your father should have cleared our little trip-back-in time to Washington with the judge. But everything's okay. Don't worry about any of it. We have everything covered. This hick is going to go away soon and everything will be fine."

"How come you're not my father's lawyer?"

"Well, I offered to help, but your father declined my services. Anyway, I haven't practiced law in twenty years."

"Did you know Bobby Lee was my father?"

"What? Yes, I did know that."

I didn't say anything.

Uncle Frank took a deep breath. "Listen. You can't let this get to you." He pulled his chair close to my bed and squinted his eyes, thinking hard. Then he looked over his shoulder as if he didn't want anyone to hear what he had to say. "I'm not very good at giving advice, especially to kids, but you're not a normal kid. You're, well, like a miniature adult. Hell, I can tell that. You're introspective. Your drawing and everything. Your grades. You don't have many friends. You're quiet all the time. You know what's going on so I'm going to level with you. Some frank talk from Uncle Frank." He pulled his chair closer, so close that I could see his nose hairs again. "Things are kind of a mess right now and until we clean this mess up, my advice to you is insulate yourself. You know what that means?"

I shook my head.

"It means kind of cover yourself up, protect yourself. You got a good imagination, so pretend that you have an invisible blanket and cover yourself with it, just cover yourself up and no one can hurt you. Think of it like a magic blanket. When you have it on, you can't get hurt." He sat back in his chair, spent. "With that, I just summed up about forty years of very expensive therapy."

"What's therapy?" I asked.

"It's like a doctor's office except for your mind. You go somewhere, tell them your problems and they listen and then they tell you how to fix your problems. It's like going to a mechanic if you were a car."

"Do you have a lot of problems?"

He shrugged. "Only one—my life." He leaned farther back in the chair and put his hands behind his head. "You know, not being a Pappas by blood has certain advantages. Maybe you won't have the melancholy and sense of despair that every Pappas greets the new day with."

"What?" I didn't understand what he was talking about.

Uncle Frank shook his head. "Never mind. Let's just say that maybe you'll escape certain things that come with being a Pappas. By nature, Greeks are depressed people. We worry about everything. We're not all Zorba."

I propped myself up against my pillows and considered Uncle Frank's comments. I understood that he was trying to make me feel better, but his talk of melancholy, despair, therapy, and imaginary blankets was falling short.

"Were some men trying to kill you and Sylvanius because you owed them money?" I asked.

He didn't seem surprised by my question. He just nodded his head. "I owed some people some money. I don't know if they would have killed us though. They weren't quite those kind of people."

"Would they have broken your knees?"

"Well, they weren't too specific on what bones they were going to crush. Let's just say that something definitely was going to get broken and I don't think it was going to be my heart. But thanks to your father, I don't have to worry about that anymore."

"Did he pay them the money you owed them?"

"He did indeed," he said. He crossed his legs and started picking some lint off of his stockings. "Your father is a generous man."

"Are you going to make any more movies?"

"Nooooo. I'm finished out there. Kaput. El fin. I'm dedicating myself to the book now."

"About the human condition?"

"Yes," Uncle Frank said. "About the human condition."

"What about your talk show? The one you were going to do on TV?"

Uncle Frank waved his hand, then wistfully shook his head. "I don't think America is ready for that type of, well, that type of forum yet. I think I'll have to flesh a few things out, tweak the concept. Right now, I got that on the back burner. In the meantime I'm going to focus on my writing. I've never written before, it's harder than you think, turning thoughts to words. Words that make sense, I mean. That's key."

He fell quiet again. Outside, I heard a police siren grow close then drift away.

"Do you know who the Chicken Man was?" I asked.

"What?"

"Spiro, the Chicken Man. Aunt Bess wanted to marry him."

"Oh. Jesus, that old guy. I heard he's still alive. He stunk. No matter how many baths he took, he had this odor about him. The whole neighborhood knew about it. I didn't hold it against him though. He was a nice man. He married the Mole Lady. Maria. We all went to the same church. Hell, he was all right. She had all these moles. I don't know what the hell their kids look like though. The guy looked like a chicken."

"How long is Sylvanius going to live with us?" I asked.

At the mention of Sylvanius's name, Uncle Frank grimaced, like he had just accidentally stepped in Stavros's kitty litter. "Your aunt likes him. I don't know why, but she wants him around."

"It's because he's famous, probably," I said.

Uncle Frank scowled. "He's not famous. He's a trivia question. He's not going to stay here for long though. Sooner or later, your aunt is going to get tired of him. Right now though, he seems to make her happy and Aunt Bess should be happy. It might make her less miserable."

He stood up and stretched his arms and then turned his neck to one side and then the other. "I'm stiff," he said. "I need some exercise. I need to do something. Anything." I thought he might leave, but he sat back down.

"What was my father like when he was young?" I asked. I didn't want him to leave. I was tired of being alone.

"Your father. Well, he was smart. Very smart. And quiet. I shared a room with him and a week would go by without him saying anything to me. I thought it was because he didn't like me. It was years before I realized that I was right."

"My father likes you."

Uncle Frank didn't say anything to that. He just shook his head. "Your father was quiet and smart. Everyone thought he'd go to Harvard, which he did. The rest is history, literally, in his case."

I considered Uncle Frank's assessment of my father.

"He is pretty quiet," I said.

"Yeah, but don't be fooled by it. Down deep he's a tough old Greek. He's tougher then he looks. Old Hillbilly Boy won't know what hit him when this is over. Your dad is like one of his Civil War generals downstairs right now, going over the battle plans."

"Like Stonewall Jackson?"

Uncle Frank laughed, a loud, unexpected bark. "Yeah, like Stonewall Jackson." Then he laughed again. "Stonewall Pappas," he said. "He's god-damn Stonewall Pappas."

THE NEXT FEW WEEKS were odd around our house, things sliding off-balance and in and out of place. My father's behavior, which I monitored closely for clues, was erratic, swinging from surprisingly abrupt—I heard him once raise his voice on the phone to one of his lawyers—to predictably passive. A number of times I walked by his study and saw him staring numbly out the window, a lost and left behind look on his face and a pile of papers in his lap. Despite these lapses however, I sensed an undercurrent of urgency coming from him, an unfamiliar single-mindedness and I did my best not to disturb him.

I knew that my fate was quietly being decided during the days while I was at school and at nights while I slept. I knew that somewhere meetings were taking place, arguments being won and lost. I was kept completely in the dark on the specifics, though the strained look on my father's face told me that a battle was being waged nearby and that the fighting was fierce. I did not ask questions, or seek reassurances. I just waited, knowing that sooner or later, things would find me.

"Now, how are you today, Mr. Teddy Pappas?" Maurice asked as he walked me to school. It was a few days before Halloween and most of the trees were bare now, giving Wilton a lonely, remote planet look. Tommy didn't have kindergarten that day so it was just Maurice and I walking over and around the leaf piles when we crossed streets.

"I'm okay," I said.

"Just okay?" he asked.

I looked over at Maurice. Ever since Manassas, he had made a serious effort to talk during our walks to and from school, initiating conversation on a wide range of topics, from the weather to soccer. I knew it was his way of showing concern and sympathy over Bobby Lee and I appreciated his effort though, like most things now, it worried me.

"I'm pretty good," I said, though without much conviction. The night before, I had dreamt of my mother and of the colliding comets and when I woke up, my pillow had been wet, leaving me with that stranded, empty feeling again.

Maurice looked up at the low clouds that were hanging close, just inches it seemed, above our heads. "Gloomy day," he said. "The TV says it might rain. Hope it's dry for trick-or-treating though. Wouldn't want all those costumes to get wet." He paused for a moment. "What are you and your brother going as? What are you wearing?"

"Aunt Bess is buying our costumes," I said. I had given no thought to Halloween, a holiday that used to consume me.

"Well, I'm sure she'll buy the right costume. I know your brother wants to go as one of those Nintendo characters. You know, when I was a young boy, I once went as Wilt Chamberlain, the basketball player. I had an old Laker's jersey and carried a basketball around with me. Wasn't much of a costume really, I just loved Wilt the Stilt though. Liked the way he carried himself. He was a confident man."

"Do you think I'll have to go live with Bobby Lee?" I suddenly asked.

Maurice's head rose up slightly when I asked that question and I thought I heard him exhale. "No," he said after a moment. He looked straight ahead and kept walking. "No, I think your father has things pretty much under control in that regard. In a little while, things will be back to the way they were. Things will work out."

We crossed another street. Up ahead, I could see St. Pius come into view, the gray day a perfect backdrop for its brooding shape.

"Are you scared?" Maurice asked.

I waited a few moments before admitting that I was. "Yes," I said. "A little. I don't want to go live with Bobby Lee."

"Your father's doing everything he can right now. From what I hear, things are going well. It's just a matter of time."

Then I said something that I had been thinking, something that had been waiting and breathing just beneath the surface of my thoughts. "I don't know why he wants to keep me," I said. "I'm not his son. And my mom was going to divorce him. She didn't want to stay married to him."

Maurice looked down at me sharply. "Now where did you hear that?"

"My father told me."

Maurice looked away from me, down the street. "Your father cares for you," he said.

I didn't say anything, I didn't know if I believed him, didn't know what I believed. But Maurice's words and the soft way he said them, opened something inside me and made me feel like crying.

"Things will be fine. Your father's a smart man. You gotta have faith now." Maurice put his arm around me and that's when I finally did start to cry. Maurice stopped walking and knelt down and hugged me, his sweet tobacco smell surrounding and holding me close. "You just cry now," he whispered. "You just cry."

AS SOON AS WE got in line on the playground, Johnny Cezzaro told me that we should have Bobby Lee killed.

"Two shots," he said, pointing his finger first behind his head, then on the side of it. "Here, then here. You gotta do it right. You don't want to leave him paralyzed. He might still be able to testify. Then you'd really be screwed. Then you'd have to kill the shooter who messed up because he would know too much."

I nodded my head. "That would be bad," I said. I kept my eyes trained on the school doors, once again praying they would miraculously open and deliver me from Johnny. I was fresh from crying with Maurice and wanted to be alone at my desk and stare at Miss Grace for awhile.

"They could kill him and then leave him in the trunk of a car at the airport. That's where most bodies are dumped now. Airports. My dad says they don't use rivers anymore. You can't drag an airport parking lot."

"I don't think we're going to have him killed," I finally said.

"You should, man. He's white trash. My dad said he just wants your money. That if you weren't rich, he wouldn't even want you. Hey," Johnny said, turning. "Here comes Wilcott."

I turned around and saw Benjamin walking in my direction, his hands in his pockets, concealed weapons. Despite his general rough appearance—he currently was sporting a large scab on the end of his nose, allegedly the result of another fight—he didn't scare me much anymore. Ever since Tommy started playing on the junior soccer team that Benjamin helped coach, his attitude toward me had softened. Rather than threats and stares, he now treated me with a benign indifference that bordered at times on the friendly. I concluded it was because he wouldn't mind having Tommy as a little brother. I also concluded it had something to do with the Cezzaro brothers' threats to kill him if he so much as looked at me the wrong way. For this protection, I was to pay Johnny $100,000 a year, Big Tony getting half.

"Hey," Benjamin said as he walked up to me.

Johnny stepped between us. "What do you want, Benji?" he said, smirking. Out of the corner of my eye, I saw Big Tony detach himself from a group of older boys and slowly begin to drift over in our direction.

"Hi, Benjamin," I said. I tried to seem oblivious to the fact that Big Tony was rapidly approaching.

"I think that guy's a real creep," Benjamin said. "That guy who says he's your father. He's not trying to say he's Tommy's father too, is he?"

"No," I said. "Just me."

"That's what my mom and I figured. He's shit, man."

I nodded my head. "Yes," I said, "he is."

"We're going to make him go away," Johnny said matter-of-factly. "Which is something maybe you should do."

"I'm just talking to him," Benjamin said, but then Miss Polk opened the doors and the line began to move forward.

While I was at my locker, Mrs. Plank summoned me to her office. Over the past few days, she had been issuing grave Catholic looks, peering out over her glasses at me in the hallways and in the lunchroom. I knew an audience in her office, the Dust Chamber, was only a matter of time.

Sitting in my now customary spot in the wooden chair in front of her desk, waiting for her to, once again, get off the phone, I allowed myself to study the Earless Jesus. He looked more worried than usual, his smile tinged with apprehension and concern. His eyebrows were arched up higher than I remembered and his Cheerio eyes had a sad and consoling look in them that I now found comforting.

"Well, Teddy," she said when she got off the phone. "How are you holding up?"

"Okay," I said. I looked down at the floor. Mrs. Plank looked particularly ancient this morning, her wrinkles rising up like waves on her face, her mouth a small pinched hole. On the other side of her dark office, tumbleweed stirred.

"Well, I know you've been through so much. It must be very difficult."

I didn't say anything. I started to feel like I might have to go to the bathroom.

"Teddy, look up, please. It's not polite to stare at the ground. Don't slouch." I looked up at Mrs. Plank. "I just want you to know that if things get too difficult, you know where you can turn," she said. "Don't you?"

"Yes," I said automatically. "Jesus."

Mrs. Plank looked surprised and I thought she started to say "Who?" but instead said, "Oh, yes. You can turn to us too, though. Miss Polk or me. Or Miss Grace. And Jesus too, of course."

"Okay," I said. I focused my gaze on a small area between her chin and mouth that didn't look too wrinkled.

"Have you received any other communication from your friend, that person from Gabon? Your pen pal?"

"Ergu?"

"Yes, him."

"No." I hadn't thought much about Ergu over the past few weeks. Between Manassas and Bobby Lee, I had more or less forgotten about him.

"I want you to know that we forwarded that letter you received to the proper authorities. They've asked that you keep us informed if he tries to contact you again. He shouldn't have been asking you for money. We don't believe a child wrote that letter."

"You don't? Who wrote it then?"

"Obviously an adult."

"Oh," I said. "Ergu isn't a boy?"

Mrs. Plank's mouth twitched once and she took her glasses off, then rubbed the bridge of her nose. "The person who wrote that letter wasn't a child, Teddy. He or she was someone who was trying to take advantage of you and your family. The State Department believes it was someone who works in the American Embassy in Gabon. We have received, or intercepted really, a number of other letters from him. The last one was somewhat threatening."

I nodded my head. The news that Ergu wasn't Ergu, that he didn't live in a mud hut and eat bark, that he wasn't a good Christian praying for a short flood season, didn't surprise me. Nothing was like it seemed anymore. I was now beginning to see things clearly, understand that people were always going to want things from me and my father. The Ergu Adult, Mrs. Wilcott, Bobby Lee, the Cezzaro brothers, even Mrs. Plank and St. Pius. They all wanted something. I sat back in the wooden chair wondering if this was what Uncle Frank meant when he talked about the human condition, every-one wanting something.

I looked up at the Earless Jesus just in time to see Him nod.

MY FATHER WAS waiting for us at the front door when I got home from school. When I saw his face, my stomach started to hurt again, a deep dull pain that I imagined as a small thorny ball, all bristles and blood. He looked worried.

"Thank you, Mr. Jackson. We'll see you shortly," he said. He closed the door and led me up to his study. The thorny ball in my stomach expanded, scratching the sides of my stomach.

"Teddy," my father said after I sat down in the chair against the wall. "You are going to have to spend a little time with, ah, with . . ."

"Bobby Lee," I said.

"Yes." My father walked over and sat down behind his cluttered desk with a thud. Off in the corner a fax machine that my father had just bought spit out documents, all of them I was sure, concerning Bobby Lee and me.

He cleared his throat. "The court has ruled that until this is resolved, he is entitled to visit you. He has requested this. We have insisted that those meetings be supervised however."

"Will you be there?" I asked.

"No."

"Will Uncle Frank or Aunt Bess?"

"No, they won't be there either. Part of the agreement is that no family members can be present. We'll be around though. Mr. Jackson will be there however. In the room with you. We agreed to that."

Knowing that Maurice was going to be there with me made the Stomach Ball shrink, but just a little.

"When do I have to talk to him?"

My father cleared his throat, then rubbed his chin with his hand.

"He's here, isn't he?" I asked.

My father looked at his watch and said, "No, but he'll be here shortly." He sighed, looked down at the desk and arranged some papers. Then he quickly looked up, his face brightening for a moment. "Oh. I almost forgot. Aunt Bess has made a snack for you."

"I'm not hungry," I said.

"Well, you should try to eat something."

"I'm not hungry," I repeated. But I got up and headed for the bathroom.

While washing my hands, Uncle Frank stuck his head in the doorway of the bathroom.

"Oh, there you are," he said. He lowered his voice. "How are you doing?"

"Okay," I said. I had accepted the fact that people were going to be asking me that question for the rest of my life.

Uncle Frank looked over his shoulder, back out into the hallway.

"Remember our little talk the other night, remember what I told you about that imaginary blanket?" His voice was still low.

"Yes," I said. I turned off the faucet, turned, and faced him.

"Well," he said. "Throw it on now."

BOBBY LEE kept coughing and drinking water.

"Your name wasn't Teddy when you was born, you know that? It was Ryan. Amy always liked that name. Ryan Lee."

He was sitting on the black couch in our living room on top of the two puncture holes Tommy had made with a pencil, holding a football in his hands. Maurice was sitting on the other side of the room, looking at the floor. In the kitchen, I could hear my father's and Bobby Lee's lawyers, talking quietly, their voices a flat mumble.

"I got this for you," Bobby Lee said, holding up the football. "You like football?" he asked.

I didn't say anything. I just looked at the football.

"I hear you play soccer. Hell, that's a phony sport. You never see soccer on TV." Bobby Lee looked over at Maurice. "Do you like soccer? Hell, you used to play pro ball, I heard. Bet you got your bell rung a few times."

Maurice looked up at Bobby Lee. "I did. I rang a few of my own too," he said.

Bobby Lee laughed. "You were all-pro two years. That's what the paper said. What are you doing being a bodyguard? Seems to me like you be doing something else. Maybe own a bar or restaurant, or something. Lot of ex-athletes do that. Cash in on the name. Good P. R. brings in the people."

"I enjoy my work," Maurice said.

"Who else did you ever bodyguard?"

"You and me can talk later. You're here to talk to Teddy," Maurice said. "We only have the hour. You were late."

"Yeah, well, I got stuck in that damn traffic. Still not used to it." He looked over at me. "Have to learn how to gauge it better. You know, figure out how long it takes to get somewhere."

I looked back down at the floor. Bobby Lee took a deep breath. He seemed nervous. He kept running his hands down the side of his pants.

"You don't remember me at all then, huh?" he asked.

I shook my head slowly. In the bathroom before I came down, I had decided on a strategy of not speaking to Bobby Lee, my hope being that he would find me dull, even unintelligent and consequently lose interest in me.

"Well," he said, "we used to live in Memphis. Do you know where Memphis is?"

I shook my head. A perceived lack of geographical knowledge might also aid my case, I thought.

"It's in Tennessee. On the Mississippi River. Well, you, me and Amy, your mom, we used to go to Beale Street once in awhile and walk around, buy ice cream. You were in a little buggy. You don't remember any of that?"

I looked at the floor.

"Yeah, well, I didn't think so. You were just a pup an'all." Bobby Lee started to cough and then took a sip from the glass of water he asked for when he came in.

"Gotta quit smoking," he said. "It's messin' me up." He coughed again, a raspy, raw sound. "You don't smoke, do you?"

I shook my head again. I was surprised by the question until I realized that hillbilly boys probably started smoking when they were four or five.

"That's good. I discourage smoking," he said.

"I hear you're a regular artist," he said after awhile. "Heard you can really draw. Your mom, she liked to draw too. They always hung her pictures and stuff in the halls at school. She had talent they said. They say the same thing about you too now. That's good. I got some pictures your mother drew when she was about your age, maybe a little older. She drew this one of the stars and the planets, she called it 'The Galaxy at Night.' It won all sorts of awards. Awards for kid artists, I mean. I got that one with me. I got to show it to you one time. Maybe next time I visit."

Bobby Lee's comments about my mother's drawing interested me. Though I was determined not to ask any questions, I was curious to see her work.

"Yeah, she had talent," Bobby Lee continued. "Me, I never could draw much. All the teachers said that my pictures looked like monsters or aliens. Hell, I should have gone to Hollywood and made monster movies."

I kept looking at the floor. Bobby Lee's boots were old and had a thin film of dust and dried mud on them and the cuffs of his jeans were frayed. He was clean-shaven though and was wearing what looked to be an uncomfortable but new blue shirt and tie.

"You ever been back to Tennessee, to Memphis?"

I shook my head.

"It's nice down there. Warm winters. Don't get snow. Looks like you get a lot of snow up here."

"We get some," I said for some reason.

234

"You do, do ya?" Bobby Lee smiled, relieved that I had actually spoken. He looked over at Maurice and nodded his head.

"You play hockey?" he asked.

I quickly shook my head, angered at my lapse.

"I thought everyone in Chicago played hockey. With all this snow you get I mean."

"I don't play any sports," I said. I concluded this warranted communicating. Not liking sports would be another negative in his eyes. Bobby Lee definitely seemed like the type of person who would want a sports-liking son.

"I don't like sports that much either. I just watch it on TV once in awhile. Bunch of whiny millionaire jocks. Hell," he said looking over at Maurice, "no offense." Then he looked back at me and laughed. "And no offense to you, millionaire."

Bobby Lee coughed and took another sip of water. Quinn, my father's lawyer, a slight quiet man with large glasses, walked in the room and pointed to his watch, then left. Bobby Lee rubbed the side of his pants again and took a deep breath.

"You know, I'm real sorry about what happened to your mother. If I had known where she was living, I would have come to the funeral or sent flowers. I thought she was in Georgia though. She had some cousins down there. I didn't know she was dead until I saw you all on TV. Then I drove right up here to meet you. I swear that's the truth. I didn't want none of this to happen. All the commotion. I want you to know that. I just wanted to see you. You're my blood. Hell, I remember the day you were born. I held you in my arms in the hospital, came and visited you and your mom. I'm your daddy. That's still worth something, ain't it?"

Quinn came back in the living room and Bobby Lee stood up to leave. He handed me the football. "Hey, maybe we can throw this around next time," he said. "All right then. I'll be seeing you soon." Then he left.

CHAPTER ELEVEN

I WAS STANDING in the front hallway watching my father try to flatten his Jiffy Pop popcorn hair with the carnival comb again. This act alone, hair flattening, underscored the importance of the occasion. Unless Mrs. Wilcott was coming over, my father seldom acknowledged what passed for his hair and the determined way he was now pressing down on his head once again made me wonder about where we were going and why.

"Are we all set then?" he asked. I looked up at my father as his hair sprang back to life, lifting gracefully off the sides of his head.

"Yes," I said.

"Where is your uncle?"

"In the car."

"Well, then," my father said, opening the front door. "Are you all set?"

I grabbed my backpack and walked outside.

We were on our way to see Dr. Hugh Spiral, the family therapist who was going to help me cope with my shattered world, restore my sense of self-esteem and give me a new foundation to grow on, according to Mrs. Wilcott. He apparently had done the same thing for Benjamin after Dr. Wilcott ran away with Sally Daker, the tennis pro at the Wilton Country Club. Mrs. Wilcott said visiting Dr. Spiral had made a big difference in reducing Benjamin's hostility to his environment.

"What the hell kind of name is Spiral?" Uncle Frank asked as he started the old Buick.

"I'm not exactly sure," my father said.

"Well, I think it's a goddamn strange name for a shrink."

"He's a therapist," my father said quietly. "A family therapist."

It was the day before Halloween and as we drove through the streets of Wilton, I studied the different decorations that had magically appeared overnight. Ghosts hanging from trees twisted strangely in the wind, witches with black capes sat propped up on porches, cardboard tombstones stood silently on front lawns. Wilton had a tradition of having excellent holiday spirit, a fact recognized by a magazine that once described it as "Chicago's most festive suburb." My mother used to feel pressure to keep up with the neighbors, working late into the night, stuffing life-sized scarecrows with straw and cutting slanty-eyed goblins out of black vinyl. She liked Halloween though and didn't really mind the work. "Halloween doesn't try to be anything more than it is," she used to say. "It's just fun."

"Teddy," my father said. He turned around a bit in the front seat and looked at me sideways with one eye. "As you know, Dr. Spiral is going to ask you some questions. About things."

"Okay," I said.

"He's probably going to ask you how things are going. About," my father cleared his throat, "what you're feeling."

"He's probably going to ask you some questions about Catfish Mouth too," Uncle Frank said. "About how much you hate him. You owe it to yourself to be honest on that point."

"Frank, please."

We drove in silence until we got to the expressway. Then we sat perched on the lip on the entry ramp, waiting for traffic to subside. Behind us, I heard horns honking and the muffled voices of people screaming. The reason Uncle Frank was coming with us, I was sure, was to maneuver through the traffic, something my father had little practice or skill doing.

"Shut the hell up!" Uncle Frank yelled. Then he raised the window. "You know, Theo, if we had a car that was built this century, I wouldn't have to plan an extra three hours for every trip just for merging," he said. "This car has no pick up."

"Well, just be careful, Frank," my father said, looking out at the flowing traffic. "Just take your time, please. There's no need to rush."

"I don't think rushing is possible in this car."

After a few more minutes, Uncle Frank finally eased the Buick onto the expressway, the car shuddering and straining as it picked up speed.

"We cheat death again," Uncle Frank said.

As we drove, I sat silently and tried to prepare for the upcoming meeting. I knew that my answers to any questions would have consequences, knew that everything I said and did would be weighed in some manner. I viewed my upcoming session with Dr. Spiral as a test, an examination I unfortunately had no way of preparing for. Other than imaginary blankets, I knew little about therapy.

I sat back in the car and looked out the window. Up ahead, I could see the skyline of Chicago coming closer, filling our windshield. I regretted not packing my sketch pad. I had never drawn buildings before and suddenly, their angles, shapes, and shadows, seemed interesting.

My father cleared his throat. "Well, then, how are things going, Teddy? Is everything all right at school?"

"Yes," I said.

"Do you see much of Benjamin Wilcott?"

"A little."

"He seems like a nice boy. I was wondering if you would like to have him over some time?"

I didn't respond. Instead, I opened my backpack and took out the book, *Grant and Lee*. I wanted to leave my father with one last positive image of me before I met with Dr. Spiral. I began reading about Lee's involvement in the Mexican War, trudging through dates and locations, trying to focus in case my father asked me any questions on the book.

The traffic was heavy and we drove without speaking. Uncle Frank kept honking the horn, something my father never did.

"That show called again," Uncle Frank said quietly as he changed lanes.

My father was startled. He had been reading some documents that he had spread over his lap. "What? I'm sorry?"

"That show. The one I told you about."

"Oh, yes, that television show."

"They said that Anderson contacted them but they don't want him. They want you."

"Well, I'm not interested. We've been through this, Frank."

"Yes, but this show is different. She's classier than the rest. She's big time."

My father was silent. I looked at the back of his bald head and wondered what he was thinking, then wondered if he was ever jealous of Uncle Frank's thick, luxurious toupée which sat just inches from his own barren head.

Uncle Frank continued in a low voice. "I just thought this show could balance some of the crap that's being written right now. You know about that picture, don't you?"

My father looked out the window. "Aunt Bess mentioned something about it, yes."

Uncle Frank was referring to the photo of my father dressed as Stonewall Jackson that had appeared on the cover of a magazine with the headline, LOTTO LOONY THINKS HE'S ROBERT E. LEE! Aunt Bess had brought two copies home from the supermarket because she was thinking about starting a scrapbook.

"You should at least consider it, Theo."

"I don't think that would be appropriate, Frank," my father said.

Uncle Frank honked the horn. "You know, I can go on with you," he said. "On that show. I can do most of the talking. You can just sit there. Jump in when you want."

My father picked up his papers and began reading again.

We drove for what seemed forever, creeping through a sea of red tail-lights, the traffic thick. When we finally got to downtown Chicago, we parked in an underground lot and walked a few blocks in a soft rain. Dr. Hugh Spiral's office was in a tall glass building that sparkled with wetness. Once inside, we had to take two sets of elevators up to the eighty-eighth floor. When we finally got to his office, we sat in a small, dark waiting room for close to an hour because my father had gotten the times mixed up and despite the long merge, we were still early.

"Would you like something to drink?" the receptionist asked. She was an older woman with frosted hair and a bored look on her face that she wore like a medal.

My father shook his head and Uncle Frank said, "What I want, you ain't got."

My father started to pace back and forth, clearing his throat with every other step. Occasionally he stopped and pretended to study some pictures of cows and sheep that were on the wall.

I opened *Grant and Lee* again and attempted to read about Grant's days at West Point. Despite my apprehension over the meeting however, I began to feel drowsy and my mind soon wandered, drifting into a dream about Miss Grace. She had worn high heel shoes and a shorter skirt than usual the day before, a new look I had found stirring. I had spent a good portion of the day memorizing her slim ankles and calves.

"Interesting book, Teddy? Are you enjoying it?" I glanced up. My father was looking at me with a small smile.

"What?"

"Where are you now?"

"Grant is wearing high heels," I blurted out.

"I'm sorry?"

"Grant is at school, at West Point."

"Ah, Grant wasn't much of a student, I'm afraid."

"No," I said. "He wasn't."

"You're early," a voice said. We all looked up to see a large bald man with a short gray and black beard walking toward us, a friendly panda bear.

"Hello, Theo," Dr. Spiral said, extending his hand.

"Hello," my father said. I was surprised that Dr. Spiral used my father's first name.

"And hello to you, buddy. I already know who you are," he said, turning to face me. I nodded. His eyes sparkled like his building and I knew that he had a deep laugh.

"Great artwork, huh," he said, motioning toward the pictures of the sheep and cows. "They were here when I moved in." He rolled his eyes a bit. "I tried to get the former tenant as a patient, but he was seeing someone else." He turned and looked over at Uncle Frank. "And you are?"

"Oh, I'm sorry," my father said. "This is my brother, Frank Pappas. He drove us down." Uncle Frank pointed his jaw at Dr. Spiral as he shook his hand.

"Oh, that's right. Nice to meet you, Frank. I loved *The French Maid Murders*. Got a big kick out of it," Dr. Hugh Spiral said.

Uncle Frank's eyes narrowed with surprise and suspicion. He looked over at my father then back at Dr. Spiral. "Is that some kind of joke?" he asked.

"No, I liked it. I really did. Camp horror. I like Ed Wood too."

Uncle Frank processed this information in silence, mulling. Finally he said, "Camp horror, hey? Camp horror. Well, that was one of the effects I was going for. I was going to make *French Maids Two,* but then I thought, hey, let's be realistic, how many French maids are there?"

Dr. Spiral laughed. "Good point," he said. Then he said, "Unless you two want to stay in this cell and look at barnyard animals, there's a nice little restaurant on the fortieth floor with a good view. Why don't you go grab a cup?"

My father hesitated but Uncle Frank asked, "Do you think they have cappuccino?"

When Dr. Spiral said, "I know they do," they left.

Dr. Spiral led me to a bright office in the corner that had a large, wide window overlooking Lake Michigan. I sat on the couch against the wall and watched fog drift over the lake, toward us. On the wall next to the window, was a framed picture of four men in black suits, sitting on some steps.

"The Beatles," Dr. Spiral said, sitting down on the other end of the couch. "I saw them at Shea Stadium when I was twelve years old. I won a radio contest and my sister and I went to the concert and got to meet Ringo afterwards." He pointed his finger at the picture. "He signed it on the bottom, over there, in the corner. I know it's just Ringo, but it was still very, very cool."

I nodded my head and looked at the picture. My mother had liked the Beatles too and I decided to tell him this. I thought such information, being the son of a Beatles fan, might cast a favorable light on me. When I tried to speak though, I found my mouth pinned shut, unable to open.

Dr. Spiral seemed to know this. He walked over to a small refrigerator by his desk and took out two Cokes and handed me one without saying anything. Then he asked me if I had a dog.

I shook my head.

"Ah, let me tell you about Ralph then," he said.

For the next half hour, Dr. Spiral told me funny stories about Ralph, his twenty-five-year-old basset hound. I listened at first with great apprehension, convinced the story contained some hidden message related to my situation. I thought the dog might represent Bobby Lee or my father. But after awhile, my apprehension melted and I found myself laughing at Dr. Spiral's stories about Ralph.

Soon and without me noticing exactly when and how, we were talking about other things: my mother, father, Tommy. We talked for a long time, Dr. Spiral's eyes soaking everything in like soft sponges. I told him about my mother's accident, about Manassas, about Tommy starting the fire at St. Pius, things that made me feel like I led a full and interesting life.

Then I told him that I didn't want to live with Bobby Lee. I said this quietly but firmly while looking out the window at a distant point out on the gray lake. He didn't seem surprised by my declaration, instead he just said, "So you want to stay put."

"I want to stay at home," I said. "In Wilton."

He nodded his head and wrote something down on a piece of paper. Then he asked, "How does it feel to be a little rich kid?"

"Okay."

"Do you feel people treat you differently now?"

I shrugged. "I don't think so."

"Are people nicer to you?"

I considered his question. "A little. A lady on our block keeps giving us pies."

"Pies," Dr. Spiral repeated.

"Sometimes apple turnovers."

"Tarts too," he said. "How is the old man doing?"

"Who?"

"Pops, your dad. You know, the guy in the lobby who dropped you off?"

"Oh. Okay."

"He must be under an enormous amount of stress. How does he relieve it? Does he exercise?"

"No."

"Does he drink?"

"Yes. He drinks coffee."

"Does he yell and scream?"

"No."

"Does he ever hug and kiss you?"

"No."

"How does that make you feel?" he asked.

"I don't know. Okay."

"Would you feel more okay if he hugged and kissed you and told you that he loved you?"

"I don't know," I said. I was starting to feel dizzy, like electricity was running through my arms and legs.

Dr. Spiral scratched his elbow. "How did you feel when you learned that he wasn't really your father?"

I shrugged and looked down at the floor.

"He is my father," I said.

Dr. Spiral looked at me a long time. "Do you love him?" he asked.

I didn't say anything. I had never been asked that question before and the direct way Dr. Spiral asked it, startled me. If someone had asked me if I'd loved my mother, I wouldn't have hesitated to answer. I loved her and I knew she loved me.

Dr. Spiral stood up from the couch and walked over to the front of his desk and picked up a crystal paperweight which he juggled from hand to hand. "Do you think you love your dad, Teddy?"

I watched Dr. Spiral toss the paperweight and thought of my father, saw his worried face, saw him sitting on his bed, holding the lottery ticket the night we won, the night everything started, his eyes rimmed red, his hair jumbled and confused. "I think I do," I said after some time.

"You think you do what?" Dr. Spiral asked.

"I think I love him," I said. Then I swallowed and said, "But I don't think he loves me."

"Why would you say that?"

"I don't know," I said. The electricity was running through me hard and fast now, surging and searching for someplace to go. "He doesn't talk much to me and do things with me."

"Are you mad at him ever?"

"Sometimes. Not a lot though."

"Why do you get mad at him?"

"I don't know." I shrugged. I wanted to tell Dr. Spiral it was because he never hugged me or kissed me, because he was probably having sex with Mrs. Wilcott, because he was always so far away, even when I was standing next to him, but all I said was, "Because he won't spend any of the money we won." I looked up at Dr. Spiral. "We won the lottery."

Dr. Spiral threw his head back and laughed, a deep clear laugh that sounded like it was starting from someplace far underground. "I know that, Teddy. I think everyone in America knows that now." He took a deep breath. "So you want your dad to spend some of the cash, huh. That would make you happy?"

I shrugged again and looked back down at the floor. "A little," I said. "Maybe. I just want him to do something with it."

"Well, Teddy," Dr. Spiral said, leaning back on his desk, still holding the paperweight in one hand. "I'm going to let you in on a little secret. How would you feel if I told you that your father has been spending a lot of money lately? A lot."

I looked up at him, confused. "He has? What's he buying?"

"He isn't buying anything. He's giving it away." He smiled again and scratched his beard. "Do you remember that little baby that was left on your front porch? The baby you found?"

I nodded. "Baby Girl," I said. "He gave some money to Baby Girl?" This news shocked me. "How much did he give her?"

"I don't know specifics," Dr. Spiral said. "But I'm pretty sure that little girl isn't going to have to work a day in her life. He's given money to other people too. To your uncle, to your uncle's friend. To your school."

"St. Pius?" I had a hard time believing any of this.

Dr. Spiral nodded and grinned. "He's given a lot of money to charities too. Hospitals, shelters. I would say your father is definitely doing something with that money. He's a very generous man."

I sat there, holding onto the arm of the couch as the fog moved close to the window. My world had shifted again, an unseen force had rearranged the order of things. I felt at once proud and deceived; my father, a generous man.

Dr. Spiral laughed. "If you could see the look on your face, kiddo." Then he put the paperweight back down on his desk and walked over to the window and stood, staring out. "You know, Teddy, on a clear day you can see all the way to Indiana and Michigan," he said. "Not that I really want to see Indiana and Michigan, but it's still impressive. Sometimes I imagine that I'm up here in this watchtower and that I'm watching over everything, watching over the whole universe." He put his hands in his pockets and kept looking out the window. "I like to watch things," he said. "You do too, that's why you're an artist, that's why you like to draw."

I nodded my head.

"But watching things is different than seeing things," Dr. Spiral said. He turned away from the window and looked at me. "You're a wonderful artist, your father showed me some of your work. He's very proud."

This surprised me also. "He is?"

"Yes. He showed me dozens of your sketches. You like to draw people, don't you?"

I thought about this for awhile before answering. "Yes," I said.

"I used to draw too, especially when I was your age. And I remember that how I drew things, especially people, depended on where I was drawing them from. From what angle. Are you following me on this?"

I nodded my head even though I wasn't really sure.

"No, you aren't." Dr. Spiral smiled. "You're not a good liar, Teddy. Okay, say I was trying to draw a house but I couldn't get it right. The door, the window things would be out of balance. So, instead of giving up, I would just try to approach it from a different angle. Instead of drawing from the front, I would draw it from the side, maybe. Instead of drawing it up close, I would draw if from farther away and add some other houses to give it context. Do you know what I mean?"

This time I understood. I frequently did the same things when I drew.

Dr. Spiral walked back over to his desk and looked through some papers. "You watch your father all the time, don't you?" He said this without looking up at me.

I nodded. "I watch him sometimes."

"Did you ever think that maybe you're not watching him, seeing him, the right way?"

"I don't know," I said truthfully. I was watching Dr. Spiral closely now. I felt that he knew secrets, suddenly thought that he knew everything.

He walked back to the couch and sat down. For the first time I noticed that the tie he was wearing had a little picture of Donald Duck on the very tip, Donald Duck holding an umbrella.

"I've had the opportunity to meet with your father three times already," he said. "Got a chance to know him a little bit. He has some things he has to work out. Things about your mother, about his life, and about you. Your father is a hard man to figure out, he keeps a lot of things inside. But one thing I know for certain about him is that he loves you." Dr. Spiral smiled a smile I sometimes still see to this day, a smile that would sustain me in the terrible days that would soon follow. "Trust me, Teddy. He loves you more than you'll ever know."

SYLVANIUS WALKED down the stairs slowly, his face chalky white, his lips a deep, disturbing red. His hair was wet and slicked back high, his lizard eyes black and cold. When he came to the foot of the stairs, he draped his cape over his shoulder and smiled, a cruel smile, then bowed deeply. I took Tommy's hand and backed away. Despite myself, I was scared.

"It is indeed my pleasure to make your fair acquaintance," he said in a strange voice, thick and musical.

"Oh my God, where's my camera?" Aunt Bess said. "Quick, where is it?"

It was Halloween and Sylvanius was a vampire once again. He had bought a cape and some makeup and was going to take us trick-or-treating. It had been his idea and his offer seemed to excite Aunt Bess almost as much as it did Tommy and me.

"It is so charming to see you," Sylvanius said again in his new voice. "You look so robust, so full of health." He stopped and gazed at our necks. "So full of life."

"Sylvanius, look over here, over here!" Aunt Bess cried as her camera flashed.

Sylvanius looked at me and Tommy and smiled again, his lips curling back. Even though he wasn't wearing fangs, I moved farther away from him, toward Aunt Bess who kept clicking away.

"I am a shadow," he said. "I am the nightmare you are afraid to remember. The black bird outside your window watching. The stray dog in the woods waiting. The darkness in the night. Come dance with me in my death." Then he started sneezing. "Dear God, this makeup seems to be causing some sort of allergic reaction," he said in his own voice. "It's not my usual brand."

"I always thought that speech was beautiful," Aunt Bess said. She turned and faced me. "He always gave that speech before he bit someone."

"Yes," Sylvanius said. "By my estimates, I recited that particular speech more than a thousand times during my tenure as the king of the undead of Lake Rohan. I actually *memorized* it. I referred to it as my soliloquy."

"You never really said anything else," Aunt Bess said. "You were mostly in the background."

Sylvanius considered Aunt Bess's comment, his head cocked to one side. "Yes," he said. "I spent most of those years hiding silently behind doors, I'm afraid. Lurking really." He sighed, lost in thought. "I was always after the writers to give me more lines. There was so much more I could have done with that part." He sighed again. "Well, that was a long time ago. We really should be going now. I'd like to be back in time to watch *The Larry King Show*. Sophia Loren is on. I'd like to catch up with her doings."

"Do you have everything you need?" Aunt Bess asked us. "Do you have all of your costumes on?"

"Yes," I said. Tommy and I were dressed as vampires, wearing the thin plastic capes and white fangs that Aunt Bess had bought the day before at the supermarket. The costumes weren't anything like the ones my mother used to make for us, but I didn't point this out to Aunt Bess. She was proud of them and I appreciated her effort. My old love of Halloween had returned earlier in the day at the St. Pius Halloween party and I was glad we were going trick-or-treating, even if we were wearing cheap store-bought costumes and even if it was just until Sophia Loren filled us in on her doings.

Maurice was waiting for us outside at the end of the driveway. As we approached him, Sylvanius bowed his head and said, "Good evening. It is indeed my pleasure to make your fair acquaintance."

Maurice looked at Sylvanius a long time before returning the bow. The look on his face made me think that he probably hadn't watched much of *Dark Towers*. He puffed on his pipe and took Tommy's hand.

We stopped at Mrs. Rhodebush's house first and found a basket of red apples on her porch with a sign TAKE JUST ONE! taped to the handle. When we walked back down her driveway, I saw her in the window, watching us. I held up my apple to show that I had only taken one. When she saw me though, she just pulled the shade down.

"I'm afraid that Emily is not overly fond of holidays," Sylvanius said as we passed. "Too many memories I suppose."

We made our way slowly up and down Stone Avenue, causing a commotion everywhere we went. Most of the younger children who came to the door stared blankly at Sylvanius, frightened and, I thought, probably confused. He was by far the oldest trick-or-treater making the rounds in the neighborhood. Mrs. Hanrahan who lived on the far end of our block and was close to Aunt Bess's age, put her hand over her mouth when she saw us and said, "Well, I'll be damned." Then she asked Sylvanius for his autograph.

When we got to the Wilcotts', Mrs. Wilcott greeted us wearing a long white dress, with paper wings on her back that flapped helplessly when she walked. She was also wearing a shiny gold crown that had a red stone in the front that caught and reflected the bright porch light.

"Can you guess who I am?" she asked when she opened the door.

"My goodness! You're a nurse!" Sylvanius said, snapping his fingers.

Mrs. Wilcott smiled at Sylvanius, but her eyes fell a bit. "No," she said slowly, making that one word seem like a full sentence. "I'm Belinda, the Good Witch of the West."

"Of course, of course, the wings," Sylvanius said. Then he took a taffy apple that Mrs. Wilcott presented on a silver tray.

"Teddy, this one is for you," she said. "I made it special." She handed me a large apple that had my name written on it with sugar icing.

"Thanks," I said, though it occurred to me that on two different occasions I had recently told Mrs. Wilcott I didn't like apples.

"Mr. Sylvanius, I have a request," Mrs. Wilcott said. "I would love to take a picture of you for my column. Would you mind?" She opened the door wide.

"A photo, of course, of course," Sylvanius said. "I would be happy to accommodate you."

We walked in and waited for Mrs. Wilcott to get her camera. "Hurry up!" Tommy yelled. He wanted to visit as many houses as he could and fill his plastic trick-or-treat bag to the brim.

Mrs. Wilcott posed us by the front door, Sylvanius standing between Tommy and I, a bony hand on each of our shoulders. Maurice waited outside on the front steps with his pipe. She took several pictures, moving closer with every flash, her paper wings bouncing behind her as she moved. I thought she was going to walk right into us, she was so close. "I want to get some head shots," she said.

After she was finally finished, she pulled me aside and took my hand. "I'm praying for you," she said, her eyes wide and earnest. "So is Benjamin. He prays every night. And I know he's praying for you."

I nodded my head. I didn't believe this. I couldn't imagine Benjamin praying for anything other than the Cezzaro brothers getting hit by a truck.

As we were about to leave, Mrs. Wilcott asked Sylvanius if he could reenact his favorite scene from *Dark Towers*. She wanted to videotape it and show it on the noncooking part of *Access Wilton*.

"I couldn't possibly," Sylvanius said. "It's been so many years."

"Let's go!" Tommy yelled. He pulled on Sylvanius's cape.

"Oh, Mr. Sylvanius, please," Mrs. Wilcott urged, her blue eyes expanding, swallowing us whole. She walked over to the dining room and returned with a small video camera which she held carefully with two hands. "I would just love to have something on tape. I know you have quite a few fans living in Wilton. It would be such an honor."

With that, Sylvanius bowed his head. "Since you put it so graciously." He put his hand over his face and mumbled, "Yes, yes." Suddenly and with great flair, he threw his cape over his shoulder. "I am a shadow," he said softly, his voice building. "I am the nightmare you are afraid to remember. The black bird outside your window watching. The stray dog in the woods waiting. The darkness in the night. Come dance with me in my death." Then he did something I wasn't expecting, he pushed past us and jumped onto the first step of the hallway stairs. "Fools!" he cried. "I can never be defeated. Not by you. Not by your God! Not by your weapons. And not by your love!" He cast a dark look down at us, his eyes blazing. I was amazed at his quick transformation, as well as with what he was saying. This didn't seem like part of his soliloquy. "You may think you have defeated me, but it is an illusion," he continued, his voice, sweet, rich chocolate. "I have allowed you to win. Now, as the sun burns, I will sleep. But I shall return and welcome you to your eternity." With this, he turned and ran up the stairs, his thick, wet hair jiggling madly like a tower of Jell-O. When he reached the top, he clutched his chest and fell backward, rolling down fast and hard.

Mrs. Wilcott screamed. "Oh my God!"

"Wow!" Tommy yelled.

"Help me," Sylvanius said weakly as he lay on the bottom of the stairs. "I think I'm having a heart attack."

AFTER THE AMBULANCE drove away, my father shut the front door then locked it.

"Well," he said, as we walked back upstairs. "That was unfortunate."

"Unfortunate for us," Uncle Frank said. "He was leaving in a few days. Now, Christ." Then he said, "It's those goddamn shoes he wears."

Instead of having a heart attack, Sylvanius had broken his foot and was resting in my father's bed. When we walked into the room, Aunt Bess was in the process of bathing his forehead with a cool cloth and administering generous doses of foot-healing 7-Up, straight from a can into Sylvanius's outstretched glass. The paramedics had wanted to take him to the hospital for X rays, but Sylvanius had refused, saying that he was tired and would go the next day.

"Jesus Christ," Uncle Frank said when he saw Sylvanius's feet. "Those are the ugliest feet I have ever seen. Ever." He left quickly with his head bowed and his hand over his mouth.

Sylvanius did have ugly feet. They were long, bony and bunioned. Their ghastly appearance was punctuated by yellowish-orange toe nails that were horribly chipped, as if something wild had gnawed on them. The foot that was broken was laying-in-state, propped up on the mountain of pillows Aunt Bess had arranged on the bed. Every so often, Aunt Bess would gently soothe it with another wet cloth.

Sylvanius sighed, then sipped 7-Up from a straw. He was a sad serpent now, his thick hair a jumbled mess, his red vampire lips a washed-out mortal pink. "I'm afraid Frank's right. I have spent my life neglecting, no, punishing my feet, I'm afraid," he said.

"Everyone takes their feet for granted," Aunt Bess said as she filled his glass with more 7-Up. "I never think of mine. I have so many other things to think of."

"True, this is true," Sylvanius said. "I pledge though that this abuse will stop. I pledge that from this day on, I will treat my feet with renewed respect and admiration. They have been dependable appendages and are worthy of my attention. At the very least, I plan on cutting my toe nails more often."

"I can do that for you," Aunt Bess said.

"You are a saint," Sylvanius said. He took another sip of his drink.

"The problem might be those shoes," Aunt Bess said after she had wiped his chin.

"Ah, yes," Sylvanius said. "They are very awkward."

"Are they special shoes? Orthopedic shoes?"

"No, they're very large though and I find them comfortable. I have very long feet." Sylvanius said, sipping again on his straw. "They're props, actually. From a movie I was in."

This interested me. "What movie?" I asked.

"I believe it was *Dance of Blood, Blood Dance*, something along those lines," he said. "I stomp some people to death and . . ." he stopped here and caught his breath.

"What's wrong?" Aunt Bess cried, reaching for him. "Tell me!"

Sylvanius smiled weakly and patted the tops of her hands. "Nothing, Bess. Just a wave of pain washing over me." Then he sank back farther into the other tower of pillows Aunt Bess had constructed at his head. "Oh, for something sweet. It would be comforting."

"I have a cherry pie cooling downstairs."

"Cherry?" Sylvanius asked sadly.

"I have some butterscotch cookies too, the ones you like."

"You are too kind, Bess." He patted her hand again then whispered. "Too kind."

When Aunt Bess left, Sylvanius looked over at us. "As are you, Theodore. I feel just terrible, commandeering your bedroom like this. And all these pillows. I feel like a sultan."

My father cleared his throat. He had been silent the whole time, in shock I thought at the condition of Sylvanius's feet, as well as with the prospect of sleeping down in the basement with Uncle Frank whose snores shook the house. "Yes, well, it can't be helped," he said.

"Well, I'm sure I'll be up and about in no time."

My father nodded. "Well, thank you for taking the boys trick-or-treating. Tommy and Teddy said they enjoyed themselves. Until the accident, of course."

Sylvanius suddenly reached out and took my father's hand. "You have a fine family," he said. "Good sons. You've done a fine job raising them." He closed his eyes and whispered, "You're a good father, Theo, a good father."

I looked up at my father, bracing for the symphony of embarrassed throat-clearing that would normally follow such a personal comment. He was silent though and when I looked over at him, I noticed a faint smile at the corners of his mouth and an unfamiliar look in his eye. He slowly withdrew his hand from Sylvanius's.

"Well," he whispered to me. "You should go to sleep now, Teddy. And don't forget to brush your teeth after all that candy." Then he smiled at me and patted me on the head and walked out.

I was stunned. My father had never told me to brush my teeth before, much less patted me on the head. I walked dazed into the bathroom where I spent several minutes brushing hard for my father.

After I finished and was getting in bed, Tommy asked me if I was still his brother. He was sitting on the floor, sucking his thumb and hugging his candy bag with his free arm, like a life preserver.

"Jerry Ryan says you're just a half-brother."

"I don't know," I said. Tommy's question made my heart drop. "I guess I'm your half-brother."

Tommy continued to suck his thumb, a sure sign that he was deep in thought.

"What half of you is my brother?" he asked.

"What? I don't know. It doesn't work that way."

"I think this half here is my brother," he said, putting his hand on his waist and moving it up, toward his head. "This half here."

"You boys should be sleeping." It was my father. He was standing in our doorway, holding an old green sleeping bag I remembered my mother buying at Wilton's Garage Sale A Go-Go, an annual fundraiser that featured rock music and old furniture. At first I thought he was just passing by, on his way to his study to read more documents. I had heard the fax machine running earlier that evening and I was sure there was a small stack of papers waiting for him to review. Instead though, he walked over to my desk and turned off the small lamp. Then he cleared his throat.

"Boys," he said. "I have something I must ask you."

My throat went dry. I assumed it had something to do with Bobby Lee. The day before, I had overheard Uncle Frank tell Aunt Bess that a judge was reviewing the case and might make some type of decision soon because of all the publicity.

"I was wondering if I might sleep in here tonight. Your uncle is snoring very loudly. Would that be all right with you? The couch in the living room is too small and I don't really want to sleep in the kitchen."

"It's okay," I said. I tried to keep the excitement and disbelief out of my voice. I couldn't imagine my father sleeping with us, much less on the floor.

"All right then," my father said as he spread the sleeping bag out carefully in the middle of the floor, between Tommy and me.

"Teddy, Daddy is going to sleep with us," Tommy whispered loudly as he got into bed.

"Well, just for this one night. I imagine I'll end up in the basement soon enough," my father said as he slowly got into the sleeping bag. Once he was settled he said, "It's very late. Close to midnight. We should try to get some sleep now."

We were quiet for a moment and I feared my father would immediately fall asleep. I couldn't let this moment pass in silence, however.

"Is the floor hard?" I asked. I had trouble making him out, my eyes had not yet adjusted to the darkness and when I looked in his direction, all I could see was a dark, round shape.

"Well," I heard him say, "I'll get used to it. I used to sleep on the floor quite often in college. My roommate, Mr. Quinn actually, our lawyer, was quite a snorer too. So I used to sleep in another classmate's room, down the hall."

"At Harvard?"

"Yes. There." I heard him moving in the sleeping bag.

"Did you go trick-or-treating when you were little?" Tommy asked. His voice was soft and tiny and I knew that he was already falling asleep.

My father cleared his throat. "Yes, I did. With your uncle. We would go up and down the neighborhood together. I remember doing that, yes."

The image of my father trick-or-treating, of being young and having fun, fascinated me.

"What did you go as?" I asked. "What costume did you wear?"

"Oh, well, I don't really remember," he said quietly. I thought he would fall silent, but then he said. "Once I went as a gangster. Gangsters were very popular back then. I wore my father's hat, I remember that, an old felt hat. We both had toy machine guns. Black machine guns. They were very realistic." He spoke tentatively, like someone making his way through a dark, cluttered room. "Mrs. Frosso, an elderly woman, a neighbor, she called the police when she saw us coming down the street to her flat. When we got to her door, the police were already waiting for us so we started running away."

"Why did you run?" I asked.

"I'm not sure. I guess we were scared. You didn't see the police in our neighborhood very often, and they, the police, started chasing us." My father then laughed, a dry, rusted sound, totally unfamiliar and totally wonderful. "Yes," he said. He was speaking faster now, his words coming out in bunches. "They chased us for blocks, through alleys, through the park. The only reason they were chasing us was because we were running. I remember, we finally hid in a garage, inside of a car. That was where they found us."

"What happened then?"

"We were taken down to the station house and our parents were called. It turns out that the police were looking for two young toughs who had been vandalizing the neighborhood. It was all a misunderstanding, but very exciting. We were terrified. At least I was. Frank didn't seem very fazed by it, as I recall. It was the talk of the neighborhood for some time, though."

"How old were you?"

"Oh, about ten or twelve. Your age. Frank was seven or eight."

"Where did you live then? You didn't live in Wilton, did you?"

My father chuckled, another new and odd sound. "No, no. At that time, we lived on the north side of Chicago, in the city, by Lawrence Avenue. It was a Greek community. Everyone was Greek."

"Can we go there some time?" I asked.

There was a pause. "Why, of course," my father finally said. "We could go down there. That might be enjoyable. I haven't been back in thirty years."

The room fell quiet. I was thrilled with my father's story and the way he had told it. I planned to ask him more questions about his life, to talk all night, but it was late and I was beyond tired. Laying in my bed with my father so close, I felt safe in a way I hadn't felt since my mother died. I closed my eyes for what I thought would be just a moment.

"Well, then," I heard my father say. "I suppose that's enough talking for tonight. We should get some sleep now. Good night, boys."

Tommy was silent. But I managed to whisper, "Good night, Dad," before slipping away.

CHAPTER TWELVE

"I CAN'T HELP IT, I love cheeseburgers, any kind, any way," Bobby Lee said as he poured a pool of ketchup onto his plate that spread like an oil slick. "I know they ain't the best thing for me, but I can't help it. Everyone's got a vice I suppose. What's yours?" he asked as he took a bite of the burger. "Fast little girls?"

I ignored him and tried to swallow a thick french fry. Bobby Lee's persistent questions were making it difficult to keep to my strategy of silence. Sooner or later I was going to have to speak.

"Yeah, well, you are a little young for women," he said.

We were sitting in Will's New Family Restaurant eating an early dinner. Originally, Bobby Lee had wanted to go to McDonald's but after talking to the lawyers it was decided that we would have more privacy at Will's. They were right, we were the only people there other than Bobby Lee's and my father's lawyer who were at a nearby table drinking coffee. Outside, I could see Maurice, who had dropped me off, sitting and smoking in his car, the window down a crack.

"Kind of a nice place," Bobby Lee said, looking around the empty restaurant, his mouth now full of cheeseburger.

I looked around with him. He was right. Over the past few months, Will's had undergone a drastic transformation. Its heavy layer of grease and slime had been stripped away to reveal a brighter, cleaner, almost cheerful surface. The old, stained, and ripped booths had vanished, replaced with sleek black lacquer tables and the slippery floor was now a dazzling checkerboard of black and white. Even the menus were new and colorful, offering selections under impressive headings such as "May We Suggest . . ." and "A Few Wonders from Will's Grill." Off in the far corner, some remodeling was evidently in progress; a wall had been knocked down and behind a hanging sheet I caught glimpses of ladders and buckets of paint. A sign on a nearby easel read, PARDON OUR DUST. When Will seated us, he briefly explained that he was building a small banquet room for special occasions such as funerals.

"So, do you think you'd ever like to come visit me in Tennessee sometime?" I shrugged.

"I think you'd like it," Bobby Lee said, chewing on a french fry. Then his expression changed and he looked down at his plate. "These fries suck," he said and waved the waitress over. Despite all the new changes at Will's, I recognized the waitress as the same one who had waited on Tommy, Uncle Frank, and me awhile back, the last time we were at Will's. Her teeth still looked like they needed to be shined.

"Get me some more of these. I got a bad batch here."

The waitress gave Bobby Lee a long look before walking away.

"You like burgers?" he asked.

I nodded.

"Your mom, she liked hamburgers too. That's about all we ate down in Memphis. You remember ever eatin' hamburgers down in Memphis?"

"No," I said. I allowed myself to speak. I figured having no recall of my prior life was a point I should communicate.

"Yeah, well, you were just a babe." He took a long drink of his Coke, pulling hard on his straw. "So," he said, swallowing. "What do you want to be when you grow up? A doctor or lawyer or something? I heard you get good grades. I know you like to draw. You want to be some kind of artist?"

I nodded. Apparently, my silent strategy was having little impact on Bobby Lee. He seemed oblivious of the fact that I wasn't talking or responding to his questions. I sipped my Coke and wondered if a new strategy, one that focused on short, dull answers, would be more effective.

"Yeah, well, you're young. You got plenty of time. You can do what you want to do. Just don't go join the army. That's all I can say. I tried it for awhile and I hated it, didn't like it one bit. My brother Carl joined too. He's your uncle. He liked it enough. But he's always been a little off. He and my sister Barbara are different. She'd be your aunt. We called her Barbi growing up. She and Carl were always ganging up on me like they were my parents. She lives in Kentucky, Barbi, in Lexington, I think. Haven't seen her in awhile."

I continued to say nothing. I wanted to tell Bobby Lee that I had no interest in these people, Carl and Barbi, had no interest in who they were and what they did. I knew he was trying to construct bridges to me, connect me to his life, but I just wanted to go home.

"So, you and Amy used to draw a lot. She liked to draw all right. And dance. Hell, she could dance. Was a shame what happened to her. She wasn't a very good driver. Drove reckless. I used to tell her to slow down. I don't think she had very good eyesight either. I remember her telling me that she needed glasses or contact lenses. But she never got them. Vain. Did she ever get them up here?"

I shook my head.

"Maybe if she got them, she would have seen that exit ramp. I heard that she was decapitated."

My stomach turned around and I tasted something terrible in the back of my throat. "What's that mean?" I asked, though I was afraid I knew. I remembered hearing that word whispered around our house soon after the accident.

"It meant her head was chopped off," he said. "Or knocked off maybe."

I felt a hole open in my stomach, felt my heart fall through it. I swallowed hard and looked back out the window at Maurice's car.

"Your mother was pretty. Hard to imagine her without her head. Did you go to the funeral?"

I kept looking out the window. Maurice was leaning back in his seat, barely visible. I was hoping to make eye contact with him. I wanted to give him a look that he would immediately understand as a plea. The taste in my throat was getting worse.

"Must have been a sad affair, her funeral. Wish I had known about it.

Would have made the effort to be there. Despite everything, I would have come. Did they reattach her head?" he asked as he took another sip from his Coke. "For the funeral? Did they put it back on? Hell, they can do anything nowadays. I knew a guy who had his hand chopped off once fixing a lawn mower and he just picked it up and went to the hospital and they just sewed it back on. A year later, he chopped off the other hand and they fixed that one too. When I saw him after that second time, I just said, hell, man, get rid of that lawn mower."

He sucked hard on his straw again, emptying his glass. "Where's she buried? Is she buried around here, nearby?"

I nodded my head.

"I guess I should go there," he said. "Pay my respects. Despite everything, we had some good times. Especially in high school. We ran around with some wild kids but we had fun. She ever tell you about those times? She ever tell you the time that she did that hand stand in church? Right in front of the whole congregation. She was about fourteen. Right next to the priest. She had just given a little talk, she was representing her Sunday school class. She used to go to church a lot back then. St. Agnes. And after she finished the talk she stood on her hands and walked on them a little. She said she would do it if I ever went to church. So when I finally went, she did it. Hell, that was funny. Always thought we'd get back together. Guess I should visit her grave. Maybe you want to come with me. Pay respects together." He wiped his hands on a napkin and I noticed his fingernails were rimmed with dirt.

"What kind of name is Pappas?" he asked suddenly.

"It's my last name," I said. I was so shaken by the image of my mother without a head that I could no longer focus on my silence strategy.

"Hell, I know that. I mean, what kind of nationality is it? What country?"

"It's Greek. My father is Greek."

Bobby Lee shot me a look when I said "father," then picked up what was left of his cheeseburger and bit down hard. "Greek. Hell, I don't know many Greeks. Knew one one time. But I didn't like him. He was short and walked around like he owned everything and everyone and he hardly could speak English."

"My father isn't like that," I said.

Bobby Lee stopped chewing and leaned over the table and whispered, "He ain't your father. He's your guardian. Or something."

"He's my father," I said, looking down at the table. "And I'm staying with him and Tommy."

Bobby Lee started to say something when the waitress came back with a new plate of french fries. I felt his eyes on me and saw his hand reach out for a fry then quickly throw it back on the plate.

"Hey, lady, come back here, these fries are cold and probably still taste like piss," he said. I looked up. His hawk eyes had narrowed and his face was red.

"Oh, so you know what piss tastes like?" The waitress said. She looked angry too.

"Hell, you been eye-balling me since I came in here," Bobby Lee said. "You got a problem with me?"

"Yeah," the waitress whispered. "I got a big problem with you. Why don't you go back to your swamp and leave this family alone?"

"You get the fuck out of here," Bobby Lee said. But he said it too loud and the lawyers stopped talking and Gus came out from behind his shiny new counter holding a very old baseball bat.

"What the fuck's your problem?" Bobby Lee yelled to Gus.

The lawyers jumped up and rushed over to our table. Bobby Lee stood up, waiting for them. He stood straight with his chest out, his arms bent slightly, his hands in fists.

"Get the hell away from me you bunch of piss ants. I'm getting sick and tired of being abused by everyone in this goddamn city. Goddamn sick and tired, you hear me?"

"Robert, this is not the time," Bobby Lee's lawyer said.

"Hell, you shut your face! I'm paying you money I ain't got and all I'm doing is sitting around waiting for nothing. You've been telling me to stay quiet, lay low, and I have been. But I'm sick and tired of waiting. Something's gotta give." He grabbed my shoulder. "This boy is mine. I never wanted to give him up. Didn't know what happened to him. Now I found him and I want him back. Now everyone's making me out to be some type of criminal."

"These meetings should have been better supervised," Quinn, my father's lawyer, said. "Let go of the boy."

"You don't tell me what to do with my son," Bobby Lee said.

"Let go of that boy," I heard a voice say. I looked over toward the door and saw Maurice moving quickly toward us. "You let go of him right now." He had a look on his face I had never seen before, a fire in his eyes.

"What do you want?" Bobby Lee asked.

Maurice stopped inches from Bobby Lee and stood silently, coiled and a million miles tall. Bobby Lee looked around the room at everyone, at the lawyers, at Gus, then back at Maurice. Then I felt him loosen his grip on my shoulder.

"You outnumber me, boy," he said to Maurice. "You might not next time." Then he let me go.

THE DAYS PASSED slowly and a quiet fear fell over our house, a worry that I could read in Aunt Bess's eyes and hear in Uncle Frank's suddenly mellow voice. I seldom saw my father, he was either in his study or meeting with the lawyers downtown. Bobby Lee, for his part, vanished. After the incident at Will's, we didn't see or hear from him, except through his lawyer. I spent most of those dreary days in my room, doing my homework, reviewing my List of Things and waiting.

I suspected the battle against Bobby Lee wasn't going well. Once, after dinner, I briefly overheard Uncle Frank and my father discussing a compromise Bobby Lee had apparently offered, the terms of which weren't discussed. In the end, my father would have none of it, however.

"Under no circumstances," I heard him say, his voice firm. "That is completely unacceptable. I will not negotiate."

Faced with what I thought was the increasing possibility of my having to move to Tennessee, I decided to take matters into my own hands and began to formulate an alternative plan, a plan that, while risky, offered me some hope: I would stage my own death.

I would write a suicide note announcing my decision to take my life rather than go live with Bobby Lee in the hills. I had yet to work out the exact wording of this letter which was to be several pages long, illustrated and in fact resemble a short book, but it would be hopefully convincing enough that Bobby Lee would believe it and leave me alone.

My plan, while simple in theory, had one major flaw however: most suicide notes were usually accompanied by a dead body. The absence of my body, I feared, would cause serious credibility problems with my scheme, causing more problems than it solved. I wrestled with this issue for days, considering various options, until I came up with what I thought was a solution. About five miles away, in the nearby suburb of Wilton Highlands, there was a small river, the Pepper Creek, which eventually ran into the larger Brandon River, a legendary cauldron of smoldering pollution and toxic waste. My Suicide Book would reveal my plans to throw myself into the creek and drown. It would also stress the futility of searching for my body since the toxins in the Brandon River would destroy all trace.

My Pepper Creek plan also called for the leaving of shoes and an old pair of pants on the Creek's bank, as well as a hiding place, possibly Montana or Charlie Governs's basement. After a suitable amount of time, I would somehow get word to my family about my condition—living. We would then construct a new life together, one that would include a permanent relocation to a remote island or mountain top and the wearing of disguises.

One Saturday afternoon, while I was in the middle of the first chapter of my Suicide Book, I heard my father approaching my room, his heavy step unmistakable. I sat up straight in my chair, bracing for some type of bad news. He had been on the phone most of the day, talking low and taking notes with his gold fountain pen, his face grim. I feared the worst.

"Teddy," my father said as he entered my room. I looked up at him. I had just finished sketching a pair of lonely shoes laying in some weeds besides the Pepper Creek. Underneath the sketch I had already written the words *"Gone Forever, Do Not Search For."*

"Teddy," he said again, apologetically. It was then that I noticed the strange way he was dressed. He was wearing tight fitting white shorts and an equally tight fitting white shirt. He looked at me, an uncertain snowman. "Would you," he said, "would you like to play tennis?"

"KEEP YOUR EYE on the ball, Theo," Mrs. Wilcott said. Then she said quietly, "Maybe we should have just had a late lunch."

Mrs. Wilcott and I were sitting on a bench at the indoor court of the Wilton Country Club watching my father swing and miss tennis balls with a frequency that defied the law of averages. Sooner or later he had to hit something.

Joining the Wilton Country Club was Mrs. Wilcott's idea, I knew that as soon as I saw her waiting by the front door of the club, standing underneath the gold-and-green club crest, wearing a short white skirt and delicate white bow in her hair that looked like it had fallen softly and with perfect aim from a cloud. Despite my feelings toward her, I continued to grant her credit for her beauty. Standing with a white sweater draped over her shoulders, she looked like a shiny-faced angel playing hostess at the gates of heaven.

On the drive over, my father had attempted to explain why we were joining the club, the oldest and most prestigious in Wilton. Located on the outskirts of town, on the area's only real hill, it was a remote place I had given little thought to until now.

"I just thought we could enjoy some of the activities they offer, as a family," my father said. "They have two pools, a golf course, tennis, and supposedly an excellent restaurant which I thought your aunt might enjoy."

Instead of being thrilled—the club definitely had an *Eastern Estates'* look and feel about it—I was plunged into a near state of panic over this new development: country clubs today, Tennessee tomorrow, I thought.

"Are you all right?" Mrs. Wilcott now yelled to my father. He had slipped on the court, falling briefly to one knee. He waved and stood back up, his hand on the arch of his back.

My father continued to swing at balls. With each miss, he seemed to grow smaller, shrinking until it appeared that he was hovering just inches above the court. I found it difficult to watch him in this diminished state and instead turned my attention to his tennis instructor, Miss Cahill, who I thought was very pretty in a sympathetic nurse way. Mrs. Wilcott had thought starting with a lesson might make sense after my father informed her that neither he nor I had ever played tennis before. He had volunteered to take the first lesson, the reasoning being that I could study and learn from him.

"Good effort," Miss Cahill yelled as my father missed yet again, twirling and twitching in a violent manner that reminded me of a PBS series I had once seen on seizures.

"Try to keep from dropping the tennis racket, though," she yelled across the net. "Hold on tight. Contact will come."

My father nodded, then bent forward in the peculiar, hunched-over stance that Miss Cahill had taught him, his arms dangling lifelessly in front of him. Miss Cahill lobbed the ball over her own head and gracefully tapped it in his direction. I watched as the ball gently arched into the air, flew harmlessly over the net, bounced once, then quietly hit him directly in the middle of his forehead. He hadn't even attempted to swing.

"Are you all right?" Miss Cahill called.

"Yes, I'm fine," my father said. He offered no explanation for not swinging his racket.

Miss Cahill looked at him then said, "I think that might be it for today,"

"My timing seems to be a bit off," my father said as he walked painfully over to where we were sitting. Up close he looked terrible. His face was blotched red and his hair was sticking out perpendicular to his head. He was breathing so hard that I considered offering him the antiheart-attack pill I had smuggled out of the house and now had in my pocket.

"The timing will come. With practice," Miss Cahill said. "Overall, how did you feel out there?"

"Well, to be honest, a bit awkward," my father said. "I've never had much eye-hand coordination, but I enjoyed the exercise nonetheless."

"I think you did just great," Miss Cahill said and smiled. Then she leaned over and dabbed some sweat off my father's forehead with the corner of a towel. She was about to do it again when Mrs. Wilcott suddenly stood up and stepped in between them.

"Theo, you look like you could use a tall glass of lemonade in the clubhouse," she said.

"Oh, yes, I imagine I could," my father said. "Yes. I'm, I'm afraid I'm paying a price for all those wonderful pies you've been making for us, Gloria," he said.

"Those pies will slow you down," Miss Cahill said. "You really should be watching what you eat. A lower fat, higher protein diet will give you more energy."

My father looked embarrassed and said, "Yes."

Mrs. Wilcott smiled, but only for a second.

"Teddy, are you interested in playing a little?" my father asked.

"No," I said simply.

Miss Cahill flicked some hair away from her eyes. "Are you sure? It'll be fun."

"If he doesn't want to, he doesn't have to," Mrs. Wilcott said, her voice now full of small edges. "He's really a soccer player, aren't you, Teddy?"

I shrugged.

"We'll just reschedule for another time," Mrs. Wilcott said.

Miss Cahill looked over at Mrs. Wilcott. She was young and lean and had misty gray eyes that looked mysterious. "Okay," she finally said. "Well, just call me here at the club to schedule. I'm here most days." She gave my father a half-smile, one corner of her mouth up just slightly, and walked slowly away, her arms swinging at her sides, in perfect rhythm with her short white skirt.

Mrs. Wilcott watched Miss Cahill leave, a flat and focused expression on her face. Then she suddenly came back to life, cocking her head to one side and smiling.

"Lemonade anyone?" she chirped.

THE WILTON COUNTRY Club was long and sprawling, a maze of thickly carpeted hallways and dark, mahogany-paneled rooms. Despite its pools, tennis courts and golf courses, the club was shrouded in stillness, a forced, tight quiet that the members, mostly older people of or about my father's age, seemed afraid or unwilling to disturb. The club, built in 1901, had been renovated just twice, the last time being more than twenty-five years ago, a fact that Mrs. Wilcott, who headed the renovation committee, found simply unacceptable.

"Quite a bit of work has to be done," she said as she sipped her bottled water.

"Yes, I imagine it does," my father said.

We were sitting in the Clubhouse Room, by a huge window that overlooked the first fairway of the golf course, a wide avenue of browning grass that unfolded before us like a soft airport runway. According to Mrs. Wilcott, the Western Open had been played here many years ago and Arnold Palmer himself had walked these very grounds.

"Very impressive," my father said.

I sipped my lemonade and looked out the window. We were the only ones in the clubhouse. The old empty room, with its high, remote ceilings and dark brown carpet vaguely reminded me of Mrs. Plank's Dust Chamber. Somewhere in the middle of my first glass of lemonade, I decided I wanted to go home.

"We need to raise two-point-five-million dollars over the next six months," Mrs. Wilcott said.

My father, who also had been looking out the window, deep (I was sure) in Bobby Lee thoughts, turned to face her. "I'm sorry?"

Mrs. Wilcott smiled. "We need to raise two-point-five-million for the club."

My father's eyes widened. "Why?"

"To preserve the integrity of the building."

My father was silent for a moment, then nodded his head. "Oh," he said. "Yes, integrity."

"We're all set for the fund-raiser next week. The Gala. I hope you remembered to keep that on your calendar, Theo." She reached over and briefly touched my father's arm. "You asked me to remind you."

"Oh, yes, of course. The fund-raiser. Yes. We're planning on attending. I meant to mention that to you, Teddy," he said, turning to me.

"You'll have to rent another tuxedo," Mrs. Wilcott said. "You should really just buy one. It would make more sense."

"A tuxedo, yes."

Mrs. Wilcott looked at me. "You're coming too, Teddy, you and the whole family. We've hired a wonderful band. I'm sure you and Benjamin will be able to persuade a few young ladies to dance."

I nodded my head, the image she described inconceivable.

"Your aunt is invited to the Gala too," Mrs. Wilcott said. "As is your Uncle Frank, of course. We're all sitting at the same table. We always have a wonderful time at the Gala."

I finished my lemonade, my straw scraping the bottom of my tall thin glass. The casual but affirmative way Mrs. Wilcott referred to the Gala made me wonder if it had recently been established as a national religious holiday, like Christmas or Easter.

"It's a shame about Mr. Sylvanius's foot. I hope he'll be able to make it to our house for Thanksgiving," she said. She turned to face me. "Benjamin is very excited about having you over. I'm baking a special apple pie for you."

I was surprised by this announcement. Uncle Frank's birthday was on Thanksgiving and I knew Aunt Bess was planning a special meal for him. My father though didn't catch my glance and continued to look out the window.

"Mr. Sylvanius was also going to do a dramatic reading during the talent hour," Mrs. Wilcott said.

My father finally looked up at this, focusing. "I'm sorry? Talent hour?"

Mrs. Wilcott smiled and rearranged a cloth napkin on the table, pressing down hard on it with both hands. "Yes, he had committed to participating. A handful of members perform every year."

My father nodded.

"I've been asked to sing," Mrs. Wilcott said. She looked at my father expectantly as if she had just made an important announcement, her proud but hesitant expression on her face managing to make me feel sad. I knew that she wanted my father to react in a certain way, to congratulate her, but he merely looked back out the window. I glanced away and tried to dig a last remaining ice cube out of the bottom of my glass with my straw. I didn't want to see her disappointment.

"It's just two songs," she said quickly. "Cindy Watson of the committee asked me. I haven't sung in years. But she was very persistent. Very." Mrs. Wilcott folded then refolded the napkin.

"Well. We're looking forward to the evening," my father said, unconvincingly. "Are the tuxedos necessary?"

"Not for the boys. But you'll have to wear one, yes. Especially since you'll be sitting at the head table."

My father nodded and said nothing. I could tell that he was tired and wanted to be going. The late nights with the lawyers and the tennis lesson had done him in. I thought he might fall asleep at the table.

Mrs. Wilcott didn't seem to be concerned or even notice my father's state however. For the next twenty minutes, she talked urgently about seating arrangements, agendas, menus and floral arrangements for the Gala, her voice picking up speed in the face of my father's silence. Twice the waiter came and refilled our glasses and I began to swim in lemonade.

"Oh, Theo," Mrs. Wilcott said, as she sipped her water. A sudden transformation came over her and she looked strangely awkward and nervous. She folded the napkin again and fixed her eyes on my father. "I hate to pester you about this, but the committee is wondering if you've agreed to serve as honorary chairperson of the event. I mentioned it to you last month. You said you'd consider it."

My father had no reaction. He continued to look out the window, distracted. I finished another lemonade and this time tried to dig the ice cube out of my glass with my hand. When I tilted my glass, two melting cubes slipped out and onto the table.

Mrs. Wilcott glanced at me, an unusual look of annoyance on her face. Then she stopped folding the napkin and leaned toward my father. "Theo? I said the committee asked that you serve as honorary chairperson. Nothing's really required. You just have to say a few words."

My father finally turned to face her, a faint light of recognition flickering in his eyes. "I'm sorry? Oh, that's right, the chairperson." He grimaced. "Gloria, I've given it some thought and I don't think I'd be right for such a role."

Mrs. Wilcott sat up straight in her chair and began to finger a small gold necklace that hung between her breasts.

"Why not?"

My father shook his head. "Well, as I've mentioned, I'm not even a member yet. We haven't officially signed all the papers."

"That's just a formality." She leaned over the table. "Oh, Theo, you'd be perfect. You're a well-known historian. A successful writer and a wonderful parent." She smiled at me when she said this.

My father exhaled slowly. I was surprised that he was putting up any resistance. He seemed incapable of independent thought where Mrs. Wilcott was concerned. I attributed this change to the strain of the past few weeks, a strain that seemed to be hardening him. "I don't think I would feel comfortable," he finally said.

"You will add quite a bit of credibility to the event. To the cause."

"The cause," my father repeated. "I think there might be better, more appropriate . . ." he stopped and quickly picked up his glass of iced tea.

Mrs. Wilcott studied my father for a moment, then smiled and leaned halfway across the table. I stopped sucking on my straw. Through her tennis blouse, I could clearly see her brassiere and the tops of her breasts as they pressed against it. Some strands of hair fell free across her forehead and when she moved her hand to slowly brush them aside, I thought she might very well be the most beautiful woman in the world.

"All you have to do," she said softly, "is talk a few minutes about the history of Wilton and the club's role, then announce the totals collected from the silent auction. I'll be onstage with you. You said you would do it when I first asked."

"Well," my father said. He was about to say something else, but stopped. Instead he smiled weakly and leaned back, far away from Mrs. Wilcott and looked at her for a moment as if he were trying to balance something. Then he did something that shocked me. He cleared his throat and stood up. Mrs. Wilcott sat back, surprised, her eyes a mixture of confusion and anger. As far as I knew, it was the first time he had ever ended a visit with her first.

"We really have to be going," he said.

CHAPTER THIRTEEN

M RS. WILCOTT WAS standing perfectly still as the curtains drew back to reveal her standing slightly off to the side of the stage. She had a happily expectant look on her face, as if she was about to receive good news. When the music began, she walked toward the center of the stage, moving with a casual grace in a slow, smooth walk that put the audience at ease. As I watched her in her short black dress, black stockings and high heels, I believed I was watching the devil's wife herself.

"Killer legs," Uncle Frank said as he reached for his Diet Coke. "I'll give her that. Killer legs."

When she reached the microphone she sat down on a tall stool next to the large white piano and surveyed the crowd one last time, a calm, almost holy expression on her face. She then nodded to the piano player, a small man with wire spectacles and began to sing.

Her first song was sweet and sad, a song I didn't recognize about lost love. As she sang, she put her hand on her chest and when she reached what I assumed was the saddest part of the song, she closed her eyes and shook her head in a way that reminded me that Dr. Wilcott had abandoned her for a tennis pro. When she was done, she hung her head limply, her chin almost bouncing off her chest. The room filled with applause.

She adjusted herself on the stool and smiled. "Now," she said. "We're going to lighten things up a bit." When she crossed her legs, there was a silent sigh from every man in the room.

"Raindrops keep falling on my head . . ."

Uncle Frank looked across the table at me and shook his head. "You're too young to remember *The Gong Show*," he said.

"And just like the guy whose feet are too big for his bed."

Listening to Mrs. Wilcott sing was less embarrassing than I had thought it would be. I had hoped for some mishap, forgotten lyrics, a collapsing chair, a ripped dress but, as usual, she was in command of the moment. That evening months ago when she sang for my family after dinner, her voice had been deep and bold. Tonight though, it was light and soft and entranced the room. Sitting onstage with her killer legs crossed, she seemed to be hovering a few feet above the rest of us in a special, reserved space. I looked over for Tommy's reaction, but he was sleeping, his head down on the table. I glanced my father's way, but couldn't see his face either because of the darkness. Resigned to my fate, the Gala was at least an hour or so from being over, I sat back in my chair and lost myself in thought.

The week prior to the Gala had been hectic. My father's lawyer, Quinn, was frequently at our house working late into the night with my father. Despite his schedule, Mrs. Wilcott managed a number of visits, urging my father to accept the honorary chairperson position of the Gala. Her requests, and the timing of them, infuriated Uncle Frank.

"Doesn't this broad realize that you might have more important things to worry about right now?" he blurted out one night after dinner. "Hell, it's pretty obvious what she's trying to do. She figures making you the head guy of this party is going to force you into giving money. You're her prize, Theo, her goddamn prize. She wants to show you off. Look, I bagged Mr. Money-bags. I still got it. She doesn't give a shit about anything else. I know her type, believe me."

"I don't think that's the case at all," my father had said quietly. It wasn't until the ride over to the country club that he told us that he had agreed to be introduced as honorary chairperson and say a few words about the history of Wilton.

The Gala itself had been predictably boring, with a series of speeches and toasts to the future of the Wilton Country Club filling the evening. The talent hour had been equally dull. Prior to Mrs. Wilcott, there had been a dance number, two husband and wife duets, a violin solo, and a painful comedy monologue by the teenage son of a prominent lawyer. It was during this monologue that Benjamin, who had been sitting at our table ignoring me, had disappeared to go play in the club gym.

Despite my boredom, the evening appeared to be a success. Hundreds of people were there, drinks in hand, greeting one another with smooth faces, pats on the back and kisses on the cheek. The grand ballroom was suitably impressive. Large and dimly lit, with dark wood-trimmed doorways and cathedral windows, it reminded me of an immense funeral parlor. The floral centerpieces that Mrs. Wilcott had ultimately chosen were a spectacular combination of colors and sweet scents. Aunt Bess asked the waitress if she could take ours home.

It was the women of Wilton that caught and held my attention though. They were beautiful in their short and shimmering dresses, their backs and arms naked and free for my inspection. Despite their outfits however, none came close to approaching the appearance of Mrs. Wilcott.

She looked particularly beautiful, her dress catching the stares of both men and women as she made her way through the ballroom during the cocktail hour, touching people's elbows and smiling in a way I didn't believe. She seemed illuminated as she glided through the crowd, my father and family following her trailing light. Several people tried to engage my father in conversation as we walked about, inquiring about my situation and wishing us well, but he remained silent. He hadn't said more than three words all evening and I wondered how he was going to manage his brief speech.

"Thank God, she's done," Uncle Frank said.

Mrs. Wilcott ended her song, and hung her head shyly again while waiting for the applause. The men in particular seemed to appreciate her performance. Dr. McDonnell, an orthodontist who was sitting at the next table, stood as he clapped.

While people were still clapping, she made her way slowly back to our table, acknowledging the audience with a smile and a strange wave of her hand, her wrist turning slowly and mechanically to one side and back. When she sat down between Tommy and me, I could feel heat coming off her body.

"Where's Benjamin?" she whispered to me. Mrs. Wilcott remained convinced that Benjamin and I were friends, despite the fact that we had not spoken all night.

"I think he's playing basketball," I said. I kept my eyes on the stage where the piano player was furiously playing, the tempo quickening.

Mrs. Wilcott didn't seem to hear me. She kept looking around the room, smiling and offering small waves. I moved my chair away from her. Early in the evening, when we first arrived, she matter-of-factly told me that I needed a haircut and new shoes.

"Theo, we're on in a few minutes," she whispered across the table. My father nodded. It was then that I noticed his face. He looked stricken, his eyes glassy, his face chalk.

"Gloria, I don't think I'm up to this," he said quietly. "I am sorry."

"What?"

"I don't think I can go through with this."

Mrs. Wilcott yanked on her gold necklace. "Oh, Theo, we've been through this before. All you have to do is say a few things. Your speech. Just say your speech. The one we practiced. You'll only be up there for three minutes. I'll be right beside you."

My father licked his lips and coughed once into his hand. "I don't think I'm up to this," he said again. "Not this evening."

"Are you all right, Theo?" Aunt Bess asked. "Is it your heart?"

"I'll be fine," he said. "I just don't feel comfortable speaking in front of crowds, this size. I haven't lectured in awhile. And even when I did, they were small groups, really."

"He can't do it, Gloria," Aunt Bess said. "He can't do it."

"He *has* to do it," Mrs. Wilcott said quickly, her voice flat. "It's printed in the program. I promised everyone."

Immediately after saying this, she smiled and her voice once again sounded like a chipmunk's. "I'm sorry, Theo," she said. "If you're truly not up to this, I guess I can do this alone. If you *truly* can't do this." Then she said, "But I wish you would try. It's only a few minutes."

My father sighed and looked down at the table. "Well," he said. "I might be able to manage." But when he stood up, he wavered for a moment and grabbed onto the table. As I watched him steady himself, an unfamiliar feeling rose inside me, a growing anger.

"Jesus, Theo, you look like hell," Uncle Frank said. "Sit down."

"No, I'll be fine," he said, though it was obvious he wasn't. Mrs. Wilcott quickly stood up.

"He's fine," she said.

"No, he's not," I said. I found myself jumping out of my chair and moving toward my father. "Leave him alone. He's not feeling good. Just leave us all alone." I was now standing between my father and Mrs. Wilcott. I was vaguely aware that the music had stopped and that people were clapping. Mrs. Wilcott tried to walk past me, but I held my position.

She stopped and regarded me in a peculiar way, as if she was examining a faraway object up close for the first time. I felt the heat coming off her body, could feel her self-restraint giving way, the bounds loosening.

"He's not feeling good," I said again, but this time I said it quietly.

"You be quiet!" she snapped. "Sit down. Sit down in your chair right now, young man. I've worked so hard on this event. You people are impossible!" Her voice sounded like it might break in half and that the raw edges would cut me.

"You don't talk to him like that," Aunt Bess said. She struggled to her feet. "And what do you mean, 'you people'?"

"Jesus Christ, everyone sit down, we're making a scene here," Uncle Frank said. He glanced around the room which was growing quiet. A few people at nearby tables were looking our way. Dr. McDonnell turned completely around in his chair and stared at us, his mouth open. Then Uncle Frank said, "Hey, yeah, what do you mean, 'you people'?"

Mrs. Wilcott fingered her necklace roughly, sliding her hand up and down the slight chain so hard I thought it would break.

"Are you coming?" she asked my father quietly.

My father looked directly at her and straightened his back. "No," he said. "I'm not." But his eyes were clear and he didn't look sick anymore.

AFTER MRS. WILCOTT presented the totals for the silent auction and thanked everyone for coming, Uncle Frank, Aunt Bess, Tommy, and I left. As planned, my father stayed with Mrs. Wilcott for dancing and drinks, though I assumed he would be doing neither.

"That woman is a solid gold bitch," Uncle Frank said when we got into the old Buick. "She reminds me of Corky."

"Who?" I asked as I buckled my seat belt.

"Corky Patterson. An ex-wife of mine, one of the many former aunts of yours you never had the pleasure of meeting. This one in particular was a special lady," he said. "In so many ways, a special lady."

When we got home, I went straight to bed. I was exhausted. Tommy was asleep in minutes, breathing slow and loud. I tried to sleep, but found myself thinking of Mrs. Wilcott and my behavior. While I was embarrassed and surprised by what I had done, I wasn't sorry. After her final presentation onstage, Mrs. Wilcott had ignored me and we left without saying good-bye.

I was mulling over the evening, finally drifting toward the edge of sleep when I heard my father's voice.

"Teddy? Are you awake?"

I sat up. "No, yes, I mean. How come you're home now?"

He made his way to my bed in the darkness, stepping around Tommy's clothes which lay in a pile on the floor.

"I called a taxicab and left a little early," he said. "I don't think I'll be missed." He sat down on my bed. Even in the darkness, I could see how tired he was. The circles under his eyes looked like soft ridges. "Did you enjoy the party, the Gala?"

"No," I said. He sat there a moment, his shoulders rounding into an arch. "Are you feeling okay now?" I asked.

"Yes, yes, I'm fine. I think I just, I think I suffered from a bit of stage fright perhaps. I used to get light-headed when I first started lecturing. I hadn't had that sensation in years though, that feeling that things were," he paused here, "well, beyond me. Everything beyond me." He coughed and cleared his throat.

"I don't like Mrs. Wilcott," I said. I knew this comment might have ramifications, but it was late, I was tired, and I didn't care. I expected a stern response, or at least surprise, but my father was silent.

"Well," he finally said. "She was very tense tonight. She had quite a bit of responsibility, organizing such an event. I never should have committed to speaking." He sighed here. "Though she shouldn't have spoken to you like that, in that manner. I told her that."

"You did?"

He cleared his throat. "Yes. Yes, I did. I expressed my disappointment."

I was stunned. I couldn't imagine him doing that.

"What did she say?"

"Well, I'd rather not get into that right now. It's for the best though."

"Are you going to marry her?" I asked.

He made a strange sound that I recognized as his rusty chuckle. "Oh, no, no. I assure you, that won't happen."

We sat together on the bed and listened to Tommy breathe. "Teddy," he finally said. "We should be hearing very shortly about our situation. I received a call earlier, as we were leaving for the party. Our lawyer called," he stopped here. I felt dizzy and closed my eyes for a moment, waiting for him to tell me the news that I was leaving. But instead, he just coughed. "We don't know anything yet, but we should know within the next few days. About the outcome. They're coming to a decision much sooner than we expected, anticipated. I'm sure everything will be fine though," he added hastily.

I couldn't think of anything to say so I was quiet.

"Well." He stood up, pressing down on my bed with his hand to raise himself. He started for the door.

"Do you miss mom?" I asked.

His shoulders shook at the directness of my question, but his voice was steady. He turned back to face me. "We all do." He paused. "I know she tried. With me, with us. With everything. She wanted things to work. And she wanted everyone to be happy, especially you and Tommy. But unfortunately, things didn't work out the way she envisioned." He smiled at me in a way that made me want to cry. "You have her good qualities, you and Tommy. Her spirit." He didn't say anything else. He just stood there. Outside, a car drove by, its headlights bright against the walls, then gone. "Despite everything, I miss her. I miss her every day," he finally said and then he too was gone, disappearing with the light.

WE DIDN'T GO to the Wilcotts' for Thanksgiving. Instead, we stayed home and celebrated Uncle Frank's birthday by eating lamb. My father offered no reason or explanation for this change of plans, nor did he return any of Mrs. Wilcott's many phone calls. Instead, the night before Thanksgiving he simply brought home a large leg of lamb from DeVries, the local supermarket.

I was pleased with the change of plans, content to sit on the living room floor, watching the flames lick the bricks of our little used fireplace, eating feta cheese and olives. Aunt Bess had prepared an immense tray of appetizers for us but I focused most of my efforts on the Greek olives, a treat I found irresistible.

"This is all rather quaint," Sylvanius said. He was sitting in a gleaming, new wheelchair my father had bought him, a bright red blanket draped over his legs, a glass of wine in his hand. "This all reminds me of a Norman Rockwell movie."

Uncle Frank looked up at him, then over at Maurice who was sitting quietly on the couch, reading an old issue of *National Geographic* by the firelight. In the dining room I could hear Aunt Bess asking my father when he wanted to slice the lamb.

"There is something so, so, well so nice about a fire," Sylvanius said.

Uncle Frank shook his head. "You have a poet's eye, you know that, Sylvanius? A poet's eye."

Sylvanius smiled at Uncle Frank's comment. "Dear, dear Frank. Tell us, do you feel any wiser today? You certainly are older. Has your great advanced age, brought on any great insights?"

Uncle Frank silently stared into the fire, his jaw at a reflective angle. He had been quiet all day, moping around the house in blacker than usual clothes, leafing unenthusiastically through the special holiday issue of *Luxury Living!*, with its cover story on amphibious snowmobiles and ice cruising yachts. Aunt Bess said he never liked his birthdays because they reminded him of death and all the money he never made.

"Penny for your thoughts, Frank," Sylvanius said.

Uncle Frank grunted. "That's about all you could afford."

Sylvanius laughed. "Oh, Frank, always thinking about money. Even on your fifty-third birthday."

"My fiftieth," Uncle Frank said.

"Ah, of course," Sylvanius said. "I've forgotten your unique way of marking time." Sylvanius took a sip of wine.

Maurice turned the page of the magazine.

"I remember when I was fifty-three. It seems like yesterday. Teddy, let that be a lesson to you. Time flies so enjoy it while you can."

"You should write for Hallmark," Uncle Frank said.

"Speaking of writing, how's your book going?" Sylvanius asked. "I haven't seen you writing much lately."

Uncle Frank shrugged. "Slow," he said.

"Are you blocked?"

"What?"

"Are you blocked?" Sylvanius asked again.

"What do you mean, like writer's block?"

"Yes."

"No," Uncle Frank said.

Everyone was quiet again. Maurice turned another page.

"I think you're blocked," Sylvanius said again.

"Goddamnit, I'm not blocked. I've taken a little time off from it. Now stop talking to me."

"My, my," Sylvanius said. "So much for the lively art of conversation." He sipped some more wine as I reached for my fifth and last olive. Aunt Bess had said I could only have five so I ate it slowly, rolling it around luxuriously inside my mouth before biting all the way down through the soft, bitter skin to the pit.

"So, Maurice," Sylvanius said. "You're so quiet sitting over there. What are you thinking?"

Maurice looked up, distracted. "I'm reading," he said softly.

"Oh, and what are you reading?"

"About an ancient Indian burial ground they discovered in New Mexico."

"Ah," Sylvanius said. "Of course. Burial grounds. Very appropriate for today's celebration. Have you given much thought to where you'll be buried, Frank?"

Uncle Frank grunted again and kept staring into the fire.

"I will be cremated, of course," Sylvanius said. "Burned to ashes."

This interested me. "Why?" I asked.

Sylvanius finished his wine and placed the empty glass on the coffee table. Then he brought both his index fingers together and tapped them back and forth, thinking. "Elvis," he said after some time.

No one said anything. Maurice looked up briefly from his magazine, then back down again. I took the olive pit out of my mouth and laid it carefully on my plate, next to the others I had lined up in a row. I guiltily reached for another.

"Yes, Elvis Presley," Sylvanius continued. "Many years ago, I visited Graceland where he's dead and buried. In Memphis."

"Memphis?" I asked. "In Tennessee?"

"Yes, I believe it's around there. And I remember thinking what a spectacle all this is, his fans waiting in line, people leaving things on the grave. Horrid, really. I do have a dedicated group of fans and I don't wish that on myself. No, I'll be burned and my ashes will be scattered. On Broadway, of course."

"Try the Poconos," Uncle Frank said. "Or the parking lot of a dinner theater."

Sylvanius shot Uncle Frank a sly, serpent smile. "Very clever, Frank. As always, very, very, clever." He sighed. "Well, I can see my attempts at thoughtful and provocative conversation are going nowhere so I'll just contemplate the fire and warm my old and broken bones."

"Broken bones." Uncle Frank spat the words. "Let me ask you something here. How long are you going to milk this foot thing?"

Sylvanius fixed Uncle Frank with another serpent stare. "Excuse me?"

"You heard me. How long are you going to be pulling this FDR act? When are you going to get the hell out of here?"

"If your brother asked me that question I would feel compelled to answer it since this is his house. But since you yourself are nothing but a guest I do not feel I have to respond. Besides, as we speak, my foot is throbbing and in need of medication."

Sylvanius reached over and picked up his glass, raised it high in the air, and smiled at Uncle Frank. "Oh, Bess," he called. "Oh, Bess, dear."

My father entered the room instead with Tommy walking stiffly by his side. They both sat down on the leather couch next to Maurice. It was then that I noticed that my father was holding a children's book.

My father looked apologetically around the room, which had fallen completely silent and said, "Excuse us." Then he picked up the book and cleared his throat while Tommy, expressionless, stared straight ahead into nothing. He seemed to be in a state of shock.

"What are you doing, Theo?" Uncle Frank asked. "What the hell's going on?"

My father cleared his throat again and held the book up for everyone to see. "I just thought Tommy and I would read this book," he said. "By the fire. This one here. Together. While we wait for dinner. Aunt Bess is almost ready."

Sylvanius looked over at Uncle Frank who nodded his head, then leaned back in his chair.

Maurice stood up from the couch. "Let me give you more room, Mr. Pappas."

"No, please, Mr. Jackson, I didn't mean to chase you . . ."

"It's no problem. I have to get something from my car. I'll be right back in a minute. Besides," he said, "you need some peace and quiet to do some reading together with your boys. Isn't that right?" He looked at Uncle Frank and Sylvanius, neither of whom said anything or made any effort to move.

"What?" Uncle Frank asked.

"I just thought . . ." Maurice's voice trailed off into silence.

Uncle Frank just sat there, stretched out low in his chair, looking bored and depressed while Sylvanius rearranged his blanket across his knees.

"I'll be back," Maurice said quietly and was gone.

"Well, then," my father said. He cleared his throat and took out his rectangle glasses from his front pocket and put them on the edge of his nose. Tommy remained completely silent and continued staring. I knew he was nervous. While my mother had frequently read to us, my father never had.

"May I ask, what are you reading, Theo?" Sylvanius asked.

"Oh," my father said. He closed the book he had just opened and studied its cover. "*If You Give a Mouse a Cookie,*" he said. "Tommy chose this. I asked him what book he wanted me to read and he chose this one, this book."

"*If You Give a Mouse a Cookie,*" Uncle Frank repeated. "What's it about, Tommy?"

Tommy looked down at the floor. "About what happens when you give a mouse a cookie."

Uncle Frank nodded. "Hence the title."

"And then, after he gets the cookie, he wants a lot of other things too," Tommy added.

"Well," my father said, opening the book again. He cleared his throat. "Shall we begin, Tommy? To read the book?"

Tommy nodded once.

"If you give a mouse a cookie," my father began, his voice halting and tentative. "He's going to ask for a glass of milk."

Uncle Frank glanced over at me, then sat farther back in his chair.

"When you give him the milk, he'll probably ask for a straw."

Sylvanius yawned and picked up his empty wine glass, then put it back down, then once again readjusted the blanket around his knees.

"When he's finished, he'll ask for a napkin."

I sat on the ground and watched my father, his face rigid and tense. He read without interruption or pause, speaking slowly and enunciating carefully, for both Tommy's and, I suspected, his own benefit, since he was essentially attempting to master a new language. He turned each page slowly, allowing Tommy plenty of time to study the pictures.

"So, he'll probably ask for a pair of nail scissors . . ."

Throughout the first few pages of the story, Tommy continued to stare, first at the floor, then at the book. After the mouse asked to be read a story, however, he began to steal glances at my father, then smile.

My father finished the story within a matter of minutes, slowly closed the book and exhaled.

"Well," he said. "It's a bit short. Did you enjoy it though, the book?"

Tommy nodded and smiled some more.

My father looked relieved, his face broadening out, and relaxing. "Good. I'm glad. He's an interesting character. The mouse."

"Can we read it again? Later tonight?" Tommy asked.

I could tell that my father was both surprised and pleased by Tommy's request. "Yes, yes, of course, of course. Tonight. And we can read other books too. There are others we can read, as well." My father looked over at me. "We have other books here, don't we, Teddy?"

"We have a lot of books," I said. "Upstairs."

"Well, then," my father said. "We'll make a point of it then, Tommy. Yes."

"I know what books I want you to read," Tommy said. "The books mom used to read."

Mention of my mother made everyone look at the ground. Uncle Frank sat up a bit and Sylvanius picked up his empty wine glass again.

My father seemed unfazed though. "Your mother used to enjoy reading to you," he said. "I remember that. Yes. Yes, I do. And I know you enjoyed that as well." He looked up at Tommy and took a deep breath. "Well then, I think we have a few minutes before dinner. Why don't we take a look at them now, those books? Pick out which ones would be appropriate for reading later."

With that, he took Tommy's hand and slowly led him out of the room.

No one said anything for a few minutes after they left. I contemplated the scene I had just witnessed, but could draw no clear conclusions in regard to my father's strange behavior. My introspection however, quickly gave way to a more serious contemplation of the final olive that sat desperately on the tray before me.

It was Uncle Frank who finally spoke. "Interesting book, don't you think?"

"Quite," Sylvanius said.

"I was talking to Teddy," Uncle Frank said, looking over at Sylvanius. "That book was probably over your head. You probably missed the significance of it. It had significance. You don't even know what it's really about."

"Oh, Frank, really."

Uncle Frank sat up. "Okay, tell me what it's about then. Come on."

"It's a simple children's tale," Sylvanius said. He waved his hand, dismissing the subject.

Uncle Frank shook his head and smiled. Then he fixed me with a long, meaningful look. "That little book there," he said, "was about people wanting things, Teddy. It was about . . ." he stopped here and reset his jaw, giving it a good forward thrust. "The human condition."

I took in what Uncle Frank said, then stared back down at the coffee table and counted the number of brown olive pits on the tray. I now counted eleven.

"The human condition," Uncle Frank said again. The fact that he had repeated this made me feel like I had to respond. I chose my words carefully.

"Yes," I said.

"And you know the reason your father read it?"

I had a response for this. I looked back up at Uncle Frank. Out of the corner of my eye, I could see Sylvanius intently watching our exchange, looking concerned and a bit confused.

"Because it's Tommy's favorite book," I said.

"Because it had a moral." Here Uncle Frank looked at me hard and pointed his finger. "And do you know what the moral is, Teddy?"

I made no attempt to answer him. After living with Uncle Frank for more than two months, I was coming to the conclusion that not saying anything was the best way to talk with him.

"Never give people an inch or they're going to want a mile," he said. "Not an inch, Teddy. Not a goddamn inch. You know, your father was trying to send you and your brother a message with that book. A message about things." He pointed at me. "About things." With that he stood up and disappeared into the dining room.

After he was gone, I popped the final olive in my mouth and bit down hard. It was then that I noticed Sylvanius looking at me.

"Teddy," he said, speaking in an exaggerated whisper. "It was just about a mouse. Just a little, little mouse."

AT THE DINNER TABLE, my father shocked us all again by asking that someone say grace. We had never said grace in our house before, even when my mother was alive, and I was speechless, a condition my father was increasingly leaving me in.

"That's an excellent idea, Theo," Sylvanius said. "A meal like this is really a religious occasion of sorts."

"Aunt Bess, why don't you do the honors?" my father asked.

Aunt Bess stared at him, confused.

"I mean, say the prayer," my father said.

"Oh, the prayer. I'm not saying a prayer, I cooked the food. Someone else should say it. It's Frank's birthday, I think Frank should say it."

"I'm not saying any prayer," Uncle Frank said. "What would I say?"

My father looked around the table, his desperation rising. "Mr. Jackson? Would you care to say something?"

Maurice shook his head slightly and repositioned his fork and knife, moving them closer to his plate.

We all sat in silence. I was waiting for someone to ask me or Tommy to say a prayer when Sylvanius spoke.

"I would be honored to bless this food, honored." Then he cleared his throat and looked up at the ceiling. He looked at it for a long time without saying a word, his eyes wide and serious. After a while, Aunt Bess looked up too, then my father and then finally Uncle Frank and Maurice.

"What the hell are you doing?" Uncle Frank finally asked. "Praying for rain?"

"Pray out loud, Sylvanius," Aunt Bess said. "Out loud."

Sylvanius shook his head. "I'm sorry, Bess, I'm afraid anything I said would be hopelessly insignificant. I am not worthy of such responsibility. Besides," he said, reaching for his wine. "I just now realized that I don't really know any prayers. Any religious prayers that is."

My father sighed and cleared his throat. He looked in pain. "Well, I imagine I can manage something," he said. He bowed his head, his hair popping out like the arms of a cross. "Dear Lord, we thank you for this wonderful meal." He paused here and cleared his throat. "And we thank you for this opportunity to spend time together. As a family."

With that, he quickly picked up the salad bowl and passed it to Maurice.

I chose to temporarily ignore the obvious and ominous sign—my father was now praying in public—and ate with great appetite, devouring the thick slices of moist meat and spicy rice and potatoes Aunt Bess heaped on my plate. My suspicion that Bobby Lee was behind the prayer should have been reason enough for the thorny ball in my stomach to expand, but I couldn't help myself; I was famished and the food was delicious. The ball could expand after dessert.

"Oh, Bess, you've outdone yourself, outdone yourself," Sylvanius said. "I must have your recipe for this bean salad."

"It's canned," Aunt Bess said, passing him more.

"Ah."

For dessert, Aunt Bess brought out a special cake with a small vampire figurine in the middle, complete with a black cape and tiny high collar that looked stiff and sweet. I was surprised when Uncle Frank laughed. He had been glum most of the meal, wolfing down his food violently, his head inches from his plate.

"It's made of sugar," Aunt Bess said. "We can eat it later on. The boys, maybe."

"Thank you, Aunt Bess," Uncle Frank said. He carefully picked up the figurine and studied it, squinting his eyes. Then he passed it on to Sylvanius who looked overjoyed.

"Delightful Bess!" he said. When he leaned over and kissed Aunt Bess on the cheek, both Uncle Frank and my father looked away.

"Tommy, don't!" Aunt Bess said as Tommy stuck his finger in the side of the cake. Maurice quietly took Tommy's hand and removed it slowly. Then everyone sang "Happy Birthday" except my father who cleared his throat in time to the music.

"Well," my father said after we finished singing and were eating the cake, "afterwards, I was wondering if we would all like to play a game."

Everyone except Tommy stopped eating and looked at my father.

"I thought," my father continued, his eyes trained on his plate. "I thought that we could all play Monopoly, perhaps."

"Monopoly," Uncle Frank said. "What do you mean, you mean the game Monopoly? With dice?"

"Yes," my father said. His eyes were still on his plate.

"What?" Aunt Bess said. She look frightened.

"I just thought, we would all enjoy it. As a, well . . ." he paused. "A family activity. I know we have the game in the front hall closet." Everyone kept looking at my father who now decided to study his lap. "I saw it there yesterday. It's in the closet."

"I'm going to excuse myself for a bit," Maurice said. It was the first thing he had said since we had sat down. "But I want to thank you, Miss Pappas. Everything was very delicious. I enjoyed the lamb. Now, I'm going to take a walk around the block and enjoy my pipe." He stood up and carefully pushed his chair back under the table and walked out.

"Maybe he doesn't like Monopoly," Aunt Bess said. "Do blacks not like Monopoly?"

"I don't think he likes us," said Uncle Frank.

"I like him," Tommy said. "I like the Mo Man. He's the Mo Man."

"Yes, well, I'm sure he feels a bit uncomfortable in our family situations," my father said. "Mr. Jackson is a very private man. Anyway," he said. "Should we play Monopoly? Teddy, would you like that?"

I nodded my head.

"The kids are too young for Monopoly," Uncle Frank said. "They don't know how to play."

"I think I can play," I said. "I played with Charlie once."

"I don't know how to play," Aunt Bess said. Once again, she looked scared. "How do you play? Is it complicated? Do I have to read something?"

"It's not difficult, Bess," Sylvanius said, patting Aunt Bess on the hand. He gave her a meaningful look. "I have played with the best."

"Would you teach me?" she asked.

Sylvanius bowed his head deeply. "Of course, of course, Bess. I shall teach you everything I know."

We cleared the table and set up the game. Since it soon became obvious that Sylvanius didn't know how to play either, my father had to read the instructions out loud from the back of the box which made Tommy fall asleep under the table. We started the game awkwardly, frequently stopping to refer to the instructions which my father kept at his elbow. I was Aunt Bess's partner and got to roll the dice, move the thimble, and count our money. After a little while, we started winning.

"Like father like son," Uncle Frank said as he paid me some money for landing on Illinois Avenue.

"I think I would like to purchase a new hotel for that railroad," Sylvanius said.

"You can't put a hotel on a railroad," Uncle Frank said.

"Ah," Sylvanius said, rubbing his chin. He was very interested in the game though he was losing badly. "I'm afraid I'll have to revise my strategy then."

"Here, Teddy, give Sylvanius some of our money. We have so much," Aunt Bess said.

"Oh, Bess, I couldn't."

"You can't lend him money," Uncle Frank said. "It's not allowed."

"Why not?"

"Because it's not allowed," Uncle Frank said.

"I'm afraid he's right," my father said, squinting at the instructions. "I don't believe it is allowed."

"I'll be fine, Bess," Sylvanius said. "I'll be fine. My luck is turning. I feel Lady Fortune will soon be smiling upon me." Then he rolled the dice and it bounced off the board and landed on Tommy's sleeping legs.

"That's not allowed," Uncle Frank said.

"Oh, Frank, please. You and your rules. The attorney in you is coming out," Sylvanius said and everyone laughed but Uncle Frank.

After a little while, Maurice returned, smelling faintly of tobacco. He sat down and watched us.

"Maurice, I think I need your assistance," Sylvanius said.

"Do you need help going to the bathroom?" Aunt Bess asked.

"No, I need him to help me change my luck. Here," he said holding the dice out to him. "Would you be so kind?" Maurice pulled his chair close to the table. "It's been awhile," he said, but he rolled the dice.

"Remember when we used to play cards, when we were kids, Theo?" Uncle Frank asked. "Remember how we would play all night until Mom made us turn out the lights, then we would play with flashlights in our bedroom?"

"I do remember that," my father said. "Yes. I do."

"We would play with Dad too. And old Uncle George. Remember old Uncle George?"

"Of course. I remember those games," my father said. He had been mostly quiet throughout the game, hiding behind the instruction box and pretending to study the board, occasionally smiling. I once again suspected that Bobby Lee was behind our playing, suspected that Bobby Lee was behind most things we now did and said, but once more, I didn't care. For the moment, everything seemed fine, everything in place and that was enough.

"Those were the days, Theo," Uncle Frank said. "Those were the days."

"Yes, they were," my father said. "Unfortunately, you don't always know that at the time though. Not always." Then he briefly smiled at me in an embarrassed manner and picked up the dice. It was then that I realized that something had changed, that something had in fact been changing for sometime. I now knew that my father had quietly left his remote hiding place for good and was wandering, lost in the woods, looking for us. Watching him roll the dice, I had the sudden urge to tell him that everything was going to be fine, that we were all right here, waiting for him to make his way to us. The moment passed though and I didn't say anything, of course. I just picked up the dice. It was my turn to roll.

CHAPTER FOURTEEN

Fire Ants, The Rising Storm
By F. "Aris" Pappas

He was a man of action. He didn't like waiting for the phone to ring. He always made the first call. He had been married three times, to the wrong women. Now, he was married to his job. He was an entomologist at the U.S. Department of Agriculture and he was about to face the biggest challenge of his career. The biggest challenge in anyone's career.

From Florida, they had been marching forward, north, eating and destroying everything in their path. The government's war machine, used to high-tech, military strikes and high-powered weapons, was powerless to stop them. For this was a different enemy, this was an enemy that knew no rules, had no conscience, needed no supplies, followed no logic. This was an enemy that would not negotiate, would not be intimidated.

And would not surrender.

This was an enemy unlike any other. An enemy that defied all. This was an enemy that could not be stopped. For this was a fire ant, and millions of them were marching directly toward Washington, D.C., the nation's capital.

The phone rang. He answered it. It was the White House. He had expected their call.

"Chet Steel," he said laconically into the phone. It was Goldman, the Chief of Staff, and she sounded scared.

I was reading Uncle Frank's novel on the human condition on the computer in the basement, waiting for my father to return from the lawyers so we could play Stratego. That morning at breakfast, he asked me if I wanted to play the game after school. When I came home though, Aunt Bess told me that he had an unexpected meeting with the judge and that he wasn't sure when he'd be home. I instinctively took this as a bad sign—any type of meeting with the judge was serious I knew—so I vowed to complete my Suicide Book and enact my Pepper Creek plan as soon as possible. I was using the Macintosh in the basement to compose an illustrated will and testament when I stumbled upon Uncle Frank's novel. I found it interesting but short; it was only one page.

"What are you doing?" Uncle Frank asked. He had suddenly appeared behind me.

I started, popping straight up in my seat like burnt toast from a toaster, then fumbled with the computer, trying to shut it off. I was too late though.

"Hey, that's very private," he said. He leaned over and shut down the computer. I studied the floor.

"That's goddamn rude of you, Teddy. You shouldn't be nosing around other people's work. Hell, I don't nose around your work. Your pictures."

"I'm sorry." I said still looking at the floor. When I looked back up, Uncle Frank was staring at me, his eyes narrow, his chin red and angry. I looked back down, afraid to move or say anything. I planned on sitting there, motionless, until Aunt Bess called us for dinner, which was several hours away.

"Where is your father?"

"Downtown. Meeting with the lawyers," I mumbled. I continued to concentrate on the floor.

"So," Uncle Frank said. "What did you think of it?"

"What?"

"What did you think of it? So far, I mean."

I looked back up. "It's good," I answered truthfully.

He nodded his head. "I think it has potential too," he said.

"It's different than you said it would be."

His eyes narrowed. "What do you mean, different?"

I shrugged. "Than the way you described it." Then I said, "The human condition."

"The what?" Uncle Frank took a deep breath. "Oh, *that*," he said. "Well, I plan on incorporating or illustrating my point through this story."

"Through fire ants?" I asked.

Uncle Frank nodded. "More or less. And through people too. There's people in my novel. There's going to be more people in it than fire ants. Actually, that's not true, there's tens of millions of fire ants. But the people will talk so we'll get to know them better. Better than the ants. The ants are a kind of, well, kind of a metaphor."

It was my turn to nod. I had no idea what he was talking about. "Are fire ants real?"

Uncle Frank massaged his chin, his chest inflating with knowledge. "All too real, Teddy. All too real." He clasped his hands behind his back and began walking slowly back and forth, his head cast down, his face grim. He finally stopped in front of a wall that had a faded and ripped *Sesame Street* poster my mother had hung years ago. I was sure Uncle Frank wished it was a window overlooking a great valley or mountain range. "These ants, Teddy," he said, peering at Ernie and Bert hanging from the caboose of a train, "they eat everything in sight. And they only have one natural enemy. Do you know who that is?"

I thought for awhile. "Evil dolphins?"

"The phorid fly. Nothing else can really kill them." He turned and looked back at me. "I've done research," he said.

"Do you have any more pages?"

He shifted uneasily from foot to foot. "Not really. I mean I had more, but I kept editing. I may actually hire someone to write it. I'm much better with plot lines, the big picture. I don't really like writing words, per se."

I was about to ask more questions, when Aunt Bess started screaming upstairs. I popped up in my seat again. I knew she was in the kitchen watching the news on TV and I feared that there had been some announcement about my case. His lawyer had been on TV frequently over the past few days, angrily making demands and accusations.

"Oh my God," Aunt Bess screamed again.

"Wait here," Uncle Frank said. He looked nervous and walked quickly, almost running upstairs. Then I heard him yell, "Jesus Christ. I don't believe it."

I felt things leave me then, felt my breath, my hope empty out of me. Without thinking, I started praying, my mind a blur of promises and pleas. I prayed hard, squeezed my eyes shut, trying to imagine the Earless Jesus hovering nearby, listening.

"Teddy, get up here," Uncle Frank said. "You got to see this. They're going to play it again. Hurry, run, run."

I opened my eyes and ran upstairs and into the kitchen where I found Uncle Frank and Aunt Bess gathered around the small TV on the counter next to the microwave. Aunt Bess was covering her mouth with her hand and Uncle Frank was shaking his head.

"Jesus Christ," he said.

There on TV, was Sylvanius dressed as a vampire, falling down the stairs at the Wilcotts' on Halloween night. The newscaster's smiling face came on right after the fall and said that fortunately, Richard Melton, known for years as the popular vampire Sylvanius on TV's *Dark Towers* wasn't seriously hurt and is believed to be a houseguest of Dr. Theo Pappas, the multi-millionaire lottery winner, involved in a bitter child custody battle over his adopted son.

"How did they get that tape?" Aunt Bess asked.

"How the hell do you think?" Uncle Frank said. "Old hot legs down the block."

"Gloria?"

"Yes. Our good neighbor. How else would they get it? She probably sold it for a bundle." He snapped the TV off and stormed off.

I went back down to the basement and turned the computer back on, determined to make the most of what I believed was a reprieve and finish my Suicide Book. As soon as I started alphabetizing my possessions, though, the telephone rang again. Once more Aunt Bess screamed, but this time in a different way.

"Thank God, Theo, thank God, it's all over," I heard Aunt Bess cry. I turned the computer back off and just sat there, hope rising, an unexpected tide. A few seconds later, Uncle Frank bounded down the stairs, his face neon, his chin tilted in triumph.

"Good news, Teddy," he said. "Good news. Your father just called. All this bullshit is over. The whole goddamn thing is over."

A WEEK AFTER the judge decided that a just-discovered paper Bobby Lee had signed giving up his parental rights to me was valid, we bought a new car: a black Oldsmobile.

"Nice color," Uncle Frank said as he circled the car in our driveway. "Jet black?"

"Well, I'm not sure," my father said. "I think it's plain black." He paused. "Are there different shades? Of black, I mean?"

Uncle Frank shrugged. "It's jet black," he said.

"It's a very safe car," my father said. "It has quite a bit of room. We should all fit comfortably."

Uncle Frank nodded his head. "Room and safety," he said. "They are key, Theo, they are key."

My father had bought the car because the night the judge made his unexpected ruling, the old Buick died on the expressway on the way home, stranding him for hours until Maurice came to rescue him.

"What did you do with the old one, the old car? They couldn't have given you anything for that on the trade-in, did they?" Uncle Frank said. He was still walking around the driveway, circling the car suspiciously, his long black coat wrapped tightly around him. I stomped my feet and put my hands in my coat pockets. It was cold and the wind stung my face. I was due at Charlie Governs's house and though the new car interested me, I wanted to leave.

"Actually, I decided to keep the Buick," my father said.

"Keep it, why? What's with you and that car? It has some kind of significance? Abraham Lincoln drove it? What?"

"Well, actually, I thought you might be able to use it," my father said quietly.

Uncle Frank stopped walking and looked over at him, my father's words Latin to him.

"What?" Uncle Frank asked again.

"I thought that maybe you could use the car. For short errands and things," my father said. "Meetings. Very nearby meetings."

Uncle Frank continue to stare at my father, who cleared his throat.

"Well, it's just a suggestion, of course," my father said quietly. "We'll just keep the car, to have it then. I think it might come in handy."

Uncle Frank shook his head and walked slowly away.

"Well," my father said, looking over at me. "What do you think of the car, Teddy? Does it meet with your approval?"

"Yes," I said. While not quite the shiny black Lexus I had registered on my List of Things, it was such a vast improvement over the Buick that it was hard to believe that both were of the same species. "Where's the old car?"

"It's at Cezzaro's, being worked on. Well," he said again, turning to face the car, hesitant and proud. "I think it's practical. It will help us get around. Oh, Mr. Jackson, what do you think of it?"

Maurice walked up the driveway and studied the car, before nodding his head. "I think it's very nice, Mr. Pappas," he said. "You'll enjoy it, I'm sure." Then he turned to me, "Are you ready to go to your friend's?"

"Yes."

My father cleared his throat. "You'll be here at the meeting tonight?"

Maurice nodded. Despite his lawyer's objections, my father had agreed to let Bobby Lee come to our house to tell me personally how he had forgotten about the paper he had signed ten years ago. Afterward, he was going home to Tennessee for awhile, though the judge said he was allowed to visit me.

"Well, then," my father said. "Would you like me to drop you off at Charlie's house?"

"We'll walk," I said. "It's only three blocks."

"I better put the car into the garage then. They say it's going to rain hard tonight. Possibly snow."

Maurice and I walked quickly, our heads bowed into the wind. It was late afternoon, already getting dark and the street lights were beginning to flicker. I jammed my hands deeper into my pockets, regretting not having accepted my father's offer of a ride.

"So, how you doing there, Teddy Pappas?" Maurice asked. Since the judge had made his decision, Maurice had changed. He was lighter and looser in his walk and talk and sometimes hummed low tunes. The day before, my father had offered him a permanent job with us, though Maurice had seemed reluctant.

"Are you going to stay with us?" I asked as we crossed a street.

"Well, I'm considering it," he said. "Originally I was to stay on for just a few months. I'd like to stay on past Christmas. Want to make sure I'm around for that soccer awards banquet for Tommy. You know about that award, don't you?"

"Yes. Tommy told me. He's excited."

Maurice shook his head in wonderment. "Most Valuable Player and he didn't join the team till midseason. Missed half the games. That's something to be proud of. He seems happy too. He liked having your father read to him. Said he enjoyed it. He's talking more now too, you noticed that?"

"Yes." The past few days in particular, Tommy was happier than I had seen him since my mother's accident, talking excitedly about his award and wearing his uniform around the house and to bed.

"After the awards banquet, though, we'll have to see about me staying on," Maurice said. He looked down at me and smiled. "Boys your age don't need to be walked to school every day. Anyway, I think all of this will be forgotten soon and your family will go on with things and so will I. But I am considering it."

"I hope you stay," I said. Maurice looked at me again and patted me on the back. "Why, thank you, Teddy Pappas." We stopped at another block and waited for a car to pass. The wind died down for a moment and I felt my cheeks relax.

"How are things going with that Wilcott boy?" Maurice asked. He was looking straight ahead, down the block.

"Fine," I said. I was surprised by the question. I had never talked to Maurice about Benjamin. Lately, there hadn't been much to talk about though. He pretty much ignored me now. "He leaves me alone," I said. "My father isn't that friendly with Mrs. Wilcott anymore."

"I haven't seen her around much, now that you mention it."

"She doesn't stop by anymore," I said.

We turned down Charlie's block, and the wind picked up. I bent down farther, leaning into it, trying to stay low.

"So, are you looking forward to seeing Bobby Lee tonight?" Maurice asked.

"No," I said. "But it's only for a little while."

"Well, I'll be there with you," Maurice said as we walked up Charlie's driveway.

"I know," I said.

CHARLIE AND I spent the rest of the afternoon working on his computer, doing research on fire ants. I wanted to help Uncle Frank finish his novel, or at least the second page, and thought the more information I could provide the better. We didn't accomplish much though, because our efforts were constantly interrupted by Charlie's mother who kept coming into his room for different reasons, laundry, snacks, and drinks in her hands. She was a small quick woman who seemed to be in constant motion.

"She wants to make sure we're not looking at pornography," Charlie said after she left the last time. "She caught me a few weeks ago."

"I thought you said she got Kid Check."

Charlie looked at me, his face expressionless. He then closed out of the Department of Agriculture Web page. In a few seconds, there was a picture of a naked woman riding a motorcycle holding her underwear high over her head.

"I can get around all the checks," he said.

I stared at the picture. The woman was joyously naked. "That's good," I said.

We spent the next half hour searching and finding pictures of naked women in various poses, until my cheeks started to burn.

"When I get married, I'm going to make my wife walk around naked all the time," Charlie said, switching back to the Department of Agriculture website. After I agreed that was a good idea, we returned to our research on fire ants.

After awhile though, the lure of having naked women at our fingertips proved too strong so we decided to take one last stroll through the Forbidden Delights website. We didn't get far though. While the images of our favorites, Lisa and Laura, began appearing on screen, Mrs. Governs sprang into the room like an hysterical cat, screaming.

"You're disgusting!" she yelled. "Is this how you utilize technology?"

When she started pulling on Charlie's ears, I backed up into a corner and thought frantically of an explanation. Other than possibly yelling, "It was Charlie's idea," I could think of no excuse and covered my ears with my hands, my fate accepted. Mrs. Governs's full attention, however, remained on Charlie and sensing my opportunity, I slipped out of the room, down the stairs, and out of the house.

I started running. It was raining hard and I had left without my coat. I tried to cover my head with my arms, but soon gave up and let the rain soak me. I knew that Maurice and my father would be upset for my leaving without calling, but my options were limited. I would think of an excuse when I got home. I ran faster, running straight through puddles.

When I got to a corner and tried to cross the street, a dark van pulled up in front of me, cutting me off. Despite the rain, the window was down.

"Hey, there. Hey, Teddy. It's me." It was Bobby Lee.

"Oh, hi," I hadn't seen him since the outburst at Will's.

"Jump on in. I'll give you a ride. I'll take you home. Hey," he said. "I got that picture I told you about, the one your mom drew, the one with the stars and everything. 'The Galaxy at Night.' I got it back here."

"It's only another block," I said.

"Come on, boy. This is stupid. It's raining. Everyone will be mad at me if I said I just drove by and left you." He leaned over and opened the door. "Get in now. Come on."

I hesitated, standing in the rain for a moment longer. Then I got inside.

"Buckle up," he said.

"It's only another block."

"Do as your daddy says," he said. "We got a long drive ahead of us."

"Where are we going?"

"I told you," he said. "Home."

HE DROVE RIGHT past our house without slowing down. When I asked him where we were going, he said, "Taking a little ride, that's all." When we got on the expressway, I asked again but this time he didn't answer. He just pulled out a bottle from under his seat and started taking long, hard swallows. When we approached, then passed downtown Chicago, the skyline receding in the rain and fog, I asked one last time, trying not to sound scared.

"Just close your eyes and when you wake up we'll almost be there. I ain't gonna hurt you. Just relax now and leave the driving to me."

"My father is going to be worried," I said, then immediately regretted it. Bobby Lee turned and looked at me, his hawk eyes moist and burning in the darkness. I heard the rain pounding on the roof, a million drumbeats. "I'm your daddy," he said. "Now get some sleep."

I closed my eyes and tried to fight off the feeling that I was drowning, circling in a whirlpool. I was scared, wet, and cold, knew my family must be frantic, knew they would be soon looking for me.

I sat there with my eyes closed for some time, pretending to be asleep, feeling the highway, seeing my family. I must have finally fell into a little crack of sleep, because the next thing I remember, it was getting light out and I could see streaks of dirt on the windshield. It had stopped raining. I closed my eyes again.

"You gotta take a piss or anything?" Bobby Lee asked me. "Go to the bathroom? I know you're up. I can see your eyeballs moving."

"I'm okay," I said. "Where are we going?"

"Hell, I don't know," he said quietly, letting out a deep breath. "Hell, I don't know."

WE FINALLY STOPPED at a motel inches off the highway, a low one-story building with a drained swimming pool and a yellow sign that said free HBO. I waited inside the van while Bobby Lee got the key. I was starting to feel strange, lightheaded in a dangerous, crazy way. My clothes were still wet and my shoes sloshed when I moved my feet. I knew I was getting sick. I thought of Aunt Bess's cough suppressants that were light years away and sneezed.

"Room seventeen," Bobby Lee said, opening my door. He held the key up like a prize. "Let's go now."

Once we got in the room, I went into the bathroom and sat on the toilet, thinking that I might throw up. On the other side of the door, I could hear Bobby Lee pacing, turning the TV on and off, coughing.

"You all right in there?" Bobby Lee asked.

"Yes."

"I'm going to go across the street to that little store and get some more food. I'll be right back."

When I heard the door shut, I quickly walked out of the bathroom and picked up the phone but there was no dial tone, just a cut-off emptiness. I hung up and sat on the bed. The room was small and dingy. Cracks in the walls branched out like tiny veins and the carpet was spotted and thin. I considered escape, but I had no idea where we were, and no idea where to run. I suspected we were in Tennessee, Bobby Lee country, but I couldn't even be sure of that.

Despite everything, I was exhausted and was about to lay down on the bed when Bobby Lee came back to the room in a rush.

"Let's go," was all he said.

When we walked outside, I saw a police car parked across the highway at a convenience store. I thought about calling out for help, but Bobby Lee grabbed my hand and roughly pulled me along to the van.

We drove again for a long time. I sat in the back seat, my eyes pinched tight. I began to accept that we would always be driving, that Bobby Lee and I would circle the globe, a lost spinning top, forever in motion. After a while, I felt I was losing my weight, felt myself disappear and start to float. I left the van, rushed into the sky and saw things laid out beneath me: my family, my mother, my home, everything neat and safe, for one last time. Then I saw the comets collide, saw the sparks and flames dip and dance and felt everything move and change. I opened my eyes, saw burnt hills and barren trees, saw crosses on fire, vampires walking, fire ants marching, dead rebel soldiers, their eyes wide and glassy. On a hilltop I saw a solitary soldier sitting on a horse, his hands outstretched, his face up toward heaven. I hovered over him, saw Stonewall Jackson's dead eyes, his lips moving in silent prayer. Then I felt heat, and saw flames, all around me.

From far down below I heard Bobby Lee's voice say, "We're getting there. Only a few more miles."

I was quiet. I was so warm and floating so high now that I no longer cared where we were going. I closed my eyes and disappeared into the fire.

CHAPTER FIFTEEN

W E WEREN'T IN THE van anymore, that much I knew.

"You got to get that boy to a doctor," Carl the Bear was saying.

"Hell, I can't do that now."

"He's burning up. Boy, you have done it up good this time. You have done it up, special."

I opened my eyes. I was laying on a couch in a small room that had a bear's head on the wall. I stared at the bear and wondered who had killed it, how long it had been dead, then closed my eyes again and started to shiver. After I shook for awhile, I felt someone covering me with a blanket, then saw a thick, bearded face with worried eyes.

"Hey, Carl, you got any aspirin?"

"Hell, no. I don't have any aspirin. What do you think I am, a pharmacy?"

"Hell, everyone's got aspirin," Bobby Lee said.

"Shut up." A deep breath. "I'll go get some. And by any chance, if you were gone by the time I got back, that would be okay by me, little brother."

"We'll be here."

"I was afraid of that."

T HE BEAR ON the wall had a shadow over its face. Specks of dust danced around its nose and in and out of its open mouth. I wondered where the rest of the bear was, wondered what they did with his legs and tail.

"This ain't aspirin," I heard Bobby Lee say. "It's Tylenol. You can't give a kid that. His stomach ain't mature. Why didn't you get the aspirin?"

"I grabbed the first thing I could. Next time, I'll phone ahead and ask what they recommend for a kidnapped boy with a fever."

"He ain't kidnapped," Bobby Lee said. "He's my son."

"Your son, bullshit," Carl the Bear said. "You never were a father to this boy."

I closed my eyes and let sleep surround me.

"OKAY," I SAID even though I wasn't.

Carl the Bear had just asked me how I felt. He was sitting close to me, trying to feed me some chicken noodle soup. I had trouble swallowing the slippery noodles because my throat was on fire.

"I want you to know that I had nothing to do with you coming here," he said. "I'm just going to help you get better, then you're going to go. Sooner the better. Gonna get you back home. Your family probably's worried sick."

"Okay," I said again.

"Okay, then," Carl said. He fed me a few more spoonfuls of soup, then stood up and ran his hands through his long black hair and smoothed his beard. "You look like your mother," he said. "Just like her."

IT WAS ALMOST dark and I laid with the blanket over my face, listening to the voices floating over my head.

"Hell, I just thought that, that's all. I thought I had it planned out. But it didn't work out. I only wanted a little something to get me back on my feet. But they didn't give me a dime. Hell, he's my son. Then I figured I'd raise him and they'd probably support him. Trust fund and everything, I figured."

"What the hell do you know about trust funds?" Carl the Bear said. "It was pretty ill-conceived. And now you kidnapped him."

"Quit using that word. I didn't kidnap no one. I'm entitled to see him, so I just took him to visit my family. His family. See his roots."

"And you didn't leave any ransom note?"

Bobby Lee was quiet for a moment before saying, "I never sent any note."

"You are one sick man."

"Hey, Bear, cut the shit," Bobby Lee said. "You going to help me?"

"Hell, no. And you cut the shit and take this boy home tomorrow 'fore he starts showing up on the back of milk cartons. Say it was a misunderstanding. Goddamn, I'm glad your mother ain't alive to see this."

I didn't hear anything for awhile and was starting to fall back asleep when Carl's voice pulled me back.

"This is more than just about the boy and money, though, ain't it? It's about Amy. Ain't it?"

Bobby Lee was quiet.

"It's about her leaving you for another man, ain't it? I know you, boy. You're always looking to even the score. No one gets one over on Bobby Lee Anderson. Let me tell you something, that old man had nothing to do with what happened to you and Amy."

"That old man took my wife," Bobby Lee said. "Goddamn stole her away."

"Your wife?" Carl said. "Hell, from what I remember, you weren't there half the time. And when you were, you were knocking her around. Forced her to work in those clubs, taking her clothes off for a living while you and your buddies shot pool and drank yourself blind."

The bear was covered in deep shadows now and I fell back asleep.

WHEN I WOKE UP, dogs were barking close by. My blanket was wet but I wasn't shivering much anymore. I opened my eyes, pulled the blanket off my head, and looked around for Bobby Lee and Carl the Bear. I couldn't see them but I could hear their voices outside.

"Damn dogs don't shut up," Carl the Bear said. "Bark at every damn squirrel."

"You still working at the distillery?" Bobby Lee asked.

"Hell, yes. After Heaven Hill burned down, I got on with Beam. Got lucky, they're probably the best."

"You get me a job there?"

"Right now they ain't exactly looking for extortionists and kidnappers."

"I'm serious, Bear. I might be ready for a change."

"What do you know about making bourbon?"

"Hell, I like to drink it, that's a start. Got a natural interest."

Carl the Bear let out a laugh. "I haven't seen you in ten years but you haven't changed. In all your traveling, have you even been to your wife's grave, paid your respects?"

"No, not yet. Been busy. I'm going though. Probably after I leave here. Gonna plant something. A flower or something."

"Flower, hell. It's almost winter. I'll give you something. I got some bulbs in back I was gonna put in. I'll give you some tulips."

"Bear, you still think you're a gardener, don't you? Mr. Green Thumb."

"Hell, you come out here in spring and summer and look at my garden. I ain't embarrassed about beauty."

It was dark out now. I couldn't see anything but a shadow from a small light on the table in the middle of the room. I knew it was night and even though I didn't want to, even though I wanted to get up and run far away, back home to Wilton, I fell back asleep and floated away like a falling leaf on a windy day.

THE NEXT MORNING I was hungry and ate the three bowls of Kellogg's Corn Flakes that Carl the Bear gave me.

"Wish I had something else to make for you," he said. "Scrambled eggs or something. I can run out to the store if you want. Though it might take awhile. I'm ten miles from town."

"I'm okay," I said.

"Hey, you say that word a lot."

"What word?"

" 'Okay,' " Carl the Bear said.

I nodded my head.

"You want one more bowl?"

"Okay," I said and Carl the Bear laughed then smoothed his black beard with his paw of a hand. He was a huge man, much heavier and taller than Bobby Lee and filled space in a way that took my breath away. His arms were meat and steel, his neck a knot. Despite his size, there was a softness in him, ample room in his wide, smiling eyes and I could immediately tell that he was nothing like Bobby Lee.

"How do you like Kentucky?" he asked as I started in on another bowl of cereal.

"Kentucky?" I had assumed we were in Tennessee.

"Kentucky," Carl the Bear said. "Fifteenth state in the union. Home of fast horses and faster women. You're just outside of Bardstown. It's a nice place. Quiet and clean. Bourbon capital of the world."

I kept eating my corn flakes. They needed sugar but I didn't ask for any. Carl the Bear was being nice enough and I didn't want to make any unnecessary demands. I knew he was my salvation.

He folded his large hands on the table like he was praying. "Moved here from Memphis a long time ago. Hell, I'd like to go to Chicago sometime, but never have. Maybe I will, I don't know. Kentucky kind of gets a hold of you. Of course, I'd probably say that if I lived in Iowa. I don't like to travel, I guess."

"Are you Bobby Lee's brother?"

Carl the Bear stood up from the table and walked over to the small kitchen counter where he poured himself a cup of coffee. "Unfortunately, I am. There are two things a man can't control and who your family is is one of them. The weather is the other in case you're ever asked."

He sat back down and blew on his coffee before taking a sip.

"You know your father is misguided," he said. "I'm talking about Bobby Lee here, not your Chicago father. He's always been on the wrong side of everything." He blew again and sipped. "I want you to know something about your blood. We ain't all trash like him. I went to the army and spent three years at Bowling Green University. The folks over at Jim Beam are high on me, say I got a future. I got to go back and get my degree though, if I'm going to move farther ahead. I pulled myself up, he didn't. It was his choice. Our sister did okay too. She's an emergency room nurse in Lexington. She's the head nurse now, runs the show. Hell, she's talking about going on to med school. Hell, if anyone can do it, she can. You look a little like her, now that I think about it."

He got up and walked over to the counter and poured more coffee, then sat back down at the table, the wooden chair creaking. "You know, he shouldn't have taken you on this little trip, but I figure that if he returns you himself, he'll get off light. He won't hurt you. So you just hang in there. You'll be home soon, probably tomorrow night, depending on traffic. I know I'm taking a risk by not calling the police, but he's my brother. I'm doing this for my mother."

Mention of his mother made him fall silent. He sipped his coffee, his mouth a hole in his beard. Glancing through the window over the kitchen sink, I saw slants of sun shining through bare trees. I didn't see any other houses and sensed that we were deep in the woods. Carl the Bear's house was small, just two rooms, but it was clean. Books lined one wall and pictures of fish and dogs lined the other. On the table, there was a small vase with dried yellow flowers.

He saw me looking around. "What do you think of my bear?" he asked.

I looked up at the bear. Its mouth was terrifying, but its teeth looked yellow and faded, its eyes glassy marbles.

"It's okay. It's big, I mean."

"In case you're wondering, I won it in a poker game about twenty years ago, while I was in college. I tell women that I killed it though, it impresses them, especially if they ain't educated. Uneducated women impress easily. Hell, I don't bring many women back here now though. I'm getting old. Old as that bear."

When I finished my cereal, he picked up my bowl and brought it over to the small sink in the corner, where he rinsed it out and carefully dried it using a bright red cloth. He turned around and crossed his huge arms in front of him. "Wish the circumstances were different so you could stay awhile, get to know each other," he said with a small smile.

Then he shook his head. "But circumstances ain't different, so you gotta go. Your family's up north."

AFTER I FINISHED breakfast, Bobby Lee came back from the gas station and I got in the van, in the backseat, ready to leave. I still wasn't feeling very well, but my fever was gone and I was riding a wave of hope that I was going home.

"Take care, Mr. Okay," Carl said, leaning through the window and handing me a piece of paper with a phone number on it. He turned to Bobby Lee and said, "I don't get a call from this boy's father in twelve hours saying that he's safe, I'm calling the cops and they'll hunt you down like the goddamn dog that you are, little brother. You returning him is your only chance and I'm giving it to you, out of respect for our mother. And once you get back to Chicago, keep driving north into Canada. They ain't very smart up there and maybe they'll fall for some of your shit."

Bobby Lee stared straight ahead, quiet.

"Here," Carl said. He handed Bobby Lee two brown bags. "Some soda and snacks for the boy in one, and those tulip bulbs in the other, for the cemetery. If you ever get around to goin', that is. Knew that woman since kindergarten and you still ain't paid your respects. Kind of man are you?"

"Hell, I just found out where she was and I'm going to see her," Bobby Lee said. "Going straight there." He took the bags and put them on the front seat next to him. Then he started the van up and pulled out, shooting gravel and smoke.

We drove through country that any other time I would have thought pretty, past hills that Bobby Lee called knobs. "They're just like hills but they call them knobs here for some reason." Bobby Lee talked softly, looked almost peaceful, driving with one arm out the window, his hair blowing back in the breeze. Every so often, he would point something out to me. "Over there's a buzzard roost, or used to be at least," he said, pointing to a strand of trees. "Behind the trees, buzzards flocked there, hang out together. Quite a site. I remember coming up this way before with your mom. We were thinking of moving here. Long time ago. Used to come here a lot, she had family in Louisville. A cousin."

When we passed a bronze historical marker by the side of the road, he slowed down and pointed. "Over there's Knob Creek," Bobby Lee said. "Abe Lincoln was born near here."

"I thought he was born in Illinois," I asked, honestly interested.

He shook his head. "Nope, Old Abe's a southern boy." He smiled. "See what you learn from your daddy?"

We drove for awhile longer on winding roads that weaved and dipped, past more knobs and wide, rolling fields. It was a clear, unseasonably warm day and I could smell the earth through Bobby Lee's open window, raw and fresh. Soon, the hills flattened out and we passed through a small town of clean, bright store fronts.

"Bardstown," Bobby Lee said. "Used to drive up here with my high school buds all the time. Visit the distilleries, see if we could get some samples. It was a long drive up from Memphis, but one of my buddies had a brother who worked at one of the stills, in shipping. Used to give us two, three cases. Made the trip worthwhile. You ever been to a distillery? Where they make bourbon? Hell, we'll drive by one in a few minutes, I think. Used to be right off the main road."

We were through the streets of Bardstown and back out on the main road in minutes, Bobby Lee driving leisurely, his eyes at ease, the ride and the countryside calming us both. I opened my window a crack to let the warm air in.

"What are those?" I asked. Up ahead, I saw several large black buildings emerging in the distance. Dozens stood on the hills, watching us in silence like brooding sentries. As we approached them, they looked old and weathered and I was sure they creaked and swayed in the slightest wind.

"Those're rackhouses," Bobby Lee said. "Got whiskey aging in them. Open your window more, go on now, all the way down. Now smell that Kentucky air. Take a deep breath. Go on. Smells sweet, don't it? Lots of the bourbon in those rackhouses goes straight up into the air. The angel's share, they call it. The angel's share. Hell," he said, "hope your mom's getting her share up there. Old Amy liked her bourbon."

We passed a final grouping of rackhouses, then the road opened up to a four-lane highway. Bobby Lee shut the window, and ran his hand through his hair. "I miss your mom. I didn't think I did, but I do." He looked over at me and started to say something else but stopped short. Then he leaned forward and turned the radio on. "Getting hungry," was all he said.

I fell asleep after we crossed a large bridge that seemed to stretch on forever. When I woke up, Bobby Lee was studying a map, his face scrunched up. We were in a gas station, parked in back, under a light by the men's room. He was drinking from a new bottle, taking hard pulls again. A lit cigarette burned in the ashtray. My heart sank.

"Maybe we'll head out to Utah," he said. "Ever been to Utah? They got Mormons out there. Might be a nice place to grow up. They got mountains, lakes. Not many people and the Mormons are supposed to be nice enough. They respect privacy."

"I want to go home," I said.

"Home?" Bobby Lee said. He put down the map and turned the key in the ignition. "Home is where the heart is. Didn't you know that? Ain't your heart with me now? Your blood daddy?" He took another drink from the bottle with one hand, the other still on the steering wheel. "Hell, we got a lot of catching up to do, you and me. You know, we didn't do much talking at those meetings before. All those blood-sucking lawyers watching us. I never felt comfortable and I know you didn't either. So I only think it's right that we spend some unsupervised time together."

"Then can I go home?"

"We'll see what happens. Let's go get something to eat now though. I'm hungry and need some burgers."

We stopped at a restaurant off the highway and sat in a booth in the very back against the wall. After we ordered, Bobby Lee made me change seats with him so he could look at the door. "I want to see who's coming and going," he said. "I'm a people-watcher."

I tried to eat the pancakes he ordered me, but my stomach started to hurt, so I just ate a little bacon and drank water. Bobby Lee ate his cheeseburgers like a rabbit, sinking his two front teeth into them and swallowing in noisy gulps. The peaceful look was gone now, in its place hard tightness.

"So what you think of my big fat big brother, Carl?"

"He's okay."

"Yeah, I think he's an asshole. Always has been. Don't know why I wasted my gas to go see him. He's always putting me down. Never had much of a relationship with him. Brothers supposed to get along. Not us though. He's difficult. You know what a contrarian is? It's someone who always does the opposite of everyone else. That's what Carl calls himself. A contrarian, like it's a doctor or something. Hell, contrarian is just another word for asshole as far as I'm concerned. He can't get along with society. That's why he never married and lives alone in that little house in the middle of nowhere. He's a misfit."

The waitress came by with a beer for Bobby Lee. While she was refilling my water glass, a large man, wearing blue overalls and a baseball cap sat down at the table next to us and picked up a menu.

"So, what's it like being rich and everything? That old man buy you anything? Hope he did, he won a hundred-and-ninety million, shit. I read that he got it all in one check too. One goddamn check. He's a goddamn greedy bastard. He didn't do anything to earn that money. It's taxpayers' money. He should have spread it around, made other people happy. What's he do with all that money?"

"I don't know," I said.

"You don't know, huh? Hell, I know what I do. Spend it, even though I probably couldn't spend it all. I'd buy a big house though, a ranch or a farm. Pay cash too. No mortgage. 'Right here, boy,' I'd say and hand over the money to buy it. Got it right here."

I drank some more water and looked around the restaurant. A few more people had filtered in, sitting down at the counter and around the small tables with an experienced weariness. Most of them were men wearing baseball caps and smoking cigarettes. They all had a dusty, worn-out look about them. Out in the parking lot, silent trucks threw huge shadows.

Bobby Lee finished his cheeseburger. "So what did you do all that time up there with your mother?" he said.

"We drew pictures sometimes."

"Hell, I can't imagine her up there with that old guy. Hell, she never loved him. She just felt safe with him, that's all. Hell, he's ancient."

"He's not so old," I said.

"Hell, he's older than shit. And he knew she didn't love him too. That's why he don't love you. You ain't his son," Bobby Lee said, his eyes on fire. I looked down at the table.

He lit a cigarette, waved the match out, then blew smoke up in the air. "Hey, you driving that truck out there?" he asked the large man at the table next to us. "That bourbon truck?"

"Yes, sir, I am," the man said, wiping his mouth with a napkin. "But that ain't bourbon. That's Jack Daniels."

"That's bourbon," Bobby Lee said.

"No, it's not," the man said and kept eating. "That's Old Number Seven and that's Tennessee Whiskey." He smiled. "Know you Kentuckians don't hold it in high regard, know you like your Jim Beam."

"What's the difference?" Bobby Lee asked.

"Way it's made." He took a sip from his coffee. "Run it through some charcoal. I really don't know how they make it; I just drive the truck and load and unload."

"You drink a lot of that stuff?"

"I don't drink any of it. I don't believe in it."

"You don't believe in what? Drinking? Hell, what's to believe in, you just open your mouth and pour it in."

"I know a lot of decent people who drink, but I choose not to. I don't believe it's God's way."

"God's way," Bobby Lee repeated. He blew smoke straight up in the air again. "So God don't like bourbon, huh? What, he a Scotch man then?"

The man laughed. "I doubt that."

"Oh, that's right, he probably likes wine."

The man kept eating his dinner, chewing loudly. Bobby Lee blew some more smoke and coughed a little. Outside, I could hear trucks roaring past on the highway.

"So, you like driving that truck?" Bobby Lee asked.

"Yes, sir. It's a living and a good one. It provides."

"Provides what?"

"A living."

"Oh. You got kids?"

"I got four."

"Four kids," Bobby Lee said. "I got just the one here." The man looked over and smiled at me. "Just the one," Bobby Lee said. "Hey, they hiring over at Jack Daniels?"

"They might be. Always looking for good drivers."

"Hell, I could drive," Bobby Lee said. "Man, I know how to drive. They pay okay?"

"Yes, sir," the man said, swallowing. "They pay fine."

"My brother works down at Beam."

"Fine place to work, I've heard."

Bobby Lee took another drink from his bottle of beer. "I don't know, driving a truck all day, must get boring. Monotonous like. Same thing all the time. Same roads."

"I like the quiet. Good time to reflect," the man said.

"Reflect on what, like God stuff?"

"Sometimes, I think of the Lord, yes, I do."

"You really believe in God then?" Bobby Lee said. "I don't. You can if you want, but I don't believe in anything invisible."

"God's not invisible. He's everywhere you look."

"Yeah, well, I guess I need glasses then."

"You gotta look hard, but if you do, you'll see him."

"Yeah, well, he can come looking for me, if he wants. I ain't hard to find. How come you're so sure that He exists?"

"I just know He does. He saved my life once."

"Saved your life once. You in a war or something?"

"No. But I almost choked to death. On a chicken bone at a barbecue."

"So, what did God do? Bang you on the back?"

"No. But I almost died and then I felt His presence and then the bone was dislodged from my esophagus."

Bobby Lee didn't say anything. He just repeated "esophagus" under his breath and let smoke stream out his nose like an angry bull. "Yeah, well, I don't like chicken," he said.

After a little while, the man finished eating and stood up, wiping his hands on the back of his overalls. He winked at me as he walked past and said, "Good night now."

"Yeah, see you in heaven there, old boy," Bobby Lee said. "And watch the old esophagus." Then he grew quiet and lit another cigarette.

"You believe in God?" he asked.

"Yes," I said.

"Yeah, your mother did too. Figured you would. You pray a lot?"

"Sometimes," I said.

"Yeah, well, I don't think He exists. If He did, how come bad things keep happening? How come your mom got decapitated? Think she's floating around up in heaven without her head? Shit."

"I don't know," I said. I was getting tired again and I felt the thorny ball flip over and start growing in my stomach.

"You think praying won you the lottery?"

"No."

"Hell, if praying worked, I'd do it. I'd do it all the time. I ain't going to pray to air though. Shit, fuck God."

Bobby Lee was frightening me. He was acting different now, growing sharp edges, his eyes dark, moving razors. I thought about asking some of the dusty men at the counter for help, but before I could move, he grabbed my hand and said that we were leaving and right away.

We drove for a long time, Bobby Lee singing along to the scratchy radio in a sad voice that sounded like rain at night.

"Bet you didn't know your daddy was a singer," he said. "Your mom and I used to sing a lot together. She had a pretty voice, I remember that." He was quiet for a long time.

The sun was disappearing in the sky, sinking low and flooding our windshield in a soft, orange color that made me think of summer. I watched the Kentucky light slowly fade away, watched it become thinner and thinner and wished that I could follow the light, disappear with it to some hidden, safe place. Then I shut my eyes and started praying even though I wasn't sure God was listening to me anymore.

"YOU THIRSTY? I could use one. Maybe two," Bobby Lee said as he pulled into the parking lot of Tyrone's Lounge. It was dark out, and we had been driving for awhile, off the highway, on one-lane roads. The parking lot was gravel and when Bobby Lee got out of the van, I could hear his dirty boots scrunching and scraping stones when he walked.

"Come on, boy," he said, opening my door. "You can get a Coke or something. Come on now, I know it's late, but when I say go, let's go."

I followed Bobby Lee toward Tyrone's, a low building that was sagging to one side. There were only two other cars in the parking lot, and as we approached the door, I could hear faraway music, getting louder.

When we got to the entryway, Bobby Lee paused, his hand on the door. "Anyone ask you, you just tell them you're my nephew from Lexington," he said. "Don't mention Chicago or nothing. No one's going to ask though. Not here."

It was dark and hot inside Tyrone's, a sticky, steamy hot that reminded me of the St. Pius gym. A few dim lights with green shades hung from the ceiling. Off in the corner, some men played pool, cigarettes loose in their mouths. Mirrors advertising beers hung from the walls. Behind the bar, was a large picture of a woman laying on the beach in a bathing suit.

"Like to go swimming with her," Bobby Lee said.

The bartender didn't look up when we approached. He kept his eyes on a magazine.

"Need a drink here, boy," Bobby Lee said. "Need two."

The bartender glanced up, then returned to his magazine. "He don't look twenty-one," he said.

"Yeah, well, he's a little midget," Bobby Lee said. "Give me a Bud. The boy wants a Coke." The man handed Bobby Lee our drinks and Bobby Lee paid him with some money that he dug out of the front of his jeans pockets.

We stood by the bar with our drinks. I wasn't very thirsty, so I just held onto my plastic cup, the cold feeling good against my hot hands. Bobby Lee, though, drained his bottle in three or four swallows then ordered another one, paying with two more crumpled-up dollar bills. He was halfway through that bottle when he took notice of the pool table located in the far corner. A thin man and a fat man, both wearing baseball caps, were playing, the balls moving silently over the green table. Bobby Lee finished his new beer and watched the game with growing interest.

"Those boys any good?" he asked the bartender.

The bartender didn't say anything. He just started drying off the inside of some glasses with a white towel. He was a beefy looking man with a thick gray mustache and long sideburns. When he turned away from us, I saw a small gold earring glitter in one of his ears.

"Boy over there's all right," he finally said. "Slap Dog over there can play some." He pointed toward one of the men.

"Slap Dog?"

"Slap Dog Jack. He'll take your money."

"Won't take mine," Bobby Lee said. Then he held up his empty beer bottle. "Fill 'er up, premium, one more time there, old boy."

BOBBY LEE WON the first game easily, walking around the table in a quick, graceful manner I had never seen before. In his tight T-shirt, he looked young and thin, the pool stick light in his hands. After the game, he snatched up the twenty-dollar bill Slap Dog laid on the table and held it up to the light.

"Sure looks pretty, don't it, Teddy," he said, calling over to me. "Specially when you earn it."

"One more time," Slap Dog said. He took out a cigarette. "Double it up."

"You must be a rich man," Bobby Lee said. "Or generous."

I sat at a table off in the corner, and watched Bobby Lee rack up the balls again. My head had begun to hurt and the wet heat of the bar gave everything a blurry, slow-motion look and feel. I shook my head and took deep breaths, trying to make the blurriness go away. But I was beyond tired and my hopes for a brief stay at Tyrone's were fading. I no longer believed we would be back home in Wilton by morning. I no longer believed we were ever going home.

Slap Dog had been entirely quiet during the first game. He moved slowly, leaning down low to the table, one eye closed as he lined up his shots. His arms were long and wiry and he was as thin as Bobby Lee. His friend, the fat man who had been playing before we came, sat on a bar stool near the juke-box, shaking and rocking his head to a song. Every so often he would close his eyes and sing along. Other than the bartender, we were the only ones in the bar.

"Hey, how come they call you Slap Dog Jack?" Bobby Lee said as he chalked his pool cue.

Slap Dog didn't take his eyes from the table. He had a long drooping mustache that hid his mouth. "Name's Jack. Not sure why they call me the other part." He nodded toward the table. "You break."

I closed my eyes and listened to the balls gently bump into each other, then put my head down on the small table and began to drift away, my mind on home. I wondered what my father was doing, worried how he was han-dling my disappearance. Aunt Bess, I was sure, was frantic and Uncle Frank, swearing and pacing. I closed my eyes tight and wished my self away.

When I opened my eyes some time later, things had changed. The man at the jukebox was standing close to Slap Dog, whispering something. The bartender had come out from behind the bar and was standing close to the table too, his arms crossed against his chest. The jukebox was silent and the room seemed hotter and smaller.

"Side," Slap Dog said. I looked up just as a ball streaked across the table, and disappeared down a pocket. Slap Dog stood up straight after the shot and from beneath his mustache I thought I saw a smile.

Bobby Lee stared at Slap Dog for a long time. Then he looked slowly around the room at the other men who stared back.

"You boys think you're something, don't you," he said. He reached into his front pocket and pulled out a wad of bills, and threw them on the pool table. Some of the money fell onto the floor.

Then without taking his eyes off Slap Dog he said, "Let's go, Teddy."

We waited in the van across the road from Tyrone's in the deserted parking lot of a muffler shop for close to an hour. When I asked Bobby Lee what we were doing, he said shut up and sipped from a bottle that he kept under the seat.

I fell in and out of sleep, had pictures for dreams. My father reading a book to Tommy. Waiting in line for the doors of St. Pius to open. Miss Grace. Charlie.

Then I dreamt about my tenth birthday party, saw my mother again standing in the doorway of the Laser Zone in her white T-shirt and ponytail, saw her lips moving. This time, though, I could hear her over the noise of the party, this time I could hear her words. "Be careful," I heard her say. "Be careful."

A car door slam woke me, then voices yelling. I sat up and looked out the window.

There, across the street, I saw Bobby Lee standing in the parking lot of Tyrone's under the one street lamp. He was yelling to someone. When I opened the door and got out, I saw Slap Dog and the man at the jukebox walking slowly toward him.

"You boys hustled me and I want my money back," Bobby Lee yelled. "Give it up, boys."

I crossed the road and stood near Bobby Lee, who didn't notice me. From inside Tyrone's I could hear music once again.

"Come into our place, think you can take our money. You're a dumb shit," Slap Dog said.

"He's trying to kidnap me," I blurted out. I was breathing hard, my heart pounding. I had not planned to yell this, the words had just exploded from my mouth. "Call the police, please call my father."

Both Slap Dog and the other man stared at me confused and startled. But before they could react, Bobby Lee was on them, kicking and punching and yelling. Slap Dog, went down first, holding his stomach then his head, which Bobby Lee kicked, his boots making thick, dull sounds.

315

"I ain't no dog you can slap," Bobby Lee yelled. He whirled around. "Where you going, boy?"

The fat man was trying to run back to the bar, but Bobby Lee caught him and knocked him down with a hit to the back of the head. The man fell in a heap and while he was still on the ground, Bobby Lee hit and kicked him until he stopped moving.

"Stupid fat fuck," he yelled. "Think I'm some dumb-ass redneck. Take my fucking money. Set me up. Came in for a game and a beer and you rip me off. Teach you fucks a lesson. You goddamn motherfuckers."

The quickness and completeness of Bobby Lee's attack shocked me. That he could beat two men so savagely by himself was something I could not understand. Yet rather than fear, I felt a rising fury.

"You goddamn motherfuckers!" Bobby Lee yelled.

Slap Dog rose unsteadily to his feet, holding his head. He staggered back a bit then fell down, his face looking up toward the night. I could hear him gasping for breath as he lay there. Bobby Lee walked slowly back to him and stood over him, his fist clenched high in the air.

"Stop hitting him!" I yelled. "Stop hitting him!" I rushed toward Bobby Lee, swinging my fists. "Stop it! Stop it! Stop it!"

At first Bobby Lee backed away from me, then he reached out and snatched my hands and held them. It was then that I saw that he was holding a thin black metal bar. "Get in the car," he yelled. "Get in the damn car."

"I want to go home! I want to go home. Take me home. I hate you," I yelled. I tried to kick him but he backed away. "I hate you. I hate you."

"Shut up! I said shut the fuck up!"

With a twist, I broke free and ran. When I got to the end of the parking lot, I turned to face him, picked up some stones and threw them at him. He danced and dodged the stones as he made his way toward me. When he was just a few feet away, I hit him square in the face with a good size rock.

He grabbed his nose and screamed.

"You goddamn little bastard!"

He reached for me and caught my hands again, squeezed them until they hurt. He was taking short wild breaths, his face soaked with sweat and blood. Then he raised an arm to hit me. When I looked up, I saw the black metal bar directly over my head. I tried to kick him again, then closed my eyes and waited for the bar to fall.

"You're just like your fucking mother!" he yelled.

I opened my eyes. He was still standing there, the metal bar raised.

Then I heard someone yell. It was the beefy bartender. He was standing by the open door of Tyrone's.

"What the hell happened here?" he yelled. "What the hell is going on?"

"Get in the van," Bobby Lee said. He put the bar down and began pushing me. "Get in the damn van now."

CHAPTER SIXTEEN

IT WAS GETTING dark out. The sky was doing somersaults, turning from blue to gray to black and I could see a handful of stars in the sky, blinking silently, watching us. We were in the cemetery where my mother was buried and it was cold.

"Where, that way?" Bobby Lee asked. He was holding the bag of tulip bulbs Carl the Bear had given him and walking unsteadily.

"Over there," I said pointing.

After the fight at Tyrone's I had fallen asleep in the van, everything poured out of me. When I woke, I recognized the Chicago skyline and my hopes surged. But rather than drive to Wilton, Bobby Lee got off the expressway and told me we were going to see my mother's grave before we drove out to Utah to start our new life.

"There," I said. "It's right there."

Bobby Lee stumbled over a branch and said, "Shit." I waited behind him as he stood slowly up and wiped mud off his pants. "Goddamnit," he said. "These are the only pants I got. I was hoping Carl could lend me some clothes but he's so damn fat now, I didn't even bother to ask. Is that it?"

"Yes," I said. I was standing a few feet away, over by a larger tombstone with a cross on top.

Bobby Lee stared at my mother's tombstone but didn't say anything. He just laid the bag of tulip bulbs down on the ground and put his hands in his pockets. I stood behind him and tried to look at the tombstone too, but I was starting to float again, so I looked down, concentrating on the ground.

"Come on here, boy, let's pay our respects as a family. The two men in her life." He grabbed my hand and made me walk closer to the grave.

"Hey Amy," he said. He took out his bottle and swigged. "Oh, man," he said. "This is weirder than I thought."

He sat down on the ground, crossing his legs Indian-style, like Tommy did when he watched TV. "You loved your mother?" he asked. "Did you love your mother? I know she loved you. Hell, she loved you more than she loved me. But that's okay, that's all right. Mother's supposed to love her children. Hey, now, what are you doing, quit that and sit down next to me."

I kept standing and wiped the tears from my cheeks with the back of my hand. The wind made my wet face sting, my lips salty. I wasn't sure when I had started crying.

"Yeah, well, it's okay to cry over your mother I guess. That's okay," he said. He took another drink. "I'd offer you some of this medication but I need all I can get right now. Sit down now. We'll be going soon so say your good-byes."

I sat down next to him on the cold ground and looked at the tombstone. Since the fight, he had been calm and quiet. I thought that he might try to hit me once we had left the parking lot of Tyrone's, but it was as if a storm had passed and we drove for hours in silence, the radio low. Twice he offered me snacks from Carl's bag.

"Amy Elizabeth Pappas," he said. "Loving mother and wife." I looked at the tombstone until I couldn't see it anymore through my tears.

"You know things turned out different," Bobby Lee said. "Different than I thought. I didn't want them to turn out this way. I wanted to stay married to your mother, be a father and have more kids. But things took their own course. The comets collided somewhere and everything changed I guess." I looked over at Bobby Lee when he mentioned the comets.

"Amy made up this fairy tale about comets colliding and when they did people's lives changed. Hell, they've been colliding a lot I guess. Things keep changing. You can't figure on anything."

I dug my hands deep into my pockets and put my face down into my coat to hide against the wind. Overhead, I heard an airplane flying, a low distant sound that moved away and left us. Even though I feared we were going to Utah, I wanted to get back in the van where it was warm. I stopped crying and started sniffling.

"She and I were together for a long time, since grade school. I miss her a lot. We had some fun together. Made each other laugh. We were just kids. Man, we were just kids."

Bobby Lee slowly began to dig a shallow hole in the ground with his hands, scooping dirt out.

"Ground is almost frozen. It's hard," he said.

After he dug for a while, he opened the brown bag and dropped some bulbs into the earth, then covered them back up quickly. While he was doing this, I thought about trying to run back to the parking lot and look for help, but I was floating now, rising above the ground and I knew that Bobby Lee would catch me no matter what I tried.

"You got Amy's big eyes. She had big eyes. Pretty eyes. I used to try and draw them in school, but I wasn't no artist. I made them too big, she used to say. Hell, she was the artist. Yes, she was." Then Bobby Lee said something that I didn't expect him to say. "I loved her," he said. "Shouldn't have turned out this way. That old man took her away from me." He put his head down between his legs and I thought I heard him crying. "Well," he said after some time. "You and me are quite a pair, ain't we? Quite a pair. Crying like this." He wiped his eyes with his hand and sniffled too. "So, you believe in God. Then what do you think He thinks of me? Doing what I did? He probably doesn't like me much, wouldn't dislodge nothing from my esophagus." He started to take another drink then stopped and put the bottle back down. "Well, you just, you just tell God, that I ain't as bad as everyone said, all the newspapers and everything. I loved your mother. I ain't evil or nothing. Didn't mean for any of this to happen."

I crouched lower in my coat. The wind blew and bare branches scratched the air. Bobby Lee wiped his eyes again.

"I wasn't going to hurt you back there in the parking lot," he said. "Hell, at least I don't think I was. I lose my temper sometimes, lose control. Don't know what I'm going to do. Hell, you got a spark in you too," he said. He gingerly touched his nose which was slightly swollen. "Should forget about the drawing and think about baseball, boy. You got aim."

I had nothing to say to any of this. I just crouched lower and felt the wind blow through me. "Oh, hell," he finally said, standing up. "Let's go. All this is just crazy."

"Where are we going?" I asked, and when I stood up, I felt myself starting to shake from the cold.

"I don't know. All I know is that I don't have any money. It's cold and I'm hungry. Let's go."

I followed him back to the van, walking around tombstones, my head down, my feet moving one after another. My stomach was hurting badly now and I was trying hard to keep from floating higher even though I was feeling strange and light.

When we got to the van, I saw someone standing under a light pole. A shadow, then a voice.

"Let the boy go," my father said. He was holding something in his hand, down by the side of his leg.

Bobby Lee grabbed me and stepped back. "What the hell you doing?"

"Please, Mr. Anderson, I came for Teddy. If you wish to go, then you may go. I just want Teddy. You had no right to take him. No right at all." My father's voice was firm. I didn't recognize it, didn't know it.

"How did you find us?" Bobby Lee asked. Then he said, "Goddamn Carl," under his breath.

"Give me the boy," my father said and started walking toward us. It was then that the light caught the object in his hand and I saw that he was carrying Stonewall Jackson's sword.

When Bobby Lee saw the sword, he pulled me back farther, holding me tight. A sudden surge of panic cut through my light-headedness. I knew that even with the sword, my father was no match for Bobby Lee.

"You think that just because you won all that money, you gonna win my boy. Bet you paid off that judge."

"Give me the boy," my father said. "I don't want any trouble, Mr. Anderson. I gave your brother my word I would not involve the authorities. But if pressed, I said I might be forced to."

"You took my wife. You ain't getting my son," Bobby Lee said. I felt his body tensing, and wondered where the black metal bar was.

"Let Teddy go," my father said. He began to circle us, taking slow steps in a wide arc, pointing his sword at us with one arm. Bobby Lee and I turned to follow him.

"Put that sword down, old man, before I hurt you. Throw your car keys and your wallet on the ground too. I'm short on cash. Throw them both this way."

"Let Teddy go," my father repeated. "Let him go. You may leave here, if you wish, but let him go." He kept circling us slowly, pointing the sword.

"Shut the hell up!" Bobby Lee yelled. "This boy's mine. You listening to me? I said drop that thing and give me your money. You damn old fool. Before I take you apart."

"Dad," I yelled. "He has a metal bar. Please, do what he says. He beat up two men at the same time."

My father kept walking, never taking his eyes off of Bobby Lee. "Things are going to be fine, Teddy," he said calmly.

"You old stupid ass," I heard Bobby Lee say. He tightened his grip on me, turning me in the direction of my father, who continued to circle us. "Stop goddamn moving and listen to the boy," Bobby Lee said. "I ain't telling you again."

"And I'm not asking you again, either," my father said. Then he put his sword down and sadly shook his head. "I'm sorry about all this, Mr. Anderson. But you gave us no choice." That's when I heard something behind us, the scrape of gravel. Bobby Lee and I turned at the same time to discover Maurice looming over us, his eyes wide, his fist raised high behind his head.

"What the hell?" Bobby Lee yelled.

When Maurice swung, he hit Bobby Lee square in the nose.

Bobby Lee let go of me, covering his face with his hands. "Goddamnit!" he yelled. "Goddamnit!"

When Maurice hit him again, Bobby Lee flew backward into the air, then fell to the ground in a broken silent pile. He stayed there without moving until the police came and took him away.

CHAPTER SEVENTEEN

UNCLE FRANK STOOD in front of the hallway mirror trying to straighten my tie, his hands moving quickly as he rearranged my collar and smoothed my shirt.

"You can make an entrance wearing a suit like this," he said. "People respect suits. They're like military uniforms. That was one of my problems in L.A., I think. I didn't wear enough suits. Suits scare people."

Aunt Bess had wanted us to wear our Confederate uniforms to her wedding but my father convinced her otherwise, saying they would be inappropriate. Earlier in the week, he took Tommy and me downtown and bought us each a blue suit, red tie, and white shirt. When we came home and showed Uncle Frank the dark conservative suits, Uncle Frank said we looked like Secret Service agents and asked my father if we had been assigned to guard the president's motorcade. The next day, after school, Uncle Frank took us back downtown and spent several tedious hours, going from store to store, considering dozens of suits until finally deciding on two double-breasted, jet black suits he thought appropriately stylish.

"Dress for success," he said on the way home. "I don't make the rules."

The wedding had been hastily organized. Sylvanius had asked Aunt Bess to marry him just the week before, falling, very gradually, to a knee one night at dinner after drinking an entire bottle of red wine. Speaking in his melodi-

323

ous voice, his words sloshing like water against the insides of a bucket, he asked Aunt Bess to make him the happiest man in the world. Despite Uncle Frank's objections and demands for an airtight prenuptial agreement, my father quietly approved the marriage, smiling broadly after Aunt Bess accepted, and shaking Sylvanius's hand. "I know this is what she's wanted for some time now," he said to Sylvanius. "And I'm happy for you both."

"We got to get the hell out of here," Uncle Frank now said, taking Tommy by one hand and opening the front door with another. "We're going to be late. Not that that would be such a bad thing."

"Why is Aunt Bess marrying the old monster?" Tommy asked.

"Because he asked her," Uncle Frank said.

"He's going to make her a vampire."

"That's highly possible."

Maurice was waiting for us in the driveway by the car, hands in his pockets, pipe in his mouth. It was snowing and large wet flakes hit my face, clinging to my eyelashes.

"Goddamn snow. Who would've predicted this?" Uncle Frank said as we got into the old Buick.

Maurice opened the back door for Tommy and me. "I don't think it's all that unexpected," he said. "It is January."

Uncle Frank scowled up at the sky, the time of year no excuse. Snow piled up on his toupée, frosting on chocolate cake. "Well, hopefully this weather will delay things for a while. For a couple of years if we're lucky." He got in the car and adjusted his seat, moving it forward. "You got enough room there, Maurice? Move the seat all the way back. The kids don't need any space."

"I'm fine," Maurice said. "Does everybody have their seat belts on? Tommy? How about you, Mr. Pappas?"

"I don't wear seat belts. This car is indestructible."

"That can be dangerous," Maurice said.

Uncle Frank started the car. "I live on the edge."

I spent a week in bed after my journey with Bobby Lee, sleeping and talking to my father, Aunt Bess, and Uncle Frank, my strength returning, my fever and the floating feeling slowly then finally disappearing forever. During that period, we were once again overwhelmed with phone calls from TV and radio stations, all hoping for interviews. Both my father and Maurice refused the requests, saying they had no interest in discussing private family matters. Disregarding my father's pleas however, Uncle Frank appeared on show after show, telling our story with moving sincerity and drama, attributing everything that happened ultimately to the human condition. He proved so interesting that he had recently been offered a job as temporary host of *Night Chat*, a late night radio show in Chicago that he immediately renamed *Frankly Speaking*. He seemed happy and talked grandly at breakfast about taking the show national and eventually expanding into network TV and challenging "the big boys."

"Did you hear my show last night?" Uncle Frank asked Maurice as he stopped at a red light. "We had that astrologer on. The one that predicts things."

"I'm sorry, I missed that," Maurice said.

"I'll send you a tape." Then he said, "You know, my invitation still stands."

"Thank you, but I wouldn't feel comfortable talking on the radio."

"Well, if you change your mind," Uncle Frank said. "I could use the ratings. My deal ends in six weeks." The light changed and the old Buick lurched forward.

It was snowing heavily now and we slipped and skidded as much as drove to Will's where Aunt Bess was waiting to begin her new life in a nearby condominium my father had bought her as a wedding gift. She wasn't getting married in a church because at the very last moment, Sylvanius remembered he was Jewish.

"This whole thing is depressing," Uncle Frank now said as we pulled into the parking lot. "This whole thing. I blame myself. I brought that guy into our family. She's going to spend her last years giving him foot rubs."

"He seems to make her happy," Maurice said as the car pulled to a stop.

"She's seventy-seven years old. She's too old to be happy."

"You're never too old to be happy," Maurice said, opening the door.

SYLVANIUS AND MY father were waiting for us in Will's new banquet room, which Gus had built primarily for funeral luncheons. Sylvanius rushed to greet us at the door, resplendent in a light blue tuxedo, complete with a pink and white bow tie that reminded me of peppermint ice cream.

"Jesus Christ," Uncle Frank said. "You look like Liberace."

Sylvanius smiled, perspiration beading his forehead. "These are my winter colors," he said. "Bess selected the entire ensemble." He looked down at me and smiled, a serpent in love. "I must admit I am excited," he said. "I haven't been married in *years*."

Quinn the lawyer and Mrs. Rhodebush were the only other people at the wedding besides our family. Mrs. Rhodebush smiled when she saw me so I could see that her false teeth were secure and operational. I hadn't seen her in quite some time, since Halloween, and was happy she was here. "You've had quite an adventure," she said.

The banquet room had two large windows that overlooked the parking lot, empty except for our cars. Gus had closed the restaurant in honor of the occasion, the least he could do, according to Uncle Frank, since my father had given him the money to remodel. I stood by the windows and watched the snow fall, the old Buick slowly disappearing in a delicate and dignified manner.

I watched the snow for awhile, then pulled out a worn note I had in my pocket. It was from my mother, written when she was my age. Bobby Lee had sent it to me that day from prison, along with the drawing, a startling picture of bright stars and planets against a dark backdrop: "The Galaxy at Night." Written on plain paper in young handwriting I didn't recognize, the note described the picture: "The Galaxy at Night, all the stars and planets in perfect place, safe and sound. Depending on each other until morning."

"Very picturesque. The snow. Very pretty, don't you think, Teddy?" It was my father.

"Yes," I said. I put the note away.

Since that night when he and Maurice flanked Bobby Lee in the parking lot, he had been trying to spend as much time as possible with Tommy and me and though I knew it sometimes required an effort, things seemed to be getting easier for him. While he still wandered at times, his thoughts remote and elsewhere, I now knew he was close by and would always be so.

"I think they're starting. We should probably sit down," he said. I followed him to a short row of chairs that faced the window.

When Aunt Bess entered the room, wearing a long blue dress and holding a single white rose, she started crying and said, "Oh God." Then she walked toward Sylvanius.

"You are a vision," he said as she took her place next to him before the judge, a friend of Quinn's. The service proceeded smoothly until Sylvanius tried to say a poem he had memorized and began stumbling over the words. When Aunt Bess said, "They're waiting to serve the food," he finally stopped and simply kissed her on the lips.

"I have one more thing to read," Sylvanius said, unfolding a piece of paper. Uncle Frank mumbled Jesus Christ and Aunt Bess said something about the food again, but Sylvanius insisted. "It will only take a moment."

He put on a pair of small glasses that I had never seen him wear before, looked around the room and smiled, stretching the moment. He then folded the paper back up and put it away.

"A man's life is made up of people," he began in his musical voice. "And if you are fortunate enough to find good people, people that you love, then keep them close. For together you will find things, together you will learn things. About each other and about yourself."

When he finished, he kissed Aunt Bess.

"Those lines were from our last movie," Uncle Frank said, looking proudly around the room. "From the last scene."

We all stood there for a moment and watched Aunt Bess dry her eyes with Sylvanius's handkerchief.

My father then turned to me. "Well," he said after he cleared this throat. "Will you sit by me, Teddy?" Over his shoulder, I could see the snow swirling, doing a dance in the lights, falling like pieces of clouds and heaven.

"Okay," I said as he took my hand and led me over to the table. "Okay."